Praise for Abigail Wilson

"Shimmering with atmosphere and suspense, *Twilight at Moorington Cross* weaves classic Regency romance with threads of Gothic mystery to page-turning effect. An absolute pleasure to read."

—MIMI MATTHEWS, *USA TODAY* BESTSELLING AUTHOR

"Readers will be on the edge of their seats as the romance unfolds in Wilson's newest novel, *Twilight at Moorington Cross*. The best of Regency combines with the best of Gothic to create a unique mood enhanced by excellent story-telling, compelling characters, and an intriguing romance that keeps the pages turning!"

—JOSI S. KILPACK, AWARD-WINNING AUTHOR OF *LOVE AND LAVENDER*

"An enigmatic illness, a mysterious manor, an unforeseen inheritance, and a suspicious death all add up to a maelstrom of misfortune for Wilson's stout-hearted and winsome heroine, especially when she's falling in love with the 'wrong' man. *Twilight at Moorington Cross* has all the atmospheric trappings of a classic Regency Gothic along with a sweet and stirring romance. Perfect for fans of Julie Klassen and Kristi Ann Hunter."

—ANNA LEE HUBER, *USA TODAY* BESTSELLING AUTHOR

"Murder, intrigue, and a possible marriage of convenience all in one Regency romance—it's enough to make a reader swoon! This is a well-told tale, and I can't wait to read more by its author."

—SALLY BRITTON, AUTHOR OF *COPPER FOR THE COUNTESS* AND THE *CLAIRVOIR CASTLE* ROMANCES

"An absolutely mesmerizing read! *Twilight at Moorrington Cross* is seeped through with so much delicious romance and heart-pounding suspense that you'll be madly turning the pages until the thrilling end."

—JOANNA BARKER, AUTHOR OF *OTHERWISE ENGAGED*

"I was drawn in from the very first page of this unique Regency story. Wilson's engaging prose and expert mystery-telling kept me turning pages and left me guessing until the end."

—KASEY STOCKTON, AUTHOR OF THE *LADIES OF DEVON* SERIES, FOR *TWILIGHT AT MOORINGTON CROSS*

"*The Vanishing at Loxby Manor* cleverly combines Regency romance with Gothic intrigue, and the result is a suspenseful, thoroughly entertaining read."

—TASHA ALEXANDER, *NEW YORK TIMES* BESTSELLING AUTHOR OF *IN THE SHADOW OF VESUVIUS*

TWILIGHT AT MOORINGTON CROSS

ABIGAIL WILSON

THOMAS NELSON

Since 1798

Published in Nashville, Tennessee, by Thomas Nelson. Thomas Nelson is a registered trademark of HarperCollins Christian Publishing, Inc.

Thomas Nelson titles may be purchased in bulk for educational, business, fundraising, or sales promotional use. For information, please email SpecialMarkets@ThomasNelson.com.

Scripture quotations are taken from the King James Version. Public domain.

Library of Congress Cataloging-in-Publication Data

Names: Wilson, Abigail, author.
Title: Twilight at Moorington Cross / Abigail Wilson.
Description: Nashville, Tennessee : Thomas Nelson, [2022] | Description based on print version record and CIP data provided by publisher; resource not viewed.
Identifiers: LCCN 2021032851 (print) | LCCN 2021032852 (ebook) | ISBN 9780785253297 | ISBN 9780785253280 (epub) | ISBN 9780785253273 (paperback)
Subjects: | BISAC: FICTION / Mystery & Detective / Historical | FICTION / Romance / Historical / Regency | GSAFD: Love stories.
Classification: LCC PS3623.I57778 (ebook) | LCC PS3623.I57778 T85 2022 (print) | DDC 813/.6--dc23

Printed in the United States of America

22 23 24 25 26 BRR 5 4 3 2 1

*For Megan Besing, my fabulous critique partner
and more importantly my dear friend.*

*Thank you for your heartfelt encouragement, for your godly
wisdom, and for simply sharing the road of writing and life
with me. I can't imagine one step of this journey without you.*

#iheartyou

CHAPTER 1

1819
KENT, ENGLAND

I t was entirely possible that I spent more time lying on the floor of
Cluett's Mesmeric Hospital than standing upon it.

Splayed out prone on the carpet once again with nothing but broken recollections of what had transpired, I gathered the rug's corner
into a tight fist, willing myself not to pound the floor. My arm shook
as I pulled myself into a sitting position and wiped away the dirt still
clinging to my forehead. Thankfully no one had witnessed my latest
episode. I fumbled to restore the potted plant on its stand in the hall
before assessing my body for bruises.

I had been leaning over. Yes, that I remembered. Then I was peer-
ing beneath the drapes. Or was it the hall table? I rubbed my eyes.
Either way, this latest sleeping spell had certainly been a revealing one.
For, regardless of how much Mr. Cluett believed his mesmeric treat-
ments were helping, I was no better off than when I arrived. Moreover,
I was getting worse.

I was still a bit dazed as my attention drifted to my lap, and my
heart turned. Oh dear. "Chauncey."

The word seemed to echo like a whisper in my mind, and I
couldn't help but touch my mouth. Had I spoken the name aloud? If
only these horrid periods of distorted reality didn't follow my bouts
of unintended sleep.

I pushed myself up to stand and caught hold of a nearby door-frame with my left hand. At least I was on my feet now. And a good thing, too, as a figure rounded the corner in a rush—a man, tall and lithe, wearing a sleek green jacket. He stopped short at the sight of me.

I mirrored his look of surprise.

"I beg your pardon. I—" There was a moment of hesitation, the man's lips parting into a delightful curve, then he took a quick glance behind him, his trove of rebellious blond curls dancing with the movement. "I was led to believe all the rooms in this hall were empty, that I could expect privacy in this wing."

A rake of fingers through his hair, then a tug on his jacket, and my attention snapped to the man's chest. My eyes widened. He'd prematurely untied his cravat, no doubt on his way to his bedchamber. And here I was—an unwanted visitor staring just so.

"I . . ." What reason could I give for wandering into this part of the house?

He fumbled with his neckcloth a moment, his other hand in his pocket, a telltale half smile creeping from one corner of his mouth, before his head suddenly popped up at my silence. "I'm sorry, but are you well, ma'am?"

Well? Why did I feel like laughing? I pressed my palm to my forehead, adding a small huff I only hoped would be believed. "Quite well indeed." The statement might have been convincing if a section of my hair hadn't chosen that exact moment to slip from my coiffure and flop over my eye.

He fought a full grin as he moved in closer. "I did hear someone earlier calling out the name Chauncey. Was that in fact you?"

I tucked the loose hair behind my ear. "Yes . . . Chauncey." His inquiry jerked me back to reality and my earlier quest. I narrowed my eyes, far more logical considerations finally seeping to the surface. Who on earth was this person? Goodness knows I wasn't accustomed to strangers roaming the various wings of the house. A new patient perhaps? But we'd not been informed of an arrival.

"I, uh, didn't mean to disturb anyone. You see, Chauncey is—" Unprepared for the thoughtful intensity of the man's brown eyes, I tore away my gaze, adding a mumbled, "I cannot imagine where the dear has gone off to."

The man watched me a moment before settling his hand on his chin. "I do apologize if I overstep my bounds, but I believe I know who you are." His words were slow to come yet equally steady. "In fact, I've been hoping to meet you since yesterday. My name is Ewan Hawkins."

Was I supposed to recognize the name Ewan Hawkins? I gave him something of a smile. After all, how could I not? The man was all ease and confidence and, if I was to be honest with myself, terribly well put together. Granted, my mind was still a bit hazy from my sleep episode.

"No need for an apology, sir. It's a pleasure to meet you. I'm Mrs. Pembroke. I've been a patient here at Cluett's Hospital for almost two years."

He nodded to himself. "And in need of some assistance this morning, I gather? May I offer you my own?"

Something within that cultured voice sent warmth rushing to my cheeks, and I only hoped it wouldn't be regarded. Generally I was not one to be taken in by a handsome face, but a deep voice was quite a different matter.

I shook off the notion at once. "I was only looking for someone . . . Well, not exactly."

His eyebrows shot up. "Not *exactly*?"

"Chauncey's not a person at all."

"No?"

"He's my guinea pig."

The man stared at me a moment then lightly shook his head. "Your *guinea pig*?"

I gave a breathy laugh. "This whole situation, my being in your

3

private apartments, is quite silly actually. One moment the little dear was having a snack of carrots on my coverlet and the next he up and vanished. I thought perhaps he'd decided to take a stroll to freedom out my bedchamber door. I was sure I heard him down your hall, and . . . then . . . well . . . something else happened . . . Oh never mind. I'm sorry to have got in your way. Really, if you'll just excuse me, I shall return to my hunt at once."

I spun to face the dark room behind me. "I doubt Chauncey would even come this far. He's not all that adventurous of a pig, but I did think I heard his squeak before and right this way."

I felt Mr. Hawkins move in close behind me at the door.

"Well, that does present a rather interesting predicament. The room you've got your sights set on searching at present happens to be my bedchamber. I'll admit, I'm not all that excited about an uninvited rodent taking up residence inside"—he laughed—"particularly if he wishes to hide under my bed and come out at the most inauspicious moment—"

"Oh dear. I'm afraid that's just the sort of thing he'd do. Maybe we better give the room a once-over. I'm well versed in Chauncey's preferences—for hiding spaces I mean. Among other things."

"You must be an animal lover then."

"More of a naturalist, I'd say."

"A naturalist? Now that's unusual for a lady."

I lowered my attention to the floor in pretense of searching for Chauncey, but I couldn't hide the grit in my voice. "Is it?"

Mr. Hawkins's arm brushed mine as he slipped past me into the room then turned, drifting back against the opposing doorframe. "I daresay you'd better advise me on all this. Other than horses, I have little experience with four-legged creatures. Should I check all my boots and pumps?"

"That's a good idea, particularly if they've fallen to the side." The fact that I was invading a man's personal space was not lost on me as

I raked my gaze over the room. "Really, it shouldn't take me all that long to poke about, and it will give you peace of mind."

Mr. Hawkins cut another far-too-attractive smile, as if enjoying a private joke. His pleasure, however, dissolved just as quickly as he moved to check his pocket watch. "Clearly you've hit upon the best course of action, yet I'm afraid I've an appointment with Mr. Cluett I'm already late for." He tossed his cravat on the bed, his resulting look a bit direct. "But don't worry, I'll be sure to send word if the fellow turns up."

"Yes, well . . ." Obviously *de trop*, I withdrew a hasty step, lost as to the best way to gracefully make an exit. "Thank you, Mr. Hawkins." My mind seemed to freeze in place, but I heard myself jabber on. "I'm, of course, unaware of the reason you've sought treatment here; nevertheless, I do hope your mesmeric session with Mr. Cluett is helpful."

A slight furrow formed on Mr. Hawkins's forehead as he grasped the bed's poster. "I'm afraid you've misunderstood the reason for my sudden arrival at Moorington Cross. I'm not a patient here at the hospital. I'm Mr. Cluett's newest solicitor—from Pembroke and Huxley."

A solicitor . . . Pembroke and Huxley? My heart stilled.

He opened his mouth as if he might say more but simply pressed his lips together, finally adding a rather mournful, "Good day, Mrs. Pembroke."

"Good day."

Images of my late husband—the perfect solicitor—flashed through my mind as I quit the room.

"Not again," I said beneath my breath. Inwardly I shook myself free from the unwanted memories as I kept my attention steady on the floor. Handsome solicitor indeed. What on earth had I been thinking?

I swallowed hard. Chauncey would simply have to find his own way back to my room. I wouldn't stay one more second with a solicitor from Pembroke and Huxley. One who, in all likelihood, would have been well acquainted with my late husband.

CHAPTER 2

M r. Cluett had been pacing the carpet like a caged animal ever
since I'd entered his office.

His nurse and assistant, Miss Seton, plunked away at the pianoforte in the next room. But what should have been a soothing back-
ground melody for my daily mesmeric session sounded more like tiny
daggers, piercing my anxious ears one by one.

All at once Mr. Cluett halted directly in front of me. His calm
voice and the warmth of his hands on my scalp usually accompanied
such a keen gaze, but he didn't move, not today. He just stood there,
watching me.

My heart sank. Was something amiss? Another problem with
my treatments?

He pressed his fist to his chin and a flash of gooseflesh littered
my arms.

Unsure what to do or say, I reached for the iron rod submerged
in the *baquet* in front of my chair. Regardless of my increasing sleep
attacks and my questions regarding the therapy, I meant to continue
with every idea he suggested. What other hope did I have?

As Mr. Cluett had already added iron fillings to the wooden tub,
I dipped my head to press the metal rod against my forehead, but
his voice stopped me cold. "Not yet, Mrs. Pembroke. I've something

important I wish to discuss with you first, and I must admit, I'm at a loss as to how it will be received."

He carelessly tossed his wand onto the desk, freeing his hand to claw at the collar of his purple cloak. "As you are no doubt aware, I've been closeted with my solicitor, Mr. Hawkins, nearly the whole of this past week. But what you cannot know is that *you*, my dear, have been the central topic of conversation." He looked up belatedly at me and narrowed his eyes, almost as if . . . What, exactly?

His lips twitched. "I daresay Mr. Hawkins should be present if I'm to carry on. The last thing I would want is to confuse you. This is far too important."

He yelled over his right shoulder. "Miss Seton, please fetch the apprentice solicitor for us."

The music ceased, and Miss Seton's scratchy voice barely breached the closed connecting door. "Sir?"

There was a moan of wood then the clip-clop of shoes before she appeared at the connecting door. Her icy gaze swept the room, her frail body lengthening in the doorway.

Mr. Cluett measured his voice, that familiar hesitancy he always affected in her presence taking over. "If you, uh, wouldn't mind, Miss Seton, we have need of Mr. Hawkins."

She clenched her arthritic fingers before eventually nodding and disappearing from the room.

A repressed sigh and Mr. Cluett spun back to face me, his fingers busy with the lace lining his cloak as that odd delicacy returned to his voice. "We'll have to resume your mesmeric session a bit later on—tomorrow even. I daresay you'll have much to think about tonight, and I wouldn't wish to overload the magnetic fluids at work in your body." His eyes were almost sheepish in the dim light.

Was he embarrassed? All at once I couldn't stop my toes from curling in my half boots. What did his solicitor have to do with me?

Then my stomach turned. Surely Mr. Cluett knew I was in no condition to entertain a suitor at present. I gripped the armrest, my focus roving the shadows of the room. Or did he?

Mr. Cluett had remarked endlessly in the past about how I needed stability in my life. Had he somehow learned of my misplaced attraction to Mr. Hawkins and taken it to heart? My chest felt heavy. I never should have spilled one single word to Mrs. Fitzroy about how attractive he was. What if she'd spoken out of turn during one of her trances?

The constant tick of the mantel clock filled the silence between us, and I was compelled to give him a wan smile. Mr. Cluett returned a nod, the sort only a man of his paternal charm and respectability could perfect, but there was an element of mystery about his demeanor that sent a fresh wave of nerves prickling up my back.

I rushed to speak. "I do thank you for your concern, but tomorrow will do just as well for my session. I've had a couple good days."

He nodded. "Yes, you have."

My shoulders relaxed a bit. Surely I was mistaken in my suppositions. After I lost my parents to the fever at a young age, then one guardian after another to selfish abandonment, and finally my controlling husband to an early death, Mr. Cluett and I had waded past the invisible boundaries of doctor and patient into the realm of surrogate family or good friends. He would never play matchmaker now.

He rested back against the desk, his attention on the floor. "I'd planned to speak with you this afternoon along with everyone else; however, as I attempted to concentrate at the start of your session, I realized waiting might indeed be easier for me but hardly fair to you. No, my dear, you must hear it all before the other patients."

I angled my chin, completely lost.

"There's really no easy way to broach certain difficult topics, and what I'm about to tell you is unfortunately one of them." He pushed his spectacles up his nose. "I presume it does no good to delay the truth now. Mrs. Pembroke"—he lifted his eyes to reveal a glassy sheen about the edges—"over the course of the last few weeks I've discovered something about myself. It's a small complaint really, merely a disorder of the humors of the body. But the sudden change to my otherwise exceptional health has shaken me more than I'd like to admit."

Numbness filled my core. "Are you trying to tell me you're unwell?"

"Nothing to worry you, my dear, but—"

A brief knock and the office door swung open, silencing Mr. Cluett and averting our attention to the front of the room. Mr. Hawkins paused a moment on the threshold before searching the dim space for Mr. Cluett and angling forward on a cold draft from the landing.

Mr. Cluett sprang to his feet and motioned him forward. The already strained undercurrents of the room shifted as Mr. Hawkins crossed the carpet, a book in one hand, the other in his pocket, his sharp brown eyes sweeping the area. For a passing moment it almost felt as if Mr. Cluett and I had been waiting all this time in Mr. Hawkins's office instead of Mr. Cluett's.

Still riding a wave of confusion, I remained seated but no less attentive as Mr. Hawkins stopped but a foot from my chair. The startling interest I'd experienced previously hadn't diminished. If anything, the anticipation of why he was here only made it stronger.

The curly blond hair I'd found unruly yet attractive before had been brushed neatly into place for our meeting today. He glanced first to me then to Mr. Cluett. "How may I be of service?"

Mr. Cluett motioned toward me. "You remember Mrs. Pembroke?"

Mr. Hawkins bowed. "Yes, we had a rather informal introduction in the corridor earlier this week. You'd lost a pet if I remember correctly."

"Yes . . . my guinea pig, Chauncey."

He cracked a smile. "That's right, your guinea pig. And did you find the little devil?"

"I did. Thankfully he was only hidden in the pillows on my bed . . . and . . ." I touched my throat, suddenly all too conscious of the depth of Mr. Hawkins's gaze and the resulting thickness of my tongue. What had I meant to say about Chauncey?

Mr. Cluett chuckled. "I haven't seen Chauncey in ages. Perhaps you should bring him with you to your next session."

My next session.

No matter how much I wanted to, I couldn't hold my smile. Mr. Cluett had never meant to draw attention to my disorder, but the uncomfortable reminder that I was a patient at the hospital and not simply a random young lady felt distinctly like I'd been tipped forward into the cold waters of the *baquet.*

Unaware of my embarrassment, Mr. Cluett ushered Mr. Hawkins and me over to a nearby sofa and chairs where we all took a seat. It was in that uncomfortable moment of adjustment that I first noticed Mr. Hawkins's left hand—the strange stitching of his glove, the sharp, unnatural bend.

Mrs. Fitzroy had mentioned Mr. Hawkins hid a deformity, and in all honesty I hadn't meant to stare. I was still reeling from my own mortification. But he caught me looking nonetheless. He didn't say a word, merely retucked his hand into his pocket and gave me a perceptive glance.

I could have sunk into the floor. I knew better than anyone what it was like to be different.

Mr. Cluett, clearly misreading my discomfiture, adjusted his purple cloak about his legs. "I appreciate that this is a great deal to take in all at once, Mrs. Pembroke, but I beg you to keep an open mind."

Though I had been nervous before, something about the turn of his voice sparked a deeper level of tension. "By all means, I'll do my best."

Mr. Cluett motioned to Mr. Hawkins. "My solicitor can explain the details far better than I."

Mr. Hawkins's face went slack, and for the first time since he'd waltzed into the room, I thought him a bit off stride. He moved to adjust the sleeve of his jacket then cleared his throat. "Certainly, I would be happy to discuss the particulars, but may I inquire how much the young lady is privy to at present? I—"

Mr. Cluett flicked his fingers in the air. "Just start at the beginning, my good man."

Mr. Hawkins leaned forward, taking his precious time to find his way to the start. In fact, I could have sworn his eyes rounded before he dutifully regained his composure. "Mrs. Pembroke, Mr. Cluett brought me to Moorington Cross to make a rather unusual change to his will. And, as you can surely guess at this point, this change chiefly concerns you."

I crossed my feet at the floor to keep them still. "Me?"

"As it now stands, you are to be the main beneficiary of Mr. Cluett's vast estate as well as a good portion of his rather sizable fortune. However, you must understand that this inheritance comes with an important stipulation."

I nearly fell off the sofa. *I* was in Mr. Cluett's will? . . . How? . . . Why? "You can't be serious. I—"

Mr. Cluett held up his hand. "Let him finish, my dear. Then you may ask all the questions you desire."

Mr. Hawkins rubbed the back of his neck, a thread of discomfort lining his movements. "As per the updated will, as I said, you stand to inherit a great deal, but let me get to the rather important clause. Mr. Cluett has made your inheritance conditional upon your marriage to one of two named gentlemen, and if you haven't already done so, you must wed one of them within thirty days of his death."

The room seemed to tilt, then swirl, and I was forced to blink to right it. Desperately I sought out Mr. Cluett's kind eyes. "Marriage? I don't understand."

He leaned forward. "Not to just anyone, my dear. I've done the work for you. I've selected two very fine gentlemen for you to choose between."

I shook my head, frantic to process each new revelation. "And the house, the money . . . *an arranged marriage* . . . Why me?"

Carefully he took my hands into his. "Who else would I give it all to but you? Miss Seton will have a large sum, naturally. But over the past two years I've come to think of you as a daughter. I've no offspring, no close family. What kind of man would I be if I didn't find the perfect way to provide for your future? It was Mr. Hawkins who assisted me in coming to a seamless solution. Marriage for security, a house for comfort, and money for your prosperity."

My jaw clenched as Mr. Cluett's words echoed in my mind, "*It was Mr. Hawkins who assisted me* . . ." I swallowed a bitter sigh. Leave it to the solicitor to find a way to tie up my future in what looked like a package with a pretty little bow.

Granted, Mr. Cluett and I both knew another marriage would not come about naturally for me, not with my sleeping spells. Yet why bother with an arranged one? Couldn't he have simply willed me a bit of money and allowed me to sort out my own future—like Miss Seton?

I stole a wild glance at Mr. Hawkins, expecting him to echo Mr. Cluett's sentiment, but his eyes were glazed over, uncertain even.

I whirled back to Mr. Cluett. "Do I know either of the gentlemen you speak of?"

He patted my hand. "No, my dear. They are both strangers to you, but I think you shall be well pleased." There was a moment of awkward silence as he stood. "I did anticipate your desire to meet them. I am not wholly remiss as a stand-in father. The gentlemen are to arrive this very afternoon."

I rose as well, my legs a bit shakier than I'd anticipated. "They are coming here today?"

"To be informed of their position in the will, of course, and to spend some time over the next few weeks acquainting themselves with you. I've planned a short stay for now, but I hope we shall have some time to fully familiarize ourselves with one another before you will be required to make your final decision. Don't you see? This is why I've chosen to reveal the details of my will directly and not upon my death. So you have plenty of opportunity to make an informed decision."

My lips parted. "You mean to tell me, the gentlemen coming to Moorington Cross are not aware of any of this?"

He turned to his desk, hunting for the wand he'd discarded earlier. "No, indeed they are not, but you mustn't worry. You do that a great deal, you know. You always have. All will be well, my dear. I've made certain of it. Now, if the two of you will excuse me, Major Balfour should be arriving for his session in the next few minutes, and I need some time to ready my mind."

So much for answering any questions I had. Lovely.

Like a child dismissed from the presence of a father, I was forced to follow Mr. Hawkins out the door, my mind awash with my present situation. Yet, as we crossed the landing and made our way down the opposing hall, I thrust out my arm.

"Was this really *your* idea, Mr. Hawkins?"

My outburst seemed to catch him off guard. His right hand retreated to his chin while he kept the other behind his back. "You mean adding you into the will?"

"No, the arranged marriage part. I cannot imagine Mr. Cluett coming up with such an outlandish idea, not when he could have simply willed the money to me. I—"

"Can't you?" Mr. Hawkins released a slow breath, his eyes attuned to mine, the intensity of his voice quick to mirror my own. "First of all, please acquit me of inserting such an extraordinary clause on my own.

Mr. Cluett had marriage on his mind for you long before Mr. Huxley, my employer, and I were summoned to this house. Let me assure you, providing for you was first and foremost on Mr. Cluett's mind." He dipped his head. "I am glad he decided to give you something of a choice."

"Ah—a choice. Is that what you call it?" The cold feeling that had been hovering over me since I'd stepped foot in Mr. Cluett's office settled in the pit of my stomach. I'd been married before, tricked into the arrangement, and that had ended in disaster. Mr. Cluett knew that—I thought I might be sick.

Confusion seized Mr. Hawkins's face as he waited for me to say something further. After all, in his eyes I'd just been handed a fortune. I should be giddy. He hesitated as he breached the silence. "And you're disappointed?"

"Not exactly. I mean, not yet. But what if I meet the gentlemen this afternoon and neither is worthy of marriage or the least interested in me? Where will I be then?"

"With better prospects than you had three days ago, I daresay. You hold all the cards, remember?" There was a bit of exasperation in his voice, yet I could see his mind at work, turning over what I'd said, examining my plight from different angles. However, he hadn't lived through what I had.

"I don't mean to pry and I certainly don't mean to lecture you, Mrs. Pembroke, but Mr. Cluett has told me a great deal about your situation. With no family and no hope of any sort of a future, I would have thought you'd be glad of his generosity, thankful he would arrange something so entirely suitable. He has gone to an abundance of trouble for you."

His statements did make some sense on the surface, yet I'd learned over my unfortunate marriage that solicitors knew how to twist their words, to control every situation to their benefit. My last guardian, Mr. Stanley, came rushing into my mind as well—barristers were even worse.

I glanced up, my stomach souring as I took in Mr. Hawkins's strained countenance. Interesting how the sheen to his handsome demeanor had faded over the course of our conversation. He certainly wasn't the dashing gentleman I'd thought—more of an intelligent shrew.

"Tell me, Mr. Hawkins, how many years have you been a solicitor?"

"This is my first real position." He shuffled his feet. "I'm still an apprentice. I've a few years yet before—"

"Then I doubt you've had the time, the opportunity, or the inclination to meet someone like me." I felt the sweat on my palms as I folded my fingers into a fist. "Inheritance or no, upon my marriage, all that I have will become my husband's. Surely you can see any woman's difficulty there. I, nonetheless, am left with one prayer—that Mr. Cluett has picked two honorable gentlemen for me to choose from. Because as a widow, a woman with little means, and a condition that brought me to Cluett's Mesmeric Hospital in the first place, believe me when I tell you, Mr. Hawkins, I could find myself in a far worse situation than I am in now. I could very well be locked away."

CHAPTER 3

I escaped to the blue salon as I did every morning after my mesmeric session, but I had no intention of partaking in the selection of cold meats or breads and cheeses, not after the morning I'd had. My mind was far too unsettled.

I could see from the doorway that Mrs. Fitzroy, eager to enjoy her luncheon, had already filled her plate and taken a seat at the small round table by the fire. Her attention, however, was across the room on Major Balfour, her finger tapping on the tabletop.

She swallowed a hasty bite of cheese. "I do agree with what you are saying to some extent, but it would behoove you to attempt to understand me as well."

She must not have heard my approach as her gaze remained fixed on Mr. Cluett's only other live-in patient. A scowl joined the wrinkles on her face. "I did not expect the treatments to take so long. This very morning I received a letter from my son, and he has begun asking uncomfortable questions."

Major Balfour raised his voice. "Yes, but—"

"Listen"—she crinkled her nose—"I've come to crisis more than twelve times since arrival. Twelve! Yet my nerves day in and day out are no less ripe." She picked at her bread. "And your feet? Hmm? Are they really any better than when you arrived? I've certainly not seen you walking without a cane."

Major Balfour passed a shaky hand through his dark hair before running it down his face. "Mr. Cluett assures me I'm able to traverse the room on my own power during my trances. If only I could remember doing so, it might change my outlook." He gave a weighted sigh. "At present, all I can do is hope."

I snuck across the carpet and took a seat at Mrs. Fitzroy's table before casting a quick glance at both occupants. "We're all hopeful. Are we not?"

Mrs. Fitzroy lifted her thick gray eyebrows. "Hope can be a dangerous thing. Particularly if it empties your pocketbook when you're not looking." She touched my hand. "Good morning, Amelia, darling." She stared at the empty space on the table in front of me. "Why aren't you eating? Did something happen during your session?"

I tried my best to sound nonchalant. "I didn't end up having a session this morning."

"But weren't you supposed to increase the magnetized water treatments today?"

"Yes. However, Mr. Cluett decided it would be best to wait until tomorrow. He said he didn't want to stress the fluids in my body."

How I wished I were free to disclose the truth about Mr. Cluett's illness as well as the will, but I had little choice except to wait for the official announcement he'd promised to share later in the afternoon. I could only imagine what my fellow patients would think of me then.

Major Balfour clawed at the armrest and staggered to his feet. "Magnetized water treatments indeed." He flipped open the top of his cane to take a whiff of the vinaigrette he kept there. "I don't put much faith in whatever chemical concoction he's brewed up in that *baquet* of his. The iron rod's not been a friend of mine. Now, Mr. Cluett's trances . . . Well, I daresay it's past time I head upstairs." His legs wobbled as he inched across the room. "We're so close to making a breakthrough. I can feel it." He turned back and gave us a wink. "By this time tomorrow I may be Mr. Cluett's first patient to learn how to self-mesmerize."

Mrs. Fitzroy nodded, but I saw the doubt in her eyes. "I do hope so, Major Balfour. You've certainly put in the work."

We watched in silence as he ambled through the door and disappeared from sight. It was several seconds before Mrs. Fitzroy motioned me forward, her lavender scent infusing the air. "The poor man's had a rough go of it today. The ache in his feet kept him up most of the night."

I cast a wayward glance at the door. "It's been four years since Waterloo. Is there nothing else that can be done?"

"A surgeon in London warned him he might never walk again. It's a miracle he's been able to do so for the last few months. I don't know how much longer he can bear the pain. As he said, Mr. Cluett is his last hope." She leaned forward. "I'm afraid I still see flashes of his dark mood when the light all but goes out of his eyes. He had quite a time of it when his cousin—whom he was terribly close to—died so suddenly, you know. It was why he bought that commission in the first place—to forget."

She secured another square of cheese with her fork. "Won't you at least have some tea? You do look a trifle out of sorts."

My stomach clenched. "Tea certainly smooths over a great deal of evils." I stood and idled to the nearby sideboard. "And I can use all the help I can get at present. This morning has been difficult to take in."

Mrs. Fitzroy fanned herself with her free hand. "You must be extremely disappointed to have your treatment delayed. Of course, you've Mr. Pembroke's money to support you here for several years. As I was telling Major Balfour, I received a letter from my son, John, earlier this morning, and he was quite angry with my progress."

"Oh?"

"John doesn't possess the least understanding about Mr. Cluett's methods or the hospital. By the end of his shocking missive, he saw fit to use the word *fraud*." She mouthed the last part as if someone might overhear our conversation.

I slipped back into the seat at her side, positioning my teacup and saucer in front of me. "Is that what you believe? That Mr. Cluett is a fraud?"

Her eyes widened. "I don't know what I thought yesterday or even today, for that matter. I cannot account for vast periods of time I've spent rather pleasantly in a trance in his office. And then when I emerge from the fog, I really do feel far calmer than when I went in. It's inexplicable, really. But when I'm alone in my room at night or this morning while reading John's letter, my heart still quivers as it did before. My legs still shake, and I'm so terribly afraid."

She stared down at her plate of food. "What if Mr. Cluett really isn't making any progress at all with my anxiety? You and Major Balfour have been here longer than me, and you've said yourself you've seen little improvement. What scares me the most is that I haven't the resources to stay here indefinitely."

She shoved another bite of bread into her mouth. "And then I think about what it will be like when I have to leave. I'm well aware John doesn't want me to live with him. He never has, and I've felt such a connection here to you and Major Balfour." She buried her face in her hands. "I don't know what I'll do if John stops paying. I'm not ready to go home . . . to be alone. My nerves will get the better of me then."

I reached for her elbow as Mr. Cluett's will trickled into my mind. And for the first time I thought I might be glad of the provisions. Perhaps some good would come of my difficult situation after all. "Please don't be anxious, Mrs. Fitzroy. We're like family—you, Major Balfour, and me. I promise that whatever happens, the three of us will find a way to help each other."

"You've always been so good to me." She released a sigh. "And I'm well aware you know what it feels like to be forced to live with a relative who doesn't want you. I daresay you've seen little else in your life."

"Yes." I nodded slowly. "Every last guardian but my uncle William.

He was the only one of my relatives who ever showed even a spark of kindness. I think if I could have stayed with him, things would have been different."

Mrs. Fitzroy paused to examine her plate. "Why did he rescind the guardianship and send you away?"

"I was only five years old at the time, but from what I remember he already lived on the Continent. He had business there, and it was no place for a child at the time."

"Sometimes people have little choice in the matter. The hands of fate can be cruel ones."

I leaned forward. "Maybe so, but like I said, this time around it's going to be different. I'm determined we'll find a way to stay together, to care for one another."

Mrs. Fitzroy's smile when genuine crinkled her eyes at the corners, and this was no exception. "Whenever you speak, Amelia dear, you almost make me believe that extraordinary things are possible."

I was summoned to the drawing room at half past three that afternoon. Though I'd conjured up all the courage I could muster to meet the two gentlemen I'd be choosing between, nothing could have prepared me for the uncomfortable wave of fear that followed me down the grand staircase.

At the same time, I knew I could no longer focus on my future alone. I had Mrs. Fitzroy and Major Balfour to consider. My decision as to whom to marry would affect us all.

I'd donned my best round gown of pink sarcenet, and my maid drew up my hair in elegant yet disheveled curls. Deep within, however, I felt a child—the same one who'd been paraded before guardian after guardian in hopes they would offer me a home that would last forever. But they never had, had they?

Not for the little girl with the transient sleeping spells.

It had been the same vicious cycle over and over again. My guardians, my husband. They all thought me lazy at first. That I was avoiding things—a nap in the stables here, a lengthy doze on the sofa there. It didn't take long for them to realize something far worse was underfoot. I was sick and in a strange way they couldn't understand. So off I'd go to another situation, or in the case of my late husband, straight to Cluett's Mesmeric Hospital. If I couldn't be fixed, I'd sure as well better be hidden away.

My hand lingered on the curve of the banister. How could I possibly trust either one of the gentlemen Mr. Cluett had chosen for me? My steps ceased as my slippered foot reached the parquet floor, and I stared a long moment at the front door.

"Considering running away?"

My heart leapt, and I spun to face the voice hiding in the shadows. "Oh, Mr. Hawkins. It's only you."

He stepped into a beam of sunlight, which lay across the floor in elongated squares at the base of the window. He wore a knowing smile along with a black jacket and brocade waistcoat decorated all too perfectly. "Granted, I wouldn't blame you if you did consider bolting."

I swiped a feral glance at the drawing room door. "Have you already met the gentlemen and found them wanting?"

Mr. Hawkins's eyes widened, then he held up his hand. "Heavens, no. I was only . . ."

He gave a nervous laugh as he skulked forward, sobering as he drew up at my side. "Please, allow me to apologize at once, Mrs. Pembroke. I must be the biggest lout in the world to tease you just now. I haven't met either of the gentlemen as of yet. I"—he cocked an eyebrow—"understand they are waiting for you in the drawing room."

I let out a deep breath. "I see." I waved my fingers in the direction of the front door. "Yet your idea of running away does hold a great deal of appeal at present. An arranged marriage indeed. How could Mr. Cluett even consider such a thing?"

Mr. Hawkins bent his head downward before flicking his gaze to meet mine. "As far as I'm aware, he thinks he's doing what's best for you, and it's not exactly an arranged marriage . . ."

"I suppose not, but really, the whole idea of conditional inheritance remains nothing but a perverse extension of the antiquated notions about women that I've come to despise at every stage of my life."

Mr. Hawkins paused. "Well, that was a mouthful." His eyebrows furrowed then released, and he was quick to hold up his hand, staving off a retort. "Listen, I would be the first person to agree that women should have the right to choose their partner in marriage, but you do realize I had no say in regard to the essentials of Mr. Cluett's will?"

I nodded as a slow grin spread across his face, his tone far more than idle. "And as to all the other antiquated notions of society—that discussion, enticing as it is, will have to wait for another time. Your suitors are waiting."

Then he gave me one of those galling shrugs. "You never know. Mr. Cluett's selections may very well turn out better than you seem to think. Trust me, I was in London for the past season and ran into few gentlemen I'd consider your equal. If Mr. Cluett thinks he has found two eligible gentlemen who can string together three words that elevate conversation—"

"Ha." My chest burned. "I suppose you and Mr. Cluett consider yourselves the authority on . . . on what exactly?" I mirrored his pert smile. "Courting? The depths of the female mind?"

His eyes remained maddeningly unreadable, yet his tone was tight enough. "I was merely responding to the level of engagement you've displayed in our interactions, Mrs. Pembroke. I cannot imagine you would consider entertaining any gentleman who is not at a minimum well read."

My smile turned rigid. "If you mean to insinuate that I'm a

bluestocking, then I shall wholeheartedly agree. Curiosity and intellect have always been extremely important to me. However, I won't for one moment acquiesce to your ridiculous assertion that there are no more than two gentlemen in Britain who possess such a clarity of mind, nor that Mr. Cluett has somehow located them and strategically placed them in his drawing room like two flowers waiting for me to pluck the one I fancy."

Mr. Hawkins held my gaze for a long moment before something of a laugh emerged.

I raised my voice. "And furthermore, I imagine you were far too busy flirting and enjoying the latest on-dits of the season to expend any real time conversing with eligible men who are also—as you deem necessary for me—well read."

"Hardly." His laugh turned into a cough. "I was far too inundated with work to do anything of the sort. Although I do hate to shatter any illusions to the contrary." He moved to offer me his arm then checked. "I don't know how or why, but clearly you've labeled me your adversary in all this."

"No . . . not exactly."

"Then what the devil is behind that appalling glare? You've been looking at me like that since I walked into Mr. Cluett's office this morning."

I forced my jaw muscles to relax and managed a rather guilty, "What glare, sir?"

"Hmm . . ." He crossed his arms, his eyes glinting in the afternoon sun. He rested his shoulder against the banister as if he might not join me in the drawing room after all. "It's like you're measuring my worth and . . . I don't know . . . enjoying it."

I fought back a grin as I straightened my back. "Goodness knows you would deserve such censure." I stole a sideways glance at the door, certain it was best to avoid his enticing gaze. My face was far too hot already. "Tell me, Mr. Hawkins, do all the solicitors at Pembroke and Huxley speak so condescendingly to the people involved in their wills?"

"None whatsoever." He drew up beside me, forcing me to acknowledge him once again. "You, Mrs. Pembroke, have been fortunate enough to be associated with the only one at the firm who won't slip into one of those antiquated notions you so detest."

"What a relief." I narrowed my eyes then drew back. "As you said earlier, it is past time we joined the others."

He wriggled his hand from his pocket and extended his left arm. Unwittingly my attention slid down the sleeve of his superfine jacket to his disfigured glove.

He went on. "Your late husband was a good friend to me when I needed it, so I do hope we can find a way to begin again. Mr. Pembroke was my mentor and I'm willing to do anything I can to help his widow."

His mentor?

I took a careless step back as the specter of my late husband darkened the air between us. Inch by inch, I lifted my gaze to meet Mr. Hawkins's equally startled one, and I had to remind myself that no one knew the real Mr. Pembroke except me. At least, I hoped Mr. Hawkins hadn't.

I'd chosen long ago not to tarnish the Pembroke name. However, it also wasn't the first time I had wondered if Mr. Pembroke had mentioned me to any of his colleagues prior to his death. Granted, I had no intention of broaching that uncomfortable subject. Not now, not ever.

I accepted Mr. Hawkins's outstretched arm and spoke without thinking. "Was it an accident?"

At first he seemed lost as to what I was referring to, glancing about the room as if it might provide him the answer.

I touched his jacket sleeve. "I meant your hand."

"Oh . . . uh . . . no." His muscles tightened beneath my fingers as his voice fell flat. "It's something I've had since birth."

Suddenly I felt like an intruder, his hand no doubt a private matter I never should have questioned. "I-I didn't mean to stare earlier in Mr. Cluett's office. I—"

"Please, you needn't apologize. Heaven knows I'm used to curiosity, but"—he motioned his chin toward the drawing room door—"it really is high time we go in there. Mr. Cluett is bound to be wondering where you are."

"I suppose so."

We paced awkwardly forward, the door looming larger with each step.

"Wait!" I dragged us to a halt. "Were you serious about what you said earlier?"

"About running away?" He gave me a shrewd grin. "I don't think I would recommend that at present."

"No, about helping me." I swallowed hard. "For Mr. Pembroke's sake."

"Of course." I felt his arm tense beneath the fabric of his jacket. "Yet there is little recourse but for you to go inside that drawing room and find out about the gentlemen for yourself. Remember, at the end of the day you still have a choice. You can refuse to follow the will and give up the inheritance."

The subtlety to his voice gave me pause, and I eyed him a moment, taking in every inch of his bearing. I had to remind myself not to be fooled by a solicitor again.

Mr. Hawkins simply wanted to placate me, to make this whole process easier—for him. Once he'd wrapped up his business affairs at Moorington Cross, he would be on his way back to London, congratulating himself on a job well done. I would be the one left here to deal with the consequences.

I bit my lip then released. A solicitor could still be useful. I cast a quick glance up. "Considering you are a self-proclaimed master at examining the suitability of gentlemen for marriage, perhaps while you are here you would be willing to spend some time with these two men. You know, really try to learn who they are. Figure out that which they hope to keep hidden. It might make my decision easier to get the unbiased male perspective on things."

His tongue darted out to lick his lips. "You mean you want me to spy for you?"

"And why not? You're perfectly situated to do so, and you've already ingratiated yourself into the intricacies of my future when you wrote up that atrocious will."

"You little termagant. That was Mr. Cluett, remember? I only put his words onto paper." He reached for the doorknob, but he didn't release the latch. "All right, if I agree to help you, I need you to promise me one thing in return."

"What's that?"

"That you'll keep an open mind about this situation—for all our sakes."

"And why wouldn't I?"

He flashed me one last smile before he opened the door. "Reading a lady's thoughts is just one more of my admirable qualities."

CHAPTER 4

One measly step into the drawing room and I knew without a doubt the decision of which gentleman to marry would not be an easy one. Keeping an open mind as Mr. Hawkins had suggested hardly seemed feasible.

Mr. Cluett rose and hurried to greet us at the door. "Why, there you are, my dear girl. We have been waiting an age"—an astute widening of his eyes—"but you needn't worry. It's not been an unpleasant one."

Mr. Cluett gave Mr. Hawkins a dismissive nod, and he released my arm, retiring to the back of the room where he could no doubt watch the proceedings without putting himself forward.

If only I could do the same.

There would be none of that, of course, as Mr. Cluett urged me to the center of the blue rug like a horse led onto the field at the start of a race. His tone remained the perfect mixture of ease and gaiety. "Major Balfour has kept us entertained with whimsical stories of his childhood at the seaside. But now that you are here, I'm happy to carry on."

My nervous gaze passed over Major Balfour and Mrs. Fitzroy, who were seated on the sofa against the wall—our usual spot after dinner—each unable to conceal their confusion and anticipation. Major Balfour ran his hands down his breeches as Mrs. Fitzroy bobbed her head back and forth, whipping the ostrich feather in her hair against the wainscoting like a brush.

I gave them a quick smile, but my attention was promptly arrested by the two strangers on the opposite side of the room.

A full second of wretched throbbing assaulted my ears as my heart sought to escape my chest, then a wash of cold nerves took over. I raised my eyes to appraise my suitors, but the sights and sounds of my first meeting with Mr. Pembroke flashed into my mind and my vision blurred. I'd thought my late husband attractive and well mannered that day. How terribly wrong I'd been.

Mr. Cluett must have sensed my uneasiness as he made a great show of my presentation.

A tall brown-headed gentleman with a long face and jutting chin stepped forward and was introduced as Mr. Lymington. He looked to be around thirty and was well dressed but not ostentatious. A stilted bow followed a short greeting, and he instantly put me in mind of a giraffe—graceful yet awkward, all bones and knees, but in an agreeable sort of way.

"I am pleased to make your acquaintance." Though he spoke prettily enough, he was quick to avert his eyes, an air of irritated tolerance settling across his face.

I could only assume Mr. Cluett had not revealed the specifics of the new will as of yet.

Next came a slightly younger gentleman, who hadn't bothered to move from where he leaned against the casement of the window until Mr. Cluett called him over. His steps were lazy yet assured, and it took me all of two seconds to recognize his infamous name once announced—Mr. Montague, heir to Whitefall. Inwardly I flinched. Even with my sheltered existence, I had heard of the cad of Kent.

My world shifted as it shrank before my eyes. So this was it? My two suitors? What on earth had Mr. Cluett been thinking? Moreover, why Mr. Montague of all people? Was Mr. Cluett aware of his reputation? I managed a hasty glance at Mr. Lymington. His tight-lipped snobbery was already looking better and better.

Mr. Cluett's jovial voice finally instigated a bit of interest on Mr. Montague's part and he gave me a flowery bow. Slowly, carefully, he straightened, and all at once I was face-to-face with the cad.

Strange that I found his appearance remarkably average at first—his height, his thick black hair, his smooth features. Perhaps the rumors had been exaggerated. After all, he was only a man. Yet when he captured my hand, settled his ice-blue eyes on mine, and spread a seamless smile, I encountered the twinge of what I could only imagine scores of women had experienced before—that delicious hint of unbridled curiosity. What would it be like to kiss such a man?

My cheeks flamed, and I recovered my hand at once, turning to my friends on the sofa. Thankfully Mr. Cluett had encouraged everyone in the house to be present for his forthcoming announcement, which had always been the way with us at Moorington Cross—every patient considered family.

Mr. Cluett helped me to a chair and a cup of tea, then assumed his place at the front of the room. "I want to begin by thanking you all for coming together this afternoon. I realize both of our new arrivals made sacrifices to journey here and stay for the time being."

Mr. Montague perched himself on the edge of a nearby chair and tossed a perceptive glance at me, that wry grin never far from his lips. "You have our undivided attention, Mr. Cluett."

Yet did he? I couldn't help but notice Mr. Lymington's scowl and morose stare as he toured the left side of the room, his fingers far too busy with his watch fob to pay much attention to anything else.

Mr. Cluett didn't seem to notice or care as he puffed out his shoulders, ever the dramatic host. "Allow me to present Mr. Hawkins, my solicitor from Pembroke and Huxley. As I wrote to the both of you"—his eyes darted between Mr. Montague and Mr. Lymington—"this meeting today has everything to do with the contents of my newest will. If you would, Mr. Hawkins."

I couldn't help but notice how Mr. Lymington abruptly ceased his pacing at the word *will*.

Mr. Hawkins made his way to the front of the room and began very much like he had with me earlier in the day, the two gentlemen nodding along with him. It was only when he got to the marriage clause that Mr. Lymington gripped the back of a chair and hung his head. "You can't be serious, Cluett. Only last year you said—"

"Enough." Mr. Cluett's hand shot up, his voice razor sharp. "There will be no discussion about the contents of this will or the previous one. You may consider my decision final." He ticked his finger in the air. "Don't make the callous mistake of embarrassing yourself in front of the lady."

Mr. Lymington thrust his hand through his hair, and though he gave me something of a contrite nod, the expression on his face was clear enough. He didn't relish an alliance with me any more than I did with him.

It was Mr. Montague who surprised me.

Mr. Hawkins finished the details of the marriage clause, ushering in an uncomfortable silence. That is, until Mr. Montague clapped his hands, a smug smirk sneaking its way across his face. "Good show, Cluett. Egads, I didn't think it possible, but you've found a way to astonish me yet again." He tossed a wink at me. "But you won't hear me say it's entirely unwanted." He sent a tight glare to Mr. Hawkins. "And the choice is the lady's, you say?"

Mr. Hawkins shifted on his feet. "That it is. Hers and hers alone."

There was a tinge of laughter on Mr. Montague's breath as he glanced over his shoulder. "I daresay the game's afoot, Lymington."

Mr. Lymington returned a dead stare first at Mr. Montague, then Mr. Hawkins, before clearing his throat. "What if we think better of this whole situation and decide to leave this instant?"

Mr. Cluett fumbled with his spectacles before perching them on his nose. "Then you shall get nothing from me, young man. It was for just such a purpose that I asked Mr. Hawkins to stay in residence. Believe me, the will can be altered again." He held his posture stiff for several seconds before his shoulders slumped. "The two of you need to understand how dear Mrs. Pembroke has become to me over the past few years. In due time you'll be glad of my provisions."

Mr. Montague strolled over to the fireplace near my chair and positioned his arm on the mantel. "Who says we're not already? I, for one, find myself very well pleased."

Mr. Lymington's face flushed crimson at Mr. Montague's declaration, and he narrowed his eyes. "Naturally, *you* would after you've cut up London and disgraced yourself in every drawing room from Falmouth to Canter—"

"Gentlemen, please." A muscle twitched in Mr. Cluett's jaw. "This quibbling with one another like a pair of street urchins in my drawing room is unconscionable." A hesitant glance at me. "You should be saving your breath for Mrs. Pembroke, and respectfully at that." His voice fell. "I had planned for the both of you to spend some time acquainting yourselves with her in the coming days, but I have to admit, after your abhorrent behavior this afternoon, I begin to question whether she shall agree to such an arrangement at all." He stared out the window for a long moment. "I believe it best for us all to retire to our rooms at present. Supper shall be served promptly at six o'clock."

Mr. Montague rolled his eyes to the ceiling. "Brilliant . . . country hours. How quaint." Then a snide, "You'll be sure to enjoy that, won't you, Lymington?"

Mr. Lymington opened his mouth, yet nothing came forth. He whirled to the window, his hands clenching and releasing. A second of strained silence, then he turned back only to pitch forward into an awkward bow. He followed the display all too quickly with a nearly unintelligible, "Perhaps you're right, Cluett. Good day, Mrs. Pembroke, Mrs. Fitzroy." And stormed from the room.

His footsteps pounded down the hall until they were replaced by the emergence of Mr. Montague's petty laughter. The cad folded his arms across his chest and tipped his head back. "I've always said Lymington should be onstage at Covent Gardens. I'd pay good money to see that again. Wouldn't you?"

"Montague . . ." Mr. Cluett's voice drifted away as Mr. Montague knelt beside my chair.

"I do apologize for my"—he motioned his head to the side—"you know, I'm not sure what to call the swell. He's certainly not my friend. Either way, if Lymington's behavior in London had not already done so, Mrs. Pembroke, his thoughtless actions today lead me to question the respectability he so deftly clings to."

"I daresay he was only shocked by the wording of the will, as we all were. I—"

He wrested my hand from my lap, silencing me with a single touch. "Don't worry that pretty head of yours. I promise you, I'm not easily rattled." He drew my hand to his lips and placed a kiss on my glove. "Forget Lymington. Forget all of this. I hope you will grant me some time tomorrow as we have much to discuss. Suffice it to say, I take the contents of Cluett's will, my future, and the intricacies of my heart quite seriously. Neither of us wish to be played for a fool."

He released my hand and it drifted back to my lap, seemingly of its own accord, a touch lighter than before, but no less vulnerable. Mr. Montague made his way from the room, a certain swagger about his steps, one last shrewd look at me. I couldn't help but watch him until he disappeared from sight. We all did. But I was fairly certain I was the only one floundering internally from a vile mixture of gall and disbelief.

How could I possibly entertain either one of these gentlemen?

Yet at the same time, I perfectly understood Mr. Lymington's disgust. Had I not responded the same way hours before? And Mr. Montague—what had he meant about the intricacies of his heart? Maybe there was more to the cad than society's hostile opinions of him and a bit of misplaced wit. Thank goodness Mr. Hawkins had pledged to help me sort out the truth.

I glanced over to where he stood at the front of the room, astonished to find him staring back. He looked so hopeful, as if the meeting had gone far better than planned, as if those two gentlemen actually were the cream of London society.

Pledged to help indeed. I could have screamed.

Thankfully, Major Balfour motioned me to the sofa at just that moment, and I escaped into Mrs. Fitzroy's and his comforting hands.

But his were ice cold. "Mr. Cluett disclosed his tenuous state of health while we were awaiting you and the gentlemen earlier." The shake of Major Balfour's head was so delicate it was more like a quiver. "Mrs. Fitzroy and I are still trying to make sense of what that means for us, how long we'll have to make the necessary arrangements for our futures. But all those worries aside, I can't tell you how glad I am you're to be taken care of."

My gaze swung unbidden to the door. "Yes . . . taken care of." I shifted on the sofa. "Mr. Cluett said it was a minor complaint. I believe we will have some time before he will be unable to continue his treatments. There is hope yet. And when the unthinkable does occur, I have every intention of taking care of both you and Mrs. Fitzroy. Rest assured, you can stay at Moorington Cross as long as you wish."

I adjusted the folds of my skirt. "And I've given our situation a great deal of thought over the afternoon. I understand that Mr. Cluett trained at a mesmeric school in France, then led his own school before coming here. He actually studied directly under Franz Anton Mesmer and then Karl Wolfart. If we could somehow contact Mr. Wolfart, he might be able to recommend someone to continue our therapies. All is not lost."

Mrs. Fitzroy grasped my hand. "That sounds lovely, Amelia, but those gentlemen . . . I fear they may not be in agreement with your plans. Hiring another doctor and bringing him here to stay would involve a great deal of money."

I took a deep breath. "I will admit, the marriage stipulation does give me pause, but I mean to be certain of their agreement before making my final selection."

She gave me a wan smile. "A very good idea. What do you think, Major Balfour?"

He gripped his cane, a grimace settling on his face. "I don't like any part of it, not at all. You've been put in a difficult position, and you must be extremely careful, Mrs. Pembroke. From what I observed this afternoon, I fear both men might well have something to hide. Who do they think they are, parading around this room bickering like they lost something dear to them? It begs me to ask the question: What exactly was in Mr. Cluett's previous will?"

CHAPTER 5

I jerked awake, gasping for air.

Daring shadows took shape around me as the chilled night air crept down my throat like ice. I thrust myself into a sitting position as I scanned the depths of my bedchamber for what had brought me roaring to my senses. But my room stood motionless, the soft tick of the casement clock pricking my ears. Perhaps I'd only been dreaming.

Then I heard it again—a bone-chilling cry.

My fingers contracted against the top of my coverlet. Mrs. Fitzroy?

Somewhat dazed by my abrupt awakening, I staggered to my feet only to fumble with my robe.

Another scream rent the air, and my gaze snapped to my bedchamber door, my muscles tightening like a cord. Something was terribly wrong. My movements were jerky at best as I thrust my arms through the sleeves of my dressing gown and grappled with the ribbon, the hidden folds of darkness creeping ever closer.

Across the carpet I snatched my slippers from beneath the settee, barely managing my second shoe before escaping into the corridor.

Moonlight poured in through the leaded windows of the west wing, but an eerie haze clung to the distant light. Mrs. Fitzroy resided in the apartment next to mine, but her terrified screams had certainly come from the opposite direction. Though she was prone to bouts of anxiety, I'd never heard her cry out in such a way.

I had no time to lose. A quick glance behind me and I hastened down the long hall.

Distant footsteps echoed off the stone walls in muffled waves, the house teeming to life around me.

I erupted onto the landing at a full run, plowing headlong into a robust yet equally lithe figure shrouded in darkness. The shadowed person caught me hard against his chest, his arms quick to support my back. "What the deuce?"

My heart nearly stopped. It was Mr. Hawkins.

A moment of breathless confusion held us transfixed until his hands retreated to my shoulders and he held me at arm's length. He, too, had donned a dressing gown, his hair unbridled, his expression sharp. He must have heard my rather loud intake of breath as his eyes snapped to mine in the dim light.

"Mrs. Pembroke." His voice was nothing but a whisper. Like lightning, he released me, taking a wild step back as he readjusted his robe and plunged his left hand into his pocket. "Is something amiss? I heard someone calling for help. I"—he raked his hair with his free hand—"had a terrible inkling it might be you."

"Me?"

"With everything that has happened since the adjustment of the will . . . What I mean to say is . . ." I thought I saw his muscles stiffen beneath the thin material of his robe, and he lightly shook his head. "It's been a taxing day, and I'm relieved to find you well."

"I am well." My pulse throbbed in my ears, and I had to force myself to speak over the incessant pounding. "It was Mrs. Fitzroy you heard, but not from our hall." I glanced across the landing. "I have no idea where she is at present. I came barreling this way to find her. I apologize if my behavior seemed a bit unladylike. But, you see, Mrs. Fitzroy suffers hallucinations from time to time. I'm afraid she may be having a bad spell—"

Mr. Hawkins's focus shifted ever so slightly over my shoulder, and he silenced me with a motion of his chin.

I mouthed the word *what* before capturing his meaning and the reality of our unfortunate situation. Warmth lit my cheeks and I whirled about to find Mr. Montague cresting the grand staircase.

A drink in his hand, the cad sauntered forward. He was fully dressed but for his missing cravat and unbuttoned waistcoat. He rested his hip on the banister before settling his languid gaze on me.

"What a surprise, Mrs. Pembroke." His finger swung like an inebriated pendulum between Mr. Hawkins and me. "I never would have thought you the sort of lady who enjoyed a dalliance, but one can't really know a person on first meeting, can they?"

"Don't be ridiculous." There was a flame to Mr. Hawkins's tone as he stepped between Mr. Montague and me. "Mrs. Pembroke's and my meeting just now was nothing but a curst accident. I assume you heard the screams that brought the two of us darting from our respective rooms?"

Mr. Montague swirled the contents in his glass, his eyes still smarting with his own clever retort, before downing the remaining liquid. "I heard nothing of the kind, but I must confess I've been rather pleasantly engaged in the blue salon for the past half hour, too distracted to hear whatever it is you are referring to."

Miss Seton emerged on the stairs behind him, her hand guarding a candle as she brushed into our little circle. She took one long look at the lot of us and shook her head. "'Pon my word, the bell to the master's bedchamber is a-ringing off the hook."

Mr. Hawkins held out his arm to delay her. "Mr. Cluett's room?"

"That's what I said, didn't I?" Her voice shook, but she'd not lost the superiority she affected so well. "He never does call me at night. I'm lost as to what can be wrong now."

Mr. Hawkins angled his chin, a vacant look transforming his face. "I daresay time may be of the essence. We heard a scream just moments ago. Please, allow me to accompany you at once."

A pop of the eyebrows and Miss Seton pushed her way through

our little group, leading the way with her outstretched candle, a cautious expectancy to her steps.

I eyed Mr. Montague and he gave me a shrug, his innocent-looking inquiry somewhat at odds with his glassy eyes and full lips. Was he really curious what caused the frantic ringing of Mr. Cluett's bell, or was this simply another form of amusement for a dissolute rogue?

Either way, I had no intention of remaining on the landing with him alone at night in little else but my night rail, even for the merest second. I moved quickly to follow Mr. Hawkins down the hall, Mr. Montague trailing behind us.

The candle's winking glow revealed glimpses of an ornate hall. Dark wainscoting rose from the floor while medieval sconces littered the walls—each thread of iron swirling to form a torch-like pedestal. I was fairly certain none of us had ever stepped one foot into Mr. Cluett's private sanctuary besides Miss Seton. I certainly hadn't.

So much of Moorington Cross required money and attention that I knew very well Mr. Cluett refused to spend, from the worn carpets to the endless corridors filled with peeling wallpaper and dank odors, but the path to Mr. Cluett's private sanctuary was something out of a dream. One alcove after another housed intricate marble busts followed by the occasional rococo table. The carpet was so thick my slippers sank in with each step.

Miss Seton paused to light the sconce across from a curved doorway, then motioned forward. "His room is just there." She didn't move.

Was she afraid to enter? Or was it something else?

One glance turned into many, everyone frozen where we stood. We hadn't heard Mrs. Fitzroy's scream for some time, and it seemed we all needed a breath. It was Mr. Montague who stepped forward and banged on the door.

Silence was followed by pounding footsteps, then the door swung open.

Mrs. Fitzroy wore a nightcap and a dressing gown, her face as white as the lace on her collar. "Thank goodness. Oh my, thank good-ness." She was quivering from head to toe. "He's dead I tell you. Dead!"

Mr. Hawkins pushed forward. "Who? Mr. Cluett?"

She extended a shaky arm, lengthening her pointer finger in the direction of the far side of the room. "See for yourself. I-I cannot go over there again."

Part numb, part confused, the group of us inched forward into Mr. Cluett's large bedchamber only to stop a few feet from the edge of the rug.

My mouth fell open, my mind grappling to process what I saw.

There before a snapping fire sat a beautiful copper tub, the ghostly flames illuminating the inert form of Mr. Cluett. His legs were tucked unnaturally against his body, his face far beneath the motionless sur-face of the bathwater.

Miss Seton was the first of us to speak or move as she let out a strangled cry and rushed over to the tub's side before falling onto her knees. Mr. Montague prowled behind her. I thought he meant to lend her his support, but he merely edged in next to her and peered over the edge of the tub to get a better look at the body. "A suicide, do you think?"

"No." I shook my head, the binding clutches of my initial shock ebbing away to raw emotion. "He would never do such a thing."

A half smile crossed Mr. Montague's face as he peered over his shoulder back at the group. "Where's Lymington?"

Mr. Hawkins dipped his chin. "You don't think he has anything to do with this, do you?"

"Do with what?" As if Mr. Lymington had been waiting for a dra-matic entrance all along, he breached the door and wandered toward us. "What's to do?"

He didn't stop his advance until he was inches from the foot of the tub, his voice dropping to a strangled whisper. "Good heavens."

Mr. Montague tipped his head back and laughed. "Leave

it to Lymington for the well-timed and spectacularly apropos understatement."

Mr. Lymington ignored Mr. Montague, redirecting his inquiries to Mr. Hawkins. "How did this happen?"

"We were just beginning to sort it out. Unfortunately, Mr. Cluett was found in his current condition. No witnesses that we know of as of yet." He cast a look over the group. "Mr. Montague has offered up suicide as a possible guess."

Mr. Lymington pressed his lips together, his response slow to come. "Mr. Cluett did just square away all his affairs. The timing would certainly support such a theory. Was there a note in the room? Who discovered him?"

Tears poured down Mrs. Fitzroy's cheeks and her hand shook as she fell back against the wall. "It was me. I did." Her eyes widened like those of a scared doe. "I simply came to ask him a question about my treatments."

Her voice sounded foreign, her words suddenly uneven. "My son had . . . sent me a letter, you see, but . . . that is neither . . . here nor there. Mr. Cluett didn't answer the door, and when I came in to wait for him, he was . . . well, he was . . . as you see him now. I couldn't help but scream . . . I"—she pinched the bridge of her nose—"there was no letter or anyone else in the room. I felt faint, so very, very faint. That's when I began pulling the bell. What else could I do? There was no chance to save him."

I moved in close and took Mrs. Fitzroy's arm. "I think it's time you return to your room. The gentlemen can handle whatever must be done tonight."

Her eyes looked glazed in the moonlight. "Oh, Amelia. How can I manage the steps required?"

"You will do well enough with me beside you." I motioned to Miss Seton, and I was surprised to see a hateful scowl as she hesitated to take Mrs. Fitzroy's other arm. I sent her a harsh glare, and she finally did so, the three of us moving forward. "See, we shall all do it together."

We came upon Major Balfour at the open door, the final guest of the house entering the fray. He took one peek at Mrs. Fitzroy and his concern was instantaneous. "Are you ill? What has happened?"

I thought it best to answer in Mrs. Fitzroy's stead. "She's had a fright . . . as we all have and mustn't be importuned. Be so good as to continue on into Mr. Cluett's bedchamber. Mr. Hawkins will be more than willing to apprise you of what we have discovered this evening."

I gave him a reassuring touch on his hand perched on his cane, and he offered me a nod before trudging on into the room.

I led the ladies of the household to the landing and initiated the turn to Mrs. Fitzroy's and my hall when Miss Seton pulled away. "I've a great deal to do, of course. I daresay the two of you can manage the rest of the way."

"But—"

"I've to awaken the staff and send Andrews for the parish constable."

I was hesitant to nod, but I did so as I knew she was right. Andrews had been butler at the house for the past decade, and Mr. Cluett had always trusted him. He would get things into motion. There was much to be done in the hours ahead, and I doubted there would be any sleep for us tonight.

She whirled away and made for the stairs, pausing at the banister to crook a shrewd glare over her shoulder. "Granted, I suppose you're the lady of the house now. The servants shall await your orders."

My throat felt thick. "Do as you see fit. I'll take Mrs. Fitzroy to her room and administer a dose of her medicine to help her sleep. It may be some time, but I'll return as soon as I can to see what remains to be done."

Miss Seton's owlish look faded some and she affected a tight nod, yet I knew the motion pained her. For decades she'd reigned over everyone at the hospital. Even Mr. Cluett seemed all but defenseless against her power. So many times he'd referred to her as the true mistress of Moorington, as if she were his equal or, worse, his courtesan.

"Very well, Mrs. Pembroke." She checked, a transient smile creeping its way onto her face. "Of course, it will not be *Mrs. Pembroke* for long now, will it?"

CHAPTER 6

Mrs. Fitzroy required quite a bit of coaxing before I convinced her to lie down in her bed. Her nerves were afire as her thoughts scattered first one direction then the next. Unsure how best to help her, I found myself powerless to do so, and for several heart-pounding minutes I feared her complete collapse. But soon enough the herbal concoction of valerian, saffron, and tansy oil tea she utilized for sleep, to which I'd added a touch of laudanum, began to ease the worst of it, the jitters in her hands disappearing, her near-frantic words dwindling, then escaping into the thin night air.

Finally she tipped her head back against the pillows and I gave a sigh of relief. I scooted a slat-backed chair near her bedside and sat. Peering down at her troubled face, I inwardly cursed the chain of events that led up to this moment. Good, kind Mrs. Fitzroy was the last person in the house who should have chanced upon Mr. Cluett this evening.

The results of her medicine ushered in a rather sudden and unsettling silence—the insidious sort of gloom I didn't notice lurking in the shadows until it was upon me. The sickening remembrance of everything that had happened in Mr. Cluett's room gathered in my stomach and tightened my abdominal muscles. How could I even begin to process all this?

Before long I found myself staring over my shoulder at Mrs. Fitzroy's bedchamber door as I imagined the scenario likely playing out in Mr. Cluett's apartment. A part of me ached to be there, to help make sense of the utterly senseless discovery, but I could not leave Mrs. Fitzroy's room. Not until her medicine had soothed her to some sort of sleep.

I deigned a peek at the clock on the dresser across the room, the full weight of the evening now heavy on my shoulders. Mr. Cluett—my doctor, my counselor, my friend—was gone forever, and nothing in my world would ever be the same.

None of our worlds would.

A shaft of moonlight feathered into the room through a slit in Mrs. Fitzroy's chintz curtains and obscured the lines on her face. She was calmer now, motionless. The moonlight's muted glow exposed a glimpse of the strength I'd heard she possessed in her youth—that nearly forgotten period in her life before she'd endured a grievous assault at the hands of vagrants on the streets of London. Yet somehow that strength was accompanied by a vacant look that had crept into her eyes over the course of the evening and remained fixed in place.

What could I possibly say at such a moment?

"Do try to sleep, Mrs. Fitzroy. I don't intend to leave for some time." I wiped a stray tear from my cheek before reaching forward to adjust her blanket beneath her chin.

Her lips twitched into something resembling contrition, but it was sterile, unnatural, angst-ridden.

I waited to say more, hoping she would succumb to the medication and her eyes would drift closed, but her attention remained stationary on the ceiling. A new, deeper level of anxiety stirred within my chest. Was there more plaguing Mrs. Fitzroy's mind than the loss of our doctor and the sight of his body?

I bent forward, driven to relieve the growing tension in the air. "Would it help if I read to you from the Bible or a novel perhaps?"

Her head lolled to the side. "Thank you, my dear, but I know I couldn't focus." She glanced down at her hands, her fingers curled into balls on the coverlet, her skin stretched white across her swollen knuckles. "What do you suppose happened to him, Amelia? I . . . I just can't help but think that his death was somehow my fault."

Again, that tingle of unease. *Her* fault? I tempered my voice. "What would make you say such a thing?"

"John's letter, the one I told you about, well, you see . . . it arrived yesterday morning." She was almost breathless, each word more difficult than the last. "I read Mr. Cluett the whole wretched correspondence during my afternoon session today. I thought he might help me form a response, but I begin to wonder if John's accusations set him off. Mr. Cluett was so distant when I finished, so unnaturally cold . . . I . . . Mr. Montague did suggest it could have been a suicide."

I paused to examine my thoughts. "Mr. Cluett has certainly been questioned before about his methods. Not everyone is as keen on mesmerism as he is." I pressed my lips together. "In fact, I don't think John's letter would have come as a surprise to him at all. Nor should you consider yourself the least bit responsible."

She didn't look convinced, so I went on. "You remember the Faculty of Medicine in France, don't you? Though flawed in their methods, they evaluated Mr. Cluett's instructor, Dr. Mesmer, and found it highly unlikely that magnetic fluid even exists. That was years before Mr. Cluett trained with him. Mr. Cluett was well aware of the study and chose to utilize a *baquet* in his practice anyway. He believed quite deeply in mesmerism. After all, he's observed the effects himself. So you see, John's questions would have been nothing new to him."

Emotion crept into my voice as I took her hand. "This terrible tragedy was nothing more than an unfortunate accident. For all we know, Mr. Cluett may have simply fallen asleep at the wrong moment. His heart may have seized. He warned us he wasn't well. Any number of things could have caused him to lose consciousness and slip beneath the water, sadly ending his life."

Mrs. Fitzroy blinked, her focus darting about the room. "But if you're right, that means we may never know what truly happened. The poor, dear man. I . . . ." She reached for the glass of water beside the bed and took a long, slow drink, her eyes widening in turn. "That is, unless his death wasn't natural . . . and someone in this house sought to do him harm." Her eyes darted first one direction then the next. "Amelia . . . what would you say if I told you I saw something, or rather someone, in Mr. Cluett's private hall? Do you think that could mean something?"

"Well . . . yes—"

The glass shook in her hand, and she slammed it back on the table. "I didn't give much thought to it until now. But there was a man—at least, I think it was a man—in the corridor before I entered Mr. Cluett's apartment."

A chill washed over my body. "Go on."

"Whoever it was, he saw me. I know he did. He slunk into the shadows of the alcove by the large stone coat of arms as I approached Mr. Cluett's door. The sudden movement gave me a terrible fright." Her hand flew to her mouth. "Oh yes. I remember it all now. That's the reason I plunged into Mr. Cluett's room without an invitation in the first place. I dashed inside to tell him what I'd seen, and then I happened to glance back . . . Oh, Amelia, the figure had simply disappeared. Who would have been in Mr. Cluett's corridor at such a moment?"

I tried to stay calm, but my heart was racing. "There are several gentlemen staying at Moorington Cross at present, many with perfectly sensible reasons to be anywhere in the house—not to mention the servants. Let's not get ahead of ourselves. Why don't you start by describing exactly what you saw?"

"The man was average height, I think." She shook her head. "Or not—heavens, I don't know. He had on a long coat of some kind . . . or a lady's gown. Oh dear, I wish I could remember, but everything is hazy in my mind. All I know is that I saw a pair of devilish eyes glinting back at me in the moonlight. Everything else about the figure remained in the shadows." She flinched back slightly. "At least, I think it did . . . Wait . . . There was something—a flash, like from a spill . . . or . . . or . . . maybe a tinderbox."

"Like he was lighting a candle? Did you smell anything?"

She scrunched up her nose. "I don't think so, but I was terribly afraid at the time. I-I didn't linger. The person certainly could have been doing so."

"But why wouldn't the man declare himself if he was only lighting a candle? And you said he shrank away at first, then disappeared."

She nodded quickly. "He most certainly did. I can't put the feeling into words precisely, but I knew in that moment my life was in danger. Whoever it was, he didn't want me to discover him, but he knows I did. Oh Amelia, I begin to fear that whoever I saw carried out something frightful."

"Indeed." A knot formed on my brow. "Unfortunately, there is simply no way to identify him from what you described, not unless someone else saw this person around the same time. I think it best to disclose what you observed to Mr. Hawkins as soon as we can."

She grabbed my hand, her fingers claw-like in the darkness. "But can we trust the solicitor? You said never to do so."

I sat back in my chair, Mr. Pembroke's throaty laughter echoing in my ears. Could we trust Mr. Hawkins? Strange that I had been so quick to think of him. I gave her a reassuring squeeze. "I'm not certain we should consider anyone as absolutely trustworthy at present, but it would seem he also works for me now. I'll be forced to disclose what I know to him one way or another. Although we should proceed with extreme caution."

I tucked her arm beneath the coverlet and encouraged her to lie back down, yet her words of warning refused to leave my mind.

Why had I come upon Mr. Hawkins so suddenly on the landing?

Had he been waiting there for me all along, for everyone to emerge after Mrs. Fitzroy's screams?

No. He'd seemed as frazzled as I was at the time. Of course, he was a solicitor like my late husband, and the great Mr. Pembroke would have been calm, cool, and collected in just such a situation. He'd explained to me within my first few days of knowing him how he'd been coached to keep his emotions under control at all times. He'd thought me weak if I displayed the least sentiment or spark of passion.

Mr. Hawkins would have received the same instruction. If not at university, then by Mr. Pembroke himself. My shoulders slumped. It was entirely possible that Mr. Hawkins's kindness and lack of control had all been an act.

Mrs. Fitzroy fought a yawn, but it snuck up nonetheless. "Murder or not, this whole terrible situation puts me in mind of what happened to the elder Cluett brother."

My attention snapped to the bed. "Elder Cluett brother?"

"Surely you've heard the villagers' stories about the Cluett family curse—that the men tend to die prematurely. After today I begin to wonder if those stories have been right all along."

I tucked a stray curl behind my ear. "What on earth are you talking about?"

She eyed me beneath heavy lids, the medicine working to cloud her gaze. "You don't remember, do you?"

"Remember what?"

She licked her dry lips. "The reason Mr. Cluett went off to train in France in the first place. When the curse struck down his elder brother, our dear doctor was overcome with grief."

Her eyelids slipped closed, and I was forced to poke her arm to hear more.

"What happened to the elder brother?"

Her eyes shot open. "The poor man was murdered in cold blood."

"Murdered." My voice a bit breathless, I said it more to myself than to her, then cleared my throat. "By whom?"

"There's the rub . . . never did find out." Her sentences had begun to slur together, her mouth sliding back and forth over each word. "There was some talk of the girl's father flying into a rage after she went against his wishes, but his wife swears he never left London."

"What girl?"

"I'm not aware of her name. Really it's unimportant because the couple never made it to Gretna Green. You see, Mr. Cluett's elder brother was riding escort at the time and was shot off his horse on the way—dead on the highway. Thus Mr. Cluett inherited the whole of the estate. Soon enough, he found he could not bear to live at Moorington Cross, not for many years, mind you. It was just such a sad reminder of the brother he'd lost. Even today, he refuses to venture into the east wing where his brother used to reside. I'm told his brother's things remain just as they were, left to gather dust behind locked doors."

The air slipped slowly out of my lungs. "I have wondered a great deal about that part of the house and the eerie feeling surrounding it. I swear I fight a chill every time I pass those enormous mahogany doors. Mr. Cluett instructed me upon arrival never to go there, that the foundation was unsafe. But he never told me about his terrible loss or what remained on the other side."

"The rumors tell a bit of a different story—that it had nothing to do with sentiment about his brother. That Mr. Cluett locked up everything to avoid the curse. People say the bad luck originated from the family's possessions—secret, hidden things, perhaps even something Mr. Cluett was not entirely aware of. After all, he's said as much."

"You don't really believe that, do you?"

"I certainly didn't when I agreed to come here. A curse— ridiculous! But now . . . No one can deny that many Cluetts have met their deaths rather young. There was his grandfather with the carriage accident and his great-uncle who passed away after his first London season."

Her eyes fluttered shut, and I repositioned the blanket once again beneath her chin. Mrs. Fitzroy would not be awake much longer, and she had given me a great deal to think about.

I rested my elbow on the bed, my hand cradling my chin. Had my late husband known about all the strange, unexplained deaths in the Cluett family—especially the murder of Mr. Cluett's brother—when he arranged for me to be admitted to Cluett's Mesmeric Hospital? A chill skittered across the base of my neck. Of course he had. He would have left no stone unturned.

And he'd sent me anyway.

Hours later I found Mr. Hawkins brooding in the corridor outside Mr. Cluett's room, his hand fisted beneath his chin. Interesting that he stood so near the place where Mrs. Fitzroy had seen the shadowy figure. He'd propped his back against a large arched window filled floor to ceiling with squares of colored glass, his attention set on the opposite wall.

He straightened as I approached, his expression one of weary sympathy. "Does Mrs. Fitzroy get on any better?"

"She's asleep at present, thank goodness, but I'm afraid the dawn might bring with it more difficulty."

"Hmm . . . I imagine so." He cast me a long look before slowly nodding his head.

If his concern for Mrs. Fitzroy was another act for my benefit, I thought his performance quite well done. His voice even held a genuine quiver of concern. And there was more—the strained evening had clearly taken a toll. His blond hair lay at odd angles about his forehead, his cravat a limp mess.

Absently, he gave it a tug, and my heart checked.

Something about that subtle movement softened the edges of his superior demeanor and lent him a boyish air, reminding me all too quickly of our first meeting in the corridor and the schoolgirl thoughts I'd had. Of course, everything was different now. My future was planned out before me. I was not so green as to continue to allow a spark of feelings for the wrong man—at least not this time.

The air felt a bit thin as I took a deep breath. Attraction, however, was an entirely different animal and the resulting awkwardness a bit uncomfortable for me to manage, but I was determined to plow on. I only hoped Mr. Hawkins couldn't see the flush warming my face.

He didn't seem to notice as he gave me a wan smile. "I daresay you look about as beat down as I do."

"What? Oh—" My attention fell to my rumpled evening gown. "Indeed, I must look a fright. I . . ." I lifted my chin and my mind fell vacant.

The moon must have shaken loose from a layer of clouds beyond the wall as light suddenly poured in through the colored glass, painting Mr. Hawkins's face in soft reds and deep blues. My heart constricted, unbidden as the attraction was, and I was forced to shrug off the reaction yet again. What was it about Mr. Hawkins that dredged up such romantic notions?

I gave myself a mental shake. I'd survived one intolerable guardian after another and then a violent husband. I could certainly keep this far-too-handsome Mr. Hawkins at arm's length. Besides, he had no intentions where I was concerned. There was no mistaking that. I was merely a problem that needed solving.

The thought sobered me in an instant. "Is the constable here?"

"Yes. He's brought a few men with him as well. They are going over Mr. Cluett's bedchamber at present. Montague, Lymington, and I have all given our statements, and I'm afraid the rest of you will need to do so as well, but not tonight. The inquiry is to be set up for tomorrow morning here at Moorington Cross." His shrewd focus swung back to the alcove across from us. "Do you believe what they say about the Cluett curse?"

"Heavens." Here it was again—more about that silly curse. I tossed a peek over my shoulder.

In the shadowed recess of the wall hung a massive stone sculpture of the infamous coat of arms, which I was told by Miss Seton had been awarded to a distant Cluett family member and passed down through the male line, guarded on each side by a particularly deadly pair of colichemardes.

I eyed Mr. Hawkins before plodding a bit closer. "I've never actually seen this particular display before, only heard of it. Mr. Cluett showed me a small engraving in his office and told me how proud his father was of the family's coat of arms. As for a curse, I only just heard the absurd idea from Mrs. Fitzroy but a few minutes ago. Don't tell me you believe in such a farce."

He edged closer. "Not at all, but you must admit the Cluett family has had its fair share of tragedies. They say the imaginary scourge is tied to whichever Cluett inherits the money and all the holdings."

"Oh?" He arched his eyebrows and suddenly I felt cold. "You mean me?"

"Or whatever hapless gentleman you choose to marry." His smile turned crooked. "If the curse is to be believed, you may not have to live with the man of your choosing all that long after all."

My mouth fell open. "What a horrid thing to say. Goodness, I know you were only teasing, but really—"

"You're right, of course." His gaze dropped. "A poor sort of joke on such an evening. However . . ." He nudged my arm. "I did see the way you were looking at those two."

I stiffened. "How was I looking at them?"

"Like you'd been presented a pair of strutting peacocks—the male and the female, I daresay."

A smile fought against the tense muscles in my face. "I will admit to hesitancy regarding my options, but I would never be so indelicate."

He chuckled to himself. "You'd never say such a thing aloud, no doubt. You're too well bred for that, but your eyes more than give you away."

I met his clever expression and crossed my arms as I swallowed a scathing retort. "And what, may I ask, are they saying now?"

He leaned in close, affording me a long, hard look. "I, uh, don't believe I should admit it aloud."

"Well. Then by all means, keep it to yourself. I've had enough of your curst witticisms today." I whirled to face the coat of arms. "Besides, none of this conversation even matters as I cannot and will not be the one to inherit the curse. Thankfully I am not a Cluett, nor will I ever be."

"A lucky escape." Mr. Hawkins turned to the stone carving. "And a good thing, too, as this coat is a rather threatening one."

Chiseled masterfully into gray stone were three dragons caught at the moment of flight, each swarming the central crest with their talons bared and their wings spread wide. The vicious animals possessed pointy teeth and beady eyes, which they turned menacingly on any innocent observer who crossed their path.

We both stared at the smooth stone until I found myself rubbing a transitory chill from my arms. "Tell me, Mr. Hawkins, has everything been arranged in regard to the investigation and Mr. Cluett?"

"Officially, yes, but at some point we'll want to move his body downstairs to lie in wait for the burial."

"I'll need to speak with Miss Seton, but I'm sure she's already arranged to have him watched over by the servants. Though she doubles as a nurse, she's filled the role of housekeeper here for years."

"Mrs. Pembroke." Mr. Hawkins's voice had tightened. "I would be remiss as your solicitor if I did not take this opportunity to remind you about the various stipulations in the will."

I huffed out a laugh. "You think I've forgotten?"

Though Mr. Hawkins had appeared tired throughout our late-night encounter, the lines on his face deepened, and I wondered how much longer he could conceal his exhaustion.

He shook his head. "Unfortunately, your thirty-day clock starts today. I would recommend that first thing in the morning you approach both Lymington and Montague and ask them to stay throughout the month. I will warn you, earlier I heard Mr. Lymington allude to the fact that he plans to leave Moorington Cross as soon as possible."

"Oh dear."

Mr. Hawkins reached out as if to steady my arm, but I'd never been a simpering miss nor was I surprised by the revelation regarding my guest. Who would want to stay at the hospital after everything that had happened? Granted, Lymington's desire to leave certainly made my next moves a bit more difficult.

Mr. Hawkins's hand fell back to his side. "Remember I'm here to assist you in any way I can."

I shot him a sideways glance. "If you would but change the will—to divide it evenly between the three of us—that would be fantastic."

We watched each other a moment then shared a pent-up laugh.

"I'm afraid that ship has sailed. The will has already been submitted to the Prerogative Court of Canterbury. I have no choice but to oversee Mr. Cluett's wishes at this point."

I nodded and we lapsed into a comfortable silence. But the moonlight beyond the colored glass dimmed, ushering in the night's shadows. The gloom only brought Mrs. Fitzroy's recollections bubbling into my thoughts, and my smile faded.

A whisper of caution prickled my ear, but I banished it to the recesses of my mind. If I was to figure out a way through this madness, I had to trust someone, and Mr. Hawkins was as good a choice as any. After all, as my solicitor he was the only one whose job it was to help me. "Are you to attend the inquiry tomorrow?"

A long pause as he inspected the stained glass window. "In all likelihood, yes."

"Then there is something I believe you should be made aware of. Mrs. Fitzroy informed me earlier that she came upon a person concealed in the shadows just outside Mr. Cluett's bedchamber seconds before she entered to find him dead. She believes this person may have meant mischief—that he might be responsible for what happened."

Mr. Hawkins's eyes rounded. "A person, you say? That would shed new light on the situation indeed." He hesitated. "Of course, whoever she saw may simply have been a servant or one of the gentlemen residing at the house."

"Possibly, but Mrs. Fitzroy felt like this person was specifically hiding from her, like he might have been poised to run or attack if fully exposed. Provided, she wasn't certain, but the whole scene terrified her enough to enter Mr. Cluett's bedchamber unannounced."

Mr. Hawkins rubbed his jaw. "I have to admit, I was leaning toward believing his death a possible suicide or a terrible accident, but if there was a person in Mr. Cluett's apartments at such a time, they must answer to it"—his voice turned grim—"particularly since they've kept quiet about their whereabouts thus far. I shall speak with Mrs. Fitzroy as soon as possible to go over it all again. I suppose that will have to be tomorrow."

I nodded and turned to leave, but he grasped my arm. "Mrs. Pembroke, promise me one thing."

"Yes?"

"I need you to be careful."

"Of course I will, but—"

His fingers tightened. "I mean a great deal more so than usual. Lock your doors tonight. You might have a maid pull a trundle into Mrs. Fitzroy's room if possible. And above everything else, don't trust anyone. Not until we know exactly who might be involved in Mr. Cluett's death."

I couldn't help but think how easily I had put my faith in Mr. Hawkins, even after Mrs. Fitzroy cautioned me in the same manner. Yet for some reason, doing so felt right. My muscles relaxed. There was something about him, a well-crafted believability, like worn leather—pliable yet strong. He was nothing like my late husband, who had wormed his way into my life on a lie. Mr. Hawkins was witty but controlled, accomplished yet real . . . and smart—I'd better not forget that.

I could only hope my gut wasn't leading me down a dangerous path. "You believe someone would want to harm me?"

He moved closer, his voice like ice. "Not harm, precisely. Influence perhaps, or shall I say, *coerce* might be the better word. Keep in mind, in the new will if you do not marry one of the two named gentlemen, the entire fortune goes to the Bordeaux Mesmeric Hospital in France, which is still in business across the pond. Nobody would get anything here in Britain, including Miss Seton. Absolutely everything depends on what you decide."

CHAPTER 7

I awoke the next morning far more restive than I would have liked, my head smarting from the events of the previous night. Though my body fought new layers of exhaustion, my senses remained heightened from all I'd been through. Fear, it seemed, was an all-consuming emotion, and it wasn't finished with me yet.

I'd formulated a plan to find and meet with Mr. Lymington and Mr. Montague before the authorities could sequester me to tell my story of what happened or the gentlemen had a chance to pack their trunks and quit the hospital. Of course, neither gentleman would likely depart Moorington Cross without taking leave of me first, not with the will in play. And though I remained ignorant of their financial situations, the obvious interest they'd shown in regard to the marriage stipulation assured me they would not risk my displeasure.

The authorities were already hard at work questioning Miss Seton in the blue salon. I could only imagine the scene taking place there, the depths of her hauteur which would inevitably arise with the conversation.

She had always had a strange, tight relationship with Mr. Cluett, as she had been his nurse since he began his work in France, yet at the same time was cold and reserved with the patients here—particularly me. No one knew the intricate workings of the hospital better than she . . . nor those of the residents. She had been present for every single session Mr. Cluett performed.

The thought burned, but I knew quite well that as a nurse she was bound by the same professional care as Mr. Cluett. Now was not the time to question her loyalty. I had more pressing matters at hand.

Andrews informed me that Mr. Lymington had set off on a morning walk, so I promptly followed suit across the manicured lawns while soaking in the delicate glow of the rising sun. Waves of warmth feathered across the blades of grass as a bird perched somewhere beyond my sight filled the fragile stillness with its entrancing call.

How different the daytime world felt from the one I'd closed my eyes to only a few hours before. Yes, the sun had arisen in all its grandeur, whitewashing the specters of the distant hours, but I knew what lay beneath such a shiny veneer. If Mrs. Fitzroy's suspicions proved correct, someone within the walls of Moorington Cross had committed an unspeakable act, and we had no way of knowing who that person was.

But for now I needed to focus on the matter at hand. Andrews had also relayed to me that Mr. Lymington stomped rather dramatically out of the house and headed east. No doubt I could lay the cause for such an outburst wholly at Mr. Montague's feet. I only hoped Mr. Lymington wasn't too cross to listen to what I had to say.

I followed the rows of yews to the back of the gardens, my heartbeat a bit erratic. I'd promised Mr. Hawkins to be cautious, yet what I planned to discuss with Mr. Lymington was a delicate matter indeed; far easier to broach if I came upon him alone.

Again and again I tried to imagine Mr. Lymington as the dark figure who'd evaded Mrs. Fitzroy and hidden in the shadows of Mr. Cluett's hall, but I only shook my head. The gentleman I'd met in the drawing room yesterday didn't seem like he could murder a person. He was sulky . . . indolent . . . irritating, certainly, but a killer? That was a stretch.

The spring breeze proved a loud and playful one, running its fingers through the oak leaves, dancing its way across the hedgerows in rushed upsurges. In fact, the hollow gusts muffled a sound I'd not heard at first—a rather lively conversation taking place on the other side of the yews. At the wide opening in the path housing the juncture that led to the summer house, a deep voice managed to wriggle through the wind flurries.

The intersection was something of a grotto with an isolated, circular pool and miniature garden, which remained a favorite of the patients of Cluett's Hospital. At first I assumed I'd stumbled upon Mr. Lymington, but when I parted the yew leaves to be sure, I was surprised to see Mr. Hawkins and Major Balfour facing me, seated on the white bench beneath the willow tree.

Leaning back, but still well concealed by the hedgerow, I stayed quiet, wondering if I should make my presence known. After all, there was Major Balfour to consider. He was a dear friend but terribly long-winded, a master at keeping one pinned to his side. My erratic sleeping pattern had already left me little time with which to locate Mr. Lymington. Now was not the moment for forced pleasantries.

I parted the tiny opening in the yew leaves once again to get a last view of the pair, and a smile emerged. If the look of helpless boredom on Mr. Hawkins's handsome face was any indication of what had transpired thus far between himself and Major Balfour, I had certainly been right.

Poor Mr. Hawkins. He was clearly the latest victim of Major Balfour's whims. Of course, with Mr. Hawkins's tenuous position in the house, he had little choice but to sit and listen to the man as he prattled on. It would have been pitiful in a way if it wasn't so comical. Whenever Major Balfour got into one of his garrulous moods, he never seemed to notice his companion's apathy.

I pulled away, intending to leave them to their business, when a flash of movement on the bench jerked my attention back to the conversation at hand. Mr. Hawkins stood, his left hand jamming beneath the folds of his jacket, his right fingers drumming against his leg. "No . . . Balfour . . . I'm afraid it is you who lacks even the basic understanding of my situation."

My eyes widened, and I leaned closer. Oh dear. This was more than a simple conversation. Mr. Hawkins appeared furious.

"Must I spell it out for you? I'm an orphan . . . *sir.*" Mr. Hawkins's already enraged tone turned equally grave. "Dash it all, I was in a blasted workhouse until I was ten years old. Yes, Lord Torrington was gracious enough to take me in and raise me like a son, so I won't pretend I'm not indebted to him in innumerable ways, but I am also not as you insinuate—the heir to Middlecrest Abbey." He paused for a moment to breathe, but it didn't calm the grit in his voice. "Nor would I trade on any connections I have for a handout. I worked deuced hard for not only my position at Pembroke and Huxley but this very appointment, and I won't have anyone suggest otherwise."

Major Balfour barely moved, his eyes seemingly stunned in place. "My dear boy, forgive my hasty, ill-informed words this instant. I never meant to suggest . . ." His cane wobbled beneath his hand, but his fingers were clenched tight. "I never purported to imply you were in any way unsuitable for the position of solicitor to the Cluett family, nor remiss in regard to Mrs. Pembroke. I merely wished to question what brought about the remarkable change in the particulars of Mr. Cluett's will. You must admit, this is hardly a proper situation for the lady."

Slowly Mr. Hawkins relaxed his stance and sat down. "I will agree that Cluett has put Mrs. Pembroke in an appalling position. Her decision as to whom to marry shall be a difficult one, but I tell you again, I had little say in the matter."

A quiet pause, and he tipped his head back against the bench, his right hand at his forehead. "Please, Major Balfour, if anyone should be apologizing, I'm fully aware it's me. I know you only mean to see her taken care of, and I admire you for that. I'm not wholly ignorant of the familial affection that can develop over time between people who reside in the same house."

The statement seemed to catch Major Balfour a bit by surprise as his voice dropped to an emotional whisper. "I suppose I do think of Mrs. Pembroke as the daughter I never had."

Mr. Hawkins rubbed the back of his neck. "Regardless, I never should have lashed out at you as I did." Then somewhat at odds with the tone of the conversation thus far, the hint of a smile emerged.

He had control now, and I found myself inching forward to get a better view. Heavens, something about Mr. Hawkins was so maddeningly charming when he knew he'd got the upper hand—his rueful smile, his winsome movements—a tug on his jacket here, an arm propped just so.

This time he shrugged, and artfully at that. "I'm afraid I've a ghastly temper at times, particularly when it comes to my lamentable past. It's one of many particularly irritating flaws in my personality. I've found myself sorry for it time and again."

Major Balfour cleared his throat, still noticeably moved by the admonition. "Nonsense, I never should have presumed—"

"No." Mr. Hawkins held up his right hand. "Really, sir, I shouldn't mind explaining my position. And you've every right to question it as Mrs. Pembroke's guardian, so to speak. My humble beginnings are a part of me like everything else. It's just when people suggest I've been given a handout or whisper behind closed doors . . . I thought you'd . . . Never mind. Clearly I misunderstood your intentions. I'd be well pleased if we can simply forget the last few uncomfortable minutes." He picked a leaf from a nearby tree and rubbed it between his fingers.

Major Balfour returned a rather contrite nod. "Assuredly, but allow me to say, I can well understand your quick reaction. Believe me, I have no intention of speaking one word of our . . . shall we call it a lively discussion? Nor am I put off by a gentleman who knows his own mind." He extended his legs. "As you can see, I have my own problems to bear. With a pair of curst feet that don't quite work right—bah! I hear people talking even before I've left the room."

"Then I daresay we understand one another."

Major Balfour lifted his eyebrows. "Perfectly."

Mr. Hawkins leaned forward as if to stand, but Major Balfour was quick to still him. "An orphan though? That does change my perspective on things. You mean to tell me you've no idea who your parents are?"

There was a hesitation in Mr. Hawkins's manner, then he settled back against the bench. "Well, not that exactly."

I leaned forward to hear better.

Major Balfour's fingers were hard at work, tapping the top of his cane. "Then how—"

"Did I end up at Middlecrest Abbey with the Baron of Torrington?" Mr. Hawkins raised his chin. "A valid question, but not an easy one to answer." He stared across the pond for a long moment, a far-off look about his eyes. "Though I've never treated my past as a secret to be guarded, few know the truth, and even fewer would dare mention such a thing to me."

His voice seemed to hang on the air. "The fact is my mother was actually Torrington's first wife, Florencia. She only married him to hide an illegitimate pregnancy"—he gave another casual shrug—"me, of course. Thus, the identity of my natural father remains a mystery."

My hand retreated to my mouth.

"Hmm." Major Balfour's head bobbed as he took in the whole of what Mr. Hawkins had revealed. "I see. But if you don't mind my prying, may I ask how you then found your way to the workhouse?"

Mr. Hawkins's gaze settled hard on the far side of the pool. "At my birth my *ingenious* mother took one look at me and shipped me straight off to London. Of course, that was after she told everyone I'd died." There was a moment of charged silence as he turned to face Major Balfour and raised his left hand. "From what I understand she couldn't tolerate the sight of a child who wasn't perfect. Sometimes I want to believe she was worried Torrington wouldn't accept me, or she thought to give me a different life, but I know otherwise."

Major Balfour shook his head. "You can't be serious."

"Sadly, I am."

It took several seconds for Major Balfour to respond. "I can perfectly understand your emotions now, and I feel clumsy to have brought up your situation in such a backhanded way." Major Balfour shifted in his seat. "If you'll allow me, I must say you've done quite well for yourself."

The solicitor's practiced facade slipped back onto Mr. Hawkins's face, a mask he'd probably worn countless times before. "You were right to question my qualifications. Let me assure you once and for all that there is nothing unusual about the Cluett will. I plan to keep Mr. Huxley apprised of everything that transpires and will heed any advice he offers. Anyone would question such a strange situation, particularly with so much money at stake."

He ran his hand down his face. "And you were also correct about Lord Torrington in a way. I do owe him a great deal. He was the one who journeyed to London to search for me when I was in the workhouse. After my mother's death, he came upon the information that I hadn't died as she'd said and took great pains to find me."

"Extraordinary."

Mr. Hawkins splayed his hands wide. "In many ways I am a lucky man."

"But . . ."

Mr. Hawkins attempted to hide his laugh with a cough. "There's always more, isn't there?"

"Well, of course. Society is a cruel and vicious animal that never forgets."

"Indeed. No matter where I go or whom I marry, I wear my shame openly and, at times, as you have seen, rather defiantly."

Major Balfour paused. "You said earlier you consider your quick temper a flaw. If I may, I do have a suggestion to curb the unwanted emotion."

Mr. Hawkins pursed his lips. "Go on."

"Have you perhaps considered mesmerism? The practice would go a long way to help you control such feelings. It has done wonders for me."

I saw the smirk on Mr. Hawkins's face before I heard the resulting tinge of disbelief in his voice as he looked away. "I have not."

"Mesmerism has been a somewhat freeing experience for me, at least the trance part."

Mr. Hawkins turned toward him. "Then you believe in such things."

"Certainly. I came here specifically for Mr. Cluett. My cousin, whom I consider the wisest man I've ever known, was a great proponent of mesmerism. He died a long while ago, but when I was faced with these two feet that don't quite work right, well, I decided to try my chances as a patient here. In many ways I felt the hand of my cousin urging me to come—to see what might be done."

"Then you consider your treatments somewhat successful? I can't help but notice you still walk with a decided limp."

Major Balfour adjusted his cane. "Though I've come to understand I will always need some level of assistance, I have seen improvement, particularly recently. I won't sugarcoat the process, however. It's taken a great deal of time and work to get to this point."

Mr. Hawkins secured his watch fob as he slowly nodded. "I do apologize, but I must dash off. The inquiry begins in less than an hour, and I've been asked to be present." He stood. "I also promised Mrs. Fitzroy I'd speak with her before they convene."

"Quite right. Her thoughts must be heard and voiced. And keep a watch over Mrs. Pembroke. I daresay she could stand a friend right now. Between you and me, I fear both of those ridiculous gentlemen could be hiding something—something we'd better uncover before she makes her final decision. She and she alone will be the one who is forced to live with the consequences."

CHAPTER 8

Embarrassed by what I could only call blatant eavesdropping, I scurried off over the rise, my hand clutched to my chest, my pulse quickening. Past the conservatory and the back of the rose garden—anywhere I was sure to be alone and concealed.

Providence, however, had a different end in mind as I caught sight of Mr. Lymington's black beaver hat bobbing up and down above the garden wall. Oh dear. I fell into the shadows of the smooth stones and forced a measured breath. Apparently my hasty flight had deposited me directly in the path of my original target.

Fantastic.

I had to shake myself. It was absurd to feel anything but relief as I'd purposely set out to find Mr. Lymington in the first place. But the private conversation I'd overheard moments before would not release its claws from my mind.

Mr. Hawkins—an orphan like me? And the workhouse? I couldn't believe I'd heard it all correctly. Still panting, I ran my tongue across my dry lips. No doubt there was even more to his past than what he'd revealed to Major Balfour at the pond. I'd heard that telltale catch of protective truth in his voice, which he veiled all too carefully behind well-placed words. I'd buried such emotions often enough myself.

I worked to smooth all the rumples from my gown, but my gaze lingered uncomfortably on my twisting fingers. Mr. Hawkins was nothing to me, his difficult past none of my affair. The man was simply my solicitor, paid to placate me. My hand settled on my neck as I averted my focus to the horizon. I was a fool to give depth to an attraction I never should have entertained in the first place, nor should I award him trust he hadn't earned.

So he'd lived a rough life. Many others could say the same.

I patted the back of my coiffure before lowering my hands to my waist. But wasn't there solace in community—a sort of bond in shared experiences? At the very least, the chance for friendship?

My shoulders relaxed. If nothing else, I did understand him better—that edge to his voice, the dip of his chin. It hadn't been the smooth confidence of a solicitor that I'd perceived in his words. No. One of my guardians, Mr. Stanley, had called it street grit—a curious mix of deep-seated rebellion, relentless gratitude, and self-deprecation that far too many orphans fight within themselves.

Mr. Hawkins was simply a survivor. He'd found a way to move past rejection, past his time in the workhouse. I peered once more at the bobbing beaver hat still visible above the garden wall. Maybe, just maybe, if Mr. Hawkins could move on, I, too, could find my own way to marry again, to love.

A swell of disquiet bent my thoughts. Love indeed. I had but two possible choices before me—the taciturn Mr. Lymington or the curst cad of Kent. Mr. Cluett had essentially tied my hands in every way possible.

Defeated, I nudged the garden gate open without a sound. One last cautious glance behind me and I stole into the fragrant stillness of the small sanctuary, into the presence of the man who would in all likelihood be my future husband.

Mr. Lymington stood oddly still, deep grooves lining his forehead, his hands clenched into fists at his sides. I didn't think him aware of my approach. But having ceased his pacing, he raked his narrow focus over the rosebushes, a flaming curse on his breath.

My chest erupted into a flutter of nerves. I opened my mouth to address him, yet nothing came forth. What did one say to a man so angry with his present situation he was cursing alone in a rose garden?

I'd prepared myself to meet with both gentlemen as soon as possible, but I'd spent little to no time crafting the words needed for such an awkward discussion.

Finally I simply cleared my throat. "Mr. Lymington?"

A sharp glare to his right, and he all but stiffened at the sight of me.

Not the best of starts.

He managed a rather late, "Good morning, Mrs. Pembroke."

What remained of my errant thoughts spun wild as I cycled through each possible arrangement of sentences and the resulting embarrassment we would be forced to endure. I turned instead to the safety of the garden wall, running my fingers along the curved stone. "I do hope I'm not disturbing you."

"Disturbing *me?*" His voice came out equal parts sharp and distant. "Not at all. I simply needed some air." He allowed a clumsy pause. "Would you care to join me on the bench?"

"Oh?" I whirled to face him as warmth swept across my cheeks. Heavens, it took me more than three seconds to fully digest what he'd said, and even longer to ponder his intent. "Thank you. I believe I will."

Somewhat numbed by what I must say to him and how I must do it, I stumbled across the path and took a seat at the far end of the bench, my fingers setting out at once to worry my bonnet ribbons.

Mr. Lymington didn't join me exactly. Instead, he propped his well-polished boot on the edge of the seat before bracing his arm on his knee. The look on his face was intense, almost as if he were . . . worried? Surely not.

I waited for him to speak, but he didn't address me, and the seconds stretched out long and deep into the nervous energy of the dampened air. The resulting undercurrent of silence hit my ears like a warning.

Still hoping to salvage our relationship, I tried a smile. After all, what other choice did I have? Mr. Montague? I took a measured breath. "I understand Mr. Montague is already up and about this morning. Surprising, as I'd have pegged him for a gentleman who slept well into the afternoon."

Mr. Lymington wrinkled his nose, a pout taking up residence within his glare. "The man is something of an enigma, I'm afraid."

I lifted my eyebrows. "Then the two of you are well acquainted?"

"We don't run in the same circles if that is what you are getting at."

"Forgive me, I didn't mean to *get at* anything at all. I merely hoped to apologize for his continued rudeness. Andrews mentioned you were upset this morning. I assumed it was because of Mr. Montague."

"Oh no. *Phst.*" He flicked his wrist. "I've become somewhat accustomed to Montague's gauche behavior. I stopped regarding it years ago, and I would recommend you do the same."

I gripped the bench. "I don't mean to continue to quiz you, sir, but if it wasn't Mr. Montague who put you off this morning, who precisely were you cursing to Jericho not five minutes ago?"

Mr. Lymington gave me a daring look. "You heard that, did you?"

"Anyone within ten yards is well aware of your anger."

He nodded coolly as if I were the one being snappish. "I had every reason to believe I was alone. Forgive me for assaulting your ears with my lamentable plight."

"*Your* plight?" This time it didn't take me long to ascertain his meaning. My heart lurched and my voice lost its tone. "You mean the stipulations in the will."

I'd blurted out the statement with as much indignation as I could muster, but I wasn't able to hold my pointed glare. He tossed me a smile, and I couldn't help but stare. It was the first time he'd done so, and it was startling how much it improved his disposition.

He rested his hand on the back of the bench and offered a light chuckle. "Mrs. Pembroke, you misunderstand me entirely. I had a trying time with the parish constable is all—a personal matter I'd prefer not to discuss at present."

My eyes widened. *A personal matter? Not discuss? The constable!*

"Oh?" I'd tried to keep my voice light, but really, what on earth was he referring to? The last thing I wanted to do was begin our forced courtship with secrets.

I folded my hands in my lap. "You do realize we have thirty days to understand one another. I want to believe Mr. Cluett included you in the will for a reason. I have a difficult decision ahead. We both do. Surely you recognize that."

A muscle twitched in his jaw, but he held my gaze. "Let me assure you that my difficulty with the constable has nothing to do with you, the will, or your decision as to whom to marry. It merely keeps me in residence at Moorington Cross for the time being—something I was determined not to do, but I've since had time to think." He glanced down at his hand on the back of the bench, so close to the sleeve of my gown. "Believe me when I say that I hope my staying will prove the best decision for everyone concerned."

He gave me a rather mournful smile, and I felt a curious pull to touch his hand. And then what, exactly? Court him? It was almost as if I were watching a play and every fiber of my being yearned to know the ending. Yet upon completion of such a performance, an actress should be able to return to her own life. Not me.

I pressed my lips together. "You said earlier that you didn't wish to stay at Moorington Cross at first."

"Certainly not. I'd hoped to put a day's ride between me and this horrid house as soon as possible, but—"

"You mean to do your part?"

"Whatever is required of me." He looked away. "Not to mention I have no intention of getting on the wrong side of the law. I, for one, haven't any powerful friends."

Required. How many times had that word impacted my own life?

My chest felt hollow. I'd been so concerned about my own future that I hadn't given much thought to what the gentleman I chose would have to give up. What if he already had a lady he loved?

Seeming perceptive of my flagging mood, Mr. Lymington was quick to add, "I do wish to be of assistance to you in whatever way I can. I wasn't certain what to make of our situation at first, but I can see now you were caught as unaware as me and Montague."

"Thank you. I was, and I did worry you thought ill of me."

"Nonsense. I've simply been preoccupied." There was a shift in his bearing, a tightening of his stance. "There's— Well, let me just say this sudden passing of Mr. Cluett has overset me. I cannot believe such a gruesome death as innocent as the authorities thus far imply."

I wondered how much I should reveal to a man I hardly knew, but if this Mr. Lymington was to be my husband, I had to find a way to trust him. "Nor I. Did you hear or see something—something that led you to your assumptions?"

"No, not exactly." Hesitation laced his voice. "I heard a commotion and voices that woke me, and then, well, you were there. I entered Mr. Cluett's chamber to find him just so."

"What about earlier in the day? Did you speak with him after supper?"

His jaw clenched. "We had a bit of an argument in the office he uses for mesmerism. I came to find out later that Miss Seton was in the next room."

"Mr. Cluett has Miss Seton observe all of his interactions with patients. We were informed of this when we entered the hospital. I suppose they confer on our care."

"Then I guess she's already told you all about our encounter."

"No. Why would she?"

"Let's just say she's made a few insinuations this morning. I get the feeling I'm high on her list of possible suspects."

A jolt of concern shot through my chest, but I went on. "Miss

Seton has always had a difficult time trusting new people. Of course, how can we blame her? Someone must have had a hand in Mr. Cluett's death."

He gave me a sideways glance. "But I get the feeling you don't think that someone is me."

Slowly I shook my head, and he closed his eyes.

"I can't tell you how good it feels to know that." Then he met my gaze. "Perhaps we might forge a suitable alliance after all."

Was this just a performance, or was there more to Mr. Lymington—real sentiment buried behind that grimace of his?

As if he followed my thoughts, he went on. "Love is a fickle notion to stake a marriage upon at any rate. All I desire is a level of respect and propriety from you." The hint of a smile creased his lips. "And I cannot deny it would be a blow to Mr. Montague that I would relish. He's probably been counting his inheritance all morning."

My shoulders felt heavy. So this was the twist in the production, the uncomfortable act when the flawed character showed his true nature. My stomach turned as my heart beat a path of retreat. "Are you planning to attend the inquiry?"

"Well, yes."

"I understand it's to begin shortly."

Mr. Lymington swiped a quick check of his watch and made an even quicker thrust of his foot to the ground. "You're correct. I best make my way back to the house. Would you desire an escort?"

I shook my head. "I'd like to continue my walk just now."

He bowed, a newfound vigor to his movements. "Then I remain your servant, Mrs. Pembroke."

I stood there motionless as I watched him leave, assured of the fact he would remain at Moorington Cross for the time being. A drearier thought, however, roamed my mind—did I even want him to?

CHAPTER 9

U pon my return to the house, I managed to stumble straight into a face-to-face meeting with Mr. Hawkins.

He was pulling the drawing room door shut behind him at the same moment I attempted to enter. Caught in a rather intimate situation, my stomach did a slight tumble as the both of us skirted into the hall. Mr. Hawkins eventually settled back against the wainscoting, a reluctant half smile winding across his face.

My fingers tightened around the swath of skirt clenched in my hand as I, too, fought to regain my bearings. Something about that lighthearted smile pricked my defenses to attention.

"Good morning, Mrs. Pembroke."

I managed a quiet nod as I weighed the tone of his voice— patronizing, friendly, or something else entirely?

"I suppose you're on your way to join the inquiry. I understand it's to take place quite soon in the blue salon. The parish constable has already arrived."

"Indeed, yet . . ." He checked his watch. "I know I'm pressed for time, but if I may, I'd like to have a word with you first"—a sideways peek at the stairs—"in private."

I hesitated a moment then motioned to the drawing room door. He didn't move. His gaze only sharpened.

I expelled a small huff. "Lest you forget, Mr. Hawkins, I am a widower. There isn't the least need of a chaperone if that is what has wrought that pained look on your face."

It was late, but he did chuckle. "I fear you misunderstand me. The, uh, parish constable is in the drawing room at present speaking with Mrs. Fitzroy. What I have to say to you I'd rather not share with that deuced flat."

I blinked a few times. "Understood." Then dipped my chin. "I guess that means the rumors I've heard about him are true."

Mr. Hawkins gave an irritated sigh. "I can't begin to guess what you've heard about that man, but Constable Voss is doing everything in his power to make sure Mr. Cluett's death is ruled an accident."

"But why?"

"I have a feeling his motivation stems from a desire to keep the runners out of the area at all costs." He lowered his voice. "I was well aware people outside of London value their individual freedoms, but this is the most backward-thinking authority figure I've ever encountered. Bow Street could only help the investigation."

"I daresay you're right. But you must admit, it would be a good deal easier for Constable Voss if this entire affair is simply swept under the rug. Less work for him at any rate—he's a volunteer, and from what I've heard rarely stirs himself to seek justice. Most people around here are forced to pay for a private investigation if they want any real answers. Poor Mr. Cluett. With no family situated to request such an examination, the truth of his final hours may end up a mystery never to be rectified. And a dangerous one at that."

"Which is why I wish to speak with you. Have you a moment?"

I took another look at the drawing room door, my heart a bit unsteady. "If you will accompany me to the sitting room on the first floor, we are sure to have privacy there."

He gave me a wan smile. "After you."

An undercurrent of dread lurked in the heady stillness of the Cluett family wing. Almost as if Mr. Cluett's sudden absence had injured the very soul of the house and it might never be healed. After all, Mr. Cluett was the last of the Cluetts ever to reside within the old gray walls. Cursed or not, the family had breathed life into every stone, every floorboard, and every nook and cranny. Moorington Cross would never be the same.

Once we'd entered the first-floor sitting room, I gestured to a nearby chair and settled down on the end of the opposing sofa. "Please, have a seat, Mr. Hawkins."

There was an energy between us I'd not felt before. His hand went to his chin, then the folds of his jacket. Abruptly he turned to the fireplace and grasped the iron poker to rattle the coals. "Will you be warm enough without a fire?"

I couldn't help but rub the ghostlike chill from my arms, fully conscious it wasn't the cold of the room crawling across my skin. "You said this wouldn't take long."

"Yes . . . I . . ." A full second of charged silence ticked by before he lifted his eyes to meet my level gaze. "I spent some time with Mr. Cluett's body this morning."

I'd anticipated that something regarding Mr. Cluett's death had spurred this sudden meeting, but a heavy feeling settled into my stomach. "You went to see Mr. Cluett?"

"Miss Seton let me into the room where she'd laid out his body." He propped his arms on his knees. "I'd not felt at ease, not since our conversation last night."

"I don't think there is a single person in this house who does."

He winced a bit as he went on. "I fear what I've since discovered will only deepen those restless feelings. Yet at the same time, I know you'd agree with me that Mr. Cluett deserves a proper investigation into his death, even if it's only by me."

A numbing chill left me motionless. "Then you truly have no confidence in the upcoming inquiry?"

"None whatsoever."

I sat there in silence for a long moment then folded my hands. "I want to help in any way that I can. No doubt Mrs. Fitzroy will wish to do so as well." I peeked up. "What did you discover?"

He nodded as if in slow motion, his gaze never leaving my face. "I'm very much aware you'd go to any lengths for your friends. That is, ultimately, why I asked you here in the first place. I hoped we might combine our efforts—an investigative partnership, so to speak. But as I sit here now, I wonder if I should not simply beg your caution and leave this room at once. I have no idea who we can trust as of yet, and all of a sudden, I don't wish to burden you with the particulars of Mr. Cluett's death."

I took a deep breath, forcing a wave of irritation at bay. Mr. Hawkins probably thought he was being noble. He had no idea he'd struck a nerve. Well, I was done being left in the dark, done being sheltered away from life. If I wanted to be treated as an equal, I must remember what Mr. Pembroke had taught me: no emotions. "I'll not faint or give in to hysterics if that's what worries you. Trust me, I'm made of sterner stuff than that. Anyone would be who's lived the life I have. And I've a good mind for reason."

Something glinted in those light brown eyes. "And a well-read one, if I'm not mistaken."

My jaw tightened, but I kept my voice steady. "Indeed. Either way I have no intention of permitting Mr. Cluett's killer to get away with murder, nor will I sit here and allow you to waste our precious time. I want to know what you discovered."

"Well, I can see you'll be the taskmaster in this little endeavor." Then he held up his hand. "Allow me to say, I'd expect nothing less from Mr. Pembroke's widow. I'm fully prepared to speak plainly enough."

I almost thought he made a move to grasp my hand, but he ran his fingers down his breeches instead. "What I'm about to reveal might be unsettling."

I sat up straight and motioned for him to continue. Whatever he had to impart could not be any worse than what I'd already seen and experienced the previous night.

His fingers balled into a fist. "Mr. Cluett's body appeared strange when we discovered him last night, so I took a closer inspection. That's when I found a few mild marks on his shoulders and arms with some pooling of blood, which can only mean one thing. They were inflicted before his death."

Unbidden, my movements stilled as I rolled these details around in my head. "Do you mean to imply he was manhandled in some way?"

"Possibly. At the very least someone knows something." He stared down. "There's more. His belly was swollen, as it should have been if he'd drowned, and his skin was yellow." He bit his lip. "But he also had large patches across his abdomen that were dark in color and swollen. Poison, perhaps? He very well could have been given something. All I know is it was more than just an accident. I'm sure of it."

I turned away, my teeth clenched, my stomach unsettled. I'd expected to hear such gruesome facts, but Mr. Hawkins's discovery forced a deeper truth. I now knew without a doubt that a killer had walked the halls of Moorington Cross, and whoever the person was, he very likely was still here.

CHAPTER 10

I spent the length of the morning in the library hoping to catch Mr. Hawkins the moment he emerged from the inquiry down the hall. However, it wasn't my solicitor who swept across the threshold a half hour after I'd entered the room.

No, indeed.

Instinctively, I stood as my fingers curled around the book I'd been pretending to read before inching it onto a nearby table, my gaze fixed to the door. "Why, Mr. Montague, I thought you were with the others in the salon." My voice came out a touch cool. After all, I wasn't yet certain how to approach the gentleman.

He gave me a shrewd glance before sauntering the rest of the way into the room, his crystal-blue eyes taking a tour of the massive book-shelves behind me. "What do you know but I wasn't even invited." He paused to add a lazy shrug. "Of course, any decision regarding Mr. Cluett's death is none of my affair. I have nothing further to disclose to anyone nor anything to gain by how it is ruled."

"Nor I."

My voice had fallen to a whisper, and Mr. Montague's eyes narrowed ever so slightly, a subtle movement few would notice. This forced relationship between the two of us was anything but natural. We were complete strangers—thrown together by the worst of circumstances—and worlds apart.

If we'd chanced to meet at a ball under normal circumstances, Mr. Montague never would have asked me to dance. Yet I knew how much I would have longed for him to do so. My chest burned at the thought, and I swallowed hard.

Thirty days and I would be forced to make the decision that would change both of our lives.

As if he followed my errant thoughts, he leaned forward a touch. "Is now a good time for our little chat?"

I was slow to nod but did so realizing our relationship would be easier once we had everything out in the open.

His face softened and he motioned me to the window seat at the side of the room, then settled in next to me, mere inches away. He didn't speak at first, allowing me a precious second to gain my bearings. Though I'd seen the cad in the drawing room the day before and thought him mildly appealing, up close and alone, there could be no doubt as to what had inspired such a nickname. Mr. Montague's allure was absolute, something deep and passionate about his eyes, a startling quality to his gaze.

I clenched my hands in my lap. "We've been placed in a rather difficult situation, you and I."

He gave a slight laugh. "Cluett has always had a distinct flair for the dramatic. I'm sure by now you've observed him parading around in that purple cloak of his—the master wizard of Moorington Cross."

I smiled. "Well, yes. He thinks it helps establish his position as a true doctor of mesmerism."

"So that's what inspires such an awful display. I did wonder." Mr. Montague ran a hand down his face, his smile smoothing into a serene line. "I must admit, I am glad to find you alone. We have a great deal to discuss."

He waited for some sort of affirmation from me, but when I remained silent, he went on. "Clearly, I know little about you aside from Mr. Cluett's obvious affection, and I daresay you know even less of me." He gave his jacket sleeve a tug. "Let me begin by assuring you of my utter sincerity in all this. I mean to court you as I would any lady I'd met during the season in London, to win your affections. You deserve nothing less. And I'll have you know I've been thinking for the past few months it was high time I took a wife. Really, there's no reason in the world the two of us won't be able to find love, even under these strained circumstances." A quick grin lit up his face. "I've certainly never had a problem doing so before."

Love? With Mr. Montague? He couldn't be serious.

He peered down at my fingers, which were fidgeting in my lap. "My dear Mrs. Pembroke, allow me to say how utterly pleasant you are to look at. Not in the regular way, mind you, but in a far more enticing way. I"—he relaxed his posture—"how can I possibly explain myself? If you've heard anything of me, no doubt you are aware that I tire of most ladies in a matter of seconds, but you possess something special, a sort of charisma. It's fascinating really. I find myself wholly captured by your spell."

His hand slid carefully between mine, jerking my attention back to his face.

My heart fought wildly for control, but I managed to steady myself. "Perhaps, Mr. Montague, it is the charm of the Cluett family fortune that has you, uh, as you so deftly put it—captured."

He stilled for a moment then tipped back his head and laughed. "What a delight you are."

"I refuse to stand on pretenses."

"Nor easily flattered. However, believe me, I was in earnest just now. If you allow it, I'll find a way to your heart."

Or a well-timed set-down. I pursed my lips. Had anyone ever refused the cad anything?

"Mr. Hawkins did mention the possibility of it being a challenge, but I never expected such an enjoyable one."

I wrenched my hands free. "Mr. Hawkins?"

"Don't take a pet. I simply sought him out to gather a bit of information about you."

"Interesting that he should feel informed enough to advise you on the subject . . . as he barely knows me."

"Rest assured, he intimated as much." Amusement lingered on Mr. Montague's breath. "All the solicitor said was that you could hold your own in conversation, and I'm pleased to report you have not disappointed, my dear . . . my dear . . . Tell me, what is your Christian name? I won't presume to use it as of yet." He tapped his chin. "I remember hearing it earlier. Was it Annabella?"

I laughed. "Heavens, no. Do I look like an Annabella?"

"Agnes?"

I looked to the ceiling. "Amelia."

His grin widened. "Soon to be Mrs. Amelia Montague, I hope."

I couldn't help but glance away. The nerve of the man. "And what is your name?"

"My parents saw fit to name me Guy Frederick Montague, but—" Something caught the corner of his eye and he thrust his finger to the glass. "What the devil?"

A small group of people had gathered on the front lawn, waiting in a line beside the grand oak tree.

A furrow crossed his brow. "What are they doing?"

"They've come for treatment."

"Treatment? At a tree? Besides, don't they know Cluett is dead?"

"Yes. Mr. Cluett magnetized that oak several years ago. You see, many people lack the funds to seek official services at the hospital."

Mr. Montague didn't move. "Forgive me, as I know little of mesmerism, but he *magnetized* a tree?"

"I will admit to sharing some of your skepticism, but the gentleman who taught Mr. Cluett all he knew about mesmerism believed that those with such a gift possess the ability to pass their healing powers to other objects.

"Mr. Cluett magnetized that particular tree to provide services to the poorer villagers. It's thought not to be as beneficial as seeing him in the hospital, but many people come daily, desperate for help. I can't say I believe their time with the tree does any real good, that a living organism can even be magnetized, or that any one of them has truly recovered. So many of us are looking for answers—answers we may never find."

Mr. Montague stared back at me for a long moment before speaking. "And you would know that as you were a patient here."

"Yes, I was." I'd been terribly embarrassed every time I disclosed my condition in the past, but for some unexplained reason I raised my chin. "What brought me to Cluett's Mesmeric Hospital worsens every day. I don't know the cause of it, but I'm sleepy a good bit of the day and, worse, sometimes I can't control my own body. I was forced in here by my late husband over two years ago. He made more than certain I knew he was ashamed of me."

My attention flashed to Mr. Montague, anticipating some level of surprise and revulsion. I suppose a part of me wanted to shock him, to scare him away, but the sudden candor of my response surprised even me.

He sat there unnaturally stiff, his gaze ticking around the room. "Sleep . . . so that's the worst of it?"

I couldn't tell him about my frozen muscles, the episodes where I was conscious but couldn't move. Not yet at least. I fiddled with my necklace. Really, the more extreme spells came so infrequently, no one needed to know. "I sleep a great deal too often."

His shoulders relaxed. "Then I believe we shall get on quite well with one another. I frequent several clubs in London, and I tend to sleep as much as I like during the day. We shan't be in each other's way."

I gave him a feeble smile. If only it was as simple as he'd implied. Yet he didn't appear afraid of my confession or the least bit judgmental. It felt good to be honest and forthright, and apparently we both had our issues. If I chose him, maybe he was right. We could simply go our own way, a marriage of convenience.

Carefully, Mr. Montague reached up, sliding his hand against my chin and his thumb along my jawline. Obviously he was quite comfortable with women, his touch easy and assured . . . and so terribly frequent. He'd perfected its use to garner whatever he desired at the moment. And at present, that was me and Mr. Cluett's money.

He drew in close, his voice husky. "You mustn't worry. I don't regard such a minute deficiency of character in the least." As if he'd already ticked off every box I required in a husband, his eyes focused in on my lips.

I pulled back.

A marriage of convenience indeed. Mr. Montague had far more planned for me than that. I rose awkwardly. "I do thank you for your forbearance . . . and the sound reassurance . . ." I stumbled around the nearby sofa and took a hasty seat, glad of the distance between us. "And for being so open with me thus far." I smoothed my skirt. "I do, however, have a few questions of my own for you."

He made his way around the sofa but settled into the accompanying chair. Apparently he'd understood the message that I needed space. He raised his hand in the air. "I'm happy to answer anything you'd like to know."

I thought for a moment. "What is your current situation? I understand you are the heir to Whitefall."

"Yes, my father is the only person still living in my immediate family, and I must do his bidding at all times."

"His bidding?"

He flicked his fingers in the air. "He likes to order me around, but I realize that is not what you were getting at. I'm to inherit a rather sizable estate. I only hope my father leaves enough funds for me to be able to run it."

"Thus, what you are saying is that Mr. Cluett's fortune would be a welcome addition."

"I won't lie and tell you it's not to be considered. Of course it is. And don't let Lymington convince you otherwise. We both want a piece of it. Who wouldn't?"

He was right. I'd be a fool to believe otherwise. At least Mr. Montague was honest about his motives.

"And how do you know Mr. Cluett?"

He coughed a laugh into his hand. "Our relationship is a bit complicated. I met him for the first time a few years back."

"In a professional capacity?"

"Certainly not. My mother merely asked me to relay a message to him a few weeks before her death. I did as I was told."

Curiosity pricked my tongue, but I was hesitant to push him for specifics. "And Mr. Cluett responded to your mother's message?"

"In a way, but I don't think she was satisfied."

Slowly, I sat forward, hoping he might offer something up on his own. "Oh?"

My subtle movement, however innocently meant, must have reignited his earlier passions as he clasped my hands and leaned in even closer, his voice a whisper. "I do have—"

Footsteps sounded at the door, and Mr. Hawkins ambled into the room. His pace was lazy at first. That is, until he caught sight of Mr. Montague and me on the sofa, my hands so carefully placed in his.

Mr. Hawkins froze, his eyes rounding, then his gaze plunged to the floor. "Please excuse my intrusion. I'll be on my way at once."

"No, don't go." Recovering my fingers, I shoved to my feet, creating a bit of space between Mr. Montague and me. "I"—I swallowed hard—"I'd . . . That is, *we* were just talking of Mr. Cluett."

A tight smile disturbed Mr. Hawkins's mouth, but it only flashed for a second and was gone. Something far deeper fought for the balance of his emotions. He gave a heavy sigh. "I, uh, I'm sorry I barged in. Andrews directed me this way. I hadn't the least idea you were in company."

"Then the inquiry is complete."

"Yes, everyone has since departed the estate." He ran his hand down his face. "I've actually been searching for you for some time. Constable

Voss wanted me to inform you he plans to return later today. I daresay he means to tie up all the loose ends." Mr. Hawkins's hesitant stare slanted to Mr. Montague then back to me, his expression unreadable.

The participants from the inquiry had all left? And I'd not heard a single person in the hall? I'd been so consumed . . .

Mr. Hawkins dipped his chin. "Mr. Cluett's death was ruled an accidental drowning."

Shocked, I opened my mouth to refute such a claim before sobering at once. We were not alone after all. I gave him a weak nod.

It was Mr. Montague who spoke my thoughts aloud. "An *accident*? I don't believe that for a second."

Mr. Hawkins retreated to the window. "Yet we must abide by their decision. Mrs. Pembroke will have a little more than four weeks to make her final decision."

Mr. Montague stepped forward. "And if she chooses Lymington?" There was a slight waver to his voice I'd not heard before. "Remind me what the loser is afforded, sir."

I cringed at the word *loser*. This was not a game.

Mr. Hawkins remained solemn. "As I indicated before, Mr. Cluett left a small sum for the gentleman Mrs. Pembroke does not select."

"And if she chooses neither of us?"

"To incentivize Mrs. Pembroke's decision, he had me include a clause that addresses just such a scenario. In that case, all the money and the house will go to the mesmeric hospital he established in France."

Mr. Montague's eyebrows shot up. "Well, that's interesting." Then he looked at me, a caustic humor about his eyes. "Seems whether you like it or not, you'll have to choose between one of us . . . or none of us will inherit a farthing." He gave a breathy laugh. "Something tells me Miss Seton will not be too keen on such a happenstance. And if my observations are any indication, that woman finds a way to get whatever she wants."

CHAPTER 11

I met with Constable Voss that afternoon. The meeting was rushed, the questions pointed. In his warped little mind, I'd not witnessed any crime, and therefore I was utterly and completely dismissed.

I followed him to the front door, inwardly cursing myself for even bothering to voice my concerns in the first place. It was patently clear that Mr. Hawkins had been right about the smarmy nature of Constable Voss on all accounts. Any justice for Mr. Cluett would be wrought by a private investigation alone, which I had every intention of initiating as soon as possible.

In fact, as I watched the constable toddle up the steps of his carriage and collapse on the seat as if he'd run a mile, I began to ponder how exactly to commence my hunt for answers. The horrifying memories of the night Mr. Cluett was murdered trickled into my mind, and I tightened my fists. My dear friend and doctor would not be abandoned by me. What Mr. Hawkins and I needed now was a plan.

For some time Moorington Cross had been labeled a rambling structure, made worse every time a precocious Cluett family member inherited the estate—each of whom thought it their architectural duty to add rooms and passageways to the already swollen house. Thus, even with a distinct purpose in mind, I wasted quite a bit of time that afternoon wandering the aging corridors before I stumbled upon Mr. Hawkins in the library.

Seated at a large central table with a stack of papers spread out before him, he'd bowed his head over his work. So engrossed was he in the document before him, he didn't indicate he'd even heard me enter.

His hair lay a bit tousled on his head, his gloved left fist pressed to his chin, his lips forming inaudible words. Something about the singular focus to his study, the sort of childlike fascination on his face, arrested my steps.

I leaned back against the inside of the doorframe and watched him a silent moment. My heart felt like a distant bystander as Mrs. Fitzroy's voice thrummed in my ears: *"Wait, my dear, for the quiet. You'll know what I mean when you find it."*

Having taken me under her wing a year ago, Mrs. Fitzroy was always looking for a way to restore my lost faith in people. She'd cradled my chin into her hands at the time, begging me to listen. She promised me that even I could discern the truth of a person's character. I simply had to wait for those still, timeless seconds when a person forgets to hold their veil.

Was this such a moment? My chance to see Mr. Hawkins's true self? The dreamer within me kept perfectly still, mesmerized by the charged fervor that drove Mr. Hawkins's quill pen, the delight so obvious in his eyes. But my rational side allowed only a slight pause before it brought me roaring back to my senses and the task at hand.

I cleared my throat. "Good afternoon, Mr. Hawkins. May I ask what has so readily captured your attention?"

His head popped up and he stared at me as if he'd forgotten where he was. A guilty little smile emerged as he shuffled whatever he'd been writing into a book on the desk. He rose from his chair and tossed the quill. "Just a bit of work. Unfortunately, you are not my only client. I'm afraid I've neglected a few other, uh, pressing matters."

I forced myself to glance away from the hidden paper and gave him something of a wary look. "Allow me to apologize for commanding so much of your time. I'm quite certain you didn't plan to be at Moorington this long." I shrugged. "I daresay the last thing you expected was Mr. Cluett to change his will in such a way."

As if he suddenly remembered the state of his hair, he jerked his fingers through his messy locks, smoothing everything into place. "I will admit, I had originally hoped to be in and out of this house in little more than a sennight. But rest assured, I have no intention of leaving you now, not till we've seen this all the way through."

I hedged. "You mean the investigation?"

"That . . . or your decision of marriage, whichever comes first." He fiddled with his shirtsleeves before motioning me to a nearby chair. "Care to join me for a drink? We have much to discuss, do we not?"

I did as he asked, selecting a wingback chair near the desk and a glass of water.

After pouring himself a drink, he didn't return to his desk chair. Instead, he sank into the plush seat beside mine, his inquisitive gaze doing a bit of assessing of its own. "This has been a trying few days. Tell me, how are you holding up?"

I settled my glass on a nearby table. "I'll not mince words. It has been extremely difficult, but at the same time, in a way, I'm finding my feet—however uncomfortable they are to stand upon at present."

"What does everyone say . . . one step at a time and all that?" The flippancy of his statement didn't match the concern in his voice or the flex of his jaw. "I, uh, visited Mrs. Fitzroy this afternoon, and I am happy to report that although she means to keep to her room at this point, she seems to be steadily improving."

It was my turn to be flippant. "I've heard time can be a great healer . . . but . . ." I bit my lip and looked up. "If only we had some sort of closure in regard to Mr. Cluett's death."

Mr. Hawkins only nodded. He could easily guess how my meeting with the constable had gone. There was no real reason to ask.

I averted my attention to the window. "I am glad to hear about Mrs. Fitzroy. Thankfully Major Balfour is still in residence. He's always made her emotional well-being his top priority. I only wish I had more time to spend with her. I've been so preoccupied . . ."

Mr. Hawkins swallowed what I'd said in that thinking way of his, and I could see the obvious question forming on his lips. Yet for some reason he hesitated to give voice to his thoughts. After all, what decent gentleman would relish initiating a conversation about a young lady's suitors?

My shoulders slumped. "Please, Mr. Hawkins, if the question you're so clearly avoiding involves the two gentlemen I'm to select between, you needn't balk. I won't think ill of you for doing the very thing I requested of you in the first place, and that is to help me make a decision."

He seemed to relax. "Though I confess it feels as if I've known you for some time, just a second ago I was struck by how we are still strangers to one another. I didn't want you to think me brash . . . or overeager . . . or—"

"Nosy?" I laughed.

He tossed his fingers in the air. "There is that."

"Rest assured I'm no schoolroom miss, nor someone who needs to be coddled. I've been married before as well as lived my fair share of experiences. I understand how affairs of the heart can be tricky, even among close friends. But I assure you, Mr. Hawkins, I'm determined to make this decision in an intelligent manner, yet"—I let out a long breath—"sitting here with you, I cannot deny the need I have for an elder brother, a father, or even a guardian. Anyone who might help guide me through this difficult decision. Someone who might understand the depths of my feelings and my hopes for the future. Quite frankly, I have no one except—"

"Me." He coughed out the word before adding a tight smile, then shook his head. "What a dreadful fix you're in." He leaned forward. "Believe me, I don't take my position lightly. I'm well aware that you've been placed into my hands without much of a choice. Just keep in mind that I'm willing to assist you in whatever way you deem neces-sary, and I would never, ever divulge anything you said to me in regard to your decision and, if you choose to reveal them, the hopes in your heart."

He rubbed the back of his neck. "I do have some knowledge where gentlemen are concerned. And I promise you, I am here to serve. I'm now *your* personal solicitor. No one else's. And I shall advise you accordingly."

My very own solicitor? Odd how the thought rankled and intrigued at the same time.

He was staring at me now, clearly all too aware of the emotions roiling in my chest. "This business relationship—or, as I would like to call it, an impromptu friendship—won't work if you don't trust me."

I felt my muscles stiffen one by one. Then the image from moments before of Mr. Hawkins penning something to paper came to mind. He'd been so ardent and innocent in that quiet moment. I found myself relaxing. Agreeing but not surrendering. "All right, Mr. Hawkins. I shall choose to trust you. Right now, in this moment, but let me be perfectly clear. You've not earned that trust, not yet at least. I simply have no other choice at present." I paused to allow my words to sink in fully. "Experience has taught me to be careful in such matters. Believe me when I tell you I cannot bear the consequences of another man who deceives me."

Mr. Hawkins's jaw flexed, and I saw the questions spring into his eyes—to whom was I referring? What man had deceived me? He glanced away. "I am not, nor will I ever be, a gentleman who breaks my word, particularly not when I've given it to a lady in need."

"I'm glad." Our eyes met and I measured my tone. "Because I have two of the most peculiar gentlemen I have ever met waiting for me to decide if I wish to marry and bestow a fortune upon one of them. I need all the help you can muster."

"Indeed." Amusement lit Mr. Hawkins's brown eyes. "Why don't we begin by you telling me what you thought of Mr. Cluett's rather odd selections." He leaned back in his chair and propped his hand behind his head as if settling in for a long chat.

I adjusted my position as well, relaxing happily into the unexpected yet equally comfortable atmosphere Mr. Hawkins had created with a simple look. "I'm afraid you will think me ungrateful."

A laugh hovered on his breath. "You forget. I've met the gentlemen—unlucky, more like."

"Then you agree with me?"

"I've been introduced to Mr. Montague before, but I doubt he remembers me." A muscle twitched in his jaw. "Allow me to say, my first opinion of him has not changed."

I couldn't help but smile. "He's a flirt and probably a rogue. Believe me, I'm fully conscious of his dismal reputation, but be that as it may, when I'm alone with him . . . I can't explain it exactly. I feel like there might be another side to him. I don't think I can dismiss him so quickly."

Mr. Hawkins didn't move. "And he's handsome, no doubt."

"I'll not deny it; however, I'm not certain that's what drives his allure, not for me at least. How to put it into words? I simply find him absorbing."

Mr. Hawkins's brows shot up and heat stormed into my cheeks.

"Mr. Lymington is just the opposite, of course. He remains cold and aloof. I daresay it shall take all my female instincts to pry him out of his shell. After all, I only have thirty days to know him. What do you think?"

He laughed. "About your female instincts or Mr. Lymington?"

I shot him my own amused look. "Mr. Lymington, of course."

"I would certainly agree with your assessment, but add one of my own as well—he's hiding something."

My chest tightened. "You know, I actually thought the same. He surprised me this morning when he revealed he had something to discuss with the constable. I don't think he trusts me enough to share it yet."

Mr. Hawkins stilled. "Maybe he has a right to be cautious, or he has a reason to hide."

"I will not make any decisions without learning what it is."

"Yes, I—" Mr. Hawkins stood, his gaze captured by something beyond the far window. "Is that Miss Seton crossing the yard?" His eyes narrowed. "Seems she's in quite a hurry this afternoon. Strange that I saw her heading the same direction earlier this morning."

"She's back and forth to the outer buildings several times a day." I rose and joined him at the window. "I guess I've never really given her activities much thought. I always assumed she kept medicine or something for the hospital out there, but . . ."

Mr. Hawkins stole a quick glance at me. "But why would she choose to do so when she has such a large house with empty rooms?"

Puzzled, I reexamined Miss Seton's schedule in my mind. Why *was* she always in such a hurry? And where did she rush off to multiple times a day?

Mr. Hawkins's and my attention remained fixed on the lawn as Miss Seton disappeared over the rise. That is, until he moved in nearer the glass and the cool fabric of his jacket tickled my bare arm. His move was innocent enough, but my heart did the merest flip of curiosity as my mind danced dangerously with how natural it felt to be close to him.

Mr. Hawkins folded his arms at his chest and leaned against the window frame, ignorant of my rampant thoughts. "I daresay there isn't time before supper to follow her today, but would you care to join me for a ride tomorrow?"

A ride. On horseback. My heart stopped.

I'd not been permitted to ride since I was a little girl. Such an exercise was far too risky for a person with my condition regardless of what I wished. And though Mr. Hawkins was no doubt aware of my attacks, I found myself spouting the same story I gave everyone.

"I am sorry, but I've a small fear of horses. So as tempting as your offer is, I'm afraid I have to decline it."

He rubbed absently at his arms. "Really?" Then he dipped his head, trying to read the peculiar expression on my face. "I could secure you a tame mount if it really is a small fear. Or if you prefer, we might simply visit the stables. I know of a sweet little mare I'd love for you to—"

"No." I jerked away, startled by the tears gathering in my eyes. The truth was I loved horses. Riding was something I'd grieved over for years. It was far too difficult, too painful to watch as others enjoyed themselves. I'd not even returned to a stable since the day I was instructed never to ride again or even venture too far from the house alone.

Mr. Hawkins seemed lost at my strange behavior. "I never meant to upset you. I apologize at once for prodding. Please—"

"It isn't that." A tear slipped down my cheek, and I was forced to pull away. Why had I allowed myself to get so emotional? I'd not ridden a horse in years. "I do apologize, but I must beg leave of you. I just now remembered that I promised Mrs. Fitzroy a visit before supper."

Mr. Hawkins nodded easily enough, though the look in his eyes betrayed some layer of disbelief. I turned and fled the room nonetheless. After all, I didn't owe the man an explanation. He was only my solicitor, not one of the gentlemen vying for my heart.

CHAPTER 12

I was never more startled or more embarrassed by my sleeping disorder than the following afternoon when I blinked open my drowsy eyes to find Mr. Hawkins kneeling close beside the library sofa, concern written across his face.

He paused a moment to gauge the unusual location of my afternoon nap, then darted a quick look at the floor. "That boring, huh?"

Accepting his outstretched arm, I allowed him to pull me into a sitting position where I smoothed my hair back into place. Belatedly, I caught sight of the book that must have dropped to the floor during my spell.

"Oh . . . I wasn't reading exactly." I gave myself an inward shake, trying desperately to recall what had preceded my unwanted sleep. I'd not had an episode in over a week. "At least, I don't remember doing so."

He snatched the book from the carpet and assessed the spine. "*Letters on the Improvement of the Mind.*" An amused sideways glance at me. "How could you possibly have fallen asleep reading such entertaining literature?"

"How indeed." I took a deep breath then waited for my thoughts to clear. "Now I remember. I wasn't reading Chapone. Not today at least." I seized the book from his hands. "I was simply using the smooth surface to support Chauncey." My guinea pig's sweet face came to mind. "He was on my lap. Cook had given me a piece of lettuce, and the little dear was enjoying it excessively." I peered about the room. "I can only imagine where he's gone off to this time."

Mr. Hawkins, still kneeling beside the sofa, bent to check the underside of the furniture. "Not under here, but I wouldn't worry. He'll turn up just as he did the last time. There are all kinds of places for the creature to hide in here. What color did you say he was?"

"He's a mix of brown and white with a little cowlick right on top of his head." The previous time he went missing popped into my thoughts, and I lifted an embroidered pillow from the corner of the sofa.

Empty of the rodent himself but not entirely without Chauncey's handiwork. "Oh dear. He's been here all right."

Mr. Hawkins pushed to his feet and ambled to the sofa's end. "What makes you say that?"

I grimaced as I pointed at the small discoloration on the sofa's cushion. "I'm afraid it's still wet." I tipped my head back. "The poor thing tends to have accidents when I keep him from his cage for too long. Mr. Cluett gets so angry with me . . ." I couldn't finish the thought. There would be no reprimand for me this time.

Mr. Hawkins seemed to follow my sentiments. "Well, there's naught to appease but yourself at this point. It is your sofa now."

"Yes, I suppose so." My arms felt heavy in my lap. "I'm sure Miss Seton will know how to treat the stain. She's always found a way to do so before."

Footsteps sounded in the hall beyond the open library door. As if in response, grunting squeaks erupted from the floor-length drapes, which wrapped the window on the opposite side of the room. To Mr. Hawkins's and my great surprise, Chauncey's plump body toddled into view, supported only by a short set of legs and tiny feet. The entire scene would have been comical if it hadn't been so equally unexpected. Caught up in the moment, we simply stared as the pig took one look at me and started for the door, jogging forward as if he hadn't a care in the world.

"What on—" Mr. Hawkins sprang to intercept the little wretch but stopped short as Mrs. Fitzroy materialized in the doorway.

Chauncey met the new arrival there, his squeaks turning long and determined as he raised his chin and pawed the air with his front feet.

Mrs. Fitzroy, well acquainted with my pet, eyed him before eventually stooping to pick him up. She feigned indignation at first, but I knew quite well how fond she was of him.

"Now, what are you doing out of your cage again? Really, running about the house as if you were a common pest. You should be ashamed of yourself. No, I haven't brought you anything. It's your mama I've come for."

Her gaze turned to me. "And as for you, Amelia, I'm just as cross, as I've been looking for you everywhere this past age or more. I began to worry when you didn't come to my room as we'd arranged, that you'd had one of your"—a guilty peek at Mr. Hawkins—"well, you know what I mean. It has been several days since your last treatment and you have no idea how this sudden cessation will affect your progress."

Of course, I hadn't had much progress at all, but now was not the time to debate the merits of mesmerism. I met her at the center of the rug. "I did fall asleep, but you've found me now."

Mr. Hawkins, somewhat bewildered, continued to eye Chauncey's every move. "Am I wrong or did that animal know someone was coming through that door?"

"Well, of course he did." I smiled. "Guinea pigs get little credit for their supreme intelligence. Actually, not only did he anticipate the arrival of a visitor, but he knew just who to expect. He is well aware who brings him treats and who does not."

Mr. Hawkins narrowed his eyes. "You mean to tell me Chauncey heard someone walking in the hall and deduced it was Mrs. Fitzroy, thus worth the risk of coming out of his hiding spot?"

"He certainly did. He knows the sound of everyone's footsteps in the house. He only squeaks for Mrs. Fitzroy and myself, of course." I nestled him into my arms. "He means to entice her to bring him something to eat, and many times he gets just what he wants."

Mrs. Fitzroy shook out her hands. "Yes, yes, but that is neither here nor there. Chauncey must wait because I need to tell you something at once." She clasped her hands. "I saw a shadow a few minutes ago . . . a person really, only I couldn't tell who it was. They were going into Mr. Cluett's private wing. No livery, so it could not have been a servant."

"What?" I gasped. "Do you think it could have been the same person you saw before? Are they still there?"

"I don't know." She seemed to shrink back into herself. "The whole thing may be nothing, particularly with so many comings and goings with the funeral tonight. But I had to find you and let you know just in case."

Mr. Hawkins tramped to the door. "Certainly worth a look at any rate. You did the right thing, Mrs. Fitzroy." He tossed a determined glance at me. "I'll be right—"

"Oh no you don't." I stormed to intercept him, a knot cinching my throat. "I'm coming with you."

He stopped short. "Do you think that wise?"

Curiosity had long since won the battle over safety when it came to my friends, and really, Mr. Hawkins was simply being overcautious. "I assure you, whoever entered Mr. Cluett's private apartments in broad daylight without so much as a thought that Mrs. Fitzroy might oversee isn't too concerned with privacy, nor the least likely to be dangerous. I am coming with you whether you advise it or not." I stepped past him and added over my shoulder, "As you keep reminding me, it is my house after all."

We heard the rattle of papers and the clip-clop of shoes halfway down Mr. Cluett's private corridor. A few yards in the distance the door to our left was wide open, making it easy to ascertain where the shuffling emanated from. A flick of his wrist and Mr. Hawkins carefully guided me behind him, but he did not renew his concerns about my safety. He was as curious as I was to discover who had come up here and what they were doing.

Mr. Hawkins rounded the threshold first, but it was the sound of his voice that alerted the man ripping through an open desk drawer of our arrival. "Why, Mr. Lymington! What brings you to this part of the house?"

I was just in time to see the startled expression on my sour-faced suitor and the subsequent dropping of papers. His hands flew to his hair then went to work smoothing his jacket. "Miss Seton said I might look in here for something."

I sidestepped Mr. Hawkins, my face flaming hot. "For what purpose, sir? Those files contain private notes on patients here at the hospital."

His eyes widened, and he kicked the drawer shut, embarrassment tinging his voice. "I didn't think of that. Please excuse my intrusion." He started clumsily for the door, but Mr. Hawkins's arm shot out.

"Not yet, Lymington."

Splotches of red took up residence across Mr. Lymington's cheeks as sweat dripped down his hairline. He backed up until he was forced to plop into a nearby chair. "I certainly never meant any offense by coming here. I-I just didn't think. I needed to see . . ." His voice trailed away as he tugged at his cravat.

"See what?" I asked.

He cringed as he met my sharp gaze with a momentary licking of his lips. "The will, of course. I felt the necessity to read it for myself."

"The will?" Mr. Hawkins sounded incredulous. "And you thought such a document would be stored in here?"

Mr. Lymington covered his face with his hands. "I don't know. I mean, I hoped it would. Miss Seton thought it possible."

"I assure you, sir, that Mr. Huxley transported it to the Prerogative Court of Canterbury as soon as Mr. Cluett affixed his signature. That was over a sennight ago. I utilize a copy for myself." Mr. Hawkins jerked his shoulder to adjust his jacket. "Cluett's will was a holographic one, written in his own hand. My client was not coerced in any way, defrauded, or under the influence of another when he wrote it. Why didn't you come to me if you had questions regarding the legitimacy of the document?"

"I . . . didn't think of it . . ." For the first time his hands stilled. "You're perfectly right. I shall certainly do so in the future." Then he turned to me. "Mrs. Pembroke, if you accept my profound apology, I've something I'd like to ask you. You see, I've been hoping to speak with you alone all day." He fidgeted with his pocket watch. "Will you do me the honor of an afternoon drive tomorrow? I wish I could suggest we do so today, but with the funeral scheduled for nightfall tonight, I daresay the household shall be rather busy."

I blinked a moment as unease trickled down my scalp. A drive—alone? Now that was a bit of a stretch in our current situation. Surely Mr. Lymington was aware of what he was asking of me. I craned forward to catch the expression on Mr. Hawkins's face—distrust.

"Would you consider tea in the drawing room instead? I'm not certain I'm up for a drive at present."

There was a moment's hesitation as Mr. Lymington's appearance remained carved in stone before he opened his mouth to respond. "If that is what you prefer."

"I would, thank you."

The tension that had steadily grown over our conversation abruptly snapped as Mr. Lymington nodded with pleasure. So friendly was his reaction, I wondered if I had imagined the uncomfortable feeling in the first place.

He rose just as easily, speaking as if we were all good friends and he hadn't been caught snooping somewhere he shouldn't have been, then made his way to the door. "I shall be honored to meet you in the drawing room. Will two o'clock tomorrow be adequate?"

"Yes."

"Then good day, Mrs. Pembroke." He added a slight bow and slunk from the room.

It seemed Mr. Hawkins and I were both reluctant to speak or move for several seconds—thinking, digesting, hypothesizing.

But I was exhausted by my errant thoughts and slumped into the seat Mr. Lymington had vacated moments before, eventually glancing up. "Mr. Lymington wasn't here for the will, was he?"

Slowly, carefully, Mr. Hawkins ran his fingers through his hair. "No, I don't believe he was."

I scanned the room. "Then what could have brought him into Mr. Cluett's office? What was he hoping to find?"

"I haven't the least idea."

"You don't suppose he might be more willing to reveal what he was doing just now when we are alone tomorrow? His change of subject was shockingly abrupt after all."

Mr. Hawkins gave me a wary look. "All I know is that I'm glad you objected to his proposal for an afternoon drive. What a curst milksop. It's not safe at present, not till we know who's responsible for Mr. Cluett's death."

I crossed and uncrossed my feet. "You needn't worry. I'm not so foolish as to leave the protection of the house with someone I barely know."

"Good." He sagged against the wall, folded his arms, and eased back into his brooding thoughts. Then his eyes snapped open. "Perhaps this meeting of yours might prove fruitful in the end. I must admit, I doubt Lymington has any notion of sharing what he was about today, but that doesn't mean we can't learn something regardless."

My brow tightened. "What are you getting at exactly?"

He smiled. "Spy work, of course—the art of gathering intelligence. I've a bit of experience of that nature."

"*You* worked covertly for the government?"

"Not in any official capacity mind you, but I had my fair share of dealings with French spies in my youth."

A small laugh escaped. "Did you now?"

"All I'm saying is with a little well-placed ingenuity you might very well find a way to draw out the information we need from the gentleman."

I cocked my head. "Like if he killed Mr. Cluett? I don't think he'd be that green."

"That's not quite what I meant." There was a grin in his voice, that curious likability I'd experienced the moment I met him. He went on. "More along the lines of what his relationship with Mr. Cluett was like before the creation of the will." He nodded in thought. "Moreover, if things are going well between the two of you—and I have every confidence you will be able to get him talking—you just might learn what he spoke about with the constable. That is certainly high on my list of questions."

I drummed my fingers on the armrest. "And how precisely do you suggest I approach such topics, considering he wheedled his way around the question the last time I asked?"

Mr. Hawkins eased into the opposing chair and settled his fist at his chin, levity ripe in his eyes. "Surely you are not wholly ignorant of your many assets. Used properly, Lymington won't stand a chance."

Assets! I coughed out a laugh that turned a bit bitter on my tongue. "No one would call me pretty if that is what you're implying, nor would I ever use whatever female wiles I possess to . . . uh . . . draw him in."

Mr. Hawkins attempted to conceal his amusement. "You misunderstand me." Then steadied his gaze. "First off, I'd never use a word so common as *pretty* to describe the woman I see sitting before me, nor ask you to stoop so low." He picked up a penknife from the nearby table and rolled it in his fingers. "*Cultivated . . . urbane . . . eloquent.* Now those descriptors feel a great deal better on the tongue and settle nicely about you, don't you agree?"

"*Urbane? Eloquent?* Heavens, you sound as if you've been reading too much Byron."

He shrugged. "Perhaps I have, but I infinitely prefer William Blake."

"Ah, so you consider yourself a connoisseur of poetry?"

He chuckled. "Something like that." Then he looked away. "I only meant to imply that Mr. Lymington may need a bit of encouragement when it comes to the initiation of a relationship, particularly of the romantic sort."

"You think he's shy?"

"Careful, more like." Mr. Hawkins stared at the far bookcase. "You'll need more than drawing room conversation to crack that nut. Lymington must be able to trust you. I'm afraid you'll have to give him something deeper."

I picked at the overlay on my gown. "What do you mean, 'deeper'?"

"You may very well have to share a part of yourself."

I shrank back. "You mean I should entice him to kiss me— or what?"

"Not at all." He tugged at the sleeve of his jacket. "I meant for you to disclose a secret or, I don't know, anything that shows him you're willing to be vulnerable. In my experience such an admission might encourage him to do the same—to initiate a connection between you."

I glared down at my lap. "I'm not sure I can do that—artificially, I mean."

"Of course you can. It doesn't have to be anything too personal." Mr. Hawkins flicked his fingers in the air. "You could begin by revealing something like your fear of horses. You've shared that with me, and now I find I understand you better. All you need to do is allow

Lymington a glimpse at an intimate part of yourself. And if things go well, you might just spark a relationship with him that you both can build upon for your marriage."

"Oh, yes . . . our marriage."

Everything Mr. Hawkins said made a great deal of sense. I certainly needed to form a stronger connection with both of my suitors. So why did the recommendation feel so unpleasant at the same time? So devious?

I swallowed hard—because what he suggested seemed like something my deceased husband would have done in the same situation. If a relationship was to form, it had to be genuine, right?

My toes curled in my half boots. "Is that what you were taught to do, Mr. Hawkins—with your clients, I mean—to be a good solicitor?"

He stared a moment then slumped back in his chair. "No. I, uh, must always keep those relationships as professional as possible."

I raised my eyebrows. "I see."

He moved to rub his neck, his hands seeming a bit restless. "Mr. Cluett's will and subsequent murder elevates this case beyond any others I've been involved with." His voice lacked the enthusiasm he'd expressed just moments ago. "I'm not certain what will be required of me this go-around, but as I said before, I promise to stand your friend. I—"

I held up my hand, cutting him off. "Mr. Hawkins, I am not afraid of horses." I paused to catch his reaction, not entirely sure why I'd blurted out such a thing in the first place.

He blinked. "Come again?"

"I told you I was afraid of horses earlier, but I'm not. Not in the least bit."

He folded his fingers into a loose fist in his lap. "Then why the devil did you say you were?"

"I never meant to lie. I suppose I was simply embarrassed to tell you the real reason I couldn't take an afternoon ride with you.

Unfortunately, there will always be a part of me that longs to appear completely normal. You see, it's my condition that keeps me from riding—which, I assure you, I adored in my youth."

I shut my eyes for a second to escape his questioning gaze. "I don't know how much you're aware of in regard to my deficiencies. Mr. Cluett tried to spare me humiliation whenever possible, yet if you are to assist me in my quest to choose a husband and solve this murder, I fear you must know it all."

The carpet blurred before me. "When you found me earlier lying awkwardly on the sofa and you were forced to wake me, I'd no control over what had just happened. I'd fallen asleep against my will." I rolled my lip between my teeth. "You see, I'm sleepy all hours of the day, but sometimes uncontrollably so. I've learned to schedule breaks when I might rest to keep such situations from occurring, yet they inevitably do regardless of my plans. Mr. Cluett thought mesmerism might be the answer to my problems."

"But . . ."

"There's a great deal more to my condition than simply falling asleep at unseemly moments that inspired my husband to force my residence here. When I'm startled, even the smallest inward jump, something happens in my body. My muscles tense until they become hard as boards. I inevitably fall to the floor where I'm forced to lie captive for several minutes unable to move, yet aware of everything that happens around me. It's debilitating and terrifying to some people, and no matter what I do, it continues to happen."

I could see the pity in Mr. Hawkins's eyes. He meant to commiserate with me, and I'd have none of that. I spoke before he'd have a chance to respond. "Due to these strange occurrences, I was advised by a doctor never to ride a horse or even stray too far from the house alone. As a child I had a maid who followed me everywhere I went. As of late, however, I've gladly accepted more freedom here at the hospital, and I've allowed myself to walk a bit. But I dare not ever ride again, despite my love for it. Imagine if one of my spells struck while I was on horseback. I could very well die."

As soon as I'd said the word *die*, I wished I could take it back. The ominous nature of the word plunged the room into breathless silence. So much so, it felt only natural when Mr. Hawkins took my hands into his, a look of compassion on his face.

"I see now what a difficult road you've been forced to travel, and one not to be taken lightly. I was aware of some of your past from Mr. Cluett, but I appreciate you trusting me with the whole." His touch was gentle and kind as his fingers tightened around mine, and he offered me a crooked smile. "I'm sorry I brought up riding to you at all."

"You couldn't have known."

"No, I . . ."

He didn't finish his sentence. He didn't have to as a glorious second of complete understanding passed between us.

And then . . .

I don't believe Mr. Hawkins possessed any conscious awareness of making such a subtle movement, but his thumb slid ever so softly along the outside of my hand—and the room utterly shifted—as if it had been lying in wait to do so all along.

Almost in unison we stared down at our clasped hands, the fragile tendrils of stillness daring us ever closer. The shared compassion I'd reveled in moments ago drowned beneath the pulsing thrum of my heart and the aching brush of temptation.

I knew quite well I should pull away, but the resulting seconds stretched out as if timeless, driven by the steady rush of nerves and . . . what, exactly?

Shouldn't he say something? Shouldn't I? Or were the both of us to go on pretending as if I'd not been affected by his touch?

Dare I look up? Did he know what raged inside me?

Perhaps he did, as he released my hand, the cold air wrapping my fingers, and settled back in his chair. "I suppose it's past time I return to work." His voice was calm enough, his face unreadable. "I've a great deal to do today."

I nodded, unwilling to risk my voice.

However, neither of us moved, the rush of silence taking up residence in Mr. Hawkins's eyes. He propped his left hand on his leg, his specialized glove taking over the focus of our attention, then he shot me a wry look. "I'll have you know, I've never danced in my life."

I don't know what remark I'd anticipated in such a moment, but that certainly wasn't one of them.

A budding grin lit his face. "I learned the steps, of course, along with my two sisters, but I never could quite bring myself to perform them in company."

My lips parted. "Not even once?"

"No. I couldn't bear the stares, the whispered comments. You see, one cannot hide a hand like this while dancing."

I looked down at the glove once more, and I opened my mouth to point out how everyone was probably already aware of his deformity. He hadn't hidden it all that well, at least not around me. And he was so very handsome and gentlemanlike; any lady fortunate enough to be asked to partner him surely wouldn't remark on such a menial thing.

Empty reassurance, though, was not why he'd spoken out. I leaned forward. "Then we understand one another."

He covered his mouth with his right hand, eyeing me a long moment, the unspoken solidarity still thick between us, then he rubbed his forehead. "Well, at any rate, you know something of me, something no one else does." He took a deep breath. "You said earlier you were making the choice to trust me, which is not really the same as doing so, is it?"

"No."

"I promise you, right here and now, I mean to prove to you that you can actually do so. As you said, we're not so very different."

I met his steady gaze, desperate to make sense of the connection between us, but I couldn't wrangle my thoughts into line, not completely, not when he examined me with such intensity. How remarkable his eyes were. Had I ever noticed how the light softened the shades of complicated brown hues and darkened others? How entirely comfortable he made me feel? "It would mean a great deal to me for you to stand my friend."

"Thank you." He stood and motioned me to the door. "We'd better be going, don't you think?"

Yes . . . something I should have done long since.

I led the way out of Mr. Cluett's office with little else on my mind than the man so close behind me, which is why I was so surprised when I made the discovery. My feet were rooted to the floor as I pointed into the shadows. "That's odd."

Mr. Hawkins drew up beside me, a question clearly written on his face.

"The layout of the hallway there." I tilted my head as I urged him farther down the corridor toward Mr. Cluett's bedchamber, my heartbeat mirroring my furtive steps. "If Mrs. Fitzroy approached the bedchamber utilizing this hall as she indicated, there is no way she could have seen a man standing in the alcove at the terminus of the wall there, nor even a flash of light like she described." I glanced back at Mr. Hawkins, my eyes wide. "The wooden pillar completely blocks that section from view."

CHAPTER 13

I had to see Mrs. Fitzroy straightaway or my mind would get the best of me. My dear friend had lied about either what she'd seen or where she'd been the night Mr. Cluett was killed. Something didn't add up.

I dismissed Mr. Hawkins at once, certain I should see Mrs. Fitzroy alone. He was already asking too many pointed questions, and the truth was he simply didn't understand. Mrs. Fitzroy was no more involved in Mr. Cluett's death than I was. I'd known her well over a year and it simply wasn't in her nature. I only needed to reconcile her story with the events of the evening and figure out why she had made the mistake in the first place.

Andrews pointed me in the direction of the blue salon where I found Major Balfour and Mrs. Fitzroy initiating a game of piquet.

She seemed relieved as I entered, waving me over at once. "I've been on pins and needles since I dropped off Chauncey in his cage. Did Mr. Hawkins shed some light on our little shadow?"

For a split second I wondered if she already knew the identity of the man she'd sent us to ferret out, but the feeling quickly passed. "It was only Mr. Lymington. He apparently had some business in Mr. Cluett's office."

A nearly imperceptible wrinkle of her nose was her only response as she kept her focus on the cards in her hands.

It was Major Balfour who responded to the news. "Mr. Lymington, you say? Hmm . . . that's interesting. Tell me, how do you find your two suitors now that you're better acquainted with them?"

"Still strangers, I'm afraid." I couldn't help but steal a few glances at Mrs. Fitzroy as I spoke. "I'll need some time before I'll be able to make an informed decision, and Mr. Cluett's questionable death does make it rather difficult to distinguish what direction is best."

Major Balfour's head bobbed, his attention steady on the game. "I can well believe that. Forever is a great deal of time to live with such a decision. Your health and happiness must remain top priority." He moved one card to the far side of his hand. "Speaking of Mr. Cluett's death, has there been any progress following the inquiry? It was my understanding the whole affair was deemed an accident regardless of what anyone here may think."

I slid into an empty seat beside them at the square table. "It was, but I still intend to find out how it happened, if that's even possible."

"I should hope so." Major Balfour gave me a wan smile. "The past few days have been a trying interlude for us all. I will confess, I was thinking I might depart Moorington Cross after the funeral and head back to my estate, but Mrs. Fitzroy has convinced me otherwise. I've decided to keep her company till her son is able to make the journey here." He lifted his shoulders slightly. "Assuming I'm welcome to stay."

I smiled. "Don't be ridiculous. Of course you are." Then I turned to Mrs. Fitzroy. "But that means you intend to leave me after all?"

"Oh my darling." She expelled a loaded sigh. "I heard from John this morning. He's agreed to have me, and I know very well I can't stay here forever now, can I?"

"You most certainly can. My intention to offer the two of you a home has remained constant."

She pressed her lips together, emotion teasing the corners. "Once you make your choice and your wedding has come and gone, once the two of you are quite settled, then you may write to me. At that point if you find you need a nervous old woman to keep you company, I'll arrange travel without delay. But as I fully expect and you are content enough as you are, I shall find my own way to happiness with John."

So this was what had brought on her somber mood. She and Major Balfour had been making plans. Write to her indeed. If I had my way, she'd never leave in the first place, but maybe she was right. The transition would be a bit awkward at the beginning. I could only imagine how Mr. Lymington or Mr. Montague would respond to my plans. Her way might prove the best course.

I squeezed her hand before pivoting to my left. "And what about you, Major Balfour? Will you come back to us as well?"

His eyes crinkled at the corners. "If I am welcome."

My shoulders relaxed. "Goodness, you both had me a bit frightened a moment ago. I thought you meant to abandon me, but I'm glad to know I won't be alone in all this—not forever at least—that I shall have friends to stand by my side if I need them."

Mrs. Fitzroy covered a smile with her hand as she directed a knowing glance at Major Balfour. "And a rather zealous solicitor if I'm not mistaken."

My body froze, the feeling of Mr. Hawkins's hands wrapped around mine so fresh I could have sworn he'd reached out and touched me again. "What do you mean, a 'zealous solicitor'?"

"Nothing all that untoward, I assure you." She laid a card down, her eyes narrowed. "Simply an observation."

I stole a nervous look at Major Balfour, shocked to see the sly smile he offered Mrs. Fitzroy.

My tongue felt thick. "Let me put your fears to rest at once. There is nothing between the solicitor and me." The words popped out easily enough. Yet was I being entirely truthful? Nothing actually had happened, but why did I allow such a moment in the first place?

Mrs. Fitzroy draped her hand across her breast. "My darling, I never meant to imply a secret relationship or anything of the kind."

My voice lacked the flames from a moment earlier. They were right, of course. I had given them cause to wonder. I had been acting a fool. "Then what did you mean to *imply*?"

She peeked at me over the rim of her cards. "Simply that he's demonstrating exceptional care of you, my dear, and forgive me if I overstep my bounds as a friend, but you do not seem wholly indifferent to those ministrations. I only mean to urge caution."

Guilt recharged my words. "I'm well aware I've two gentlemen residing in my house intent on marrying me."

She gave me a wistful look. "I never said your position was a fair one or the least enviable."

Major Balfour tapped the table. "A conundrum if I ever saw one. Mr. Hawkins—a fine young man who five days ago would have been an excellent match, but difficult to think of now unless you would be willing to forgo the inheritance."

I stiffened at the idea. If I even considered such a thing, I would not be able to help Major Balfour and Mrs. Fitzroy. "Believe me, you needn't discuss the solicitor again in relation to me. Do you hear? I have but two choices on my plate and I mean to select between them." My chest felt heavy. "Besides, a bout of silly drawing room gossip does not equal genuine interest in the least. Mr. Hawkins has been kind to me, and I shall utilize his services in whatever way is helpful to me. Rest assured, he only means to complete the job he's been given. He's a professional in every sense. The two of you"—a sideways glare at Mrs. Fitzroy—"read far too deep into a passing comment I made long ago. I assure you, Mr. Hawkins has not spent one second thinking of me, and I will not spend one more moment thinking of him."

Mrs. Fitzroy drew a card from the deck. "You are perfectly right, my dear." The look in her eyes, however, said otherwise.

I gripped the chair, trying in vain to keep my voice even. "With that settled, there is something else I need to talk with you about." I hesitated. "It's in regard to the night Mr. Cluett died."

Mrs. Fitzroy went motionless for a moment then shifted in her seat. "Oh?"

"You told me you saw what you assumed was a man standing

near the wall in the alcove beyond Mr. Cluett's bedchamber door, along with a flash."

All prior thoughts vanished from her face. "Yes, it was far too dark to make out the man's features in that corner of the hall, but I did see a flash."

I placed my palms on the table, eyeing my splayed fingers as I spoke. "I was just up there, and do you know what I found?"

The cards quivered in her hands. "No."

"I couldn't see the alcove from Mr. Cluett's bedchamber door. There is a carved column that effectively blocks such a view."

"You don't say." Her words were breathy and short.

Major Balfour's gaze flicked up, the game suddenly at a halt.

I said softly, "Are you certain you actually saw someone that night?"

The bridge of her nose bunched beneath a wrinkled brow then slackened. "Of course I did. Why would I lie about such a thing?"

"And you were standing at Mr. Cluett's door when you saw him?"

"As I said." The cards, once firmly in her hand, fluttered onto the table. "Maybe the figure was in the center of the hall or . . . or something else. It was so very late and dark, but I know what I saw. There was a person there somewhere at the end of the hall. I don't know. I just don't know."

Before I had a chance to question her further, she shoved her chair back and rocked to her feet. "I find I'm not feeling all that well at present. I . . . We can talk of this more later if we must, Amelia. But for now I . . . I find I am in great need of lying down."

I watched her leave with lingering questions in my mind and the beginnings of a sour stomach. I would have to be a bit more delicate with Mrs. Fitzroy, yet I could not let this rest, not even for my dear friend.

I arrived for the arranged meeting with Mr. Lymington the following afternoon only to find the drawing room completely submerged in a milky gray haze. So much so, my usually pensive suitor hopped to his feet and lit a few more wall sconces. "Abysmal, isn't it? I daresay we shall see a storm before dinner."

"Likely so."

Though we'd had a few warm days of late, the chill in the house was absolute. I made my way to the sofa, the massive floor-length windows standing morose and framing what could only be called a dreary prospect beyond. I took a seat, glad to see a thin whiff of steam rising from the white teapot on the table and a smart fire popping in the grate.

As I filled my cup, the rich floral scent of black tea met my nose and lingered delightfully on the air.

I spoke over my shoulder to Mr. Lymington, who was rather strangely still lurking in the shadows. "Shall I pour you a cup as well?"

"Please." His movements were slow but direct as he angled his way around the sofa and seated himself opposite me at the far end. He'd donned a dark green jacket and white cravat and slicked his hair back with a bit of pomade. He rested his elbow on the armrest as his hand came to linger at his chin, his gaze stationary on the far side of the room.

I don't know why I thought we'd manage a bit more familiarity than this, yet here we were back to the dratted awkwardness of our first meeting. I extended his teacup. "Sir?"

My voice seemed to startle him, his shoulders jerking tight, then he dashed something of a smile. "Thank you."

He took his time regarding the contents of the teacup before enjoying an equally long sip.

Unsure what to do or say, I managed an even longer drink, my focus darting about the room. Clearly the incessant casement clock was the only occupant of the room with any measure of confidence as it ticked away in my ears.

Finally I could bear the forced silence no longer and slid my cup onto the table. "You said yesterday you'd been hoping to meet with me."

"Ah, yes." A hard swallow. "I've . . . uh . . . well, I've been overly concerned that I gave you the wrong impression . . . in the garden, that is, and then again, in the office."

"Oh?"

A nervous rake of his hand through his hair. "I was cross with Montague, and I hope I've not made you think ill of me. I want to assure you that I'm not overly mercenary. I'll not quibble with you; however, this inheritance would keep my estate intact and solvent for the foreseeable future. There are a great many people depending on your selection of a husband. Yet I also want you to know I mean to be a good partner in life. You'll not regret an alliance with me."

I didn't doubt he intended to treat me well, but the look in his eyes, the cadence of his voice—everything felt so clinical between us. How could I ever really know a man so guarded? Or more importantly, how could I trust him with my heart?

Mr. Hawkins's recommendation rang in my ears. *"Give him something personal to work with."* Perhaps he was right. Could I really expect to interview my prospective husbands like a gentleman interviewing a laborer without some sort of equal exchange? Mr. Lymington needed something from me.

I swallowed hard. "I think it best to explain my situation before we move forward."

"All right."

My fingers found the seam in my gown. "I have difficulty when it comes to sleep . . . I—"

"Oh—" He reached over and patted my hand in much the same way a doctor would a patient or a father a child. My skin crawled, but Mr. Lymington didn't seem to notice. "I'm well aware of all that."

My eyes widened. "You are?"

"Montague has spent the last two days quizzing Miss Seton regarding the specifics of your hospitalization."

My mouth went dry. "And the two of them felt at liberty to discuss my private affairs with you?"

"As I said, it was Montague who initiated the conversation."

My muscles constricted, my breaths turning short and quick. How dare Miss Seton feel at ease to chat about me in such a way. I closed my eyes for a moment, imagining the scene. How she'd probably enjoyed every minute of it.

The sofa whispered a squeak as Mr. Lymington repositioned his seat. "Let me assure you, I don't regard the issue. What difference does it make to me how often you sleep? You may do so at your will."

My heartbeat felt thin, ghostly even. Here I was once again being granted permission for something I had no control over. At least now I knew where the gentleman stood. I held my voice steady. "Thank you."

He gave me a tight-lipped grin and without warning my deceased husband flashed into my mind's eye. A warning? Or a challenge?

I tossed Mr. Lymington's patronizing look right back at him. After all, I had decided I was done taking orders. "If I'm to consider your suit, sir, there is one thing I absolutely demand between the two of us—honesty."

"Certainly." He blinked rapidly as he spoke, and I began to wonder if he'd always had the flutter or if it had been brought about by my pointed response.

"Then I'd like to know how you knew Mr. Cluett. Why did he write you into his will . . . for me?"

Mr. Lymington tapped his knee with his first finger as if considering his answer, then met my glare. "He knew my mother, actually. She was once an admirer of his."

I sucked in a quiet breath. "An admirer?"

"Yes. She was paired up with him by her father . . . until . . ."

I leaned forward, waiting for more. "Until what?"

He shrugged. "I really couldn't say. I'm not at all certain. All I know is it did not end well between them. She actually begged me not to come here at all."

"What reason did she give for the interference?"

"I didn't feel it my place to ask. I got the feeling she was not open to discussing the topic further. I simply informed her I must make my own way in the world and did so. She did not put up too much of a fight."

I pulled back. "But if Mr. Cluett and your mother were not on good terms, then why on earth would he include you in his will?"

A muscle tensed in his jaw. "I really couldn't say. The entire ordeal was a shock to my family, most of all me."

"I imagine it was."

We sat a moment in quiet, uncertain how to carry on when a flash of color caught my eye. "Oh!" I stood and pointed out the window. "There goes Miss Seton now."

Beyond the recessed glass, Cluett's nurse hastened down the path, a scrambling urgency to her walk along with a harried expression. And all at once I had to know what she was about. Mr. Hawkins had been right to question her strange movements the day before. None of those daily trips from the house made any sense, and so many of my questions at present led back to her.

I edged a glance at my current companion. It was unfortunate the opportunity presented itself at such a moment, but it wasn't to be wasted. "Mr. Lymington, I do believe if we hurry"—my face felt hot— "we can ask Miss Seton about . . ." What reason to give him? "Her loose tongue . . ." She had been rather free with Mr. Montague about me. "And just what she does around here. It's high time she answered a few pointed questions about herself. Discussing my sleeping issues indeed."

"Loose tongue?"

I started for the door.

"Mrs. Pembroke, I don't think that—"

I was already beyond the drawing room, however, shouting over my shoulder. "If you prefer not to escort me at present, I'll be happy enough to speak with Miss Seton on my own. In fact, you needn't—"

"But you promised me tea and—" Mr. Lymington had to sprint to catch me at the front door, but he did so, slamming his palm against the mahogany wood at the last second. "Careful, Mrs. Pembroke. Miss Seton is a powerful force. I would recommend playing nice for the time being."

Trapped, I crossed my arms. "Really, your concern is noted, but also wholly unnecessary. Miss Seton only continues on in this household with my approval. If you would but step aside, I simply mean to remind her of that fact."

He gave a pointed shrug, his arm falling lifeless to his side. "Whatever you think is best. Just remember, she's been the eyes and the ears of the hospital for some time. You may yet need her cooperation at some point."

I clenched my teeth, digesting with irritation the truth of his statement. No matter how angry she'd made me, I might very well require Miss Seton's vast knowledge and experience. She was simply too important to the workings of Cluett's Hospital and the inhabitants within. But I could still follow her, learn something about her curious movements on the estate. "I shan't corner her if that is what you're implying. A simple reminder, nothing more."

He offered his arm. "Then I shall be pleased to escort you." Quite properly he led me through the door and down the front steps, his chin high. "And it's a good sign for the future, I daresay."

I glanced up. "What sign?"

A toothy grin. "Our working together so easily."

Working together? He'd spoken and I'd obeyed—only because he was in the right of it this time. But what if he hadn't been? What if I'd been forced to stand my ground?

I shook off the mounting concerns as Mr. Lymington's true nature remained too difficult to discern, and I found myself occupied with something else entirely, something far more uncomfortable—the complete lack of attraction I felt in holding his arm.

Oh, it was warm enough. Steady and hardly repulsive, but the truth was I felt nothing at all, no spark of interest. A loveless marriage was not all that rare, but could I bear such an arrangement again?

Possibly, but when I was abandoned at the hospital by Mr. Pembroke, I promised myself I'd find my way to complete independence. Did a convenient marriage even offer that?

I regarded Mr. Lymington once more, the resolute curve to his chin, the slight bulge of his eyes, and sighed. At the very least he was consistent. I knew what to expect where he was concerned. And with an escort beside me, any person really, I could venture farther from the house than I usually allowed myself. I sucked in a deep breath. There was a decided benefit to companionship for me, passionate or not, the very thing Mr. Cluett may have seen that I was unable to—a husband at my side would be a ticket to return to life.

CHAPTER 14

M r. Lymington didn't even spare a glance back at the house as it hid behind a veil of trees and the lurking fog, but I did. Never in my life was I more keenly aware of the freedom company brought with it.

"Where do you think Miss Seton went from here?"

His steps slowed. "There's no way to know. If only we'd not lost sight of her when she scampered into the woods—and this mist is so thick . . . Have you any idea what might be out here? A structure of some sort? A tenant's property?"

"I usually don't wander so far from the house, but as far as I know, most of Cluett's tenants live nearer the village on the opposite side of the estate."

We both looked left then right, squinting to see anything amid the gray trees. A transient breeze slithered through the overhead branches, a hushed rustle encircling the surrounding woods.

Mr. Lymington released my hand to duck around a tree. "Perhaps she's simply on her way to Plattsdale."

"Walking?" I planted my hands on my hips. "And she'd not choose this direction—not through the woods in this weather. Plattsdale is really more that way, and the River Grey runs all along this side of the property."

"Well," he huffed. "She's lost us at any rate. Shall we make our way back?"

I was less than a second from nodding when I caught a glimpse of white several yards ahead. "What was that?"

Mr. Lymington turned, following the direction of my finger. He stared a long moment at the lonely trees. "All I see is fog."

I narrowed my eyes. "Something or someone was there . . . at least I think so." A chill skirted across my shoulders. "I don't know what I saw, but I don't think we're alone."

"I can check if you'd like." His tone remained skeptical, but he edged a step forward.

"Please, I—"

He held up his hand. "You needn't explain. I've not been at ease myself since Mr. Cluett's death. I'd rather be sure. Wait here."

I watched in nerve-racking anticipation as he crept farther and farther into the misty trees, leaving me alone to mull over my dark thoughts. Whoever I'd seen ahead was probably long gone. Yet the pulsing fear of someone concealed in the shroud of fog took root in my imagination and began to grow.

The ground felt damp beneath my half boots, the tree trunks glistening from the moisture-rich air as the mist gathered in clumps about the underbrush. Silence descended as the crunch of Mr. Lymington's boots vanished into shadows, the breeze utterly still.

"Mr. Lymington?"

I received no answer. Nothing but the wild beat of my heart.

Then I heard it—a *whoosh*—from somewhere behind me. The hairs on my arms prickled to attention. The sound had been subtle, yes, but certainly there. I whirled around, lifting my hands as if to defend myself, yet I knew very well I was at the mercy of whoever lurked in the fog.

"Mr. Lymington." I tried again in vain, glaring over my shoulder, willing him to appear. I spun first one way then the next.

Then a branch snapped at my back, and I was forced to whirl around again and face what appeared to be empty woods. But I was wrong. A man sprang out of the haze—impossibly large, hairy, clad in trousers and a dirty shirt. He gripped a shovel, which he swung menacingly over his head.

A scream tore from my throat a second before my muscles contracted. Dread filled my chest as I inwardly shouted for my legs to move, but my body had already begun to betray me. Like a tree chopped down at the base, I crashed to the earthen floor, my face pressed to the wet leaves and the hard, muddy ground.

I could hear the man breathing hard, circling my position, his steps sloshing through the wet leaves, but I was completely frozen by one of my extreme spells, brought on by the sudden fright.

"Mrs. Pembroke?" It was Mr. Lymington's voice on the breeze. He was not yet at my side, but he was close.

I tried to call out, but my tongue wouldn't move, my jaw wouldn't open.

Could he see me lying in the dirt?

Perhaps he thought the figure in the woods was me as his voice remained jovial enough. "What do you know, but there's a cottage just ahead. I found Mr. Hawkins walking there as well. He . . . Oh my."

I heard a burst of footsteps behind me, followed by the *whoosh* of branches, then the slow shuffle of a man at my far side. The person's hands were on my back and my arms, then my shoulders, before I was gently but urgently flipped to my backside.

"Mrs. Pembroke?" It was Mr. Hawkins who'd knelt near my head and his warm fingers that crossed my forehead.

The numbing contractions were waning some, and I blinked to remind him what I'd told him in the library. He gave me a wan smile, assessing my situation immediately. He turned to Mr. Lymington. "I believe Mrs. Pembroke has had a spell. I understand they pass in a few moments."

A few moments indeed. It was torturous to simply lie there under Mr. Hawkins's careful gaze. Eventually he spoke again to Mr. Lymington. "Why don't you alert one of the grooms to our situation? My curricle must be brought around at once. Mrs. Pembroke should not walk back."

Mr. Lymington nodded, but his expression was wary, as if he was wholly uncertain how to proceed before he stomped off.

"Now." Mr. Hawkins grasped my hand, finding it less rigid than before. "Can you speak yet? Can you sit?"

Over several minutes, in a cascade of firing nerves, my body tingled slowly back to life, and I was finally able to sit up with his help. "Thank you. It's nearly passed."

He gave me a wry look. "Now that was far more impressive than I was expecting."

I coughed out a laugh. "What did you think I meant when I described it?"

"I'm not certain, but the image of my swooning sister came to mind at the time. This was nothing like that. Did you injure anything? You've a bit of mud on your cheek here."

"No, nothing a day's rest won't fix." I ran my hand down my face, but my kid gloves proved to be just as dirty as everything else.

"Allow me." Mr. Hawkins edged in close beside me on the ground, his hand gentle as his fingers glided over my injured cheek.

My eyes fluttered shut, my heart lapsing into the same quivering mess I'd experienced in the office, the feelings I'd no business entertaining still so delightfully near the surface. I didn't pull away like I promised myself. I couldn't, not when every inch of my body craved the feel of connection. How few times in my life had I been held so tenderly by another person, particularly after one of my accidents.

It wasn't until Mr. Hawkins's hand slid to the curve of my face and his thumb, once busy with the work of cleaning my cheek, stilled against my skin that my eyes popped open. He was watching me, studying me, then glanced away.

His face was grim. "What started this spell?"

I glanced at the trees about us, combing back through what had caused the whole episode in the first place. "There was a man. He had a shovel."

Mr. Hawkins tensed. "You mean someone was out here?"

"Yes, right before you found me. It was a strange-looking person. He must have run off when he heard Mr. Lymington talking."

Mr. Hawkins pressed his lips together. "There was nobody here when we arrived, but I'm beginning to think the gentleman you describe might be the very individual Miss Seton intended to meet today."

"You were with her?"

"Not exactly. I saw her leave the house a few moments ago and followed her to a cottage where I proceeded to watch her from afar. But when no one answered the door, she became agitated. I decided it best to approach her at that point, and you know, she denied anyone lived there quite prettily. Although obviously the evidence suggests otherwise."

"The man was waving a shovel over his head."

Mr. Hawkins shook his head. "Then you think he could be violent?"

"I don't know what I think. All I can be certain of is Miss Seton must be hiding something."

He lifted an eyebrow. "Or rather, someone."

"Precisely."

He rubbed his chin. "But why would she do such a thing?"

"I don't know, but I believe it's high time we confront her. This is my estate after all. She cannot refuse to answer me. The secrecy has gone on long enough."

We found Miss Seton deathly still, seated at the pianoforte in the connecting room where she used to play for Mr. Cluett's mesmeric sessions. Her back was to us, the instrument looming large before her. Her bony fingers stretched out motionless, poised above the ivory keys, her posture sickeningly straight. It almost felt as if she might be waiting for a cue from beyond the door to begin to play.

The musty scent of aging wood and coarse oil filled my nose as an empty feeling settled into my stomach.

Though we hadn't made a sound, something must have alerted her to our presence, for her fingers contracted and a dissonant chord rent across the stale air, reverberating off the paneled walls. Then as if calculated for maximum effect, she pivoted to face us, a hard scowl upon her face.

"Why, Mr. Hawkins." A slight smile. "Am I to be quizzed again about my choice of walking paths today, or have you something more valuable with which to fill my time?"

Mr. Hawkins strode right up to the pianoforte and propped his arm on the lid, a sharp glint to his gaze. I followed him across the crimson rug. He was in his element now, controlling the room before he'd even said a word.

He raised his eyebrows. "That is precisely why I have come to speak with you. Only this round, I won't allow you to fob me off." A sideways glance at me. "We know all about the man in the cottage."

Miss Seton's face wrenched inward, her muscles twitching to life as she stuttered her way through something of a response. "I, uh, didn't, uh, realize . . . Really, I wasn't aware you had met Mr. Cluett's good friend . . ." She lifted a shoulder. "I'd promised to keep him a secret, you see, and I don't go back on my word, not for anyone. Of course, none of that signifies now, I suppose. It was only a matter of time before I was forced to discuss the whole with Mrs. Pembroke."

I inched onto a nearby chair. "What do you mean, Mr. Cluett's friend? I know nothing of this person."

She remained solemn, but there was a flicker of satisfaction in the curve of her mouth. "He's been a well-kept secret here at Moorington Cross for a great many years." Her expelled breath seemed to suggest we should keep it that way.

Mr. Hawkins's hand thudded onto the hard surface of the piano-forte. "Considering there was a brutal murder in this very house but a few days ago, I suggest you no longer withhold any information."

Her hands slid to the bench and she gripped the edge, her knuck-les gleaming white. "As you say." Then she pressed her lips together. "We are not at cross purposes, Mr. Hawkins. I, too, wish to discover who had a hand in Mr. Cluett's death."

I ran my fingers across my forehead. "Then tell us who this person is. He currently lives in the cottage? I saw the man myself, and he was a frightful sight. I shudder to think what he might be capable of. He had a shovel over his head."

Her eyes widened. "Had he?"

Mr. Hawkins leaned toward her. "The truth now, if you please, Miss Seton. Identify the man at once."

She took her time answering, clearing her throat and wetting her lips. "He is Mr. Cluett's patient from the Continent."

"His patient?" I couldn't hide the surprise in my voice. "Then why is he here in Britain?"

"He was introduced to me at Mr. Cluett's mesmeric school in France. Henry is his name. From what I observed at the time, he became a good friend of Mr. Cluett's in the early days. He was a bright young man who came to the school in search of help for what we learned later was a deteriorating mind. Mr. Cluett initially had great hopes to use mesmerism to help Henry and thought to teach him how to manage his own condition, but his situation only worsened, eventually dipping into moments of madness followed by rounds of listlessness."

"How on earth did he end up here?"

"Mr. Cluett always felt responsible for him, since the very begin-ning, he did. And with Henry not having any other friends or family, Mr. Cluett couldn't just leave him when he journeyed back to England to take his place at Moorington Cross, so he simply brought him along. Mr. Cluett and I have been caring for Henry ever since."

Mr. Hawkins crossed his arms. "Then why all the secrecy?"

"Mr. Cluett did not want anyone to know of his utter failure surrounding the patient. There were so many others he helped a great deal over the years. Simply put, it wouldn't have been good for business."

I glanced out the window. "Is Henry dangerous?"

"You mean, is he capable of killing Mr. Cluett?" She seemed almost pleased with herself, and I wondered why that emotion continued to hover so close to the surface.

She added a tight smile. "Not usually, no. I've spent time with Henry every day. I assure you, he has moments of confusion, but most of the time, he barely stirs from his bed."

"And he has no family to speak of?"

"None that I am aware of." She rose from the bench, her black muslin swishing against her legs. "I would advise you to keep his routine intact. Mr. Cluett devised it over many years, and the schedule has proved a calming influence on a troubled man. I'm certainly happy to continue tending to his needs."

She slid the bench closer to the pianoforte, and I watched in silence as her fingers slithered across the ivory keys. I didn't trust a word of what she'd said. She'd taken every opportunity to ingratiate herself into the estate, and she was determined to stay on—at any cost.

"I think that will be best for the time being." I rose beside her. "Thank you, and please continue your work with the man as you have been. However"—I motioned for the group to head for the door— "from this point on I expect to be consulted on his condition as well as any changes to his health, no matter how insignificant you deem them. This man is my responsibility now too."

The three of us filed to the door and into the hallway before Miss Seton turned to lock the chamber behind us. "I will be sure to keep you aware of his care."

I gave her a nod as we crossed into the open landing together, but I tugged Mr. Hawkins aside, waiting until Miss Seton was out of earshot. "If Henry was Mr. Cluett's patient, there will be documents in Cluett's office. I think it prudent we take another look there, but not now, not under the prying eyes of the house."

He thought for a moment. "Tonight after nightfall?"

"Perfect. I'll meet you here on the landing at midnight. I don't know who to trust, and I don't want anyone aware of our investigation or Henry as of yet."

A smile creased his lips. "What exactly is it you hope to find?"

"Anything about that man in the cottage—who he is, where he came from. I cannot believe Miss Seton has revealed the whole. And eventually decisions will have to be made for his welfare. I need to know who I'm dealing with."

"Agreed."

I glared down the grand staircase. "Unfortunately, at present I'm engaged to one of the gentlemen for a tête-à-tête in the drawing room."

Mr. Hawkins checked. "Which gentleman?"

"Mr. Montague."

Mr. Hawkins paused, his mouth pressed tight. "Do you think it might be wiser for you to employ some sort of an escort when it comes to your time with Mr. Montague? Or even better, a chaperone?"

"Goodness, no." My response came out firm and quick, but Mr. Hawkins's words sank in deep. Mr. Montague was a rake after all, and I was not unaffected by him. Granted, he could very well be my future husband. I closed my eyes for a moment. "At least not yet."

CHAPTER 15

It was too soon, far too soon, for either gentleman to greet me with such a disarming smile, but of course Mr. Montague flashed his attractive one with abandon, a dimple forming on his cheek.

"Mrs. Pembroke." His arms shot out to greet me as I entered the drawing room. "You look ravishing this afternoon."

Embarrassed by the clearly artificial attentions, I had to force myself to respond naturally. "Good afternoon, Mr. Montague."

As his fingers wrapped mine, the hairs on my arms rose, bringing to mind what Mr. Hawkins had implied only minutes before.

He led me over to the sofa and edged in beside me as close as propriety would allow, his leg brushing mine. Once settled, he twirled his watch fob in his fingers and eyed me a moment. "You've not been entirely forthcoming with me."

More prickles. "Whatever do you mean?"

"Have you forgotten you promised to allot me ample time to woo you? The days are ticking by." He made a show of searching his pockets. "Last I checked I'm not Cupid. I haven't any arrows hidden in the folds of my jacket with which to jab you into eternal love."

His hands grew still, dropping like rocks onto his lap. "Don't tell me you've already decided against me."

"Not at all." Suddenly conscious of the complexities of his blue eyes, I straightened in my seat. "I've simply had a great deal to do as of late."

My quick answer seemed to appease him as another grin spread across his face. "I realize you've been put to the test these last few days, but now that the funeral has *passed* . . ." He dipped his chin, motioning for me to finish his sentence.

"I shall certainly find the time to devote to my future . . . and all that entails."

His smile deepened as his daring look filled with—what, exactly? It certainly wasn't attraction. No, that tight jaw and knowing look spoke far more of a challenge than anything else.

He rested his arm on the back of the sofa and ran his finger along the seam. "What you meant to say is you'll have more time to allow yourself to fall headlong into love." A neat little sigh. "As I told you before, I shan't be satisfied with anything less."

"Nor I." My heart felt uncomfortable with my response. It was the expected answer to such a pronouncement, but did I mean such a thing?

Seemingly aware of my turn of emotions, he angled forward, his voice crafted into a caress. "We're decided then. The courting shall begin in earnest." He rested back, his gaze never leaving my face. "Tell me, what shall we busy ourselves with today?" He teased a loose curl at my ear. "I might have a few ideas."

I scooted back, my hair slipping from his eager fingers. "I haven't any suggestions at present. I-I'd offer a walk, but the clouds look awfully gray beyond the window. I'd rather not venture into that again."

"Agreed." His focus roamed the room. "I also have no intention of sitting here like two boors on a log. How about a tour of the house? The east wing perhaps?"

One nerve tumbled into the next, surging down my spine. "The east wing?" What had brought that to his mind? I hedged a peek. "I must confess I've never actually been in that part of the house. Miss Seton holds the keys if I'm not mistaken. Is there something in particular you wish to see there?"

He flicked his fingers in the air, his signet ring flashing in the late-afternoon light. "Not exactly. Just curious is all. I've never been one for secrets."

I thought a moment. "I don't believe the east wing is a secret precisely, just a sad reminder of Mr. Cluett's past that was too difficult for him to manage."

As a patient at the hospital, I'd not permitted myself to wonder about such things. Now that Mr. Cluett's murder made Moorington Cross effectively mine, it would behoove me to learn all I could. I stole a glance out the drawing room door. Yet I had no intention of bringing Mr. Montague along on such a quest.

I turned back to the room for a possible alternative. "How about a game of spillikins instead? I'm quite good."

A second of motionless silence ticked away before a laugh erupted and Mr. Montague flopped against the sofa. "Allow me to understand. I rack my brains for a well-timed adventure, something mysterious enough to lead to romance. Dash it all, my offer included a clandestine search of a deserted section of the house where we would most certainly be alone—and quite comfortably so, might I add—and you counter with a child's game held here in the busiest room of the house. Tell me, Mrs. Pembroke, are you always so wretchedly proper?"

My mouth fell open. "No more so than you are wretchedly disagreeable."

He lowered his gaze and chuckled to himself. "Only when I don't get what I want."

I skulked over to the bookcase and removed a small brown box from the lower shelf before turning back to face him. "Then I daresay you must be disagreeable a good portion of the time or quite spoiled."

He joined me at the square table in the corner and settled in, pressing his palms to the smooth wood before probing my eyes. "What do *you* think? Am I spoiled or simply disagreeable?"

I opened the box and tilted it to the side, allowing the ivory sticks to fall into a pile on the table, then took a seat next to him. "Well," I huffed. "If the ladies in London are to be believed, I'd say you must be terribly spoiled indeed."

He hesitated, a smile playing with his lips. "Is that what's got you worried about me? That I'm dangerous?"

His tone was no more than playful, but I felt warmth flooding my cheeks.

"You think I might ravish you?"

I dared a peek. "Not exactly."

"Then it's my reputation that has you concerned?"

I slid the first ivory stick from the pile without moving any of the other pieces. "Should it?"

He assessed the mound of sticks intertwined in front of him. "Some say knowledge is a virtue—that more experiences of the world help refine perspective." He flicked one of the ivory rods from the side of the bunch without any movement from the pile. Another grin. "As for me, I believe my wandering, or whatever the deuce you choose to call it, has permitted me the insight to know precisely what it is that I want out of a partner in life."

I rested my arm on the table. "And what is that, Mr. Montague?"

"Loyalty, respect—what every man wants—but there's got to be more for me. I need a wife who desires me with every last inch of her being." His fingers snaked around mine, his thumb uncovering the sensitive part of my gloved wrist. "I want fireworks, Mrs. Pembroke, but not the usual fare. I want the ones that explode high in the sky then shimmer all the way back to earth."

Mr. Montague's touch was intriguing, his words so utterly beguiling that a part of me yearned to crawl into the excitement of his thoughts and stay there forever, but was it Mr. Montague I saw residing there with me? Or was it someone else?

I jerked myself back to the present, retrieving my hand from his furtive grasp, and focused squarely on the ivory sticks on the table.

"Love, romance—the whole thing is more complicated than I once thought."

I felt his boot against my leg beneath the table and my gaze flicked up.

His voice was quite soft. "Only if you let it be."

"There's more to consider, you know, more than just"—I stared down at his empty hand still lying on the table, my throat growing thick—"more than, well, *that*."

He merely rested against the back of his chair and crossed his arms. "Yes, but all this is a necessary first step—for love, that is, not necessarily marriage. At least not the kind Lymington is offering."

How did he know what Lymington had said to me in private? Granted, I knew Mr. Montague had been talking with everyone in the house. Why not my other suitor? Or perhaps Miss Seton.

Mr. Montague craned forward once again, scattering the ivory sticks on the table. "Why won't you lower your guard, take the chance? How else will we know if we can make a go of this?"

"By talking."

He nearly laughed again. "*Talking?*"

"Yes, the other side of love. The one you might not be all that familiar with—the one necessary for true connection. Shall we begin with how you knew Mr. Cluett?"

There was a brief silence, then, "He's my father."

"Your . . . *father*? But I was under the impression you were—"

"The heir to Whitefall? Indeed I am. Thankfully, Mr. Alexander Montague, my indelible papa, was not aware he needed to disown his illegitimate son before my mother's death. She kept the secret well hidden. That is, until several years ago when Cluett sent a letter to the house informing me of my place in his will. With no other choice but to come clean, my mother finally revealed the whole tawdry affair, and I began visiting the father I never knew. I later learned of my half brother from Cluett. Montague knows now as well, but he has no stomach for a scandal. Thus, society remains ignorant, other than Lymington, whom I approached with the information last year."

He chuckled to himself. "Needless to say, my half brother did not take the truth of our connection all that well. I . . ." Something beyond the drawing room door caught his eye, and he dashed me a quick smile before projecting his voice. "Isn't that right, Lymington?"

I jerked my attention to the doorway just as Mr. Lymington crept into view. His hands were fisting a piece of paper.

He appeared defeated standing there, caught as he was. "I certainly didn't mean to disturb the two of you. I came through here simply to add this letter to the outgoing mail. If you will excuse me—"

"Not yet." Mr. Montague's smile hardened. "Tell us, who are you writing on this fine afternoon?"

Mr. Lymington looked to me as if I'd encouraged the unwanted intrusion, but my thoughts were still fluttering around what Mr. Montague had revealed.

"It's no secret. I was informing my mother of my plans to stay at Moorington Cross for the time being. She won't be pleased."

"No?" There was a hint of laughter in Mr. Montague's response. "Interesting that my father encouraged me to stay as long as needed."

Mr. Lymington stalked into the room. "That is because . . ." His voice lost tone.

Mr. Montague stood and cupped his ear. "Because what? I didn't hear you, my good man."

"I already told you . . ." He mumbled something more, something meant for Mr. Montague alone.

The latter angled his chin. "A little louder for our hostess, if you please."

Mr. Lymington turned beet red and ran a hand down his face. "You really are the worst sort of fellow."

"Don't you mean *brother*?"

Mr. Lymington's sharp gaze darted to mine. It took only a moment for him to register my lack of surprise before he went on. "Still selling that miserable story, are you?"

A careful pause. "Still denying it?"

Mr. Lymington bridged the gap between Mr. Montague and me. "I came here to ferret out the truth. No one can deny that Cluett bore no likeness to me, nor did I feel any sort of connection with him before his death."

Mr. Montague ran his hand along the nearby arm of the sofa. "Yet the two of us were placed in his will. Don't you find that intriguing?"

Mr. Lymington's jaw flexed. "Yes, but . . ." Still breathy, he turned to the window. "I've not pieced together my role in all this, but there is one thing I know for certain."

I rose, hoping to get a better glimpse of his face. "What is it?"

He offered me a quick look. "What I should have already told you. It's what I spoke with the constable about."

I checked. "Yes?"

"My mother pleaded with me not to step one foot inside this terrible house. She was anxious, you see." He glanced down at the crumpled missive in his hand. "I hoped to put her mind at ease with this letter. After all, there's no way he could touch me from the grave." Mr. Lymington shrugged off what looked like a chill. "My mother has been panicked about the entire visit. It's why I was searching Cluett's office. I was looking for evidence to back up her claim. I didn't exactly tell you everything, Mrs. Pembroke."

His eyes went vacant as he dissolved into memories. "The morning I was to leave home, my mother had reached her breaking point. She actually barred my way into the coach, screaming one final warning."

The occupants of the room exchanged a silent look.

Finally Mr. Lymington sucked in a deep breath, his eyes pinched, his muscles taut. "She swore Mr. Cluett was a dangerous man and declared me a fool to spend one second in his company. She feared for my very life."

CHAPTER 16

I couldn't get the distraught look on Mr. Lymington's face out of my mind.

The nervous behavior I'd observed at our first meeting, the anger I'd stumbled upon in the garden—it all made perfect sense now. He'd been afraid.

The problem was I knew Mr. Cluett intimately, and he was the kindest man I'd ever met. So what had upset Mr. Lymington's mother? And what made her share that fear with her son? Surely there was more to the story.

Once exposed, Mr. Lymington agreed to amend his letter immediately, begging his mother to write back as soon as possible and inducing her to include more information regarding Mr. Cluett. We all hoped news of his death might unhinge her tongue, but Mr. Lymington did not think it probable. If Mr. Montague's assertions regarding her illicit affair with Mr. Cluett were correct, I doubted she would dare to risk her standing in society any more than Mr. Lymington had been willing.

Thus, all I could focus on after leaving the drawing room was my desire to find Mr. Hawkins alone and discuss all I'd learned. Yet we'd not arranged to meet until the search of Mr. Cluett's office at midnight. No doubt Mr. Hawkins had other business to attend to, and whether I liked it or not I would simply have to wait until then.

Having made my way to the blue salon to pass the time, I took a moment to breathe outside the door, resting my hand on the edge of the wainscoting as dark thoughts shifted through my mind. If there was one thing I knew for certain, it was that Mr. Cluett had concealed a great many secrets, and one of them had led to his death.

I entered the salon to find Major Balfour and Mrs. Fitzroy seated on the scroll-end sofa. Clearly the pair wasn't expecting me, or anyone else for that matter, as they sat inches apart, wholly absorbed in one another. A smile tugged at my lips. It wasn't the first time I'd wondered if my fellow patients hid an affection they'd kept secret.

Major Balfour tenderly held Mrs. Fitzroy's hand with one of his own, a piece of paper in the other. Her eyes slipped closed. From what I could hear of it, his voice sounded steady, calming, but I couldn't quite make out what he was uttering so intimately to her. Then she nodded and blinked, and I was surprised to see her eyes wet with tears.

If the mood of the room hadn't immediately lifted, I would have tiptoed away without a sound, but I felt the delicate break in intensity and cleared my voice. "Good afternoon."

Mrs. Fitzroy released Major Balfour's hand and tugged away from him, the rustling of her gown filling the fleeting silence. My steps slowed. Had I been right? Mrs. Fitzroy's cheeks were certainly flushed, her lips all but quivering. She flicked open a tortoiseshell fan and batted it before her face. "Amelia, darling, you startled me."

I cast a peek at Major Balfour and was met with what I could only call an overly welcoming smile. He, at least, seemed perfectly composed, amused even. Perhaps the feelings weren't exactly mutual.

Maybe a little nudging was warranted. "And what have the two of you been about this afternoon?"

Major Balfour swayed to his feet with the aid of his cane. "Mrs. Fitzroy has been recounting some of her extraordinary dreams. They really are quite lively."

Major Balfour motioned me onto the seat he'd vacated, pointing his cane at the sofa. I started to protest, but I knew he would not broker any discussion about his comfort. I did as he bid me and settled down, turning belatedly to Mrs. Fitzroy. "Dreams or no, I am glad to hear you've been able to sleep. I've been quite concerned."

She waved away my worries with her gloved hand. "Yes, yes, of course, I have my medicine. Thankfully Andrews was able to secure me some more tansy oil from the apothecary. But what about you? I heard on good authority that you had another one of your incidents"—a squinting glance at Major Balfour—"one of the bad ones, I'm told."

I hadn't realized my spell in the woods was already common knowledge throughout the house. Interesting that Mr. Montague hadn't mentioned it to me. "I'm afraid you've heard correctly, but luckily the spell was of short duration and Mr. Hawkins was there to assist me."

"Mr. Hawkins, you say. Thank goodness indeed . . ." She cast another shrewd look at Major Balfour. "I shudder to think what might have taken place if you had been alone—or worse, with that Montague fellow."

The muscles in my back went rigid. Here was another person concerned about Mr. Montague's intentions. What if they were all wrong and he was simply a flirt? He was the only one speaking of love. "I daresay I shall need to be alone frequently with both of my suitors if I'm to decide between them."

"Humph." Frowning, Major Balfour eased down onto a nearby chair. "Mrs. Fitzroy and I were just discussing your situation." He settled the paper he held in his lap. "Allow me to say, I find it reprehensible."

"Reprehensible?"

"Indeed it is." He pushed a puff of air through his nose. "To be thrust into marriage in such a way. It's beyond my understanding." He absently traced the triangular pattern of the wax seal on the lip of the parchment. "We simply want to be sure you don't feel responsible for either one of us—that our friendship and care remain outside of your decision as to whom or even if you should marry at all. Mark my words, if neither of those popinjays is up to your standards, I implore you to make the best and only decision adequate for your future. *Yours,* my dear, and yours alone."

I reached across the opening between the furniture and gave his busy fingers a squeeze. If only it was merely Major Balfour and Mrs. Fitzroy to consider, but there were others depending upon my answer. Both of my suitors desperately needed their portion of the inheritance. Neither would receive a farthing if I did not ultimately choose between them. The instructions in the will were explicit. Even Miss Seton would be left without an inheritance if I didn't follow suit—all of the money would go to the teaching hospital in France.

I took a deep breath. Then there was the man at the cottage to consider. Why had Mr. Cluett left everything hinging on my decision—so many futures sitting squarely on my shoulders?

Because he was a dangerous man.

I shook off Mr. Lymington's mother's accusatory words about Mr. Cluett and pivoted once again to face Major Balfour. "Believe me, I am taking everything into account, including my own preferences. I have no intention of making a rash decision. You both know me better than anyone. I'm far too methodical for that."

He smiled, but it was a hard one. "Glad to hear it."

At that same moment Miss Seton passed the open doorway. I pushed to my feet. "I am sorry to leave so hurriedly, but you must excuse me. I need to speak with Miss Seton."

Mrs. Fitzroy nodded, and I scurried from the room.

A few yards into the corridor I was forced to call out Miss Seton's name. At first I thought she meant to ignore me completely, but at the terminus of the hall she stopped short and whirled about. "May I be of service, Mrs. Pembroke?"

I waited to speak till I was but a foot away. "I had a question in regard to the east wing."

Her eyebrows shot up. "The east wing, you say?"

"I understand you carry the key."

Her fingers contracted against her skirt. "I do . . . as I have all the keys."

"Well, as current mistress of Moorington Cross, I believe it imperative for me to take inventory of everything in the house, particularly the east wing as I've never stepped foot beyond those large mahogany doors. Would you be so kind as to hand over the key?" I extended my hand.

I could see the refusal she craved to toss my way battling against the acquiescence she ultimately must give me. Finally she angled her chin. "Be careful, Mrs. Pembroke."

She disengaged the key from a circular bundle she'd removed from her pocket. "The ceiling is not safe in that part of the house, not since the storm years ago. The supports are in disrepair—an accident waiting to happen."

"But I've seen you walking through those doors on more than one occasion. In fact, you go in there quite regularly. I saw you do so last week."

The merest hint of a smile. "I check over the space every Saturday morning as Mr. Cluett permitted, but I never walk too far down that narrow hall. Nor do I wish to risk my life."

I stared at her a moment before mumbling, "I understand."

"Do you, Mrs. Pembroke? Do you?" She shook her head with such care it reminded me of a doll I'd once had as a child. "The shadows can be deceiving at times. The walls might appear sturdy enough, but heed my words, whenever I step into the east wing I hear the moans, the cracks, the constant sway of the walls. Even with the smallest wind, the space cries out in warning to anyone who will take notice."

She narrowed her eyes. "Don't allow this sudden spark of curiosity to be the catalyst of your absolute ruin."

Moonlight joined me on the landing that night, its muted glow pouring in through a large side window where the drapes had been conveniently left wide. It was an eerie brilliance, not of the usual fare. Even the shadows seemed affected by the light as they fluttered around the edges of my vision, the carpet a gray pool at my feet.

I hardly needed a candle, but I clutched the pewter holder nonetheless.

Hidden somewhere deep within Mr. Cluett's private wing, a grandfather clock struck midnight, its metal chimes an unnatural companion to the cold, still hall. I sucked in an uneasy breath. The scent of ashes hung heavy, the household fires left to smolder in their grates.

It was then I saw a glimmer of candlelight bobbing down the far hall. Though I was fairly certain who carried the light, a chill wriggled its way up my back. Too much had transpired within the walls of Moorington Cross to assume anything. I stayed firmly within the safety of the shadows until the figure was close enough to identify.

"Good evening, Mr. Hawkins."

He lifted his candle to eye level, illuminating the whole of the corner where I stood. "Good evening yourself."

A twinge fluttered up my back. Though Mr. Hawkins remained dressed, his hair combed, his bearing proper, something about meeting him in such a way was terribly intimate. His eyes looked far murkier than I remembered; the sharp curve of his face drawn deeper by the shades of candlelight.

It was dark, late, and we were alone. All at once I became aware of the hammer in my chest.

Then he smiled and, one by one, my muscles relaxed. He motioned over his shoulder. "Shall we get on with it?"

"Yes, but—" I touched his arm, yet so quick and probing was his return glance my voice dropped to a little above a whisper. "I, uh, wondered if you might be interested in joining me on a side quest, a quick peek into the east wing before we head to the office."

"The east wing, huh?" He searched my eyes. "What brought this on?"

A nervous laugh. "Mr. Montague, actually. He thought the locked wing might prove an interesting adventure for the two of us. Of course, I refused him because, well, I-I'd rather take a look at it with you."

I wished I could see his face better in the variable moonlight, but I was fairly certain the deep lines had softened a bit.

His response was slow, yet his voice light enough. "Have you any notion of what we might find there?"

"As I understand, Mr. Cluett's elder brother's things. At least, that's what I've been told. The wing has been kept locked from the patients for as long as I've been here. Miss Seton said the entire area's not safe. There was some sort of storm several years ago that affected the roof and walls. Mr. Cluett feared it could all come down without warning."

I caught Mr. Hawkins's smile in the candlelight before he shook his head. "Therefore you thought it a good idea to take me there? To, uh, do what exactly?"

I pressed my hand to my mouth to stifle a laugh. "Goodness, not to get injured or worse, I assure you. Quite the opposite, actually. You're the only one at present I trust to assist me."

"Ah . . . well, that sounds better. I was beginning to think you found me decidedly expendable."

"Hardly."

I heard what I thought was a quick breath, and again I wished I could see the little details of his face. But it was no use as he grabbed my hand and swung me toward the grand staircase. "Either way, I'll not pass on an adventure."

We descended the carpeted steps and made our way in silence to the far corner of the ground floor. The candlelit sight of those large mahogany doors brought us both to a full, somewhat intimidating halt.

In its present state, Moorington Cross was a confusing hodgepodge of crisscrossing hallways and separated wings. This particular section of the house dated back to the origins of the estate, built sometime within the fifteenth century.

I retrieved the key from my pocket as the remaining butterflies in my stomach took flight. Images spilled into my mind—the glorious days of old, all sorts of interesting people who might have walked the ancient halls—Cluetts in chain mail or robes. After Miss Seton's peculiar warning, I had no idea what to expect on the other side of those doors. Nothing, however, would keep me from taking a look inside.

I thrust my key into the rusty lock, but the curved metal slid easily into place. Of course, Miss Seton had been in the habit of opening the door every week. A gritty turn, a momentary click, and I felt the ease of release.

I nodded at Mr. Hawkins and he grasped the door handle. A faint squeak was followed by a low moan as he eased open one of the heavy wooden doors.

He cast me a cautious look, dipped his shoulder, then crept through the entryway in the lead.

My hands shot out to grab his elbow. "Not too far in, mind you."

He nodded and extended his candle to arm's length, allowing the light to lap as best it could over several feet of dusty flooring. He pivoted a bit to the right, taking in the wooden support beams nearest the door.

"Do you believe the warnings—about the walls being unsafe?"

"I'm not sure." I padded closer to his side and a bit beyond, striving to get the best look I could into the blackened interior.

Then it was *his* strong fingers I felt on my own arm. "Either way, we need to be careful. It's far too dark to assess the area properly."

The air smelled somewhat stale, the walls dingy. The few pieces of furniture, fronting what looked to be whitewashed stone and plaster, were swathed in holland covers and liberally covered with dust. The hall was an upside down T-shape and we moved forward along the long, wide corridor.

Another step forward and the boards complained beneath my feet. I lowered my candle nearer the floor. There in the thick grime appeared a lonely set of footprints, which extended only a few more paces ahead.

Miss Seton apparently had spoken the truth. Beyond the footprints, dust coated the floor in every possible direction. Clearly no one had walked beyond that point for some time.

An eerie silence pressed against my ears as the dampened air crawled effortlessly over my skin. Miss Seton was right—the east wing was a mausoleum—not to be disturbed.

Mr. Hawkins urged me to the very edge of the footprints, where we leaned forward, peering into the only visible room to our left. It was a bedchamber sparsely furnished and covered in white sheets. I could see mounds of cobwebs from where we stood, the thick dust gathering in clumps like snow. A chill snaked across my shoulders as my focus narrowed in on the dusty remains of a black jacket that had been casually thrown across the bedsheets at some point long ago, where it had been left uncovered, waiting for its owner to return and pick it up. But he never had.

Mrs. Fitzroy said the elder Cluett brother was struck down in the prime of his life—and on the way to his wedding at that. His room, dim, sad, frozen in time, was nothing but surreal. I could perfectly understand how Mr. Cluett had been unable to reenter his brother's private sanctuary after his tragic death.

Mr. Hawkins's hand circled my arm once again. "I don't think we should go any farther, not tonight at least."

"No. It's late and we need time enough to search the office, which may very well take longer than we anticipate."

"Agreed." His voice was a bit husky at my ear. The darkness, the utter loneliness of the scene before us, no doubt moving him as it had me.

We emerged from the hall a bit subdued, and I locked the door before pocketing the key. We only spoke again when we reached the safety of Mr. Cluett's private office on the first floor. I set my candle on the desk as Mr. Hawkins sealed the door behind us.

The squarish room felt far warmer than the one in the east wing, which was somewhat puzzling as there was no fire and the previous owner of this room had all but met a similar fate.

There had always been something special about the younger Mr. Cluett. His amiable essence still lingered in the worn leather chair behind the desk and in his favorite wand that he'd pushed to the back of the sideboard. Bookshelves stacked the opposing walls of the office, and the carpet was thick beneath our feet. The entire apartment felt more like a small library, one I certainly would have sought out in the past if I'd been aware of its existence.

Mr. Hawkins swiped the arm of his jacket across his forehead before pausing to meet my gaze. A curt smile and he shrugged the jacket from his shoulders before folding and tossing it on a nearby chair. "I'm afraid it's a great deal too hot for that in this tiny room, particularly if we mean to work." He angled to the desk, appearing wholly unconcerned about any sort of reaction from me. "Shall we get on with it?"

Apparently I was to remain indifferent to the exceptional physique he'd unwittingly exposed with such a thin shirt and the neat tuck of his waistcoat. I edged over to the far side of the desk. "Any idea where we should start?"

He rubbed his chin. "I saw quite a few papers in this desk the other day, and there's the cabinet that's probably full as well."

I turned to the opposing dresser and inched out the bottom drawer. "Yes, quite a bit in here." I pulled a paper into the candlelight. "Looks like these are the notes he kept on his patients. It's probably best that I search this section as I'm already aware of many of the treatments Mr. Cluett utilized during his time here, particularly as some of the patients still live here."

"Agreed."

Mr. Hawkins settled into Mr. Cluett's desk chair to initiate his own search, and I adjusted the position of a small winged chair to make my investigation a bit more comfortable.

Papers ruffled; the candles dipped. The room sank into relative silence as we examined Mr. Cluett's private records. In fact, quite a bit of time elapsed before Mr. Hawkins cleared his throat.

I looked up to find him watching me, and he gave me an inquisitive smile. "You know, I've been pondering your plight over the course of the day."

I gave a breathy laugh. "My plight?"

He nudged his elbow onto the desk, his attention back to the drawer he was looking through. "If I'm to help you make the best selection for your health and happiness, it would behoove me to know a little bit more about you."

Not quite what I was expecting. "As in?"

"Your passions, for example. What makes you, Mrs. Pembroke, excited to take on the world?"

Goodness. How to answer such a question?

He rubbed his chin, amusement flashing in his eyes. "All right. Maybe I've got a little ahead of myself. Let's begin with something a bit easier. How about you tell me what you fill your spare time with. What brings you joy?"

I arched an eyebrow. "Well, you're already aware I love to read."

"Correction. I knew you *liked* to read, but *love* it, now that is indeed a deeper feeling—one I can certainly sympathize with."

His smile widened—a handsome one, coy yet also genuine. I felt the connection at once, but it wasn't until I returned one of my own that the room seemed to narrow before my eyes. Strange how the very nature of time softened and my world slowed. Deep within the gloom I could hear the casement clock ticking carefully in a whisper, echoing the question that had plagued my mind all day—had Mr. Hawkins formed a tender for me?

He continued to stare down as he rummaged through a drawer, but his voice felt terribly intimate. "Is it mainly novels then that captivate you?"

"Well, they are a particular favorite."

He tugged a paper from the drawer and examined it closely. I thought him distracted, but he cast me a knowing glance over the rim of the page. "You mentioned poetry earlier. Ever read E. W. Radcliff?"

I thought a moment. "That name does sound familiar, but I don't recollect any particular poems by the man. Hmm, I daresay one would come to mind if the poet were worth his mettle. Is he a favorite of yours?"

Mr. Hawkins covered his mouth to cough. "Not a favorite exactly, but I have read everything he's published. There aren't very many after all."

"Wait." I closed the drawer I had completed searching and opened the next. "I do remember something by Radcliff. Didn't he write about a swan?"

"Ah, yes, 'The Determined Swan.' His silliest poem to date, I daresay, but also the most widely read. I prefer 'Dawn's Breath.' It's a much more intelligent sample if you've a mind to read it."

"I don't believe I've seen that one. I shall certainly look for it the next time I'm in the library." I flipped through a few more papers before glancing back up. "This line of questioning does make me curious. What are *your* passions, Mr. Hawkins?"

I thought I saw him recoil, so I was quick to add, "Two can play at this game, you know. After all, it would be beneficial for me to know a little more about you so that when the time comes to make my decision, I can fully trust my solicitor's opinion."

"Passions indeed." He smiled to himself then pressed his forehead. "I'm afraid my apprenticeship with Pembroke and Huxley has demanded a great deal of my time, leaving little for anything else. The law is my one driving force." He lifted his eyebrows, his gaze sharp. "And I do believe this merely a ploy to evade my questions, Mrs. Pembroke. Surely you realize I'll need to know more about you than your love of reading if I'm truly to help you with your selection."

"I suppose so, but is there really anything more than reading?"

He laughed. "I'm not certain there is."

"I guess I enjoy watercolors, although I've had little time to create them as of late."

"So you're an artist."

"Hardly."

"You would get on well with my youngest sister, Phoebe. She recently left home to train with a renowned painter outside of Plattsdale—an exceptional talent."

Suddenly he stilled, then raised his hand to maintain silence between us.

I heard it too. Footsteps. And loud ones at that.

Who? My lips rounded in an *o*. He shook his head, his voice at a whisper. "I had hoped to keep our investigation a secret."

He motioned me over to the desk with the flick of his fingers, and I crept quickly to his side. The candles were promptly extinguished, and we turned to the dark underbelly of the desk. Though the opening looked small, it appeared sizable enough for two adults. Mr. Hawkins shot me one last urgent glance, and I led the scramble beneath the massive piece of furniture.

I could make out little in the shadowy depths, and I felt his hands guiding me into position. My right arm slid along the hard wood until Mr. Hawkins inched to the side and I was tucked into place. As he had discarded his jacket earlier, I could feel every curve of his arm beneath his thin shirt.

His chest was at my shoulder, his thigh pressing tighter and tighter to mine as he pulled his long legs in as far as they would go. I caught a laugh on his breath, then utter silence. My hand retreated to my throat as my core filled with a warmth that wriggled its way down my arms and legs.

A rather pleasing scent of leather and soap tinted the air between us, and I was momentarily transported to another place—a world where I hadn't been hidden away, where I'd been taken to London for the season. The childhood dream was still alive in my heart.

The pop of the door brought me roaring out of my reflections. Instinctively, Mr. Hawkins's arm tightened around me, and I swallowed hard. A diminutive glow of candlelight danced across the wall. Whoever had entered the office stopped short and the room fell silent. I imagined the intruder seeing the papers askew, the drawer I'd left open. Then I heard an intake of breath and the door slammed shut.

Mr. Hawkins and I didn't move, not an inch, his fingers still tight on my arm, his body rigid beside me. He was ready to bolt at a moment's notice, but the feel of the room dipped back into the calm quiet we'd enjoyed before. We were alone once again.

It was several minutes before Mr. Hawkins leaned down to my ear. "I think we're safe."

The wild thrum of my heartbeat said otherwise, but I nodded readily enough. The passing moonlight intensified and as Mr. Hawkins moved the desk chair, I could see a little better and the utter awkwardness of our situation hit me full force. Mr. Hawkins propped his left arm on the underside of the desk as he extended his legs, but he didn't exit the opening as expected.

"What the devil."

I heard a click as he leaned in close to a tiny wooden overhang at the ceiling of our little hideout. He turned to face me. "Is this what I think it is?"

I touched my mouth. "A secret drawer?"

He used his free hand to slide the compartment the rest of the way open and a small black ball launched into my lap. I stared at it a moment. That is, until the horrid beast extended its eight wiggly legs and clawed its way up my gown.

"A spider!" I groped at my gown.

"Hold still." Mr. Hawkins flicked his hand across my waist, hurling the wriggling insect into the abyss at the back corner. Immediately I scrambled out from beneath the desk and jumped to my feet while shaking out my skirt.

"Wait." Mr. Hawkins was right behind me, on his feet in an instant. "There's another one in your hair."

I let out a strangled cry. "Get it out! Get it out!"

His fingers went to work at once, picking at my coiffure. He was forced to loosen a few pins, but finally the spider fell to the floor and met his end beneath the hard sole of Mr. Hawkins's boot.

I pressed my forehead. "Check to see if there are any more. I can't rest until I know for certain."

A hint of reluctance, then he gave a solitary nod.

Carefully, he slid his hand along the edge of my hair, his fingers inching their way through what was left of my chignon. I steadied myself against the desk as a quiver plunged down my neck and feathered out across my back. I knew now why Mr. Hawkins thought twice about doing as I asked.

His touch was stirring; my own response equally frightening. I scooted away. "Thank you. I believe I'm free of all pests and petulance at this point."

There was a peculiar intensity to his gaze, almost . . . a longing?

The tension snapped and his arms hung loose at his sides.

Uncertain what to do or say, he pivoted and knelt to reexamine the secret door, his eager fingers retrieving a stack of papers from inside. He unfolded them, only to scour the documents.

"Take a look at this." A quirk of his eyebrow and he stood, extending the top sheet for me to view in the moonlight. "What do you think of that?"

It took me a minute to scan the words and steady my erratic heartbeat. "It appears to be a ledger from the initial start of Mr. Cluett's mesmeric hospital in France. It was a teaching hospital." I held the paper closer to the window. "I wonder who this Mr. Cull is. I've never heard his name mentioned before."

Mr. Hawkins moved to look over my shoulder. "From what I can tell, he was the original owner."

"So why hide this ledger in a secret drawer?"

"I'm not sure." He plopped the paper onto a growing stack on the corner of the desk. "I'd like to sort through all of these more thoroughly over the next few days."

I angled back to the dresser I'd been searching. "I wasn't expecting so many patients' notes. I never realized how many people Mr. Cluett treated in France."

Mr. Hawkins bent down behind the desk. "I've also run across several documents on the gentlemen who were training to practice mesmerism under his care. It seems Cluett kept meticulous reports on each of them as well."

A long pause was followed by an even stranger dip to Mr. Hawkins's voice. "You know, I think I favor Lymington at this point."

My fingers stilled between the pages, my gaze darting down. "Pardon?"

"Earlier you said you enjoyed reading and painting. Seems like he'd be the better match for you in regard to those hobbies."

Every muscle in my body contracted as my mind raced for clarity.

"I will agree he is the more intellectual of the two, but he's awkward and boring. A match?"

"I'm not entirely blind, Mrs. Pembroke. I know he's something of a cold fish, but . . ."

"But what?"

He shrugged. "Unfortunately, both of your remarkable suitors put me off in one way or another. I'm fully aware as your solicitor I must give you guidance concerning the will. Optimal or not, Lymington is my choice at present."

I crossed my arms as a thought from earlier came to mind. "What would you say if you learned both of my suitors may in fact be Mr. Cluett's illegitimate children?"

He straightened at once. "I would be astonished in the extreme."

"Well, that is just what we all think at present. Mr. Montague announced his suppositions this afternoon. Apparently his mother confessed as much years ago before her death, and then Mr. Cluett told him Mr. Lymington was his half brother." Almost in afterthought, "I've been waiting to tell you the news all day."

Mr. Hawkins ran his fingers through his blond locks, surprise still lurking in his eyes. "I suppose that explains their strange inclusion in the will. But are you certain?"

"As well as we can be."

"It does make a great deal of sense in a way. I've been giving a lot of thought to why Mr. Cluett picked those two since I met them." He shook his head. "I still have trouble believing that is indeed the case. Their *father*."

"Mr. Lymington, mind you, refutes the connection."

Mr. Hawkins nodded slowly. "I can well understand that. I . . ." The confidence in his voice fled beneath the weight of his thoughts, and he tore his attention back to the papers in the drawer, his jaw set.

I lowered my head, closing my eyes for a moment. Mr. Hawkins was unaware I knew of his own questionable parentage, and I was forced to bite my tongue. Yet the words ached to slip out—to somehow acknowledge the pain he so obviously carried with him daily.

When he finally lifted his head, his voice came out weak. "Does that in any way change how you think of the gentlemen? Does it put you off?"

"Certainly not. A person's past has nothing to do with their value, nor do I care a fig what society thinks of me in regard to it. I've already been labeled a pariah."

His brows drew in as he mouthed the word *pariah*. "I cannot believe that. Your husband was well thought of by everyone at Pembroke and Huxley. You would have been equally welcomed into our little circle."

"I will agree with the fact he was well thought of by most. All the more reason for him *not* to bring me to London and allow me the chance to have a spell in front of his friends."

Mr. Hawkins stared, words seeming to fail him. Finally he managed a whispered, "I didn't know it was like that."

"How could you?"

I watched as even the smallest bit of truth I offered regarding my late husband chafed against the well-established opinion Mr. Hawkins already held. Now was not the time to confuse him about his mentor. I turned to the open drawer and yawned.

Mr. Hawkins smiled. "You don't mean to fall asleep on me, do you?"

Normally a question like that would have set me on edge, but I knew Mr. Hawkins was only teasing. "I hope not. Thankfully we're almost done." I stretched. "I've just a few more papers to look through."

I tugged the last set of documents onto the desk and flipped through the pages. It wasn't until I came to the final paper that something caught my eye. "Miss Seton said Henry was Mr. Cluett's patient, correct?"

Mr. Hawkins glanced up. "I believe so, why?"

"This final record here . . . It doesn't have a name attached to it like all the rest. It's simply titled Patient A." I peeked over the top of the paper. "Considering I've not found any other notes on Henry, this could possibly be about him."

Mr. Hawkins motioned me closer where he might peruse the information as well. I pointed to the first paragraph. "Here it says Patient A presented with memory loss and agitation. Mesmeric treatments were started at once by one of the trainees."

Mr. Hawkins mumbled his answer but, clearly a faster reader than me, he was already deep into the handwritten notes, his eyes widening in turn. "It seems this patient took a wild turn—bouts of madness, increasing violence. It does sound a bit like the person Miss Seton described." Mr. Hawkins flipped to the last page. "And it looks like we're not to know what happened. The last entry is dated over ten years ago. Not much to go on there."

I wrinkled my nose. "This report could reference anyone."

Mr. Hawkins averted his attention back to the pile of papers he'd collected for further research before handling the top page. "What if we wrote to Mr. Cull from the ledger and this person listed here on this record—a Mr. Dodge? With any luck, one of them might remember Patient A, or the man who treated him."

I crossed my arms. "That, Mr. Hawkins, is an exceptional idea. I wonder I did not think of it myself."

"So do I." He laughed to himself. "You've a delightfully quick mind about you."

My chest felt light. "Granted, we have no way of knowing if either of them still resides in France."

"Worth a try though, don't you think?"

I nodded, far too conscious of how close together we'd drifted once again—like two magnets, drawn inexplicably to one another.

"I also think it prudent to observe Henry somehow, in order to understand better what we're dealing with. Perhaps we should approach Miss Seton tomorrow about a visit to the cottage." A subtle shift of his weight and Mr. Hawkins's arm pressed ever so softly against mine, the underlying warmth ebbing through his thin sleeves. The adjustment was innocent enough, but the hairs on my arms sprang to attention.

I managed a soft, "Agreed," as my body sought to betray me. Motionless, so near him, everything felt alive, but we weren't hidden in the darkness this time. No. I could see every line on his face, every delicate movement of his finger on the paper. Then he looked up.

I'm not entirely certain what possessed me to lurch back the way I did. I only remember the iron fender catching the back of my half boot, the heart-pounding moment of flailing before I careened into the small plaster lion beside the fireplace, then flopped onto the floor.

I lay there on the carpet a stunned moment before laughter erupted from deep inside. "You could have at least tried to catch me."

Mr. Hawkins was at my side at once, his hands at my head and arm. "Have you injured anything?"

His voice changed as he looked me over, a mix of fear and bewilderment overtaking his expression. "Why the devil are you laughing? I did my best. It all happened so quickly."

I shook my head, willing my emotions to calm. "I honestly don't know." My laughter only intensified and tears filled my eyes. "I suppose it's because I'm such a clod."

"Don't be ridiculous. It was an accident, nothing more."

I gasped between bursts of laughter. "Here I am . . . back on the ground . . . How on earth do you put up with me?"

He ran a hand down his face, his smile threatening to undo me further. "I daresay I've picked you up more times than I can count at present. However, I certainly enjoy a challenge."

"Indeed." He assisted me into a sitting position, my mirth finally under control, and I ran my hand along my loose hair. "Whichever gentleman I select to marry will sadly be in for quite an adventure."

His smile faded and he withdrew his hand from my arm. "Yes, yes, he will."

His gaze settled on the empty fireplace a long moment before he reached out to assist me to my feet. Just as quickly he jerked away. "Mrs. Pembroke . . . Oh no."

"Yes?" I gave him a rather blank look. "What is it?"

He seemed unable to meet my eyes, a grin sneaking on and off his face. "Your gown . . . You, uh, I believe our endeavors this evening have stressed it beyond bearing."

I stared down. There at the base of my skirt, plunging out of a large tear, lay my stockinged left leg, exposed clear to my knee. Immediately, I yanked the folds of muslin, clawing them together. Of all the things to occur in Mr. Hawkins's presence, and tonight of all nights. I could have sunk into the floor.

I stared blankly at the wall a moment, deciding how I should respond, before facing him. "I'm so sorry—"

"Don't be." His eyes danced in the moonlight. "Not for such a well-turned ankle."

My heart turned violent. "You'll not breathe a word of this? Any of this?"

He leaned in close. "Let me assure you, Mrs. Pembroke, whatever has passed or will pass between us shall remain a secret forever." He mumbled something more as he stood, and I tried my best to piece together his fleeting words.

Had he said privacy? Something about extending to his clients, or was it something else entirely? I fisted the material of my gown and made my way to the door, realizing all too dismally I would never have the nerve to ask him.

CHAPTER 17

The following morning I received a note from Mr. Hawkins, urging me to meet him in the garden instead of the house. I assumed the abrupt change of location the logical first step toward reining in our relationship back to the proper bounds of client and solicitor. The momentary looks, the warmth of his laugh, the feel of his touch—it had all gone on long enough!

However, I was never more shocked than when he arrived, flashed that sweet smile of his, and greeted me with, "You know, Mrs. Pembroke, I'm quite pleased we've had more time to acquaint ourselves with one another. It has . . . well, it'll prove quite helpful in the investigation and on a whole has made my job as your solicitor decidedly easier."

Made his job easier?

Coated with delicate white flowers, a blackthorn's branches hung low over our heads, shading the lines of Mr. Hawkins's ever-shifting countenance. A subtle breeze swirled the air and gave the garden a touch of life, leaving my body terribly cold.

What did he mean by such a statement? I tightened my bonnet ribbons and glanced away. After all, I dared not give a response as my mind raced once again around what he'd implied.

Had I been a fool to waste an entire night reading into every movement, every look since I first met him? Apparently he'd meant to be a good solicitor, nothing more. I smashed my eyes closed. Wasn't that what I'd feared all along? The perfect solicitor. So how had I misconstrued his feigned compassion for something I never should have entertained?

Granted, I was a complete novice at love. I'd not experienced any affection from a gentleman before, certainly not of that sort. I took a deep breath. I knew now Mr. Hawkins's care meant nothing more than friendship. His words were quite clear.

I thrust my humiliation down deep within and gave him a sideways glance. "What do you think our next steps should be?"

He looked up, almost appearing shaken for a moment—as if my question had unwittingly snagged an errant thought. But it passed soon enough, and he affected his charming solicitor's smile as he leaned against a nearby tree. "You mean about the investigation?"

I picked a nearby white flower and twirled it in my fingers. "What else could I mean?"

"Oh . . ." He was in control as always, his voice that of a well-versed gentleman. "Nothing really. I suppose I thought you might be referring to your suitors. I . . ." He didn't finish his sentence, his voice lost on tendrils of wind.

"I figured after what we decided last night, we should visit Henry at the cottage as soon as can be arranged."

Mr. Hawkins nodded to himself, but his expression remained unreadable. "Agreed." He smiled. "We've like minds and all that." Then he checked his watch. "For that is just what I had planned for our meeting today—why I asked you to the garden in the first place. Miss Seton should be at the cottage already. I informed her on my way out of the house that you wished to assess him before making any decisions about his care, and I mean to accompany you in doing so. She wasn't pleased but did acquiesce to the plan."

"I'm sure she wasn't pleased. She seems to want to keep him sheltered away from us all."

A shove off the tree with his boot and Mr. Hawkins offered me his arm. I gladly took it, his jacket warm beneath my fingers and his gait comfortable as we made our way through the garden gate and down the path. Yet I felt a distance growing between us. Perhaps we both did, as Mr. Hawkins seemed anxious to fill the silence.

"I daresay it's been a difficult time for Miss Seton since Mr. Cluett's death. Her position has changed so drastically, and I don't believe she's a person who adapts very quickly."

"Nor does she relish relinquishing her power."

The carefully trimmed hedgerows rose and fell to our right, pointing our way onward until we reached the far side of the manicured lawns and the path ducked into the cover of the trees. Strange how the air felt so much cooler within the grove, the shadows freer to roam. We walked several minutes uphill before the thatched roof of the cottage appeared at the clearing, a thin line of smoke wriggling into the blue sky.

The trail we'd followed up to this point had been designed for little more than a horse cart, but when we breached the crest of the hill a wider lane emerged, perpendicular in the long grass. Mr. Hawkins gave me a cautious look as we traversed the lane and swung open the small white cottage gate.

At the terminus of the drive, Miss Seton stood on the terrace, effectively barring our way, her arms folded across her chest, her expression severe. "Henry's been a bit agitated this morning. Nothing extreme, but I think it best for me to bring him out to the yard for your assessment as opposed to the confines of the house."

There was something unnerving about the way she emphasized the s's in the word *assessment* that sent a chill shooting up my back. I glanced over at Mr. Hawkins for reassurance, then back to Miss Seton. "If you think that's best."

"I do." If possible, her face seemed to tighten further, her movements pointed. "You may wait over there by the fence. It is time for his daily exercise." A huff. "It may take a moment for me to convince him to allow the two of you to join us on his walk."

I trailed behind Mr. Hawkins to the spot Miss Seton had indicated, all my senses on full alert. He propped his back against a fence post and stared at the cottage door.

I spoke out of the side of my mouth, my voice low. "I'm not sure I like this arrangement. Do you?"

"I don't know what to think."

A commotion originating from somewhere within the house rent the air, then the cottage door was flung wide. The man I remembered from my spell in the woods tottered onto the step. His vacant stare was wild about the yard until it settled on us. I edged closer to Mr. Hawkins, the memory of that shovel lofted above the man's head charging my nerves.

I felt Mr. Hawkins's hand firm at my back, and he leaned close to my ear. "Don't allow him to get too close to you."

Henry was smiling, however, as he approached, the expression so at odds with the daring look about his eyes. "I've not had visitors, not in a long while." His fingers plunged into wild tufts of gray hair on the sides of his head, twisting and pulling, his stormy gaze never quite meeting my eyes. As I'd noticed before, he was stocky and tall, thin in some places, pudgy in others, and a tense energy surrounded him. He didn't really stop to converse, his legs always moving, carrying him to the fence and back again.

Miss Seton motioned us to follow as she angled his progression in the direction of a small path. "This is where we like to take our afternoon strolls. Don't we, Henry? I'm sure you shall be very happy to have friends join you today." The bend of her tone said otherwise.

Mr. Hawkins's arm was tense at my side, his steps determined. His first question was a harmless one. He no doubt only meant to engage Henry, but Henry ignored Mr. Hawkins as he did all else. Everything, that is, except the plants lining the path. Each twisting ivy leaf was slid through his fingers. He reminded me of a small boy in many ways; his attention flitting one direction then the next, an insatiable thirst for adventure coupled with an endless drive.

We'd circled a small garden behind the cottage and had nearly reached the house again when Henry spun to face us, his focus unnervingly keen on me. There was a ghostly second of unnatural stillness as his dark eyes narrowed and his breathing slowed.

He stepped closer to me. "It wasn't supposed to be this way, you know."

Then Henry's face all but changed before our eyes, his cheeks reddening. If I hadn't been so shocked, the transformation would have frightened me to the extreme, but all I could feel in that very second was intrigue. Who was this man Mr. Cluett had been hiding, and worse, what dwelt in his mind?

As quickly as it erupted, the tension ebbed away and Henry's arms fell loose at his sides, swinging back and forth, his emotions falling like a surge of wind from the north. His voice turned light as he spoke, more to himself than anyone else. "Not this way, no."

Caught up in the confusion, I crept forward, speaking as calmly as I could. "What do you mean, Henry?"

Again, that vacant look as if he saw straight through me. He held it for a long minute before a crooked smile emerged.

Mr. Hawkins's strong arm jerked me back, and Miss Seton's voice broke the mawkish calm. "Shall we head back to the house, Henry?" She gave me a hard glare as she drew up at his side.

Henry didn't seem fazed in the least; he jabbered on about a nearby bush, the passion in his voice lost on the breeze.

Miss Seton gently grasped his hand. "I think we've had a long enough walk for today."

Mr. Hawkins edged forward. "He seems to be calm again. Why not wait a moment?"

She shook her head, her eyes wide, then motioned for Henry to continue into the house. "As I said before, his nurse, Miss Brisbane, reported to me earlier that he's been agitated off and on all day." Then just for us to hear, "I'll not allow either of you to start anything dreadful. I think you've seen enough."

The crunch of gravel and the creak of wood drew our focus back to Henry as he stumbled up the cottage steps.

Miss Seton's face tightened, hardening her wrinkles into straight lines. "Excuse me. At present I need to see to my patient."

Mr. Hawkins and I watched in silence as she supported Henry into the cottage. The thin wooden door slapped shut behind them.

Mr. Hawkins turned to look at me, pity driving his expression. "Mr. Cluett should have provided for this man in his will." He toed a clump of grass with his boot. "Which begs the question, why didn't he?"

It took the whole of the night and a good deal of the next morning to fully rid myself of the restlessness Henry had wrought with a single look. The notes Mr. Cluett had left behind regarding Patient A were not flattering—bouts of madness and violence. I couldn't help but wonder if Henry was too dangerous to keep on the estate.

Miss Seton believed he could be managed, and she'd been his nurse for years. I wasn't even certain Henry was indeed Patient A, although Mr. Cluett's descriptions did seem to match Henry in a way. Mr. Hawkins had reminded me of that fact after dinner the previous evening and begged further caution. But what was best to be done while we awaited the probate of the will? Should I not speak openly with the rest of the household?

My intuition said no. I was not yet familiar enough with Mr. Montague's or Mr. Lymington's character to trust them with such information. If Henry was controllable, he must be protected. I understood that more than anyone.

Still gripped by my never-ending circle of thoughts as I sat on the back terrace, I caught sight of Mr. Hawkins marching from the stables. He wore what looked like a doubtful expression but waved as he approached, his grit morphing rather quickly to pleasure. He didn't slow till he was but a step away, where he halted and propped his boot upon a low stone wall before flashing a grin. "I had a thought this morning."

I tipped my bonnet rim to shield my eyes from the sun. "Did you? Tell me, what did that feel like?"

He laughed then cast a look over his shoulder, a light nervousness to his movements. "I heard on good authority—from Major Balfour to be exact—that your suitors have taken leave of the estate for the morning."

"Yes, they've business in town, although Mr. Lymington requested a meeting with me later this afternoon."

"Then you've no plans for the morning?"

"None whatsoever." My attention had been on the lawns, and I looked up to see him staring at me, a touch of mischievousness about his eyes. "Have you something in mind, Mr. Hawkins?"

"It just so happens I do." He offered me his arm. "It will require a short walk into the trees over there—that is, if you're up for a little adventure."

I hesitated, and he held up his finger. "You'll have to come with me if you wish to know what I have planned."

My lips scrunched into the corner of my mouth. "All right, I'll come with you, but I must warn you, I'm not all that keen on surprises."

He smiled, the gentle one that was unmistakably his. "Truth be told, neither am I, but I'm glad you're willing to indulge me this one time. I don't think you will be disappointed." He guided me onto my feet and tucked my arm in close to his side. "I have a mind to spend a few hours away from the house and thought you might like to join me."

I slowed. "Then we're to leave the estate?"

"Not exactly." He rested his hand on mine, nestled in the crook of his arm. "I will confess, this idea is a bit of a ramshackle notion and will require trust on your part." As he spoke his eyes glinted in the sunlight, flecks of yellow and amber melding into the light brown rings. "Do you think you can do that, Mrs. Pembroke? Will you trust me with your care?"

"You are my very own solicitor."

He gave me a wink. "Precisely."

I was led down the gradual slope of the hillside, past the drive, and into the dense woods that wrapped a good portion of the back half of the estate. Once we were surrounded by oak trees, Mr. Hawkins sauntered forward but a few yards before he nudged us to a halt. Ahead, tethered to a tree, stood a large black horse nibbling on a patch of grass.

"Scout," Mr. Hawkins called out. "I'd like to introduce you to a lady friend of mine."

The horse lifted his head and cast a seedy look at both of us before promptly returning to his grass.

"He's beautiful. May I?"

He released my hand from his arm and we approached the animal. "Scout is the only thing I took from Middlecrest Abbey when I left."

"I can certainly see why." Tall, sleek, majestic—the stallion had an elegance about him I couldn't help but admire; a dark beauty that contrasted wildly with the greenery around him. His glassy eyes followed my approach as I neared and rested my hand on his silky nose. "He's glorious. But I don't understand . . ." I gave a curious glance back at my companion. "What exactly do you have planned, sir?"

Mr. Hawkins grasped the bridle, running the leather through his fingers as he prepared an answer, which I was forced to wait for. "I thought we might go for a ride."

My muscles stiffened. "You know I can't . . ."

He sidestepped Scout's nose to get a clear look at me. "Hear me out. You said it was dangerous for you to ride alone, but this morning while I was tending to Scout, an idea popped into my mind. What if you rode with me?"

My eyes snapped to the solitary saddle then the empty forest around us. "You mean you want us to ride *together* . . . on Scout?"

"I agree it's not optimal, nor practical, nor all that proper, but Scout is easy mannered and quite strong. Besides, I've never been all that conventional of a gentleman. Just ask my sisters." He expelled a loaded breath. "I simply don't think it's fair that you should have to give up something you've always loved, not when it is possible to enjoy it another way. I promise we'll go slow, and I'll stay firmly within the back acres. I've been out quite often this time of day, and I can assure you there won't be anyone around for the next few hours." A hint of unease snuck into his voice. "You did say you loved to ride. I guess I thought you might appreciate the chance to do so again. And if you're worried about Scout, he would never buck with two riders. I can promise you that."

I toyed with the edge of my lip, every inch of my body aching to agree, but should I? Dare I?

Mr. Hawkins circled the horse, drawing up close at my side. "I haven't thought out all the particulars, of course, but I'm fairly certain we can find a way to seat ourselves comfortably enough." His lips curved so charmingly into a tease. "What do you say? Shall we try it?"

I felt myself nodding before I'd even made my decision, my hips swaying toward Scout of their own accord. I wanted to go. I needed to go. Mr. Hawkins was right. This half-baked idea of his might possibly work, offering me a precious chance to venture farther from the house than I'd been permitted to go in more than two years. Moreover, it would be a break from the relentless fears and anxiety of the past few days.

I touched Scout's lustrous coat, his strong muscles layered beneath. I'd dreamed of a moment like this for so long. My shoulders lightened as I felt myself fully agreeing to the plan. Today, even if it was only in my imagination, I would not be a patient of Cluett's Hospital, but a young lady asked to take a ride into Hyde Park with her gentleman escort.

Mr. Hawkins motioned me closer. "I think if I get in the saddle and you ride astride behind . . ." His voice trailed away, replaced all too quickly by a coy smile. "Do you think I'm insane for even suggesting this?"

I shook my head, still lost in my own thoughts, as tears threatened to emerge. "No. I think you're wonderful."

I can't say for certain whether it was the honest depths of my response or the subtle fluctuations of the wind, but a beat of silence gripped the forest, seizing the pair of us along with it.

My heart pounded its way into my throat before Mr. Hawkins finally gave me a hopeful shrug. "Then you're game?"

I wanted to laugh and cry, to twirl with joy from the tingling warmth spreading throughout my chest. The entire idea was indeed ridiculous but, at the same time, remarkable. Mr. Hawkins had gone to all this trouble—for me. Solicitor or no, he was a good friend. I lifted my chin. "I believe at this point I would follow you just about anywhere."

He nodded rather shyly as a smile lit his face. He gave me one last glance before gripping Scout's mane to mount. There was a caution to his movements, a protective pause before he spoke over his shoulder. "I'll pull you up once I'm settled."

He lunged off the ground and swung his leg over Scout's broad back before shifting into place. Then he looked down at me. "Are you ready?"

The words were simple enough, but my voice cracked. "I've been ready for years."

He lowered his arm, locking mine against his. "On three, you jump. All right?"

I nodded and waited as he counted, then thrust myself upward on three as hard as I could. I'd imagined a struggle, but Mr. Hawkins strong-armed me onto Scout's back in one fell swoop.

For a breathless moment I sat there stunned in disbelief. I was on the back of a horse. Astride!

Belatedly I adjusted my skirt as best I could, but my legs were clearly exposed. I didn't even own a riding habit anymore and, in truth, the whole situation was terribly awkward. But Mr. Hawkins was facing away from me, and he swore we wouldn't encounter a soul. Far too eager to enjoy myself, I shoved all qualms aside. After all, I was on the back of a horse, and it had been so incredibly long . . . and Mr. Hawkins was so near.

"Can you move in a bit closer? I don't want too much pressure on Scout's hindquarters." Mr. Hawkins reached back to guide me forward. "I'm afraid you'll need to hold on . . . well . . . to me if we're to make this work." He laughed to himself. "I suppose I should have imagined this part. Are you quite comfortable?"

My cheeks flamed. How to answer such a question? "I'm fine."

Carefully I inched forward, easing against his strong back. Then I closed my eyes, swallowed hard, and wrapped my arms around his torso. His jacket felt cool from the breeze at first, but his warmth quickly replaced it, and I could feel every tightening of his muscles, every breath he took.

"Is this better . . . for Scout, I mean?"

He must have heard the emotion in my voice but misunderstood the cause. "I'll keep him to a walk on level ground. You needn't worry. I've got you."

I tipped my head forward against his back. "Then I guess I have nothing to lose at this point. Carry on."

"Gladly." Scout seemed to respond to nothing more than a flexing of Mr. Hawkins's legs and we sidled forward.

"That's right, boy. Nothing but a stroll today."

The trees crawled by, slowly at first before we settled into a brisk walk. "Do you think the added weight will be a struggle for him?"

"Not Scout. And if I may be so bold, you are rather tiny, Mrs. Pembroke. I seriously doubt Scout even notices the difference all that much. I'm fairly certain I've loaded up a saddle bag with more than what you weigh."

I could feel Mr. Hawkins dipping his head forward to look down, and I wondered if he might be staring at my hands, which were clasped about his middle. A ping of anticipation stirred within me and all too easily I dreamed it was true.

"I used to take my sister Phoebe on Scout when she was younger. Of course, she'd sit up front and demand to take the reins."

"You were a good elder brother, then."

"That was years ago, but in many ways it feels like yesterday."

"Do you miss your family?"

"I haven't been home in two years." A sigh. "I miss them very much indeed. When I first left, I'd planned to visit often, but the apprenticeship at Pembroke and Huxley has been rather demanding. I'd hoped to be . . ."

I waited, but he didn't finish. "Hoped to be what?"

"Well . . ." Strain crept into his voice. "When Mr. Pembroke passed over a year ago, I was forced to begin again with a new instructor solicitor—all that time 'eating my dinners' wasted." I felt a sharp intake of breath. "Forgive me. I certainly don't wish to make light of not only your loss, but your general situation. I—"

"Please, you mustn't concern yourself. Though the loss of any man's life is a tragedy, let me assure you, Mr. Pembroke and I were not in love."

Mr. Hawkins didn't move. "I didn't know."

"I barely knew my husband before our wedding, and my guardian proved less than honest with him before the marriage. You see, I thought he already knew about my condition when he proposed. I was told he did, that he still wanted the connection, but I was a fool. I was too busy dreaming of an escort to London to see Vauxhall Gardens and the Royal Menagerie, and as an older, disagreeable man, Mr. Pembroke simply wanted the pleasure and status of possessing a young, proper wife. Our rushed engagement and the passing of money, however, turned out to be nothing more than a business transaction. He was not the least interested in me as a person, contrary to his declaration at our engagement. His affections were all a lie. One spell into our sham of a marriage and I was admitted to Cluett's Mesmeric Hospital posthaste. So anything you say regarding Mr. Pembroke will not affect me. I was only in his house a week."

Mr. Hawkins stiffened. "He sent you away . . . just like that?"

I nodded against his back, and he adjusted his seat on the horse as if to look back at me. The subtle movement must have alerted Scout because I could feel his pace accelerating with each stride, but Mr. Hawkins kept him firmly in hand.

His voice sounded strange. "I certainly don't mean to pry, but I must ask. Was he unkind to you, Mrs. Pembroke?"

My jaw clenched as my eyes slammed shut. I'd promised myself not to think of those dangerous few days ever again. *Unkind* was an understatement. When I didn't answer, Mr. Hawkins directed Scout into a nearby meadow and pulled him to a halt beneath a large willow tree. "Not exactly," I finally whispered, but it sounded like a stretch, even to me.

It was several seconds before Mr. Hawkins spoke again. "We're here—the place I wanted to show you."

He assisted me to the ground and then swung down at my side, his gaze roaming the nearby hillside. "Pretty little spot." But his heart was not fully in the words.

"That it is." And it was.

Drops of morning dew clung to my half boots as I walked into the meadow, a slosh marking each step. The warmth of the sun caressed my back as my focus settled on a lovely little copse of trees ahead.

New trees—ones I'd never seen before. The thought sent my pulse racing, my mind closing the door on my painful past. Mr. Hawkins had promised me an adventure after all, and I wasn't going to miss it.

"Where are you off to?"

I smiled back at him. "I'd like to see what's ahead."

Mr. Hawkins secured Scout to a tree limb before rushing to catch up with me. "Not without me you don't."

Across the small meadow I could hear the rush of a nearby brook. The surrounding bushes and trees seemed to wave me forward, their gnarled branches caught up in a delicious breeze.

Mr. Hawkins was but a step behind me when I ducked beneath the low-hanging branches. The surge of water met my ears; a layer of mist hung on the air. As I looked across the rippling waves to the far shore, my breath caught. There were so many sweet, delicate blue flowers—forget-me-nots, if I was not mistaken. They had claimed every inch of green space as their own. Wreathed in tiny petals, each flower bud tilted its head as if watching me, wondering if I would join them.

I took an impish glance at Mr. Hawkins. "Shall we?"

He nodded, and I hiked up my skirt. One stone, then another, and I crossed the creek, landing with a squish on the far shore where I waited for Mr. Hawkins to join me.

My lips parted, my dreams even now fresh in my mind. The cozy area looked just like nature's version of a ballroom, a secret haven untouched for some time. I whirled about soaking in the beauty. The oak trees were the columned walls; the clear sky its painted ceiling; the blue flowers a magnificent floor.

Breathless, I extended my hand. "Now it's your turn, Mr. Hawkins."

He eyed me a moment then smiled. "For what?"

"If I can bring myself to cross the estate on the back of a horse . . ."

He looked around. "Yes . . ."

"It's past time you finally danced."

CHAPTER 18

S hock overtook Mr. Hawkins's face. "You want to *dance . . . here?*"
"Why not?" Suddenly aware of the recklessness of such an impulsive idea, I tucked my hands behind my back and rocked up onto my toes. "Can you think of a place better to do so than nature's glorious ballroom?"

"I suppose not, but . . ." A confused look preceded a tentative smile. "For one thing, there isn't any music."

The whim that had inspired my offer in the first place now taunted me to continue. I drew in a sharp breath. "No, but we can still count the figures, can we not?" I gave a little sigh. "How long has it been, Mr. Hawkins?"

His gaze snapped to mine.

"Since you danced? You said you don't do so in company."

He ran his hand down his face, his voice stirred by a laugh. "Too long, I'm afraid."

"Well?" I extended my hand, ignoring the increasing thrum of my heart. "I daresay it is time we remedied such an unfortunate situation. A quadrille perhaps? 'La Poule'?"

"You're not serious." He pressed his lips together, watching me with that intelligent look of his. "But you are. And I don't think you mean to let this rest, do you?"

"No."

A little shake of his head, and then he glanced to his left and right as if we might not be alone. Yet we both knew there was no one in that little grove but us. A momentary smile peeked from the corners of his mouth as he clasped my hand. "Will you do me the honor, Mrs. Pembroke?"

"I believe I will." I'd been so determined to give him a taste of his own medicine that I hadn't anticipated what came next—the sudden spark of nerves, the rush of embarrassment as I moved into place across from him. His brief touch, though initially sought, lingered on my hand. How quickly lighthearted fun had shifted into something else entirely. Why had I ever thought this a good idea in the first place?

Slowly, carefully, I lifted my eyes to his, and my chest constricted. It wasn't the first time I'd stared into the depths of his eyes, but it felt that way. As I moved forward, the backdrop of the woods took on a dreamlike appearance, the grove curving inward, lulling me into a precious moment meant only for us.

A swallow sang from somewhere in the distance. Nature's soothing hum. The sun shook free of a blanket of clouds and lit the morning dew as it glinted across the flowers like tiny diamonds at our feet.

Some part of my mind must have triggered the count because whispered numbers escaped my lips, "One . . . two . . . three . . ."

Mr. Hawkins stood somewhat aloof awaiting his turn, regarding me with a solemn intensity. My cheeks felt hot as my legs began turning the figures, back and forth, near and far.

With each step I was plagued by one thought alone. What did he think of me? Moreover, what did I think of him?

Our hands met as we turned, each of us leaving a space for the pretend other couples. The underbrush swished at our feet as the sun warmed our skin. We smiled. We laughed as I hooked my arm through the air like it was a person time and again.

Mr. Hawkins proved light on his feet as the pass of the dance brought us ever closer. Then his hand covered mine at my waist, his gentle touch so intimate, so stirring, I was late to lift my other hand. The mistake brought my gaze rushing to his and my muscles contracting.

We were but an inch from each other, seconds from turning to the side as the dance dictated. But neither of us moved, the air alive between us. It was the first time I'd allowed myself to imagine kissing him, to wonder what it would feel like to be drawn into his arms.

An attractive flush colored Mr. Hawkins's cheeks, a breath of anticipation curving his lips. All too quickly he stepped back a pace, his voice low. "I daresay I've embarrassed myself enough for the morning."

"Nonsense." I tried a laugh, but it wasn't a comfortable one as I fought to regain my composure. "I'm the one who forgot the count."

He rubbed his left hand with his right, a curious sentiment taking hold between us, a feeling I couldn't quite place. Then he bowed his head. "Thank you, Mrs. Pem—"

"Won't you call me Amelia?" What inspired the question, I'll never know. The words felt ghostly thin.

He opened his mouth to speak then glanced away. "It's getting late. We should head back."

A waft of cold air washed over me, and I rubbed the chill from my arms. Why on earth had I presumed to ask such a thing? What had come over me?

Mr. Hawkins was right to be disturbed by my actions. I never should have initiated the dance in the first place, let alone allowed such familiarity between us. This wasn't a dream. This was real life—his and mine—and soon enough I would be announcing my engagement to one of the other two gentlemen.

It wasn't, however, until I once again crossed the stones of the brook and stood waiting as Mr. Hawkins leapfrogged one rock after another that my breath gathered in my chest, and I finally recognized the emotion that had eluded my identification up until that point—it was hope. Raw, unadulterated hope. Which I knew very well I could never entertain again.

Silence reigned king over our ride back to Moorington Cross. I held tight to Mr. Hawkins, relishing the warmth of his safety and strength, but my escort was a million miles away—a stranger taking me back to the prison of my responsibilities.

Scout's steady canter didn't slow until we crested the last hill into the edge of the forest. Mr. Hawkins and I must have seen the woman beneath the great oak in the courtyard at the same time. He jerked Scout to a halt.

"Who is that just ahead? I've seen her out my window before."

I watched the woman a moment as she pressed her hands on the thick bark and closed her eyes. "One of the villagers. If I remember correctly, her name is Miss Parsons. Mr. Cluett once told me that she suffers from an arthritic condition. She used to work as a scullery maid at the house, but she was unable to continue. I've never spoken with her, but I understand she comes to the magnetized tree quite regularly."

I felt Mr. Hawkins's muscles tense beneath the layers of his jacket. "Hope can be a powerful force."

"Yes, it can." I took a deep breath. "Shall we dismount? I have an engagement with Mr. Lymington this afternoon and I need time to dress."

He dipped his head again as if he might be looking at my hands. "I am glad we had the morning." His voice was soft, uncertain even.

I pressed my forehead to the back of his jacket, a catch in my voice. "Me too."

Mr. Hawkins helped me to the ground before sliding down next to me, the air ripe with unsaid words, but he only gave me a slight nod.

I tried a smile. "I cannot thank you enough for the adventure. It was a thoughtful gesture from a true friend. I'll remember it always."

"As will I." He moved a step closer, and I thought I saw a quiver on his lips. "Amelia . . ."

The hairs on my neck rose, my mouth dry.

He raked his hand through his hair, his eyes glossing over. "I need to say something." But then he stepped away from me.

Speechless, I watched as he busied himself with Scout's saddle before meeting my gaze over the horse's back. "I haven't entirely decided, mind you, but I do hope you have Lymington at the top of your list."

My vision went blurry as I attempted to digest his remark. After all, how could I possibly consider Mr. Lymington when every last muscle in my body urged me to throw the dratted will away? To take a chance at my own happiness, not anyone else's. To seize the third painful option that I'd never even considered until this blessed moment.

But all too quickly a cold, antsy feeling crawled around in my chest. Had a simple morning alone with Mr. Hawkins truly altered anything for me? Could I start down a road that would spell ruin for so many people besides us?

As if he followed the swing of my emotions, Mr. Hawkins rounded his horse. "You have a difficult decision ahead, and I mean to support you, whichever of the two gentlemen you decide upon."

My stomach clenched. Nothing had changed for Mr. Hawkins. There was no real third option, not where he was concerned. He had his position to think of, his own life. For me it would be Mr. Lymington or Mr. Montague.

I managed a rather trite, "Thank you," before fleeing the woods.

Though I intended to court Mr. Lymington directly upon returning to the house, I was met with a message from his valet. He'd been delayed in London and would be forced to take his meal on the road.

Thus it was quite late that evening before he finally waltzed into the drawing room to find none but the ladies of the household in attendance as the gentlemen were still finishing their port. He seemed quite pleased with the arrangement, and truth be told, I was as well. It would be far easier to better acquaint myself with him without my all-too-attractive solicitor continually getting in the way of things.

Miss Seton was engaged in a song at the pianoforte; Mrs. Fitzroy lost in thought at the window. I was in the perfect position on the sofa to receive him in the intimate fashion I preferred.

He had a travel-weary look about him, yet as he crossed the room I couldn't help but notice how the outside air had done him a service. His cheeks were full of color, and the innate nervousness he fell into in my presence had not yet reared its ugly head.

I did wonder, however, at his choice of tailor as the cut of his blue jacket did little for his figure. But his smile was warm enough, which in that moment I found relaxing.

He stopped but a foot from the sofa and gave me a slight bow. "Mrs. Pembroke, allow me to say how aggrieved I am to have missed our time together this afternoon. I assure you, it couldn't be helped."

I returned a smile. Though he was proving an awkward gentleman to better acquaint myself with, I was determined to start afresh and bring him out of his shell. "You have nothing to apologize for. I enjoyed an otherwise relaxing afternoon within the pages of a book."

He nodded once, his throat bobbing with a swallow.

"Do you like to read, Mr. Lymington?"

Though he'd initiated our conversation with marked attention, I felt myself losing him already as his gaze shifted back and forth from my face to the door. "As well as the next person, I suppose." He flipped his coattails out of the way and sat at my side, a scowl on his face.

Silence prevailed and I was forced to absorb the insult. Apparently this was going to be a bit more difficult than I thought.

I drummed the sofa cushion beneath the folds of my skirt. "If not reading, Mr. Lymington, then what is it you like to do? What interests you?"

He didn't even seem to hear my question, his own fingers busy at the base of his neck, his attention glued to the door.

My heartbeat turned sluggish. Did he no longer wish to court me? Was it the incident near the cottage? "Mr. Lymington?"

He gave a slight start at the mention of his name, but there was a rigid control about him.

I followed his gaze to the door. "Is something amiss?"

A well-placed pause. "No . . . not at all."

"Then what, may I ask, are you brooding over? You've hardly heard two words I've said thus far."

He let out a tight breath. "I'm not brooding exactly"—a sideways glance at me and his face slowly relaxed—"or perhaps I am. I apologize. I'm simply pondering our situation. We've only twenty-five days left, and I know little about you or where you stand in regard to your decision. I realize those concerns can be laid at my own feet, but not entirely. I had hoped to spend more time with you by now. My delay this afternoon was . . . disappointing."

Did he suspect something between Mr. Hawkins and me? "As I've told you, I'm at your disposal. I, too, wish to make an informed decision."

He nodded, almost more to himself than for my benefit. "If you will, I've, uh, some business to attend to first thing tomorrow, but I will send a note when I am free. Will that be acceptable?"

"Of course." I lifted my eyebrows. "But I'm also free now. Shall we not waste this moment?"

A smile dashed across his face. "I do realize we're alone just now. It's only . . ." He folded his hands in his lap, a frown forming once again as he took in the room, then leaned in close and lowered his voice. "We have little to discuss but business at this point. I met with my man today, and I am now fully prepared to discuss the particulars with you about my current situation."

We only had business to discuss?

He picked at his gloves, irritation lacing his voice. "Does that concern you, Mrs. Pembroke—potential surprises in regard to my financial position?"

"No. I assumed that would all be forthcoming. I would prefer—"

He cocked an eyebrow. "That is good to hear but equally puzzling. You see, I received an account of a rather distressing nature today. Just as I was leaving London, a courier of my land agent brought a message. It seems a man, wholly unknown to my family, has been asking personal questions about not only my estate but the details surrounding my living as well. Do you know anything about this?"

My lips parted. "Certainly not. You think I would hire someone to spy on you and Mr. Montague?"

He closed his eyes for a long second. "I didn't want to believe such a thing. I-I don't believe it. My honesty up until this point has been obvious, has it not? There will certainly be a marriage settlement between us. No need for anything clandestine on your part."

"I don't know who is asking questions, but I assure you, it is no one connected with me."

His shoulders dipped forward. "Thank you for putting my mind at ease. Only, that leaves me questioning who else could possibly be interested in such information."

We stared at each other a moment, the answer materializing in the air between us. "You believe it was Mr. Montague."

He rubbed his forehead. "I do know him to be less than honest, horribly divisive, and the worst sort of cad, but I cannot ascertain why he would stoop to bother with my situation. He sees this marriage arrangement as some sort of perverse game. I heard him say something of that sort to Miss Seton just a few days ago."

"He did, did he?"

Mr. Lymington scooted a bit closer to me on the sofa. "You must be made aware of who you are dealing with. Did he happen to mention to you where he went today?"

"I thought he had business in London as well."

"That's what he would like you to believe, but he went to Maple Court—to end things with Miss Allen, of course. Do you know of her?"

I shook my head.

"The gossips have tied the two of them together for some time. You see, Miss Allen has few prospects and little to recommend her—not the sort of lady Mr. Montague would generally waste his time on. However, his finances continue to worsen. He's been forced to keep the chit in his back pocket for over a year—for her twenty thousand pounds, of course. I don't think he wanted you to get wind of anything in that quarter, if you get my meaning."

"I see."

"And what of Mr. Hawkins?"

The air left my lungs. Had he noticed a partiality on my part? I cleared my throat. "Sir?"

"Has he made any recommendations about your decision?"

"Oh." I crossed my feet at the floor and took in a measured breath. "Nothing definite yet. He's still considering."

"Then I shall endeavor to speak with him as soon as may be arranged. As a man of business, I daresay he'll be better with the figures I have to present than you would." He followed up his declaration with a patronizing smile. "But I assure you my estate is solvent enough with or without your money."

Solvent was reassuring to hear, but he'd not said *prosperous*. I itched to inform him how I'd kept the books for my guardian Mr. Stanley for two years or more; however, the other gentlemen entered the room.

Mr. Lymington was on his feet in an instant. "If you will excuse me."

I watched him leave with a heavy heart. Better with the figures indeed. I was the one who would ultimately be marrying that cold fish, not Mr. Hawkins. Goodness, if the gentlemen had their way with it, they would be happy to leave me out of the decision entirely.

Well, little did they know I had a mind of my own. The scared, pliable mouse who consented to marry Mr. Pembroke two years before had grown up—desperation does that to a person, and I had indeed been desperate.

I caught Mr. Montague's smile from across the room and headed straight that way. He was a cad, yes, but also an amusing one. I would be a fool not to consider all my options, however limited they were at present.

CHAPTER 19

M r. Montague's expert fawning put me in a dangerous mood, one I certainly should have checked before waltzing out the drawing room doors onto the terrace, determined to confront not only Mr. Hawkins but my own inner demons as well.

I found him standing there facing a blackened night, his blue jacket taut across his broad shoulders, his palms flat against the stone balustrade.

He hadn't heard my approach, so I quietly folded my arms across my chest and leaned against a nearby wall. "What on earth are you doing out here all alone?"

His shoulders stiffened before he ambled around to face me, a look of subtle longing about his eyes. Moonlit tree branches swayed in the night air, forming shadows that twisted in and out of his thick blond hair. I hadn't been prepared for such a solemn countenance, nor his equally dismal voice.

He gave me a light shrug. "I suppose I'm just soaking in the last effervescent threads of moonlight carelessly tossed about by an eager breeze."

"More E. H. Radcliff?"

"Not exactly." He laughed to himself a moment before his smile fell. Then he stared down at his hands. "I couldn't help but notice that you've enjoyed quite a bit of Montague's company tonight. I found that a bit remarkable after my suggestion this morning."

I walked over and settled in beside him next to the terrace wall, resting my elbows against the cold stone. "Mr. Montague is a charming man, and I have little recourse but to keep all my options open at present."

"Ah." Mr. Hawkins fixed his gaze once again on the dark horizon.

We stood like that a good while before I finally nudged him. "What are you thinking of?"

He didn't answer right away. When he did speak, he was all business. "The murder, Mr. Cluett's documents that I've been reviewing, possible suspects. The list is endless."

"Have you formed any new conclusions?"

He pressed his lips together. "I've found the location of one of the gentlemen listed on the papers we discovered in the hidden drawer—Mr. Dodge, the person listed on the hospital record. His address was written on the back page—in Bordeaux, France. I can't be certain he still lives there, but I think it worthwhile to pursue any information we can uncover. I'll get a letter out to him straightaway."

"I agree."

"I still have no address as of yet for whoever this Mr. Cull is, and on another note, I've written to Mr. Huxley regarding the probate on the current will."

"Good idea." I rocked back on my heels, grasping the stone ledge with my fingers to keep from falling. "I've been doing a bit of reading myself—about Patient A. I can't help wondering if Henry had a hand in Mr. Cluett's death. He was treating him, after all, and there were no other notes on Henry in the cabinet. He must be Patient A. And that means . . ."

"I cannot say the thought hasn't crossed my mind, but there was no real sign of a struggle beyond the small amount of bruising on the shoulders. No other clues were left behind. I cannot imagine someone in Henry's condition could manage such a tidy crime. As far as I can tell, Mr. Cluett never saw death coming. Poison, asphyxiation—something ended Mr. Cluett's life, and I don't think it was just brute force."

I frowned, considering. "Mrs. Fitzroy saw that figure in the hallway, and as far as I can tell, everyone was accounted for that night. That is, everyone in the house."

Mr. Hawkins ran his hand down his face. "But the figure wasn't overly tall. Henry's height and bulk would have certainly stood out to her."

"True. But if not Henry, then who?"

"Mr. Cluett also treated people from the village, but the doors to Moorington Cross were locked that night. I checked with Andrews. No sign of a break-in. He doesn't think anyone could have entered without one of the staff seeing them. Everything points to a person already in residence."

"I tend to agree, but I'm at a loss as to who that could be. No one among us even has a motive."

"Will you walk me through one of your mesmeric sessions so I can better understand what Mr. Cluett did here?"

"Yes, but I'm not sure it will help." I tucked a stray hair behind my ear. "There were different types of sessions. When Mr. Cluett and I were one-on-one, he simply spoke to me softly, then observed me in silence to ensure his methods were working . . ."

"Go on."

I'd never told anyone about our sessions. It exposed a vulnerability I hadn't known resided in my heart. "Mr. Cluett would pass his hands over mine, from my wrists to my fingertips." I demonstrated. "I don't know how to explain it exactly, only it would make my skin tingle and cool. Then he would pinch my thumbs, like this, and encourage me to stare deep into his eyes without blinking."

Mr. Hawkins met my gaze. His eyes appeared almost gray in the moonlight, but soft . . . caring.

I looked away. "At that point I would get quite drowsy. I'm not really certain what happened next, not until he woke me up in the chair."

Mr. Hawkins nodded to himself. "Major Balfour has told me a great deal about his own experiences with trances. He's quite keen on them. What I don't understand is what Mr. Cluett used the *baquet* for?"

"Oh, that was usually for group mesmerism. Mr. Cluett treated several people from the village on Saturday mornings."

Mr. Hawkins arched his eyebrows. "Including the woman we saw at the tree earlier today—Miss Parsons, I believe?"

"Yes, I think so, but I didn't regularly attend those sessions, not for some time at least. Mrs. Fitzroy did. She never missed a one."

"What do you remember about them?"

"It was a completely different experience from my personal time with Mr. Cluett. He would don his purple robe and select his favorite wand. It was a great show, you see. Acceptance of his methods determined how effective the mesmerism would be, so Mr. Cluett always considered himself a showman. People would be brought into his large office on the first floor. There, Mr. Cluett arranged the drapes to allow only a thin strip of light inside. He paid a great deal of attention to detail. It was all part of the experience.

"Miss Seton would play in the connecting room to set the mood. Mr. Cluett had two large wooden tubs, the *baquets*—one for the rich and one for the poor. Each person would take a seat in front of one of the iron rods protruding from the tub's covering and bend toward it. They would press the rods to whatever part of their body possessed the complaint. I do know Mr. Cluett added magnetized iron fillings to the water in the tubs, but he also personally magnetized the phials attached to each rod where they sat in the water. All of his methods were meant to restore the balance of magnetic fluids found in nature, which were disordered in each person due to their affliction.

"Mr. Cluett would then walk the room and point the metal tip of his wand at different patients. At that moment generally one of the patients would have a convulsion and then another person, one right after the next. Miss Seton assisted them to another room to rest and begin the road to recovery, or at least until another mesmeric session was needed."

Mr. Hawkins looked incredulous, his eyes blinking rapidly. "And do you think anyone was helped by all that?"

My protective nature was roused. "I can only speak for myself, Mr. Hawkins."

"And?"

I lowered my arms to the railing. "My condition remains unchanged."

Silence prevailed as a damp cold clung to the night air, the cloudy sky working to blanket every last star. Beyond the terrace wall, somewhere within the depths of that stark gloom, hid a restful peace, a much-needed retreat for a troubled mind. Mr. Hawkins and I leaned forward against the carved stones for some time, staring out at a world concealed by nightfall but equally beautiful to the day in its own way.

"What does it feel like?"

"The mesmerism?"

"No . . . your different types of spells." As if it was the most natural thing in the world, he reached up and touched the exposed section of my arm, just above my glove. "Does it hurt?"

"It's terrifying, frustrating, consuming." I could feel emotion sneaking into my voice and I willed it away. "Sometimes I am injured when I fall."

"Is there any way to know before it happens?"

"A little. My more extreme spells are triggered by strong emotions. For instance, when I'm startled or afraid or terribly angry. The first thing I notice is my hands. By the time I realize I cannot move them, my knees buckle and I'm on the ground. Generally the whole ordeal only lasts a few minutes, but during that time I cannot speak or move. It is a total weakness throughout my body. The only way I can describe it is that it almost feels as if my muscles are shutting off.

Like someone has extinguished a candle and all I can do is wait for them to relight it."

He turned around, resting his back against the balustrade. "It's terribly important whom you choose to marry."

"No one knows that better than me." I followed his gaze, which was boring through the French doors at Mr. Montague.

A muscle twitched in his jaw. "I don't understand what Mr. Cluett was thinking when he wrote that will. He knew you better than anyone, and those gentlemen are terrible options for you. It doesn't make any sense."

"I've asked myself the same thing a thousand times before."

He lowered his head. "I cannot get out of my mind what you told me about Mr. Pembroke."

My poise was wavering. "I was young and naive, and he was a great manipulator . . . among other things. What little dowry I had was gone within six months. I understand his business flourished."

Mr. Hawkins's fingers folded into a fist. "I never even questioned him when he mentioned you. I was so thankful to have the position, for him to take a chance on . . ." His attention fell to his left hand, the moonlight highlighting the folds in his special glove. "I was blinded by my own ambition and my own inadequacies."

"You had no reason to suspect—"

"That is where you are wrong. I—" He shook his head and lowered his voice. "I came upon him one time. He was berating one of the clerks. I'd seen him do so before, but this time it was different. I suspected he might have used a bit of physical force to supplement his argument, but I had no proof. The clerk left the next day, and it was easier for me to pretend the incident never happened. I'm ashamed now of my indifference, my cowardice."

I touched his hand. "You were not in a place to confront him. As an apprentice you would have been turned off straightaway, just like the clerk. Mr. Pembroke was a master at evasion, and please don't misunderstand me when I say he probably saw your hand as a source of weakness. He eventually would have bent you to his will, just as he did me."

Mr. Hawkins released a breath. "He made me show him that first day."

"Your hand? No!"

He nodded slowly, thoughtfully. "I'd not revealed my scars to a stranger before, nor have I since, yet . . ." He glanced up at me a moment, a look of resolution across his face. Then he thrust out his left hand and tugged at the fingertips of his special glove.

"Mr. Hawkins, you needn't . . ."

"Show you?" His hand stilled as his face blanched white. "I . . . I won't if you'd prefer not to see it. I'm just basking in a rather glorious revelation. You, Mrs. Pembroke, may be the first person I've ever met who understands me." A smile crossed his face. "I find myself intrigued and strangely empowered by the discovery. I only thought that since I've seen one of your spells, it is only fair you see an intimate piece of me as well."

"It means a great deal to me that you would trust me with something so personal, but please do only what you feel comfortable with."

Meticulously, he slid the glove away. The skin was marred, his bones curved, but it was only a hand—a delicate part of the man I loved.

Loved! Warmth flooded my cheeks. My heart tumbled about in my chest. Despite all my quibbling, my dodging, and the wretched expectations of that abominable will, I had unwittingly fallen prey to the greatest power on earth—love.

And I had to do my best to hide it.

Mr. Hawkins was watching my face, dissecting every emotion trickling through my mind. Indeed, I had to be careful.

He gave me a slow nod. "Well, there it is. A mess if I ever saw one."

"Not at all." I ran my finger across a groove in his skin. "Nothing all that remarkable, nor anything to be ashamed of." I looked up at him. "Does it pain you?"

"No. It's more of an inconvenience than anything." He flexed the misshapen fingers. "I can't really grip all that well."

Without any thought at all, I slipped my hand into his, relishing the warmth of his skin and the secret he'd chosen to share with me alone. I gave him a playful shrug. "Feels pretty nice to me."

Oh dear! I'd said that aloud. The pounding rush of embarrassment that could only follow such a ridiculous blunder shot through my body like lightning, my mouth falling slack at my own stupidity.

A look of utter shock ghosted across Mr. Hawkins's face before he pivoted to the French doors.

What had I done? Was anyone watching us?

Surely it was too dark for the other residents of Moorington Cross to see us out here, but the guilt seeping onto the terrace was absolute. I could feel it in the way Mr. Hawkins recovered his hand, in the awkward turn of his voice. "Your suitors are awaiting you in the drawing room. We mustn't tarry."

Like a small child I nodded and crossed the terrace, dragging the shreds of my turbulent emotions behind me.

"Amelia?"

The sound of my Christian name stopped me cold, Mr. Hawkins's voice laced so painfully with the truth of what might have been.

"Yes?" I turned to find that his face had dropped into silhouette.

"Thank you."

My heart fluttered. "For what?"

"For being you."

CHAPTER 20

The following morning I stumbled upon Mr. Montague on my daily walk. He was lounging about at the back of the gardens near a turn in the hedgerow—the perfect spot where he was sure not to be seen till it was too late. The wretch.

A maddening natural at subdued charm and handsome coquetry, he paused for a daring look then offered me a bow. "Good morning, Mrs. Pembroke."

Not the least bit moved by his performance or his sneaky methods, I returned a nod. "A good morning it is."

There was a touch of mirth in his gaze, which only grew with his smile. He rubbed his watch fob between his fingers. "You're late, you know. I'd nigh given up on you."

"Late?" My brows drew in. "For what, pray tell?" I glanced behind me. "I don't exactly recall making any arrangements with you."

He slid out his elbow as a peace offering. "No, but you're so dashed predictable. I've been out here this past half hour or more. Surely you realize you waltz right across this section promptly at nine every morning with a determined stride, a woman with no thoughts to spare." He motioned over his shoulder with his chin. "I enjoy watching you from my window there. That is, when I'm awake enough to do so. Now, are you going to take my arm or not?"

"Dare I? All this sneaking about." I pursed my lips then swallowed my hesitation, settling my hand on his proffered arm. "I will admit, you have me somewhat intrigued."

"Good." He pulled me close to his side as he led us down the narrow path. "Because after your little tête-à-tête with Mr. Hawkins last night, I've been getting the distinct feeling you're avoiding me."

My gaze darted to the hedgerow, anywhere to evade his shifting eyes. "Not at all. I-I was only tired. When I promised you that game of whist, I hadn't intended to retire so early."

"Possibly." His arm flexed. "Or Mr. Hawkins warned you away from me. I'm quite certain that nosy solicitor of yours wishes me at Jericho right about now."

My legs stiffened, slowing my pace. "Don't be absurd. Though I value his opinion, Mr. Hawkins does not control my choice. He simply begs caution, is all, with both you and Mr. Lymington. He means to look out for me like an elder brother would."

Mr. Montague licked his lips. "An elder *brother*. Well"—a pointed huff—"I wish I could say I find that term somewhat reassuring, but, my dear Mrs. Pembroke, after my observations last night, I cannot help but wonder if that man is not indifferent to you."

He held up his hand, staving off a reply. "Andrews told me how the two of you popped into the locked wing three nights ago."

I dragged us to a halt. "Andrews . . . told you what?"

A sly dip of his chin. "Don't take a pet, my love. He wasn't spying. He merely mentioned to me how he happened to find the doors open on his nightly round, stuck his head in, and saw the two of you, nothing else, to his great relief, might I add." His smile widened. "So you may tuck that darling little lip back where it goes. I'm only teasing you where Mr. Hawkins is concerned. I haven't the least worry about a deuced solicitor. That is, unless you give me reason to." He arched his eyebrows. "I'd rather learn about the east wing. Find anything interesting?"

I took a deep breath. The east wing was certainly a safer topic at present than Mr. Hawkins. I only hoped the fright rattling around in my chest hadn't already given me away. Mr. Montague was so annoyingly clever. "First off, I hate to disappoint you, but there is nothing to see in the east wing but old furniture and holland covers. Second, everywhere I turn I hear a new report of you inquiring about me. It's beginning to feel a bit intrusive."

He shrugged. "How am I to come at information about you without a little investigation?"

"You could simply ask me."

"Of course." His eyes flashed as he eased our arms apart and clasped my hands in his. "Then put my misery to rest. Is it to be me or that straitlaced Lymington, whom I find far too ripe and ready by half?"

"You know very well I haven't made a decision as of yet."

"Well, yes." He looked down. "But I had the greatest desire to grasp your delightful little hands in desperation and stare into those green eyes of yours. Has anyone ever told you how enchanting you look in the morning?"

I jerked back, but he held me fast.

"No, and I don't take such flowery compliments seriously for an instant."

He released my left hand to pound his fist against his chest. "You wound me, Mrs. Pembroke."

I chuckled. "Much good it will do you."

"None at all, I'm afraid." He guided my hand back to the bend of his elbow. "I daresay I'm a lost cause at this point"—he shot me a sideways glance—"but an enjoyable one, I hope."

I gave him little more than a smirk, and his laugh floated away from us on the wind.

He really was a comfortable companion, but a tease and a cad who knew his way around the ladies far too well, and—if Mr. Lymington were to be believed—a fortune hunter to boot. I bit the inside of my cheek. So why was I enjoying myself? He was good, too good.

I forced myself back to the task at hand—information of a delicate nature. "I find you awfully skilled at evading any depth of conversation, Mr. Montague. Our moments together, though pleasant, rarely leave me with any more insight of your character than I had before. If I'm to make a decision, I need to know what your passions are, what you hope from the world."

"I'm not a gambler, if that is what you are getting at."

Interesting turn. My throat grew thick. I hadn't heard that vice attributed to Mr. Montague yet, but I'd better add it to my list of concerns. I swallowed hard. Now was as good a time as any to broach the more difficult questions. "I hear you went to see a friend yesterday."

"Ah, so that's what's got you excited. Dash it all, Lymington is proving to be a bit more devious than I gave him credit for." He nodded. "I'm sure the little worm has been filling you in on all my exploits; however, rest assured, I have nothing to hide about yesterday."

He adjusted his shoulders as if to shake off such an assertion. "Prior to my summons to Moorington Cross, I spent some time in London with a Miss Allen. I thought it only right to apprise her of our arrangement. I don't dabble with the hearts of well-bred ladies, Mrs. Pembroke, regardless of what you may have heard."

"I'm glad." But could I believe him?

"I stopped by Whitefall on the way back to see my father."

"Oh, is he well?"

"Perfectly. I, uh, thought it best to be the one to inform him of all the details concerning Mr. Cluett's rather tragic fate."

"I understand. And how did he receive the news?"

"Well enough, I suppose. He was startled, of course, but he was far more troubled about how I might be faring."

I stared at him a moment, searching his eyes. "And does he have reason to be concerned?"

"No." He looked away. "I'll admit, it is a strange thing to lose a father you never really knew. To have a life you were never a part of vanish just as it begins. It does make one reflect on what is really important in life."

"And what is that?"

"Seizing the day, of course. I'll not let any opportunity pass me by, not anymore." His focus shifted to the road ahead. "My father worries such an idea will make me impetuous, and maybe he's right, but I'd rather be impetuous than regretful."

"You'll need money if you're to enact such a plan. What will you do if I select Mr. Lymington?"

He clutched his chest. "Don't toy with me, love."

"I meant hypothetically."

"Well, according to the wording of the new will, I understand that if I'm not the one chosen, I will still receive a little money. There was some sort of allowance for the gentleman not selected. Not a lot, but I daresay I shall do well enough with what's provided. I've a friend near Dover who's got some rather brilliant ideas about archaeology, a business of his, I may wish to take part in."

He toed a pebble with his boot, then flicked it into the underbrush. "I believe Mr. Cluett thought it important to include such a clause—an inducement for the two of us to come and court you. He had no notion he would turn up dead that very night. Of course, all's lost if you decide not to choose Lymington or myself. Then none of us will get anything." He was watching me closely, reading me. His earlier questions regarding Mr. Hawkins were not as innocent as he would have me believe.

"I . . . realize that."

"Good." His mouth twitched. "Then let us get to the depths of conversation you seem so eager to explore. What is it you want to know about me . . . or my family?" His dimple peeked out of his cheek, dotting a wide grin. "Whitefall is one of the great gems of England. If I could, I'd take you there tomorrow. Everyone who visits is transfixed. And you needn't worry. The man who raised me shall never reveal the truth of my parentage. The estate is quite safe in my hands and will be for our children."

"I am glad to hear you won't be stripped of something you so obviously love."

"Whitefall is in my blood, whether my father put it there or not. It was my mother's home as well."

I stared off into the distance, past the rolling hills and green meadows.

Mr. Montague swayed into the view. "Is there more, Mrs. Pembroke?"

"I was simply wondering how you learned for certain you were Mr. Cluett's baseborn son."

He rubbed his chin. "I daresay you will laugh at the story."

"I won't."

He chuckled to himself. "It was my mother's uncontrolled tongue that gave up the charade. She mentioned one time in passing how shocked she was that I possessed the same freckled bum my father had. I was ten years old at the time but not clueless. Needless to say, it didn't take me long to comprehend that the man I'd known as my father did not possess such a remarkable trait. Thus the seed was planted for discovery."

"Oh dear."

"It was years before I finally confronted her, and by then she saw no reason to continue the farce, at least not with me."

"Was it a shock? To learn the truth?"

"Not really. I was never all that close with my father. He . . . tolerates me."

"Do you think it was because he knew all along about your parentage?"

"It's possible, but not likely. He is simply a man who has little patience for children." His fingers folded into a fist. "And I mean to be nothing like him."

My heartbeat quickened at the revelation as a new, possibly

dangerous thought dawned. I'd always assumed Mr. Lymington to be the only respectable choice between my two horribly inadequate suitors. But maybe I'd decided too hastily. If I couldn't be with the man I loved, was Mr. Montague an option after all?

My maid woke me from my scheduled nap with a note from Mr. Lymington. I waved her away at once and sat up on the side of the bed before holding the paper in the window's light, my hands still a bit unsteady from sleep.

> Mrs. Pembroke,
>   If you would do me the honor of joining me at the carriage house around three this afternoon, I should enjoy your company for an afternoon drive.
>   Yours,
>   Lymington

I folded the crisp paper slowly between my fingers and held it a second before sliding it onto my bedside table. Another offer for a drive, but should I trust Mr. Lymington with my welfare? I tapped my finger silently on the desk, my gaze fixed on the letter. The gentleman had given me no reason to distrust him, so why did I feel so unsettled?

I dipped my head into my hands. How was I ever going to make an informed decision if I couldn't manage time alone with each of my suitors? I lifted my eyes, my throat thick. The truth was, I wasn't.

Mr. Lymington had rushed to aid me that day in the forest. He knew what to expect from my spells now. Perhaps there was little reason at this point to be so overly cautious. Besides, I could no longer avoid the various aspects essential to a regular person's life, not when I was on the eve of an engagement.

Cluett's Mesmeric Hospital had been my haven for the past few years—for me, for Mrs. Fitzroy, for Major Balfour, and for so many others. But that place of safety didn't exist anymore—not without Mr. Cluett. Spells or not, it was past time each of us found our own way in the world.

I grasped my bonnet and hurried down the grand staircase, intending to depart Moorington Cross as Mr. Lymington had instructed in his note, but not before informing Andrews of my plans. I was not a complete fool. If I did not return by supper, Andrews was to report the details of my afternoon engagement to Mr. Hawkins at once.

Reassured, I strolled under the stone archway leading to the carriage house and found Mr. Lymington on the other side. He was dressed smartly for the occasion in a blue jacket and brocade waistcoat and stood waiting for me beside his curricle and two beautifully matched bays. He had one hand on the equipage, his other cradling his watch.

A smile dawned as he heard me approach. "Good afternoon, Mrs. Pembroke. I am pleased you were free to join me."

"As am I." The wind played with my bonnet ribbons and I was forced to hold them tight. "I confess I don't make a habit of leaving the estate these days, but an afternoon drive may be just the thing to improve my mood."

"I thought the same."

He assisted me up the steps and onto the seat before swinging up beside me and settling into place. He stole a peek at me and dipped his chin, offering me another smile. "Shall we?"

I nodded, and he slapped the ribbons, the two of us swaying with the movement.

The sun shimmered between the overhead branches, the looming shadows trickling over the curricle like a steady breeze. I tucked my hands in my lap. Any concerns I'd had earlier about joining Mr. Lymington's venture seemed miles away as the lush countryside, delightfully peppered with sweet floral scents, tickled my nose and refreshed my senses.

I looked over at my escort. "It is a fine afternoon."

"That it is." Mr. Lymington's arm muscles were taut, his gaze steady on the road, but his voice came out decidedly friendlier than I'd heard it before. "My sister used to say I was never more at ease than while I was driving. Thank you for joining me this afternoon. It means a great deal to me."

He focused on the road for a long moment before beginning again. "I daresay you'd agree that our situation is a delicate one, which is why I felt the need to leave the house. I-I have some things I need to discuss with you. I . . ."

His hand dropped to his pocket. "I received a letter from my mother this morning."

I adjusted my position on the seat. "What does she have to say?"

"I—" His fingers sprang to his forehead. "I'm not certain how to begin. The entire thing has me baffled." He inhaled a quick breath through his nose. "She writes to warn me that she believes Mr. Cluett was at one time . . . a murderer."

I touched my mouth. "What?"

"His elder brother. Years ago she came to the conclusion that Cluett was responsible for his death. She writes that he fled Britain for France to escape his demons. Took him two decades before he was able to return."

I shook my head. "I cannot believe such a thing."

"I find it quite difficult to understand myself, but there it is, plain enough."

I stared at the road ahead, blinking. "You mean, you think your mother is correct in her assumptions?"

His hands tightened on the ribbons. "The elder brother was killed on the eve of his marriage, and Cluett was the only one who stood to profit by his demise—as he very well did."

I fumbled with my fingers in my lap. "What proof does she have to back up this claim?"

"Nothing definitive. She simply stated that Cluett grew wild in the last days before he left, flying into rages, demanding perfection from the staff. Her family was friends of the Cluetts and visited often in those days. My mother was afraid of him, however, and has been all these years. She thinks everyone who knew him at that time was as well. So many left the house and never came back."

I sat forward. "But I knew him recently—for the past two years— and he was nothing like she describes. He was kind and thoughtful."

Mr. Lymington shrugged. "Maybe he mellowed some in his dotage. He could hardly be the same hotheaded fool he'd been in his youth."

"Do you think this accusation has anything to do with his death?"

"I hadn't made that connection, but I suppose such a thing would be plausible."

"But why would the killer act now after all these years?"

He pursed his lips. "Can you really assign logic to a murderer?"

"I suppose not." I took a measured breath. "It just doesn't make any sense."

"No, and even with this added information, our current situation remains unchanged." He paused to gather his thoughts, his expression—one I'd seen the first day I'd met him—changing from confusion to irritation.

"I'm not a fool, Mrs. Pembroke. I'm well aware you are not in love with me, nor have the least intention of becoming so. Clearly you'd prefer an alliance with someone else."

My mouth felt suddenly dry. Had Mr. Hawkins and I been so indiscreet as to put off both my suitors?

He coughed out a laugh. "I doubt there is a lady in London who would pick me over Montague."

I released a trapped breath. "You underestimate yourself, Mr.

Lymington." Relief tainted my words. I only hoped Mr. Lymington had not perceived it.

"A pretty thought indeed, but not a valid one. I haven't the talent some possess in regard to speeches nor the charm to pay court to you in the way a lady would wish, but let me assure you, I can offer you something he cannot." His posture seemed to lengthen the more he spoke. "Steadiness of character, loyalty, honesty, discretion. You will know just where and with whom I spend my nights, for I will always tell you."

My eyes grew round as my heart folded in on itself. *With whom he spends his nights?* A bit of bile snuck up my throat. How little he knew of me if he thought such a declaration would help his case.

"Can you say the same about Mr. Montague?"

My shoulders slumped. "Probably not."

"I'll also have you know I spoke with Mr. Hawkins, and we discussed a sizable jointure for you. If you select me, your money and future will be protected at all costs. I've seen your illness firsthand. An arranged marriage in the deft hands of a trustworthy person can provide you the protection you require for the rest of your life. Let me assure you right here and now, that is just the sort of gentleman I am. And allow me to add, Mr. Hawkins is in agreement with my sentiments. He means to see you cared for from this day on. Will you perhaps consider—"

A loud sound drew my attention to the far meadow, and my arm shot out. "Stop the carriage!"

Mr. Lymington jerked the ribbons, and the curricle rumbled to a shuddering halt. He turned and grasped the back of the seat, his eyes bearing down on me. "What on earth is the matter?"

I thrust my finger toward the meadow. "It's Henry."

"Who the devil is Henry?"

"The man from the cottage. How did he manage to wander all the way out here?"

Mr. Lymington was on his feet. "You mean to tell me that's the man who threatened you?"

"The very one, only I understand he isn't usually all that threatening. Miss Seton says he's quite docile most of the time."

"Most of the time?"

I hopped down from the carriage without assistance in a rather unladylike fashion, Mr. Lymington but a step behind me. "Mrs. Pembroke, I don't think—"

I headed straight for Henry.

"—we should concern ourselves with this man."

I glared back over my shoulder. "You'd rather we leave him out here all alone? To what end, Mr. Lymington?"

His hands were wild in the air. "It is not so very far back to the house. We can send help at once."

"Henry," I called out, and the man from the cottage turned. "Too late," I said to Mr. Lymington and couldn't help but smirk. "Thankfully you are here to protect me." Then to myself beneath my breath, "If you bother to put yourself out for it."

Part of me wished Mr. Lymington would stay with the carriage with all the good he was doing, frowning at Henry as we neared him.

I kept my voice at ease. "What brings you all the way out here, Henry?"

He had a long blade of grass in his hand that he was smoothing back and forth between his fingers. "I've been on a walk."

"I see that, but don't you think it's time you return to your nurse? She must be worried about you."

He laughed to himself. "Bet she is looking everywhere."

I cast a wary look at Mr. Lymington. "Do you realize it is nearing dinnertime? You wouldn't want to miss that."

He thrust the grass down. "No, I wouldn't." Something fixed his attention behind us, and his eyes glazed over as he shifted in place, mumbling, ". . . behind stones, hidden in dark places."

Mr. Lymington cleared his throat. "Pardon?"

"The eyes . . ." His own flashed. "They're watching, always watching. They say you'll find it—all it takes is a thorough search. Just follow the curse."

A chill skirted across my shoulder, and I hugged my arms to my chest. "What are you talking about?"

"The document. I couldn't find it. Maybe you can." A grin twitched at the edge of his mouth. "Illusions are just that, are they not?" His smile dissolved and I couldn't help but notice how his hands crunched into fists.

Mr. Lymington was equally perceptive and stepped forward, his voice filled with uncertainty. "Why don't you come with us to the carriage, my good man? It's getting late as the lady already said."

Henry's eyes narrowed to slits; his jaw clenched tight. My heart thumped away as I looked from Mr. Lymington back to Henry. Was it a sort of standoff? Mr. Lymington and he were of equal height. I couldn't be certain Lymington would prevail if it came to fisticuffs. Perhaps he had been right at the outset. I'd been far too hasty to engage Henry.

But he had been somewhat friendly with me at our previous encounter, and Miss Seton remarked on how at ease he was around me. I tried a smile. "Won't you sit in the curricle beside me? It'll be a tad crowded with the three of us, I'm sure, but I'd like to hear more about the plants you've found on your walk. I've never even been out this far before."

Henry's chin inched upward, then his arms fell loose at his sides. Apparently Miss Seton had been right. I did seem to have a calming effect on him. If only I could keep Mr. Lymington silent, I might just be able to coax Henry home.

I smoothed our way back to the curricle and then onto the seat, talking only of plants. This chatter thankfully got us back to his cottage, the ride uncomfortable but manageable—Henry docile as a lamb. I thought it a success as he turned to depart the carriage. But as soon as his feet touched the ground, Henry paused to look back up at me.

"Be careful, Mrs. Pembroke. If that document comes to light, out of everyone at Moorington Cross, you have the most to lose." He shot me one last baleful smile then toddled away to meet Miss Seton.

I, however, didn't move an inch, my heart pounding, my fingers tightening of their own accord. What document was Henry referring to? Moreover, what on earth would I lose if it came to light?

CHAPTER 21

"Y ou look as if you've seen a ghost."

I leaned sideways against my bedchamber doorframe and offered Major Balfour a wan smile. "I'm just returning from an afternoon drive with Mr. Lymington. I suppose I stayed out in the sun too long."

He directed me to continue into my room. "Then you must lie down at once."

"Yes . . ." I was surprised when he followed me into the interior. He seemed a bit lost, ushering in a moment of awkward silence before I motioned for him to take a seat in a chair beside the fireplace.

He tapped his cane on the floor, his gaze roaming the room before he eventually followed my suggestion, his legs a bit shaky with the movement.

Facing him, I sank onto the edge of the bed as he chuckled a bit to himself before looking up at me. "There is always that uncomfortable moment these days when I think I may very well fall into the chair as opposed to simply easing onto it."

"Has the pain in your feet worsened since Mr. Cluett's death?"

He popped his boots with the end of his cane. "I may be forced to search for other treatment options before I'd intended."

"If that is the case, should you not do so as soon as possible?"

He grimaced. "In all truth, yes, but Mrs. Fitzroy still needs me here."

My arms felt heavy as I moved them into my lap. How could I

even imagine a world where my dearest friends would be forced to part? "The two of you have been here for some time."

He nodded slowly. "I don't believe she's handling Mr. Cluett's death all that well. You know . . ." He rolled his hand in the air. "She was quite close to him."

"We all were."

His eyes flicked up, then a furrow snuck across his brow. "In a way, yes, but it is only natural that Mrs. Fitzroy should continue to suffer the most. I've been doing all I can to help her. I've even tried some of the mesmerism I've picked up over the years."

I thought back to what I'd seen in the blue salon when Major Balfour was sitting so close to Mrs. Fitzroy on the sofa. Her eyes had been closed. She'd been calm. "And do you think it gives her some relief?"

"Only a bit. I will never pretend to be a doctor, but she has said she appreciates my attempts." He smiled to himself. "However feeble they may be."

"I'm sure you have been a great comfort to her."

Major Balfour tipped his cane into his opposing hand and flicked open the lid of the small round vinaigrette affixed in the handle. He took a whiff from the gilded holes at the top as he lost himself in thought, the scents of cinnamon and vinegar joining us in the room.

Then suddenly he snapped it shut. "But what about you, Amelia? I cannot get the idea out of my mind of you being forced into this unwanted marriage."

"It is a difficult situation."

He wrinkled his nose. "I've spent some time with both gentlemen, and I must beg your caution once again. Marriage is forever, my dear. I cannot bear to think of you unhappy . . . or worse."

"I do appreciate your concern and I understand your meaning, but I do not think either gentleman worthy of such censure." A thick wave of sleepiness descended upon my eyelids. "Oh dear." I tried to blink the onset away, but it was no use. "I-I must beg leave of you." The room grew fuzzy around the edges. "I'm so sorry, but it's past time for my . . ."

The last thing I remember was my head hitting the bed behind me, vibrant dreams already dancing through my mind.

"There you are."

At the sound of my voice, Mr. Hawkins shoved a piece of paper into a book on the desk and peered up at me.

I couldn't help but watch the hasty movement. "I assumed you'd be dressing for dinner, but I met your valet in the hall just now, and he didn't know where you were."

"I must have lost track of time. Did you say you were looking for me?"

"I was. I—" I took one last glance over my shoulder before edging the door shut behind me. "I have something important to discuss with you alone."

A split second of thoughtful silence passed before he rose to his feet and rounded the desk. He met me in the center of the room, scouring his focus quickly over every inch of my being. Apparently mollified by what he found, he guided me to a pair of chairs nearer the fireplace. "Has something happened?"

I eased into one of the large winged chairs and crossed my feet at the floor. "First off, let me assure you I am well." His gaze was so intent, I added, "I never meant to alarm you."

His throat clenched as he swallowed. "It is no matter."

"I am, however, unsettled. For lack of a better word, it's been a notable day." I took a deep breath, then dove in to every little detail I could remember about my meeting with Henry, ending my rambling with the terribly strange remark Henry had shared with me after he exited the carriage.

As I expected, Mr. Hawkins checked, then pressed his hand to his chin. "A document, you say? That is odd. What could he be referring to?"

"An excellent question." I ran my finger along the rim of the chair's armrest. "I am beginning to wonder if Henry could have been referring to a prior version of Mr. Cluett's will. That is the only thing that makes sense if I stand to lose everything, as Henry said, with the recovery of this mysterious document."

Mr. Hawkins puffed a breath through his nose. "I assure you, Mrs. Pembroke, Mr. Cluett was of sound mind and judgment when he signed his current will. He wasn't drunk or insane or under any pressure whatsoever. The words were his. Mr. Huxley and I both witnessed him sign. Therefore, I do not believe the present will can be contested."

"No, I don't believe so either, but Henry was referring to *something* . . ."

Mr. Hawkins leaned forward and placed his elbows on his knees. "Be careful, Mrs. Pembroke. You may not wish to know what that something is." There was a note of wistfulness in his voice. "If the current will doesn't stand, everything changes."

"I only want the truth. I need to know why Mr. Cluett added me to his will in the first place—why all of this has happened."

His jaw clenched. "Then may I suggest we initiate a search? Then we shall know just what we are dealing with." He crossed the room to retrieve a piece of paper and a quill pen from the desk. "Tell me again what Henry said to you in the curricle."

I let out a slow breath, combing back through my memories. "There was nothing more about the document."

"Anything then. We cannot disregard any small phrase."

I scrunched my lips into the corner of my mouth. "I distinctly remember him saying something about eyes that were watching . . . Yes. And something about a search and an illusion. He said it was behind the stones, in the dark."

The feather on Mr. Hawkins's quill quivered as he penned out the words, and then he stared down. "Not much to go on, I'm afraid."

"No, it isn't."

He glanced at the door. "And it's nearing supper." He tapped the paper with the pen. "I'm afraid we shall have to wait until everyone retires for the night before we commence our search." He looked back down at the paper. "Darkness . . . an illusion . . . Sounds like we'll be heading back to Mr. Cluett's private office to begin our hunt. If there was one secret compartment in that room, there may very well be another."

Though our search that evening began with great enthusiasm, it proved equally fruitless and disappointing. No more secret drawers or special documents, merely plain old books and Mr. Cluett's extensive notes. Nothing of any consequence. Nothing profound that would change the current will.

Mr. Hawkins tried to remain positive, but the search of the library the following morning produced the same pitiful results. As did our investigations of the blue salon, the drawing room, and the sitting room, which, with my scheduled nap, managed to take up the whole of the afternoon. By nightfall, I could do nothing but fall into bed, irritated I'd wasted a perfectly good day hunting for something that might not even exist, particularly when Mr. Montague had offered to take me for an afternoon stroll.

It was the outside of enough!

I tugged the eiderdown beneath my chin and settled deep into my pillow, my thoughts running wild. The very idea that I might extricate myself from the terms of the will had been so tantalizing I'd lost myself to the search. But I was only chasing a ghost or a curst fabrication. Mr. Hawkins had been right from the start. There would be no way to contest the current will even if we found the previous one. If that was even what Henry had been referring to. I was no longer certain.

I'd accompanied Miss Seton earlier on her nightly round to check on Henry, hoping for more clues, but he had nothing to say to me, dismissing me even before I stepped into his room. There would be no more input from that quarter, at least for now.

Hidden in the dark indeed. There were no stones anywhere in the house.

I plumped my pillow with my fists and stared at the beams on the ceiling. Whatever Henry believed to be hidden at Moorington Cross would likely stay that way forever. I had best get back to choosing between the only two gentlemen I had no choice but to marry.

CHAPTER 22

Though I found some level of sleep that night, it was fitful, made worse by my incessant tossing and turning. Dreams were ever present, but not deep. I remember staring for prolonged periods at the drapes, my gaze following every curl of the fabric, my mind tempting me to awaken.

That was when I saw the shift. It was a subtle one, as if someone had run their fingers ever so lightly across the drapes. A cool puff of air seeped over my skin, the hairs on my arms springing to attention. At first I lay completely still, my eyes wide, my focus darting about the blackened corners of my bedchamber, but then I heard it—a whispered swish.

My heart ticked to life. Someone was in my room.

I thrust myself into a sitting position, my fingers curling around the edge of my blanket. "Who's there?"

Chauncey shuffled around in his cage. Since guinea pigs are not nocturnal rodents, his movements only heightened my growing alarm.

All of a sudden a shadow separated from the gloom, taking shape in the blackened abyss at the foot of my bed. It was a man— broad shouldered, neatly concealed in silhouette—inching across the carpet.

His arm swung upward and the moonlight exposed a knife blade in his hand as he twisted it into position.

I screamed.

As if on cue Chauncey grunted then squealed.

The unexpected sound caused the man to stop in his tracks, Chauncey's guttural cry capturing his attention for a split second.

Then, as if in slow motion, I watched the man's head twist back to me. The knife flashed in the moonlight once again.

On a cascade of nerves, I thrust the eiderdown up like a shield and ducked behind it as my heart took a wild turn. A breathless second and my hands began to tingle as my muscles went rigid beneath the bedding, now draped over my inert form.

I heard pounding footsteps, the errant *swoosh* of my door opening and closing.

All at once Mrs. Fitzroy's voice was at my ear. "My dear, whatever is the matter?"

I felt her lift my unresponsive body, then ease me backward into something of a slumped sitting position against the headboard. Her warm hands stroked my forehead. "Can you hear me, Amelia? Blink twice if you can."

I did as she directed. I could do little else. She sang as she held me cradled against her until the minutes passed and I slowly regained control of my muscles.

I moistened my lips. "Did you see him?"

"See who, my dear?" She looked around.

"There was a man in my bedchamber. He was standing right there at the foot of my bed. He had a knife in his hand. I believe he meant to kill me."

Her face bent with compassion. "It must have been another one of your dreams. You've said before sometimes you dream when you are not entirely asleep."

I shook my head. "It wasn't that." I leaned forward and felt desperately around on the bed. For a moment I did indeed think I had imagined the encounter, but then my fingers brushed over something cold and metal. Carefully, I lifted the object into the candlelight. A knife.

Mrs. Fitzroy gasped at the sight of the serrated weapon, her hands flying to her mouth. "Oh, Amelia." She glared back at the shadows in the room. "What can this mean?"

My fingers tightened around the wooden handle. "Not only do we have a murderer in this house, but he's apparently set his sights on me."

After a thorough hunt, Mr. Hawkins paced once again at the foot of my bed. "And you only heard the door open and close one time before Mrs. Fitzroy was at the bedside?"

"That's all I heard, but the drapes . . . I'm certain I saw them move."

Mrs. Fitzroy rose and Chauncey squealed for a treat. "Quiet, Chauncey!" She turned back to face me. "I've been meaning to tell you something . . . Oh, how to begin? You see, I became aware some time ago that Moorington Cross is known to have hidden passageways."

Mr. Hawkins gripped the bedpost. "Secret passageways? Here?"

She shrugged easily enough, but her gaze slowly narrowed in on her hands, clenched at her waist. "I suppose they are only secret if you don't know where they are." She gave her head a little shake. "Mr. Cluett did, you know. He-he told me one time how he utilized them."

"Do you mean to suggest that there may be a hidden passage that empties directly into my bedchamber from somewhere else in the house?"

She glanced around. "I don't know about all that, but possibly. I don't mean to make you worry. I was only thinking . . ."

Mr. Hawkins went to work at once, pawing every inch of the walls and fireplace. He scoured a large portion of the bedchamber, his fingers dipping into grooves on the surround, every facet of the wainscoting, but nothing moved, nothing jiggled.

Finally his arms fell lifeless at his sides, his voice routed. "Mrs. Pembroke should no longer be allowed to be alone. I can't imagine anyone returning tonight, but—"

Mrs. Fitzroy stood. "I completely agree." A quick look at me. "Allow me a few moments to grab my things from my room, and then I'll be right back." She held up her hand. "Now, now, I shall be far more at ease spending the night here with you than in my own room alone. A trundle for a maid can be set up tomorrow."

"But—"

She shook her head. "No disagreements. Let me do this for you this once. Goodness knows it's past time I returned a favor. You've certainly been there for me many times before."

I nodded, my stomach still sour from the encounter, my muscles weak from shock. As I watched my dear friend bustle through the door and out of sight, I was surprised by tears filling my eyes. So much so, I was forced to dab them on the coverlet.

I hadn't realized he was watching me until Mr. Hawkins pulled over a chair beside the bed. "Are you certain you wish to stay in this room?"

I generally fought such strong thoughts and emotions, pinning them deep inside where no one would know about them but me. However, as Mr. Hawkins's hand slipped so neatly around mine, something inside my heart creaked open—just enough for me to further lose my composure.

He proffered a handkerchief, and I gladly accepted it to dab my eyes. "I do apologize. I'm not usually such a lightweight."

"You have every reason to be shaken. An attempt was made on your life. I daresay I'd be screaming at the moon right about now. No reason to hold back."

"It's not that, not exactly."

His thumb moved ever so slightly across my skin. "What then?"

"It was when you declared I must never be alone."

"An important precaution, surely?"

I took a deep breath. "When I was a young lady, I had several rather terrible spells—one that left me with a broken arm. Thus, my guardian at the time resolved that I should have a maid with me at all times, and I mean all times. I could not even use . . . well . . . you know . . . the chamber pot without her watching me."

"My word! Sounds dreadful."

"It was dreadful and it went on for many years. I will admit, I've been afraid most of my life—sheltered into a practical nonexistence. All it takes is one accident, you see, one spell at the wrong moment, and my life is over. During that particularly painful time when I was never permitted a moment to myself, that was when I realized I was never more alone. It was like death walking about."

"I can't even imagine." His grip tightened around my hand. "But there's far more danger now. A risk I'm not willing to take with your life. Some protections must be put in place." He looked down at our hands. "I will promise you this. I won't let what you described happen again. Whenever you are with me or someone else in the house, like Mrs. Fitzroy or Major Balfour, you shall be entirely free of your maid." A smile curved his lips. "And when you are with me, I swear I won't watch you use the chamber pot."

I couldn't help but laugh. "I should hope not."

"In all seriousness, tonight's shocking revelations have me rethinking everything. I had begun to suspect the murderer was gone . . . or that it was Henry."

"Whoever wants me dead must be in residence in the house. How else could they move about so freely? But who?"

He raked his fingers through his hair. "And you couldn't make out any features?"

"None at all. I'm afraid I'm just as lost as Mrs. Fitzroy was when she saw the figure the night of Mr. Cluett's death. Although I am certain the person in my room was a man."

"Then we may confidently cross Miss Seton off the list, though I find her terribly tight-lipped and suspicious."

"As do I." My gaze wandered to the far side of the room. "Perhaps she's protecting someone else."

"Conceivably, but, Amelia"—he rested his left elbow on the bed—"there is something else far more concerning you need to consider."

"What is that?"

"The will. Remember how I told you that if you do not choose between the gentlemen, all the money goes to the teaching hospital in France?"

"I remember."

"Well, the same holds true if you are not alive to inherit."

I pressed my hand to my mouth. "But that would not benefit any of the people currently in the house."

"As far as we know, no." He released my hand to run his own down his face. "I cannot get this document Henry mentioned out of my mind. Such a strange revelation has to mean something. He has been in residence a great many years. He's bound to know quite a bit. And now Mrs. Fitzroy reveals there are hidden areas of the house. That means we have not even truly begun a thorough search."

The memory of him combing the walls of my bedchamber flashed into my mind. "You mean to turn this house inside out?"

"Yes, I do."

"All right, but do you not think it wise to keep this search between the two of us? I'm not even certain I should involve Mrs. Fitzroy. We don't want to inadvertently tip off the murderer. He may not be aware of what we know or what we've put together."

"Agreed. Every spare moment of my time shall be spent accordingly. With any luck something will turn up."

Mrs. Fitzroy's footsteps resounded in the hall seconds before she breached the bedchamber door. Mr. Hawkins, however, was not quite swift enough with a rather jerky scramble to his feet and a wild thrust away from the bed.

A smile lightened her face. "I am here to relieve you at last, Mr. Hawkins . . . Yet, whether you wish to be relieved or not is anybody's guess."

The following morning I began my secret search for hidden passageways in the library. After all, Mr. Cluett spent a great deal of time reading in his favorite room in the house. Draped wall to wall with massive bookcases, the space could easily conceal a doorway.

It was rather difficult as Mrs. Fitzroy dutifully had not left my side since the incident in my room, but I was determined to keep her from worry.

Swathed in a morning gown of purple sarcenet, she'd made herself quite comfortable on the long sofa, her nose tucked in a book and a cup of tea close by her side. Granted, I'd not heard a page turn in the last several minutes.

Routed from any real searching, I let out an exasperated sigh and flopped onto a nearby chair.

She stared down at her lap, her fingers suddenly of great interest. "I must say, you do look worn down, Amelia."

"Do I?" I pressed a hand to my cheek.

"It's in your eyes, my dear. There is a great deal more than the incident last night eating at you."

I feigned what I hoped was a convincing shrug. "I suppose I'm still riddled with the fact that my two suitors are not exactly what I expected."

She narrowed her eyes. "Nor is someone else, I suspect."

My heart twisted, tendrils of warmth spreading out over my face.

She pursed her lips. "I can see plain as day you are not indifferent to him."

I shoved to my feet and fled to the bookcase, ever conscious of the open door at my side. "What I feel makes no difference. You know very well I have other concerns."

"Amelia . . ." Her voice was soothing, lulling me back to the sofa where she whispered in my ear, "Why don't you just give it all up—the house, the money? You've never cared a fig for such things."

"No, but—" I stopped short, my attention arrested by a movement beyond the window. There, across the gentle slope of the manicured lawn, at the base of the grand oak tree, stood a woman. My mouth slipped open. As best as I could remember, no one had visited the magnetized tree in several days. I moved closer to the recessed glass. Yes, it was Miss Parsons, her hands flush against the bark.

A knit furrowed my brow. "Mrs. Fitzroy?"

"Yes, dear?" Her voice held a hint of concern.

"Didn't you tell me at one time that Miss Parsons was a scullery maid at Moorington Cross?"

"As far as I know she was. I heard that from Miss Seton."

"If that is true, it's possible she might have some insight about Mr. Cluett's past." Moreover, any information about the secret passageways Mrs. Fitzroy believed existed.

Mrs. Fitzroy flicked her fingers in the air. "I hear she is not all that friendly. She mightn't even receive us if we paid a call."

"I don't intend to make a call." I stole across the carpet. "Do not fear, I shall return directly." Feeling Mrs. Fitzroy's eyes boring into my back, I tossed back words I hoped would appease her: "You may watch me out the window if you like, but I haven't time to waste. Miss Parsons will be gone from the tree at any moment."

"You mean to leave the house . . . this minute . . . alone?"

"Certainly." I paused at the door to flash her a smile. "How else am I to speak with the woman?"

The countryside was unseasonably cool, the halting wind stroking the tree branches one by one as the great ocean of grass at my feet shivered in response. I watched as Miss Parsons pulled her cloak tight about her neck, her fingers gleaming white.

She caught sight of me when I was but a few paces away, and I was forced to call out her name to prevent her retreat. She fell motionless at my call, and a moment's hesitation passed before she turned around to face me. Wrinkles filled an otherwise sallow complexion. Her sunken eyes focused in on me.

I cleared my throat. "I'm sorry to bother you, but do you have a moment, Miss Parsons?"

The gnarled hand clutching her cloak shifted to her pocket. "Yes, ma'am." There was a rasp to her voice that brought out another chill.

I shook it off. "I don't believe we've ever been introduced. My name is Mrs. Amelia Pembroke. You may have seen me over the past two years. I've been a patient at the hospital. I, uh . . ." Why did my words feel so sticky in my throat? "Well, I hoped you'd be willing to answer a few questions . . . in regard to your time in service at Moorington Cross."

Her eyes widened, her face blanching in the sunlight. "My service? No one's asked me about that in some time." A sharp glance back at the house. "I'm afraid those memories have faded like the rest of me."

"I understand you were a scullery maid."

Her back stiffened. "That is correct, but like I said—"

"I was wondering, as a maid, if you might not be uniquely situated to know of any possible hidden rooms or passageways in the house. I've been told Mr. Cluett spoke of such a thing."

She let out a quiet hiss. "Rumors." A chuckle to herself. "Aren't you far too old to believe in fairy tales?"

I watched her a long moment. There had certainly been some level of interest at my question. Fairy tales indeed. What did she know?

She dipped her chin. "I don't believe I should stay out any longer in this weather. Good day, Mrs. Pembroke."

My hand shot out. "Another question, if you will?"

She angled a sharp glare at me. "If you must."

"How well did you know Mr. Cluett?"

A sudden gust of wind flapped the edges of her red cloak as a nearly imperceptible curve creased her lips. "Quite well indeed."

"Then I hope you will be willing to satisfy my curiosity. In his youth, was Mr. Cluett capable of harming his elder brother? Is that why you left the estate?"

"Not at all." Her hand groped for her pocket, and she hugged her cloak to her body. "I was dismissed."

I touched my chest. "Oh, I didn't mean to pry. Only—"

"Only, what?" Her eyes drifted into a blank stare, then her face became animated. "You're not asking the right questions, Mrs. Pembroke."

My lips parted. "What do you mean?"

She inched in close. "Don't worry. I left it where the family would have wanted it to stay." Horses' hooves sounded in the distance and she jerked away. "I dare not say anything more. Good day, Mrs. Pembroke."

She walked off briskly but drew to a halt just as quickly and whirled back to face me, a curious bend to her brow. "And please be careful. Be very, very careful. Regardless of what people may think, I did what I did for the Cluett family name."

CHAPTER 23

Mr. Montague was in a rare humor the following day in the drawing room. He met me rather dramatically at the door, took my hand into his, and directed me to the sofa—all while something simmered in those pale blue eyes.

I had the note he'd sent pressed between my fingers. "You said it was urgent."

His broad smile and the emergence of a dimple only added to my confusion. He shook his head as he ran a finger across my hand. "A bit of a stretch, I'll admit, but worth it at any rate."

I cocked my eyebrows. "You mean I left a perfectly good novel for nothing?"

"I certainly hope not." He inched closer on the sofa, grinning to himself. "Either way, I fully intend to make it up to you."

I noticed his gaze drifting dangerously to my mouth, and I pulled away. Had he been drinking? I stood and retreated to the bow window, all the while chastising myself. Why on earth had I dispensed with Mrs. Fitzroy's company in order to meet Mr. Montague alone? What a fool I was.

All too quickly he drew up beside me, leaning rakishly against the window casement, his hair tussled just so by his artful hand. He watched me a long moment before breaking the mounting silence. "I must know what you think of me, Mrs. Pembroke."

Though I expected some such instigation on his part, the merest hint of vulnerability in his words surprised me. I folded my hands at my waist. "I find you an amiable conversationalist, too handsome for your own good, and polished in the ways of the world. Yet at the same time, I'm not certain I know the real you at all."

He laughed beneath his breath. "The real me? An existential ideal indeed." He edged in closer and I didn't move, not this time. If we were to make a go of this, I had to be open to more.

"I've heard the rumors." I paused, waiting.

He ran his hand down his chin. "If you mean to imply that I'm wholly ignorant of a certain deficiency of character which has been revealed over the last few days, you'd be much mistaken. My past conquests are just that—in my past. This is all so different." He reached out slowly and ran his finger through a loose curl at the nape of my neck. "I've never been more aware of what I want, nor have I desired anything this strongly before. It's a startling sensation, I assure you."

A shiver skirted across my shoulders as my heart beat a pattern of retreat. "You mean the inheritance?"

A well-timed pause preceded his whispered, "Not at all." Then he angled to face me, his gaze deepening. Carefully, he ran his finger down the length of my exposed arm before he propped his hand against the window casement over my shoulder. "You know very well I mean you."

We were so terribly close, his breath tickling the small hairs at the edge of my coiffure. All while an equally cold wave of confusion flooded my senses. Why was such an exchange so easy with Mr. Hawkins and so uncomfortable with anyone else?

Voices sounded in the hall, then footsteps. The absolute last thing I wanted was for someone to find us in such an intimate pose. I made a move to escape his embrace, but he'd cornered me too well in the crook of the bow window.

Unfortunately, his intentions were growing clearer by the second. Mr. Montague intended to overwhelm my better judgment or put Mr. Lymington in his place. Mr. Montague thought me a silly little mouse he could command with one touch. And perhaps he could have if I'd not already given my heart to another.

He leaned closer until his mouth was next to my ear. "You needn't fight it. We're practically betrothed, remember?"

My eyes rounded. "Please, Mr. Montague, don't—"

All at once his mouth was against mine, his lips demanding the answers he sought. Shock vibrated through my body, pinning me in place as he wrapped his arms around me, deepening the connection. I'd only kissed one man in my lifetime, and it had been exceedingly chaste, so detached was my late husband.

My emotions exploded first one direction then the next, the sensation overwhelming—but how to respond to such an assault? The rough hairs on Mr. Montague's cheeks scraped against my face. The scent of his pomade mixed with his breath. His body was lean, his hands eager and rather free. Heavens, I knew quite well I wasn't supposed to open my eyes in such a telling moment, but I couldn't help myself. I saw the edge of his hairline then the folds of his ears.

Here I was kissing the cad of Kent, and all I could think was . . . *This is it?* Was this what I'd wondered about since first meeting him? I felt—nothing. No, not nothing. It was more like revulsion.

He must have felt my evasion as his hand found the small of my back, drawing me closer still. He actually thought himself so skilled a lover that I couldn't possibly be indifferent.

I was forced to thrust him backward. "You forget yourself, sir!"

I'd spoken far more harshly than I'd intended, but it wasn't until I caught sight of Mr. Hawkins over Mr. Montague's shoulder that I regretted the hasty words.

Mr. Hawkins was as still as a statue, his eyes narrow, his jaw tight.

He gave me one hard questioning look before he stalked straight through the drawing room door and across the rug. Without so much as a solitary word to my ardent suitor, he clenched Mr. Montague's shoulder and spun him to face him. Silence engulfed the room as a charged second ticked away on the clock in the corner.

All it took was one smirk from Mr. Montague and Mr. Hawkins's emotions snapped. His fist flew up with such force it caught Mr. Montague unaware seconds before it slammed into his grinning face.

Mr. Montague staggered backward, clutching his chin. "What the devil?" Though he'd spit out the question as if he demanded an answer, he gave no time for one as he jerked his jacket back into place and assessed the bloodstain on his lapel. "I should call you out for this, Hawkins. If only you were not so far beneath me."

Mr. Hawkins arched an eyebrow but gave no response.

Mr. Montague cast a probing glare at me, then back at Mr. Hawkins, his finger ticking in the air between us. "Ah, so this is the way of it then?" He tutted as he shook his head. "I was right. No wonder you've been so pettish with me . . . what with your solicitor harboring a tender for you." He gave a light chuckle, but it wasn't a pleasant one.

Mr. Hawkins shied away from the uncomfortable insinuation, retreating to the safety of the fireplace where he propped his arm on the mantel. "Don't be ridiculous. I'm only in residence to offer my professional services to Mrs. Pembroke, nothing more."

Mr. Montague crossed his arms. "If that is how you wish to play it, Hawkins, so be it. But I daresay your pitiful withdrawal severely reduces my challenge." He angled to face me and took a bow. "Good day, Mrs. Pembroke. I'm afraid I must leave you at present as I must rid myself of this sullied jacket." A sideways glance at Mr. Hawkins. "We shall talk again quite soon."

Mr. Hawkins's attention remained fixed on the fire until the sound of Mr. Montague's footsteps could no longer be heard and we were alone. Finally he stole a peek over his shoulder. "I do apologize for such a rash action. I thought—"

"You thought quite right, although I did have the gentleman in hand."

He gave me a drawn smile, but it was brief. "I'm sure you did."

"Your hand . . ." I hurried over to him, the heat of the flames lapping over a host of unsettled nerves and the waves of dreaded excitement that still pulsed through my body. "You've injured it."

He cast an apathetic look at his right hand. A red stain had formed on his glove. He shrugged. "Courtesy of Mr. Montague's lip, I suspect."

I leaned in to take a closer look. "No, that blood is definitely seeping from the inside. Let's have it off."

"I'm sure my valet—"

"Now, if you please."

He gave me a knowing glare. "Are you always this demanding?"

"Only when gentlemen turn drawing rooms into boxing salons."

"Touché." He tugged his glove from his fingers, one by one, his eyes never leaving my face. "When I saw that man pawing at you . . ."

"I will admit that Mr. Montague was rather forceful, but— Oh! This looks awful."

"Nonsense." He held out his hand to get a better view of it. "Now I shall have a matching pair."

"Don't you dare kid at such a moment. This should be cleaned up and straightaway. Does it pain you?" I turned to tug the embroidered bell rope for Andrews.

"Not much, only a tingle. I suppose I caught the cad with his mouth open and snagged a tooth with my knuckle."

"Regardless, it should be washed and dressed. You're not leaving until I've done so." I led him over to a winged chair. "Care for a drink?"

His eyes widened. "What on earth do you have planned that you need an inebriated patient for?"

"Don't be absurd." I caught his wide smile and my own sprang to life. "You know quite well I'm only offering it for your refreshment."

"Then by all means."

Andrews entered the room as I was pouring Mr. Hawkins a glass, and I sent him for supplies. When I turned back to Mr. Hawkins, a curious expression greeted me.

He rested his hand on the armrest. "I'm afraid I have something to confess."

I settled his drink on the table beside his chair and took a seat in the opposing one.

"I knew you were in here with Mr. Montague. I had just left Major Balfour in the conservatory."

"Major Balfour?"

"It seems this little tête-à-tête was his idea."

I stopped short. "His idea?"

"He mentioned that Mr. Montague stumbled upon a private conversation between him and Mrs. Fitzroy. They handled it badly and encouraged Mr. Montague not to waste any more time where you were concerned. There was a great deal of worry that he might have misunderstood their meaning, which is precisely what happened in the end. I set off at once, and when I found him . . . Well, he was already with you."

I clasped my hands in my lap. "I don't know why everyone seems to think my future is their business."

He took a drink, all the while watching me over the rim of his glass. "The meddling comes from the heart. We all simply want the best for you."

"I know that. I just—"

Andrews returned with a silver platter, which he set on a small table beside me before leaving the room. At the center of the medical supplies sat a bowl of water and dressings for bandages as well as a sponge soaked in vinegar. I tugged the table closer to Mr. Hawkins's chair and knelt at his side.

"Your hand, if you please, sir."

"It's just a scratch."

"Which I don't want turning putrid." I bit my lip. "It is not simply passing interest that spurs my actions, sir. I need you to manage this horrid situation I find myself in until I've made my decision at last."

He gave me a wary look as I settled his hand on mine and tugged back his jacket sleeve. He sighed. "I can have a replacement solicitor sent from my office if you think it best. He would arrive within the next few days. I daresay Mr. Montague will demand my exit at this point anyway."

I ran the wet cloth over his battered knuckles. "You are not employed by Mr. Montague. You are employed by me, and I have no intention of letting you leave at present." His hand felt slightly rough but warm and so utterly comfortable against mine. I couldn't stop a spark of nerves, nor my heart from climbing into my throat. "After all, we have not solved the murder of Mr. Cluett or found the document Henry mentioned. How could I manage here without you?"

His fingers curled so softly around mine that I wondered if he'd even moved them. "I'll not depart Moorington Cross unless you specifically ask me to."

I returned the cloth to the bowl and retrieved the sponge. "Then we are settled on that score, for I shall do no such thing."

Like a summer storm gathering out of nowhere in a blue sky, a darkness crept into his brown eyes. When he finally strung enough words together to speak, his voice sounded pained. "I don't know if it's ever going to go away."

My hand stilled. "What?"

He glanced up and my chest tightened.

Slowly, he shook his head. "This thing between us. I—"

My hand must have stiffened because he looked down.

"Forgive me. I never should have spoken so freely. Sometimes my tongue comes unhinged."

I grabbed a fresh cloth to wrap around the wound, and I daresay we both saw my fingers quiver.

He steadied my hand with his own. "Amelia, please don't spend a single minute worrying about what I think or feel. I know my place. I always have. I'll not get in the way. In the end there's no other choice for you but Mr. Lymington or Mr. Montague."

My throat felt swollen, my tongue thick with words I couldn't say. I'd always been the dutiful ward, the proper friend, the good patient. I sank back into that old familiar heartache, looking anywhere but at Mr. Hawkins, and gave him the answer he was waiting for.

"No, there isn't."

That night the walls of my room closed in around me. Though Chauncey did his best to provide some level of comfort and my maid snored from her position on the trundle bed, I found I could not imagine away the stark realities of the past week. I had twenty days to make a final decision between Mr. Montague and Mr. Lymington, and I'd never been more confused.

I pushed another carrot in front of Chauncey as my two suitors tumbled through my mind.

Mr. Lymington had been nothing but taciturn and distant, a thinker and doer, but not a partner in life. If I chose him, he would no doubt provide for me financially. He was already well on his way to doing that, but I could also see the truth of such a future stretching out before me where the two of us would live like strangers, nothing more. Granted, Mrs. Fitzroy would be welcome in our home—anything to keep me busy and away from my husband.

Yet as I sat there in the darkness of my bedchamber, all I could think of was the feel of Mr. Hawkins's hand wrapped around mine, the layered intimacy in his gaze, the subtle beat of my heart. He was everything I'd ever dreamed of and more, yet I could not even consider him.

I gripped the coverlet as one by one those depending on me came to mind: Miss Seton, Mr. Lymington, Mr. Montague, Mrs. Fitzroy, Major Balfour, Henry. They would all be affected by such a reckless choice on my part, and the resulting devastation would be too much for me to bear.

I closed my eyes, focusing on my duty. It had to be Mr. Lymington or Mr. Montague. I had no other choice.

Mr. Montague—the cad was passionate all right and handsome and complicated. I did believe him when he said he was searching for a way to fill his heart, but the ardor wrought about in his company was solely one-sided. I knew that now, completely. How long would it be before his interest faded as well? And then what?

I wiped my eyes with the back of my hand. And then there was Mr. Cluett. He'd been like a father to me. He'd picked me up in my darkest hour, helped me find my way. And to provide for my future, he'd offered up his two illegitimate sons for me to pick between. Was I not bound to him by an invisible debt?

Conversations I'd had with Mr. Cluett bubbled to the surface. We'd spoken often of marriage for me. I'd been determined at the time to find complete independence if an offer ever came my way again. I'd been emphatic about that in our exchanges. I suppose that was why he'd given me a choice. How different I felt now. Likewise, how little I knew of myself at the time. One smile from Mr. Hawkins and everything had changed. I wanted more. Who was I kidding? I wanted it all.

But could I even believe what I was sure I knew about Mr. Cluett? Miss Parsons's chilling warning had not left my mind since the moment she'd said it. Was my dear friend capable of murder after all? Had he taken his own brother's life years ago to secure his own financial freedom? I shook my head. The person I knew could not have committed such a terrible crime.

And then, who killed Mr. Cluett? A fiend connected somehow with his late brother? Possibly. Or not. None of it made any sense.

All my searching and probing had turned up nothing. Even the secret passageway remained elusive; the document a figment of Henry's imagination.

Henry. I ran my hand down my face.

I was at a complete standstill regarding what had turned out to be naught more than a fledgling investigation. How could I have deluded myself into thinking Mr. Hawkins and I were qualified to expose a murderer? Moreover, how had I allowed myself to become so distracted by my forbidden love affair that I'd not taken my position more seriously? Someone in this house wanted me dead, and I hadn't the least clue who it was.

CHAPTER 24

A scratch at my bedchamber door forced me to my senses. I thrust myself into a sitting position, my heart crawling unbidden into my throat. As it had so many nights before, sleep remained unattainable—every noise a fresh instigator of frazzled nerves.

Though I had little intention of waking my maid, who'd fallen deeply asleep quite quickly, her presence on the trundle bed eased some of my mounting anxiety. And really, was I fooling myself? What murderer made his presence known before moving in for the kill?

The scratch sounded again. It was subtle, careful even, as if the visitor had come for a purpose. My curiosity piqued, I slipped from the warm comfort of my bed and slung on my robe, which I'd tossed across the settee, before making my way to the door. In the looking glass on my dresser, I caught a glimpse of my braided hair illuminated by the moonlight as I crossed the rug.

Standing before the door, I rested my fingers on the latch, my mind alight with who my late-night visitor could possibly be. Miss Seton, perhaps? I could just see her gnarled little finger producing such a pitiful scratch.

I cleared my throat. "Who is it?"

"Me."

The whispered voice was indistinguishable but calm. I pulled in a tight breath and released the lock, opening the door but a crack as I planted my foot firmly against its back side, a vase of flowers within easy reach. I squinted into the glow emanating from a candle, but it took me only a second to recognize my intruder.

I wrapped my robe a bit tighter around my waist. "What on earth are you doing here? You scared me half to death."

Mr. Hawkins's smile fell. "I had no intention . . . Believe me, a great deal of thought went into how I must knock . . ."

"Really? And you decided on the insipid scratch of a scullery maid?"

He stole a wild glance at his hand. "Is that what it sounded like? I was going more for a friendly solicitor who would rather not wake the maid I forced to sleep on a trundle in your room."

I crossed my arms. "But you were more than happy to wake *me*?" Wretch.

"Perfectly." His smile returned, warming his eyes. "I had a thought." A coy look as he reached out and touched the end of my braid. "I daresay you've not been asleep as of yet. Everything still in place. Maybe I don't deserve a set-down at all."

I tossed my braid over my shoulder, fighting a laugh. "You know quite well that is neither here nor there. For all you know I could sleep quite serenely."

"Serene indeed." His smile widened. "You conveniently forget I found you in the library doing just the opposite."

I opened my mouth, a retort hot on my tongue, but my maid's steady breathing shifted. Mr. Hawkins lightly tugged me into the hall and closed the door silently behind me. "My apologies, but I don't want a third person joining our little escapade tonight."

"Escapade?"

"Shh." He pressed his first finger to his lips. "Do you have your keys?"

I patted my robe pocket. "Well, yes."

"Good. Leave a quick note for your maid just in case she wakes, then come with me." He motioned down the hall with his chin.

I had no choice but to do as he asked, tightening the ribbons on my robe as I left the room and followed him. We moved quickly through the shadowed corridors before he finally cast a glance back at me and smiled. He reached down to secure my hand in his, to guide me through the darkness—as any gentleman should. Yet at the top of the stairs something occurred, something I wasn't fully prepared for.

Seamlessly, comfortably, our bare fingers slid together, one after the other, until fully entwined.

A shiver raced up my arm, and I nearly stumbled, but he only pulled me closer, leading me down the steps without a word. His touch was gentle but assured. He simply held on to me like he had every right to do so.

My mind spun, deliciously so. But what had changed?

The darkness must have made him bold, as it had me, the strange subtlety of night like a fevered dream. I attempted to steady my breath, but I couldn't seem to do so, lost as I was in the moment, driven by the truth pounding away in my heart.

I swallowed hard. Could I not enjoy some part of this wonderful man while I still had the chance to do so?

How Mr. Hawkins knew his way through the blackened halls with little more than a solitary candle, I'll never know, but we came upon the large mahogany doors nonetheless.

We stood before them in silence for a breathless moment before he released my hand and turned to face me. "I need the key."

A slight chill accompanied his words. "Why are we at the east wing?"

He set the candle on a small side table and blew it out before facing me, resting his hands on my upper arms. "This is the only place in the house we've not searched for the secret passageway or the document. We both know Miss Seton is hiding something, and after what Henry said"—he took a long look at the closed doors—"maybe she's right about the damage. The crossbeams did look pretty unstable to me, but not at risk of imminent failure, not without some degree of help. I daresay it would take a bit of force to bring the whole thing down."

"But didn't we decide it was best to wait until daylight?"

"We did, but I don't want anyone to know what we're up to, not this time. If we are lucky enough to find a passageway—or even better, the document itself—whatever it is must stay between you and me."

I narrowed my eyes. "You think you've figured something out?"

"Not entirely, but hopefully something, yes. The key now, if you please."

I fished the ring of keys from my pocket and passed it into his outstretched hand, then waited as he unlocked the door, my mind still churning.

He started to advance through the opening, but I grasped his arm. "What is it? What do you think you are looking for?"

He let out a tight breath. "I'm not certain what I'll find, but I need to get another look at that desk in Mr. Cluett's brother's room."

My gaze slid sideways. "You think there may be another hidden drawer."

"Exactly." He motioned to the side. "I think it best for you to wait here."

"I don't—"

"Like I said before, no one must know we've been inside again, not Miss Seton or Andrews. I'll need a lookout if we're to be safe, and I don't particularly wish to lead you into danger. Wait here and if you hear the least sound coming from anywhere in the house—a pop, a creak, even a ghost's footsteps, alert me at once." He directed me against the wall, his voice a tense whisper. "Slip into the shadows beside the drapes. No one will have any idea of your presence. I won't be long, I promise. Just a quick look at the desk, then I'll be back out. I won't be foolish. I promise."

"All right."

I felt him step back, but he must have waited a moment to ensure

I was completely hidden, as I heard little for several seconds. Then at last the worn, damaged flooring of the east wing moaned as he crept through the door and closed it behind him.

I tipped my head against the cold wall and held my breath. What if he did find something in that desk? What if it changed the current will?

A smile curved my lips, but I had little time to enjoy such a thought. A dull, eerie *thump* met my ears, which was followed all too quickly by the terrible sound of something collapsing onto the floor.

Frozen, I searched back and forth, probing the folds of darkness around me, my heart pumping faster each second. Then it hit me. Whatever I'd heard had come from the other side of the door, somewhere within the depths of the east wing.

Silence buzzed in my ears—no footsteps, no movement. The world had fallen utterly still.

My hands were shaking as I stood there unsure what to do, the strange thump echoing over and over again in my mind. What had I heard? Mr. Hawkins may very well need my help. I took three faltering steps forward, the hall empty around me, until I reached the wing door and opened it.

"Mr. Hawkins?" I called out breathlessly, but there was no answer.

He'd been completely swallowed up by the dank air and menacing shadows. I tried again, a little louder this time, inching forward as I squinted into the gloom.

Nothing.

I stopped short, my hand retreating to my mouth. The sound had been almost like . . .

I pushed forward, driven by a sudden and uncontrollable panic. Where was he? Wildly, I scoured the floor around the entrance, my ears attuned to the smallest noise, before I clambered forward. I kept a grasp on the wainscoting, utilizing it as a guide back to the lonely bedchamber I'd seen before.

Every hair on my arms sprang to attention, my skin alive with fear. Without warning, I reached a sudden edge to the wall and my fingers dipped inward. I sucked in a quick breath. I'd reached the bedchamber. Images of Mr. Cluett's lifeless body plagued my mind, dulling my senses, feeding my dread.

My feet felt heavy, but I kept pressing forward. The room was dimly lit as moonlight poured in through two small windows at the back, painting a silver-squared pattern across the bed and then onto the floor.

The floor!

At the corner of the muted light lay Mr. Hawkins's motionless form. A strangled cry escaped as I fell onto my knees, my hands desperate to deny what I saw right in front of me.

"Mr. Hawkins." It took some effort, but I rolled him to the side.

I touched his cheek then his chest. He was unconscious but quite warm, his heart gloriously beating beneath my fingertips. Thank God! I watched as the moonlight glinted off his watch fob with each of his steady breaths.

"You maddening, darling man. How dare you come in here all alone." I combed the shadows around us once again, searching the gloom for what had hit him. "What on earth would I do without you?"

I tapped his cheek, gently shook his shoulder, praying he would rouse.

Finally his eyes blinked open as his hand retreated to the back of his head. "What happened?"

Relief washed over me. "I haven't the least idea. I heard a crash. I came rushing in. Are you injured?"

He looked dazed, his eyes narrowing. "Someone or something hit me on the back of my head." He moved his hand into the beam of moonlight, illuminating a trail of blood dripping down his fingers.

"You're hurt. I shall send for Andrews at once."

I jumped to my feet, but the slam of a door in the distance stopped me cold, followed all too quickly by the telltale *click* of a lock. Eyes wide, I stared back at Mr. Hawkins. Someone *had* been in the east wing with us. Moreover, they had just . . .

"Wait."

I'd already started for the door, a ball of fear growing ever larger in my gut. I staggered across the dark hall, my arms thrust out in front of me. Soon enough, my fingers revealed the truth I'd already known. The large mahogany doors that separated the east wing from the rest of the house had been locked tight.

Mr. Hawkins and I were trapped.

CHAPTER 25

Quietly, carefully, I ripped the fabric from the bottom of my shift while Mr. Hawkins dabbed at his head wound with the edge of a holland cover we'd been using to staunch the blood.

A look at me and he tilted his head into the moonlight. "I do believe the oozing is waning some."

"Thank goodness, but you still need a proper bandage." Furious at the reality of our current situation, I sent my gaze rambling over the remains of the bleak room. "Particularly if we're to be trapped in here all night."

I wrestled a clean handkerchief from my pocket, my hand quivering, and eyed the gash for sizing before folding it to fit. "This shall do much better for now." Moving in close, I pressed the cloth firmly but cautiously against the wound, then wrapped the ripped cording around his head to hold it in place. "Have you the strength to hold this while I tie it off?"

A chuckle. "I believe I can manage that." His laugh was short-lived, however, as he flinched the moment we exchanged pressure on the makeshift bandage.

He must have heard my responding gasp because he resurrected a smile at once. "I assure you, Amelia, this curst wound is more of a nuisance than anything else. No need for apprehension."

"No?" I met his strained eyes. "You, sir, should be tucked in your bed under the care of a doctor right now, not lying on the floor in this dusty, dilapidated section of the house fit only for ghosts and goblins."

At the imaginary count of three in my head, I released the knot, and to my great relief, my creation held. "Well, at least the wound is covered for now."

I slumped back onto the bedchamber floor at his side and let out a tight breath. "What I don't understand is who could have known we were coming down here in the first place. I saw no one in the hall. And your injury—surely such a havey-cavey assault was not a botched attempt on your life. If the person you encountered really meant to put an end to you, they would have been far more creative than this. Of course, imprisoning us in here for the night does put you at some level of risk."

"Of a devilish headache, yes, but no more than that."

A moment of comfortable silence passed before I felt his arm snake carefully across my shoulders in the darkness, tucking me in beside him along the wall.

My eyes snapped open, my heart a thundering mess. The sudden intimacy was hardly expected, yet equally comfortable. How strange that his embrace felt so natural, the perfect balm for my tattered nerves.

Belatedly, almost thoughtfully, he rested his hand down onto my arm. "You're in the right of it, of course. Goodness knows I was nothing but shocked when I felt the blow; however, I'm also fairly certain it was me who stumbled upon our little fiend, not the other way around. He probably locked the door simply to keep us from following him." A light shrug. "Granted, there's no way to know. What's done is done at any rate. And as for the doctor you think necessary, I can't imagine the man would have any real instructions beyond rest, which is exactly what I plan to do until we can get the deuce out of here."

I gathered my knees against my chest and pulled them in tight beneath the folds of my gown, dark thoughts threatening to tip the balance of my mind. "You're probably right, and he's long gone now . . . the rascal."

I leaned my chin on my folded arms as a decided chill roamed the warped floorboards and crawled up my arms and legs. The warmth of Mr. Hawkins's side so close to mine only proved to muddle my thoughts.

We sat like that for some time before I broke the growing silence. "If only the windows weren't rusted shut, I think I might be able to wriggle through one of the openings."

He side-eyed me for a moment. "I don't think even you are small enough for such a feat."

"Am I not?" I laughed as I faced him. "You might be surprised by my hidden talents, sir. I'll have you know I once fit through a rounded barn vent no bigger than a foot across. Given, I was a child at the time, but not all that much smaller than I am now."

I felt rather than saw his smile, the subtle shift of his arm, the shadowed dip of his head, and my heart turned. Goodness, how easy it was to be alone with him. No, not easy, although that was certainly a part of the attraction—*intoxicating* would be the better word.

I picked at the wrinkles in my robe, smoothing the muslin into place over my legs. "I don't suppose it would be any use to try screaming again."

Mr. Hawkins lifted his hand, his fingers brushing back into place against my arm. "Clearly no one can hear us down here. I'm afraid we're in for the night or at least until the servants come to light the fires. That's only a few short hours from now. We shall simply have to be patient until someone is in earshot. What did you leave in the note for your maid?"

"I simply told her I'd left my bedchamber with an escort, and I would return shortly. I daresay she won't find the letter till morning and assume easily enough that I left then."

"Good."

I stared despairingly over the shadowy room. "Your injury brings our search of the east wing to an end—at least for tonight."

He winced. "Unfortunately, it does. I couldn't possibly move, not with this headache."

"And I have no intention of leaving your side."

"Thank you." He covered a yawn before repositioning his head against the wall, his eyelids drifting closed.

I watched him a moment, my heart warming at the sight before it stilled. "Mr. Hawkins . . . you mustn't." I gripped his arm, and his eyes blinked open.

Suddenly conscious of the depth of his gaze, I went on. "You mustn't go to sleep. I-I don't remember all the details, but several years ago my guardian Mr. Stanley hit his head on a tree branch while riding. The doctor who saw to his care advised us to keep him conscious, at least for the first few hours."

"Conscious, you say . . ."

The room lapsed into silence and I was forced to nudge his side. "Are you still awake?"

"Hmm?" He ran his hand down his face, his movements a bit unsteady. "I will confess to being uncommonly sleepy."

I drew up onto my knees and touched his face. His forehead, his eyelids, his cheeks, everything scrunched together in response.

"You must indeed be concussed, which means no sleep for you tonight, sir."

He tried a smile, then thought better of it. "And how exactly do you propose I do that when I can barely hold my eyes open at present?"

I thought for a moment. "Easy. I shall talk to you and prod you from time to time if it becomes necessary. And don't look at me like that. I can be a nuisance if required."

"Only when required?"

I popped his arm. "Have you a better idea then? I haven't even smelling salts to wave under your nose."

"No ideas at present, I'm afraid." He flicked his fingers, a lazy air about his movements. "Talk on, Aristotle."

My lips twitched. "Aristotle indeed. I have no intention of bloviating to you all night if that is what you expect. That really would put you to sleep. No, I think I shall ask you questions. That way I know for sure you are awake—assuming your headache is not too great to answer them."

His eyes slipped closed for a brief moment. "It is a bit stabbing at present, but not too severe." Then he shot me a sideways glance. "I will endeavor to answer whatever questions you deem necessary. However, that look in your eyes does put me a bit on edge."

"Good." I pursed my lips. "But where to begin? There is a great deal to uncover about the mysterious Mr. Ewan Hawkins."

I saw a flash of a grin in the moonlight. "As you say."

Of course, all manner of unsuitable questions instantly flitted through my mind: Had he ever gone to London for the season, or even worse, had he ever been in love? Relieved he could no more see the flush filling my cheeks than I could the subtleties to his wry expression, I latched onto the first innocuous idea that came into my head. "Will you tell me about your interest in poetry? What is it that makes you appreciate it so much?"

Though I'd come to the idea on a whim, something about the question altered the feel of the room. Mr. Hawkins's playfulness vanished; his expression turned far more serious.

He remained quiet a long moment, and I was just about to nudge him when his gaze flicked up to meet mine—searching, hoping, the intimate gleam of vulnerability so evident in his eyes. "How to answer such a question?" A thoughtful pause. "Poetry has been a part of me for some time. I suppose it provided me a unique doorway when I needed it most."

He eased himself forward, rested his elbows on his legs, and lowered his voice. "The power of verse has always been more than mere words for me. It is thoughts, feelings, hopes, and dreams—an art given to us by God. Poetry in its many forms assisted me in combing through quite a bit of cloudy emotions over the years, both joyful and difficult. Superior verse has many layers of thought. Psalms, Proverbs, Song of Solomon—really a good portion of the Bible is poetry."

He sounded almost hopeful as his eyes hazed over and he slipped into the comfort of recitation. "'Set me as a seal upon thine heart, as a seal upon thine arm: for love is strong as death; jealousy is cruel as the grave: the coals thereof are coals of fire, which hath a most vehement flame.'" Belatedly he smiled over at me. "Beautiful and stirring, is it not?"

"Song of Solomon?"

He nodded.

"You once told me E. H. Radcliff was a favorite poet of yours. Have you one of his poems at the ready?"

A curious look crossed his face as he smiled down at his lap. "No, not at present at least."

It was in that careful moment that the mood altered once again, turning rather intimate and guarded, like I'd wandered by accident into the private chamber of the master of the house.

I grappled for a way back to the levity we'd shared moments before. Of course, I ended up rambling without even considering my words. "I daresay Mr. Montague prefers Byron to any other poet. He quoted me several lines from 'She Walks in Beauty' the other day— quite possibly the only lines he's ever committed to memory. But I will admit, it wasn't entirely ineffective."

Mr. Hawkins nodded then stilled, his expression somewhat somber. He turned to the windows, his hands unsettled on his knees, before eventually angling his gaze back to his lap, hesitation lining each movement.

A light shake of his head, more for himself than me, before he finally glanced up. "I can only assume I must be suffering from a moment of madness or I've been far more affected by my injury than I originally thought"—his fingers worried the seam of his breaches—"emboldened at the very least, but there is something I feel compelled to ask you."

He was usually so collected, so calm, the tone of his voice one of steady reassurance. I closed my eyes for a quick moment to secure my own. Why did everything feel so suddenly different between us? I couldn't help but examine his shadowed face for what lay buried beneath such a cryptic statement. Yet I found no answer beyond the tingle of my skin and the aching crescendo of my heart. "Yes? Go on."

"What if . . ." He took a long, slow breath as he leaned in close, a lock of his blond hair dipping onto his forehead. "Do you think it possible that for one exceptional night we might pretend Mr. Cluett's will doesn't exist? That I'm not your solicitor and there are no infinitely superior gentlemen waiting upstairs to take your hand . . . That no one else exists in the world but us?"

The sheer boldness of his question sent a wave of shock through my body. I hardly knew how to respond, let alone look him in the eye. "The intruder must have hit your head a great deal harder than I thought, Mr. Hawkins."

"Please, won't you call me Ewan at last? And I'm perfectly serious. Why shouldn't we enjoy a singular night away from all that plagues us? One only for you and me—no one else."

Was it a rhetorical question, or did he actually desire an answer?

It seemed a long time till he spoke again, his expression still maddeningly unreadable. "After all, other than your quick wit and infectious personality, I really don't know all that much about you. I-I'd like to, and I don't mean as your solicitor. I mean as someone who cares a great deal about you." He propped up his right leg and rested his arm on his knee. "Take your past, for example. I can't even comprehend how difficult all those years must have been for you. I yearn to know what made you, well, you."

I averted my gaze to my lap, arrested not only by the kindness in his voice but also by the longing tucked so neatly in his words. Why couldn't we have one night for us? No one would ever know what we'd spoken of, what personal things we shared.

My throat felt thick. I did want him to know about all of me, and I about him. I swallowed hard. "There were moments of happiness in my childhood, particularly early on. I do remember quite fondly an uncle of mine, Uncle William, whom I knew and loved. He was always so jovial, so happy. I remember how his whole body would shake with pleasure when he laughed." I chuckled to myself. "He was quite thick about the middle, you see." My uncle's once familiar scent of tobacco and soap came to mind, and I closed my eyes for a brief second. "I was only five years old when he left England to return to France. I never saw him again, but I miss him still."

I let out a breath. "The rest, I'm afraid, is not all that pretty to speak of. As an undesirable ward, I spent a good portion of my formative years dreaming of being somewhere else." I paused. "No, that's not exactly truthful. I dreamed of being *somebody* else." My eyes found his. "Please don't think in any way I was ungrateful to the people who took me in; my situation was simply complicated. I was not only a sick child but a stranger as well. I thought marriage with Mr. Pembroke would be my escape from all that." I gave him a listless smile. "I was wrong, of course. Cluett's Mesmeric Hospital turned out to be the only place I've ever lived where I felt safe and wanted."

"And now that has been ripped away from you as well."

"Yes, it has."

"And Mr. Pembroke? I cannot help but feel you've not told me about him fully."

My fingers curled into a fist around a fold of my skirt. "You were right. He had a decided temper, and he struck me more than once. I had more spells during that frightening week in his house than I'd had in some time."

His voice was tight with emotion. "I'm so sorry, Amelia."

"I don't really know the whole of the arrangement my late husband had with my guardian, only I think it had something to do with a debt of honor. I did have a little money from my parents in a dowry and he wanted a young, healthy wife for his own pleasures."

"You've been treated ill by so many men in your life. I can see why you were angry after you learned about Cluett's will."

"A year ago, when I heard the news that Mr. Pembroke had fallen from his horse and died, I felt relief. I don't mean to be unchristian about death, but I finally felt free. I could make decisions for myself. I had a little money from the jointure, and I was determined to spend it on getting better so I could support myself."

He sighed. "Nothing has gone as planned, has it?"

As if the house itself wished to voice agreement, a sudden swell of wind rattled the windowpanes while long shadows shifted ominously over the otherwise motionless room.

I cannot say what came over me, what possessed me to touch him in just that way—maybe it was the emotive silence or the palpable whisper of genuine connection. But for the first time in my life, I forgot who I was and what was expected of me. I placed my hand into his of my own volition. The rush of warmth was instantaneous and so terribly welcome as his fingers responded in kind, tightening around mine.

I wished I could make out the intricacies of his face more clearly as the moon danced in and out of a cloudy sky beyond the windows, but I could see his eyes, the brilliant depths, the kindness, the longing—for it perfectly mirrored my own. "I don't know what I would have done if it hadn't been you who walked into Mr. Cluett's office that day."

He watched me a long moment before responding. "I don't think I even fully realized it until now—I'm the one who is glad to have found *you*." He squeezed my hand, then released it to cradle his own left hand. "I imagine you've heard the details of my tragic past, about my years in the workhouse in London as a child. It seems everyone has these days."

I bit my lip. I did know his story because I'd learned of it the day I eavesdropped behind the hedgerows, but I had no intention of revealing my indiscretion at present. I simply nodded him on.

"I won't lie. My disfigurement has found a way to haunt me at various stages of my life, but the reality of life can be quite complicated. I don't know how to describe it really. Sometimes I hate even to think about my hand, but other times it's quite different. I'm thankful for perspective. I've used my condition to push myself forward, to reach farther than I might have otherwise. These scars"—he stared long and hard at his curved fingers—"are just that. Scars. Nothing but a fold of skin here, a misshapen bone there.

"I came to realize that the inconvenience of a faulty hand was not the issue, not for me at least. I had been assigning blame that I should have laid squarely at the feet of my mother's abandonment, a hurt that runs far deeper than a simple flesh wound." He paused, then sounded almost breathless as he finished. "I don't think I've ever told anyone that."

His eyes softened as he turned to look at me. "Oh, Amelia, you have no idea how much we have in common. I . . . I've simply never met anyone like you."

Every muscle in my body seemed to relax one by one, even the stubborn ones that never would do so. Ewan Hawkins was right. The two of us were different in many ways, but we'd also walked such similar life paths. It was remarkable really. I never thought I'd find someone who could possibly understand the wretched depths of my isolation and fear.

All of a sudden I wasn't certain where to put my hands—on my lap or back with his. "Nor I, you."

A smile snuck onto his face, but it lasted only a second as he plunged his fingers through his hair, a sense of urgency to his movements. "Yet even as I sit here, proposing we pretend away the all too real and pressing world, I find I still cannot say what I feel. I'm bound by honor—"

"We promised not to talk about the will, remember?"

"It was a nice idea, wasn't it?" He shook his head. "But I was a fool to suggest such a notion in the first place. Some things can never be imagined away. That curst document plagues me more every day. Taints every good and decent thought, reminding me over and over again of obligations I cannot help but despise. I know very well I have no choice in the matter."

I ran the edge of my skirt through my fingers. "Neither of us does. If only—"

"I'm so utterly sorry." He pressed the bridge of his nose. "I've put my mind to finding a way out of this for you. Believe me, that will is both legal and binding. You have no alternative than to follow what Mr. Cluett intended for you."

A quiver wriggled up my back like an icy spider, and I tried in vain to shake away the chill.

"You're cold?" Without waiting for my answer, Ewan thrust his jacket from his shoulders and wrapped it around mine, then settled in once again at my side, defeat still so clearly between us. We were trapped in every way.

The scent of Ewan's pomade met my nose as I stared blankly at the darkened wall in front of me. "I'm not cold exactly—afraid more like."

"Of your upcoming marriage?" I felt his arm stiffen at my side. "Of your pitiful choices?"

"Of being alone, which can happen just as easily with or without a husband. Remember, I've already lived through a loveless marriage, however brief. I'm terrified of everything—being ridiculed, ignored, or worse."

Silence tainted the air between us before Ewan's voice flamed into the room. "If they so much as—" He pressed his lips together. "Believe me, I have no intention of vanishing from your life, not after you've signed the ledger at the church, or even when you've been married for twenty years. Whichever of those two gentlemen you choose, I will always stand your friend and solicitor. You need not fear ever truly being alone again."

"I-I don't know what to say." My voice came out in a choked whisper, and I forced it as close to normal as I could manage. "Granted, I do believe both of my suitors will be happy enough simply to leave me alone after the wedding. They're only here for the money, after all."

"Don't—" His hand was at my chin, urging me to look at him. He raised his eyebrows, his face so completely confident. "I won't deign to speak for the two fops upstairs, only for myself. But don't you dare underestimate your worth." He shuffled a bit closer, his eyes glinting in the moonlight. "You've a great deal to offer the world, Amelia. I see it every day."

"When I'm awake to do so—"

"Hear me out. This condition that you so obviously loathe about yourself is the same one that has made you empathetic, introspective, and, in my eyes, infinitely more desirable." He caught a loose curl of mine with his finger and tucked it behind my ear. "It's a part of you like everything else. Don't ever allow someone the ability to shame you for it, especially not the man you choose to share your life with."

He glanced down at his hand, a bend to his brow. "It's taken me a long time to understand such a simple truth: I would not be the same person I am presently without my imperfections, even my mother's rejection."

He stilled a moment as a thought took root, then spread across his face. "Yet even now I can't help but realize that I've still been hiding." His mouth fell open, and he shook his head. "I have."

"What do you mean, 'hiding'?"

His expression was incredulous. "My special glove, my tenuous position in society, all I've concentrated on for the past few years is what other people will think and say." He rubbed his forehead. "I've been avoiding even the slightest possibility of having to address my inadequacies." He attempted to straighten his bent fingers as he spoke. "What a fool I've been. Here I am preaching confidence to you when the truth is I've a great deal to learn myself."

I smiled. "I daresay we all do."

Too easily his hands were on my arms, his gaze achingly deep. I could feel his words from earlier drumming harder and harder in my mind, drawing me closer to him one inch at a time. *"One night . . . just for us."*

I was not yet engaged, nor had I made any sort of a decision. And how I loved him.

He guided me forward until I was cradled against his chest, his voice at my ear. "I promise I won't bother you again after tonight. I-I can't. I won't. But allow me this one opportunity to say I will always stand your friend should you need me."

How easy it was to relax into his embrace, so utterly safe. Even if we could only share this one timeless moment, I knew I'd not miss it for the world.

His voice dropped to a whisper. "I so desperately want you to know what's in my heart."

My throat felt thick as I closed my eyes. "You needn't say it, Ewan. I already know because it dwells in my own." My ears buzzed as his arms tightened, my pulse racing.

We held each other for what felt like an eternity before he eased back an inch. Then he trailed his fingers along my shoulders, into the back of my hair, my skin ablaze beneath his touch. There was a boyish tenderness to his movements, a respectful caution, but no less passionate, no less desirous.

He understood exactly what I meant when I lifted my head ever so slightly and our eyes met. One breathless second and his mouth was against mine, exposing the truth neither of us dared to say aloud. He cared for me, and I for him.

At first our lips were tentative, then a blessed moment of curiosity and exploration, and then he wrapped his arms around me, drawing me against him, sparking every last nerve across my skin into tiny eruptions that only heightened the intimacy between us.

I was lost—wonderfully so—in a cascade of warmth that left a delicious floating sensation and the budding desire for more. He was urgent and gentle, firm and passionate, and how terribly aware I became of my need for him, his strength and comfort.

Nothing would ever be the same for me, not my raging heart or the maddening anticipation of genuine romance. I felt it all—elation, a touch of shyness, tingling attraction, and love. Yes, love.

My head swirled as I melted into him. I would have stayed like that forever—kissing him, loving him—but I couldn't stop my thoughts from climbing to the surface, ruining every expression between us.

Yes, I'd found the person I wanted to be with for the rest of my life, but the truth was we had no hope of a future, not without injuring my dearest friends. In a few days' time, I would be forced to wed another man, to share his kisses, his embrace.

I pushed away from Ewan, cowering in the shadows of my mounting shame. It only took one look back into his eyes to know he, too, realized we'd made a terrible mistake, one we would be forced to live with for the rest of our lives.

Knowledge is power, they say, but I beg to differ. We now knew what we would be missing.

CHAPTER 26

We huddled together the length of the night—waiting, listening, hoping—conversation nearly nonexistent.

Occasionally I'd feel his hand at my hair, stroking the errant curls at the nape of my neck, reminding me that even though he was injured, he was watching over me and I was safe. I don't know when I fell asleep. I'd not meant to, but then, I'd never really had control over that aspect of my life.

Sometime in the wee hours of the morning I awoke to hear the familiar pitter-patter of my maidservant on her way to light the fires throughout the lower floor, and we were able to gain our freedom at last. It was a false freedom, however. One I could hardly find the reserves to celebrate.

Ewan was stiff and formal as he addressed my maid, then turned to assist me to my feet, his mouth pressed into a thin line.

I was slow to move as every muscle and joint screamed out in protest, but I don't think it was my achy body that weighed down my steps or whispered encouragement in my ear to linger. As I passed through those large mahogany doors, I couldn't help but glance back into the derelict east wing and relive every precious moment we'd shared within. Ewan had held me so terribly close. I could still feel his arms wrapped about me.

But that was all over now.

A beam of sunlight stretched through the hall window, bathing the carpet in its orange glow. I touched my lips. The whole night felt almost like a dream. Every last shred of intimacy wrought about by the darkness had disappeared into nothing but a memory.

Ewan was all polite consideration as he escorted me back to my room, and though he hesitated a moment as if he wished to say something, the presence of my maid ended any chance of closure between us. The look on his face betrayed his thoughts clearly enough. We would never speak of our kiss again.

He took himself off with a bow, and I knew the next time I saw him everything would return to the way it was before—a working friendship, nothing more.

My throat felt thick as I passed my maid and settled into my bed for a few hours of what could only prove to be fitful sleep. She didn't question where I'd been or what had happened. The note had apparently been enough to ease her curiosity. She must have assumed, as I'd expected, that I left my bed in the wee hours of the morning or perhaps that a widow of a certain standing could do just as she pleased. Either way, I was glad I was not forced to put words to my turbulent feelings. I wasn't even certain I could.

I slept longer and harder than I'd expected, waking hours later to hunger pains and a stiff neck. Ewan, in all likelihood, would not be about the house, not with a head wound. So I made my way downstairs to break my fast alone.

I don't know why the sight of Mr. Montague sitting before a plate of food in the parlor surprised me.

"Good morning."

I couldn't stop the heat that filled my cheeks. He settled his gaze on me in that rakish way of his, and I almost felt like he knew—that Ewan's touch had somehow left a mark.

He eyed me quizzically. "You're breaking your fast rather late today, Mrs. Pembroke."

"I suppose I am." I crossed the carpet to procure a muffin and some cold ham. Anything to escape that look. "The last few days have been exhausting."

He stood then sauntered behind me before edging his shoulder against the wall at the end of the sideboard. "I hope you don't consider me a cause of that?"

I swallowed hard. "Not at all."

"Good." A grin emerged and he motioned for the two of us to have a seat.

He was quick to scoot out my chair, and I settled in across from his half-eaten plate. He swaggered as he returned to his seat, yet as he retrieved his napkin, something of a tense vulnerability emerged about him, a stroke of concealed nervousness in his movements.

He swirled the contents of his glass before looking up. "I believe it past time we discussed the kiss, don't you?"

My heart suspended its erratic pacing with one painful squeeze, my fingers frozen on my fork. "The kiss?"

His cheeks actually flushed crimson at my halting words. "I hope you will believe me when I say I never meant to put you in such an awkward position. I was laboring under the delusion you shared my sentiments. Major Balfour seemed to suggest . . . Well . . ."

He meant *our* kiss. My muscles slowly relaxed, enabling me to move, to breathe, to think. I'd forgotten all about that.

"It is of no concern." If only he knew how true that statement was.

He angled his chin, an inquisitive twitch about his mouth. "You are too kind." The roguish demeanor returned as he gazed at me over the rim of his glass. "Will you allow me to make it up to you?"

He really was quite amiable. A cad, yes, but a likable one. Granted . . . aren't they all? I couldn't stop a small smile. "I suppose so."

In that moment of levity Ewan strolled into the room and abruptly came to a halt as if his feet had snagged on something on the floor. His eyes swung dangerously between Mr. Montague and me, a scowl on his face.

He took in a tight breath. "May I have a word with you, Mrs. Pembroke?" One more glare at Mr. Montague. "In private, if you please."

Mr. Montague chuckled, and I backed away from the table at once. "Certainly."

Ewan's steps were brisk, his posture rigid as he led me down the long hall and into the blue salon before closing the door carefully behind us.

Concerned by his strange mood and the fact he should most certainly be in bed due to his injury, I took a tentative seat as directed on a cushioned chair. Ewan, however, proceeded to pace the rug, all the while raking his hand through his hair, pausing only briefly to ensure his new bandage was still in place.

Then he stopped cold at the center of the room. "I can't, Amelia. I just can't."

I blinked. I looked around. *Can't what?*

He stared at me. "I cannot allow you to marry either of those men."

I gripped the armrest. "What do you mean?"

His hands became animated, plunging into the air. "I thought I could do it. I told myself I had to. I meant to walk away. It was the right thing to do, the noble thing to do, but, Amelia . . . oh, Amelia." He pressed his forehead. "I love you far too much to do that now. I can't let you place your future, your happiness, your very life in the hands of those men. It would be unconscionable. I've spent the last few hours in utter agony until a stark realization hit. I cannot, I will not stand by and watch you marry one of those idiots . . . not when I can do something."

My mouth fell open, my chest a muddied mess of shock and anticipation. What could he possibly do?

"And don't say one more word about that curst will. I loathe the day Mr. Huxley and I allowed Mr. Cluett to sign that thing, but I didn't know you then. It's not the money with you; it never has been.

I know you'd give all that up in an instant. You'd leave with me right now if I asked—if only it wasn't for your friends. You mean to protect them."

"Yes." I sat in silence a moment. "You're right. It's not the money." Then my shoulders slumped. "And I would . . . leave with you . . . if it was at all possible."

He shook his head. "I'm sorry I haven't more to offer, but I promise you, I will not turn my back on your friends. And you have to acknowledge, there would be no certainty where they're concerned anyway, not when the whole of Mr. Cluett's money is passed to your husband upon your marriage."

My head swirled. "But I could make it a condition. Don't you think—"

"Oh, Amelia, I'm not standing here pretending to have the perfect answer. All I really can offer you . . . is me—all of me—every last beat of my heart." He knelt beside the chair. "I simply cannot walk away from Moorington Cross knowing I didn't exhaust every possible hope for us to be together."

"I care for you, Ewan, you know that, but if I do as you suggest, I would be robbing Mr. Lymington and Mr. Montague of their inheritance."

"Hear me out." Ewan clasped my hands into his. "What if we find the document Henry was referring to?"

"But we've looked everywhere."

"Then we'll look again. I'll tear this place apart if I have to."

I narrowed my eyes. "And then what? You know the current will cannot be contested."

"That is what I spend every waking hour pondering. Mr. Cluett was murdered right after he made the current will."

"Then you think someone else was involved?"

"Possibly. We won't know anything until we get our hands on this elusive document."

"But Henry could simply be mad."

"I don't have much experience with people in his condition, but Mr. Cluett has been supporting him for years, watching over him, isolating him. Henry was even with Mr. Cluett in France. I cannot believe Mr. Cluett's actions were completely out of the goodness of his heart, nor that Henry knows nothing. There must be some reason he spoke to you that day."

"He was warning me."

Ewan's fingers tightened around mine. "Another reason I want you out of this house and removed from the will. You're not safe until this is all over and done with." He cast a quick look at the door then smiled.

My heart barely had time to flutter before his lips were against mine, the scent of fresh soap enveloping me. His kiss was urgent but sweet, laced with the tantalizing promise of more.

He pulled back only slightly, his eyes on his fingers running down my arm. "If you think for one second I could let you walk away after that kiss last night, you've a great deal still to learn about me." He settled into a smile. "In fact, let me educate you now. I'm yours forever, Amelia Pembroke, if you'll have me, and I mean to find a way out of this mess one way or another."

Ewan and I set to work at once on another search. Though he donned his determined solicitor mask, he couldn't hide the sparkle dancing about his eyes or the way his mouth sought to curve up at the most inopportune times.

Mr. Montague first caught wind of the change. He cornered me in the drawing room in front of everyone that night with a derisive laugh. "I do believe you no longer desire a marriage with Mr. Lymington or myself. Neither of us is compatible with you, are we?" A glance at Mr. Lymington. "Mr. Cluett had a dark humor, did he not? I suppose you do have a choice in all this. You can walk away right now and never look back."

Major Balfour piped up from the sofa behind us. "He's right, Amelia. Mr. Montague is wise to remind you of an option you should consider with great thought."

I couldn't help but turn my attention to Mr. Lymington. "But the money . . . I know Mr. Lymington is in need of it."

Mr. Lymington huffed. "I won't pretend for one second that the inheritance is not vital for my family and estate." His gaze found mine, tightening my chest. "I'm willing to work with you, Mrs. Pembroke—a convenient marriage is not the worst we could do."

"No, it's not." I swallowed hard. "And if my heart were not already engaged, I would agree to such an arrangement on the spot."

All eyes in the room shot to Mr. Hawkins before voices erupted from every angle.

"I knew it!"

"What do you mean?"

"Is such a thing even ethical?"

"He's blinded her, I tell you."

"Good show, Hawkins. You almost had me believing you'd give it all up for duty."

Ewan held up his hands. "If you'll allow me to speak . . ."

The murmurs fell to a hush, the restlessness of the drawing room growing by the second.

Ewan, however, was not ruffled, not by Major Balfour's scowl nor by Mr. Montague's smirk. He had my love and that was all he needed to press on. I could see it in his stride as he crossed the rug, in the way his shoulders straightened and the way his arms swung smoothly at each side.

He rested his hands on the back of a nearby winged chair. "I mean to take another look at the current will. Perhaps there is something I missed."

Mr. Montague laughed. "That would not be in Mrs. Pembroke's best interest."

Ewan's lips parted. "Then you know the specifics of the former will?"

"We all do, right, Lymington?"

Mr. Lymington sucked in a deep breath. "Mr. Cluett's money and properties were to be divided evenly between the three of us—Mr. Montague, Miss Seton, and myself. None of us had the least notion he meant to change it until Cluett summoned us here."

CHAPTER 27

Over the course of the following day, Ewan and I turned Moorington Cross upside down. No item, however small or seemingly insignificant, was left untouched.

Books were shaken in the library, every paper gone over two or three times, every baseboard and fireplace stone pawed over more than once. The drapes were thrust about, the rugs pulled back. We were so hopeful we would find the document Henry had referred to that day in the woods—the previous will or something else entirely. He said whatever it was would affect me. Surely this hidden document could invalidate the current will.

For several hours while we searched, my spirits brightened—somehow, some way, this would all be over for the better. The evening, however, rendered the bleak reality of darkness, which terminated our investigation and made abundantly clear the disappointing truth—we might very well never uncover what Henry had spoken of.

Ewan saw fit to return to the cottage to question Henry once again, but his communication skills proved to be at an all-time low. Nothing could prod him into producing any more clues. He had spoken his piece, and we had no alternative but to continue floundering in confusion.

And confusion it was. My elation at Ewan's declaration of love had faded over the course of the day into a sour stomach and ever-tightening shoulders. More and more it looked as if, to claim any measure of happiness, I would be forced to go against Mr. Cluett's directions in the will, thus disappointing nearly everyone in the house. That is, everyone but Ewan and myself. My one consolation.

The night was quite late when—all too aware of my looming choice and how it would affect them all—I abandoned my pursuit for the quiet of my bedchamber. However, I wasn't entirely surprised to hear Chauncey's telltale squeak a half hour later, alerting me to Mrs. Fitzroy's presence in the hall.

The calming anticipation I generally felt at her imminent arrival disappeared all too quickly, buried beneath the weight of a new, rather disturbing thought.

I stared at Chauncey a moment then back at my bedchamber door, my heart pounding wildly.

Now that was odd.

Chauncey always knew exactly when Mrs. Fitzroy was in the hallway. He vocalized his excitement at the first sound of her footsteps. My toes curled in my slippers as a heavy cold sank into every last one of my muscles.

Why had I not heard him make a sound the night Mrs. Fitzroy discovered Mr. Cluett's body?

Suddenly I couldn't sit still.

There was no way my dear friend could have traversed the hall on her way out of our wing without Chauncey detecting her presence. He was so incredibly reliable. And she had no reason to hide her movements . . . or did she?

Her knock was a tentative one, but it startled me nonetheless. She must have been concerned that I was already abed.

I fought back the unnatural feeling that she might have lied to me and measured my voice. "Come in."

The latch released and the door inched open to reveal Mrs. Fitzroy's ruddy face and swollen eyes.

I softened immediately. "Are you unwell?" I urged her to join me on the bed. "Come over here at once."

"Oh, Amelia." Shaky, she closed the door behind her and crept to the side of the bed. "It is the worst. I've received another letter from John, and I'm so very afraid."

I smoothed the coverlet, urging her to sit. "What is it? Tell me all."

Her gaze darted about the room like a housefly as she settled in at my side. "I received the letter from him earlier, but I only just now read it. He cannot come for me."

My shoulders relaxed. "Then you shall stay right here for the time being. Whatever happens regarding the inheritance, Mr. Hawkins has assured me he'll extend any help needed to both you and Major Balfour. Although it may look a little different from what I previously imagined."

She touched my cheek, tears filling her eyes. "I daresay that man must adore you if he means to assist two old crows like Balfour and me." Her smile was short lived. "A happy thought, but you don't understand the whole. John apparently has already made all the arrangements. He's employed a maid as an escort and means for me to ride post to Canterbury alone. Alone!" She dabbed at her nose with her handkerchief as she sniffled. "I don't think I can do it, my dear. I will be so afraid."

I reached out for her hand. "We shall simply write him back and refuse his assistance. I'm sure we can come at another way to bring you to him."

"But it's already done. Don't you see? My departure is set for tomorrow morning."

"Tomorrow morning?" My mouth fell open. "So soon?"

"I'll have no choice but to do as he's bid. The people have already been engaged. I'm to meet the maid in Plattsdale at ten o'clock in the morning, and then we shall board the carriage."

I bit my lip. "That does sound decided, but please, allow me to talk to Mr. Hawkins in the morning. Perhaps something else may be arranged."

She managed a weak, "I would greatly appreciate that," between quiet sobs.

I looked away. Tomorrow morning. I could scarcely believe I was about to lose my dearest friend and confidante—and at such a time. My own eyes threatened tears seconds before my gaze lit once again on Chauncey's cage, ripping me back into my earlier thoughts.

My brow creased as I listened to Mrs. Fitzroy's breathing even and slow. "Mrs. Fitzroy?"

"Yes."

The last thing I wished to do was upset her again, but at the same time, there was so much I didn't understand about the night Mr. Cluett died. "There is one thing that has been puzzling me these last few minutes."

"Oh?"

"It's about Chauncey."

"The pig?"

"Well, not exactly, but it does concern him. You see, the night of Mr. Cluett's death, I never heard one squeak out of him, and I was in my room all evening." I pivoted to face her. "However did you sneak past my room without alerting him to your presence?"

Her eyes seemed to fix in place, her cheeks blanching as white as the bedsheets. Then her voice tumbled out in waves. "Oh, well . . . I guess the little devil . . . didn't hear me that time."

I narrowed my eyes, my mind combing through what I saw before me. "I don't mean to quibble with you, but I cannot help but believe you are lying."

Her breath was short, her fingers suddenly alive, pawing at the folds of her dressing gown. "Don't be ridiculous. I-I cannot be held to task over the actions of a little creature."

"Then why don't you have a better answer?" I leaned forward. "There's something you aren't telling me about that night. I can feel it charging the air between us. What do you know?"

She fanned her face. "Major Balfour has been attempting to help me remember just what I saw that night, and I have been able to discern more than before, but please don't press me about Chauncey, Amelia. The last thing I wish to do is shock you before I leave. Believe me, the truth of Chauncey's silence is not all that flattering."

"Then there is more than what you've already told me?"

She shook her head. "Not really. Well, I am certain that it was indeed a man I saw in the hall. I can almost see the color of his hair in my mind. Major Balfour says—"

"You are trying to put me off. What about Chauncey's silence?"

Her eyes widened; her words slow to come. "I . . . I promise you the answer has nothing to do with Mr. Cluett's murderer, nor will it help our current situation in any way. It's only embarrassing to me."

My muscles twitched, my heart responding in kind. "Mrs. Fitzroy, I need to know everything. It's so very important, and you have my silence. You know that."

She licked her lips, her gaze drifting to the window. "You've always stood my friend." She thrust her hands into her lap before meeting my eyes. "I should have told you before now. I almost did the night we found that knife on your bed, but I was so ashamed. You see, I utilized a secret passageway from our hall into Mr. Cluett's the night he died because . . . Well, that's why Chauncey never heard me, why he never squeaked. I didn't come this way."

"The what?" I had to temper my voice. "The what?"

"Cluett showed me the passageway months ago. I was just too embarrassed to tell you." She thrust her head back and forth.

I merely stared at her.

"Oh, Amelia, don't make me say it aloud . . . Surely you can guess at this point. It was when I began my evening visits with him."

My mind was racing. *Evening visits?* She couldn't even look me in the eye, and now I perfectly understood why. "You mean the two of you . . ."

"Were in love, yes." Then she sat up stiffly. "It started out innocently enough. He came to my room one evening to ask if I would assist him with his public mesmeric sessions."

My mind raced to follow her. "I did wonder why you attended those."

"He needed me to help the others come to crisis."

"And how did you assist with that?"

She lifted her shoulders. "You see, when Dr. Mesmer trained Mr. Cluett, he explained the necessity of employing a person at every group mesmeric session whose sole purpose was to come to crisis." She waved her hands in the air. "It apparently encourages the others to let go and do so as well. Cluett thought if he utilized the practice here, it might help."

Her hands settled hard in her lap. "I'm not proud of this, Amelia." She scowled. "During every public session here, Miss Seton would bring the music on the pianoforte to a crescendo, which was my cue to"—she cleared her throat—"fake a convulsion."

"Fake a convulsion!"

"Not for myself, but for Mr. Cluett. And he was right. As soon as I collapsed onto the floor, others quickly followed. Then I was assisted into another room to recover, and Mr. Cluett could treat the rest of his patients."

"And you never questioned this process?"

"No. It allowed me to stay at Moorington Cross for less money, which made John quite happy. I simply did the best I could. I never meant to fall in love with the man."

"And then you began visiting his room?"

"You make it sound so—so clandestine."

"Because it was."

She wrinkled up her lips as if she'd tasted something sour. "All we did was talk, Amelia, nothing more. Well, a little more, but the point is we enjoyed each other's conversation."

"I had no idea all this was going on."

"No one did."

I couldn't help but think of poor Major Balfour. Did he really hold a tender for her?

A pert little smile emerged on Mrs. Fitzroy's face. "Our relationship was something we preferred to keep a secret between the two of us, which is why Cluett thought it best to show me the secret passage, so we could visit each other without the prying eyes of the house." Her face fell. "But that's all over and done with now. Cluett's gone. Nothing shall ever be the same."

"Not for any of us." I bit my lip, belatedly taking a sideways glance at the door. "Will you show me where the passageway is?"

She sat quite still for several seconds. "I'm rather tired, but I shall do so as I'm leaving in the morning." She stood. "And I think he'd want you to know." She grasped the candle from the bedside table. "We'll need a light. It's terribly dark in there."

Like two little mice, we crept into the corridor then down the length of the hall. We finally came to a stop before a large painting. Mrs. Fitzroy cast a look back at me then reached up and twisted a piece on the base of a nearby sconce.

"This releases the latch. See the dragon there?"

I stepped forward for a better look. Sure enough, at the junction of the iron curve was a small circular dragon.

I heard a *pop*, then the painting shuddered ever so slightly. A ghostly look washed over her face as she carefully slid the artwork to the side, just enough for a person to slip into the narrow opening. She motioned to me with her chin, her voice a sickly gray. "This way."

It wasn't without trepidation that I followed her into the gloom and allowed my eyes to adjust. The dark stone of the house and crisscrossing wooden beams made up the walls of the extremely narrow passageway. And though I kept my arms tucked against my sides, I could feel the damp undercurrent, the cold permeating the ancient structure, the slithering nature of the shifting shadows.

I fought back a chill. "And you weren't afraid to come through here night after night?"

"The first time I was, of course." I saw her head bob, dithering the candlelight. "Cluett used mesmerism to help me, and it simply became a means to an end. I realized he would always be waiting for me at the other side—my haven." All of a sudden her progress came to a halt and I heard the pop of a latch. "Cluett's private hall is right through there. I-I don't think I can go back. I-I don't want to."

I gave her arm a comforting squeeze as I slunk past her to get a better look at the terminus of the corridor. The opposing wall held another latch that edged open the wainscoting on the other side— with Mr. Cluett's apartments beyond. I stepped into the opening and looked about the shadowed interior for a moment before ducking back into the secret passageway. "Perhaps it's best we return to our rooms tonight."

I didn't wait for her answer as I tugged the section of wall back into place, but my fingers rested on the latch. I would have a great deal to report to Ewan in the morning, as well as a whole new world to search. A smile inched across my mouth.

Maybe the mysterious document would be uncovered after all. Henry had spoken of a darkness and a wall, and I was most certainly behind the stones of the house.

CHAPTER 28

Mrs. Fitzroy's departure from Moorington Cross turned out not to be the nightmare she'd feared. I came upon her and Major Balfour in the front entryway a little before nine the following morning, a smile on both of their faces.

"There you are, Amelia dear." She seemed almost happy. "I was just about to ferret you out for our goodbye, although I know it shan't be forever."

I glanced at Major Balfour then back at Mrs. Fitzroy. "Then you've decided to do as John directed?"

"Yes, but not by post. Major Balfour, you see, has graciously offered to escort me to John's estate himself in his landau."

"I'm so pleased to hear it." I nodded. "That is the perfect solution."

Major Balfour edged forward a pace. "I shall return as quickly as I can, my dear, to make certain your situation is equally resolved and you don't need my further assistance. I can only depart now with the comfort of knowing I leave you in Mr. Hawkins's capable hands."

I couldn't stop a grin. "I feel quite safe. Thank you." Then I turned back to Mrs. Fitzroy. "But I shall miss you both dreadfully."

She grasped my hands. "Let us not draw this out. I don't think I could bear it. You've been like a daughter to me, and I know we shall see each other again very soon."

"You'll write every day?"

She leaned into an embrace, whispering in my ear. "Every single one."

Then I watched them leave from the drawing room—the two people who, along with Mr. Cluett, had been my whole world for the last two years—my first real friends . . . and family.

Ewan found me by the window, my forehead pressed to the glass. "It seems strange that they are gone."

I pulled back. "Very strange."

"I shall certainly miss Mrs. Fitzroy's good-humored remarks. She's been through so much life yet still manages to keep a jovial air about her."

"She has suffered greatly. Major Balfour too. Not only does he endure his worsening foot problems, but he once had a ball in his shoulder as well. I catch him rubbing the old wound from time to time—a phantom pain that will never really heal. I fear the latter years will be difficult for them both, which is why I hoped to assist them in some way, to make their lives easier."

Footsteps pounded from the hall, growing louder until Mr. Montague barreled into the room. "I've found something." He thrust out a yellowed paper toward Ewan.

"What is it?" Slowly Ewan accepted the document.

"I took a turn in the east wing, and—"

"You did what? How?" I stepped forward.

A wry smile. "Don't look at me like that. I've had a key for some time. Cluett gave it to me. Look what I found, what's written here." He motioned to the paper. "Could this be a previous will? Can you use it in some way?"

Ewan narrowed his eyes. "This is not the official one, that's for certain." He held it lower so I could read it as well. "This is odd though. It seems to be instructions for the drawing up of his earlier will, but that—"

"Doesn't make any sense." I dipped closer to the paper. Indeed. Mr. Montague, Mr. Lymington, and Miss Seton were named as the beneficiaries, but it was written in a strange way—not as instructions for the solicitor but for a third party.

Mr. Montague was growing impatient. "Does it mean anything?"

Ewan shook his head. "Not likely. Look at the date. This was written over ten years ago. All future wills would supersede this one."

Mr. Montague wrestled the paper from our hands. "I thought when I stumbled upon a secret drawer in the desk this paper must certainly mean something."

Ewan's mouth curved up at the corners, followed by a shrewd glance at me. "So there was a secret drawer?"

"All for naught, I'm afraid."

"Wait!" Something about the paper caught my eye. "Let me see that one more time."

Mr. Montague gladly handed it over as both sets of eyes turned my way.

My gaze immediately fell to the bottom of the document—the signature line—and my heart stilled. "That's not Mr. Cluett's signature!"

"What?" Mr. Montague seemed irritated.

"It's not at all." I turned the paper around. "Do either of you know his hand?"

They shook their heads.

"Well, I do. Quite well, in fact. He signed every treatment plan, every medical instruction, every dosing chart. And *that* is not his signature."

"It's a fake then?" Ewan ran his hand through his hair. "But that doesn't make any sense."

I bit my lip. "Could this be what Henry was referring to after all? A document that would change everything."

Ewan's eyes appeared strained as he looked once again over the confusing document. "What are you suggesting? How on earth would an old, fabricated document have any bearing on the here and now?"

The room fell silent, each of us lost in thought. Why didn't the signatures match? Who else would have signed Mr. Cluett's name?

Could someone have done so on his behalf? Would someone have forged it so long ago?

Mr. Montague cleared his throat. "Maybe his signature simply altered over time. Age could do that."

"Not this dramatically."

Frustrated, I watched as Mr. Montague rubbed his brow, a lock of his dark hair dropping rakishly onto his forehead. Then it hit me. Mr. Montague's handsome face, the color of his hair, even his brooding eyes. His mother told him he was Mr. Cluett's illegitimate son, yet he looked nothing like the Mr. Cluett I knew. Mr. Lymington's mother issued her son a warning, one that didn't seem to fit Mr. Cluett.

I steadied myself on the window casement. We had automatically assumed the writer of this document was the one who'd falsified the signature, but what if this was the real signature? What if the Mr. Cluett I knew and loved was actually the imposter?

I pressed a hand to my cheek, my eyes trained on Mr. Montague, my voice terribly unsteady. "What did you say earlier about a mark?"

"Pardon?"

"The marks your mother said matched your father's—Mr. Cluett?"

"Oh, you mean the freckles on my bum." He laughed.

My eyes found Ewan's in questioning alarm, and he gave an answer to the words sinking into my heart. "There were no freckles on Mr. Cluett's backside or anywhere else for that matter."

I sucked in a breath. "Which must mean . . . the man who has been treating me for over two years, who was murdered in his bathtub, could not have been the real Mr. Cluett."

A grin spread across Ewan's face. "Nor could he have signed Mr. Cluett's will."

The house fell into an uproar. Mr. Montague howling in triumph. Ewan summoning Mr. Lymington into the drawing room to disclose what we had surmised.

"The scoundrel." Mr. Montague still held a laugh on his breath. "You mean that man who pranced around in that purple cloak was not even my father?"

I shook my head. "How easy it would have been for a man of similar features to return here and assume the real Mr. Cluett's identity. None of the previous staff remained at the house. His brother had been dead for years, and he had no other family. No one could have refuted him."

Mr. Montague tapped his watch. "But the imposter would've had to know the real Mr. Cluett—intimately . . ." He fell silent as Mr. Lymington sauntered into the room.

Ewan waited only a moment for Mr. Lymington to enter fully before he made the announcement. Mr. Lymington's resulting pleasure was palpable—he couldn't stop smiling. The three of us had indeed been granted a possible reprieve, but what now?

Ewan seemed to sense my question. "I shall reach out to Mr. Huxley as soon as possible to untangle this mess. It will likely go to the courts, and I daresay it will require some time before we have an answer."

Mr. Montague flopped onto the sofa. "What if the real Mr. Cluett isn't even dead?"

My eyes widened. "He's right. The man could be anywhere."

Ewan nodded slowly as if he didn't quite believe it himself. "An investigation into the whereabouts of the real Mr. Cluett will most certainly commence, but since the man we know as Mr. Cluett has been acting as such for over ten years, I cannot imagine he still lives."

I found my way to a seat by the window and peered out into the hazy morning. How could my dear friend enact such a charade? And for what purpose? How did he even know Mr. Cluett—a man described by Mr. Lymington's mother as dangerous and unstable? A man who could have been one of his mesmeric patients.

My muscles stilled. *One of his patients.* Could it be that easy? Had the answer been staring us in the face all this time?

I pressed my fingers to my mouth as I combed through all I could remember of the documents Ewan and I perused that day in Mr. Cluett's office. The notes about Patient A.

I whirled back to the room. "We must send for Miss Seton at once."

Ewan crossed the room to yank the bell pull before drawing up close to my side. "What have you figured out? I can see clear as day something has upset you."

I heard Mr. Lymington's distant voice as he sent the butler to find the nurse. "*Patient A*, Ewan. The real Mr. Cluett could have been that first patient at the mesmeric hospital in France—the patient he kept such meticulous notes on."

A furrow creased his brow. "So you think the imposter was one of the mesmerists at the hospital? That he garnered from their sessions what he needed to know to assume Mr. Cluett's identity?"

"I'd not pieced it all together yet, but yes. Think about it. Everything we know about the young Mr. Cluett has been unfavorable in the extreme. What if he went to France to seek treatment and—"

Mr. Lymington slammed the door behind Miss Seton and we all jumped.

She was ushered to a central chair as we all gathered around her, our gazes tight on her face. We all knew she was the one person who had been in France and returned to Moorington Cross to assist Mr. Cluett's imposter as he set up a hospital in this very house. She had to be involved.

Ewan crossed his arms. "We know the man killed in his bathtub was not the real Mr. Cluett."

Her mouth fell open. "I don't know what you mean."

But she clearly did. Her legs came to life and began shifting first one direction then the next.

Mr. Lymington stepped forward. "Stop the lies. We know it all."

She fanned her hands out over her face. "He didn't do it to hurt anyone. He only meant to help."

Mr. Montague flicked his fingers in the air. "I assume you are referring to our dead imposter."

"I would just—" She repositioned herself as her eyes darted to the window. "His routine *must* stay the same. Promise me that."

"You mean Henry." Ewan's voice was incredulous. "You can't be serious. That's Mr. Cluett out there in the cottage, isn't it?"

The room collectively gasped, our startled eyes finding each other's one person at a time. My chest felt tight. "It is, isn't it?"

"Unfortunately, yes."

Mr. Montague laughed, but it was not a pleasant one. "I don't believe it."

Mr. Lymington just stood there like a curst statue.

Ewan sighed. "Tell us all, and now."

She took a measured breath, her voice a sickly gray. "It was a terrible situation in France—at the end. Mr. Selkirk was his real name. He was the head doctor at the hospital."

My gaze shot up. *Selkirk?* Strange. I'd known so many Selkirks over the years. A few within my own family in fact.

Miss Seton went on. "Selkirk was not at all certain what was best to be done, nor were any of us." At odds with the severity of her voice, a small smile snuck across her face. "The whole thing was Henry's idea, you see. *He* was the one who wanted to come home."

"Back to Moorington Cross? Henry?" Ewan sounded skeptical.

"Yes, but none of us thought it best. After Mr. Cull's unfortunate death, no one considered Henry entirely sound of mind."

The name startled me. Ewan tossed me a feral glance then leaned forward. "And who, pray tell, was Mr. Cull?"

"He was a brash new mesmerist with more money than sense who'd brought in Mr. Selkirk to run his hospital and teach him, but

Mr. Cull never listened to anyone. You see, treating a patient like Henry . . . Well, like I said, the entire situation was confusing. Mr. Cull had this horrid notion that if we provoked Henry into one of his rages we could better assess the effects of Mr. Selkirk's mesmerism—if he could really control Henry. We all believed the treatment was working, but Henry's cycles of agitation to listlessness occurred over weeks and months. Mr. Selkirk opposed the idea, of course, but Mr. Cull was eager to try his new skills—nothing but arrogance and naïveté.

"Part of me wondered if Henry could even be blamed. Cull's death was deemed an accident, and it certainly could have been. He drowned in the pond. Henry, naturally, was the only other person who was there and knew what happened. He had entered one of his hysterical episodes by the time we found them, so who can say . . ." She pursed her lips. "It was Mr. Selkirk, however, who was left to bear the guilt of it all. He never really escaped it. The death was partially his fault after all. He was the one who allowed his protégé to practice alone on an unstable patient."

My chest tightened and I took a deep breath. "What a terrible situation and loss and . . . At any rate, I can see what you mean about the confusion." I stared out the window. "But why on earth did Mr. Selkirk assume Mr. Cluett's identity?"

She shrugged. "The idea was hatched when we heard the longtime caretakers of Moorington Cross had passed away. No switch would have been possible before then. They were far too familiar with Henry and not likely to be bought off. If we'd done it earlier, they would have exposed the plan at once."

Her hands settled in her lap. "Mr. Selkirk was not keen on the idea at first. A premonition perhaps. He only agreed to the switch so he could continue treating Henry as he'd done in France. Mr. Selkirk still had hopes he could help him, and I was always there to remind him of his responsibility to help Henry.

"Henry was Mr. Selkirk's patient, and Mr. Selkirk knew deep down the only way he could possibly manage the situation would be to return to Britain with him and pose as Cluett himself. Funds were terribly low and interest in mesmerism was already fading in Parisian society. None of us could have stayed on at the hospital with the little money we were bringing in.

"It was a perfectly reasonable plan, really. Mr. Selkirk knew everything about Cluett from their mesmeric sessions. And we desperately needed the money. The two favored each other in looks, and it had been decades since Henry had been at Moorington Cross."

She smiled a bit to herself. "Henry was right. The whole thing went off without a hitch. No one questioned our little ruse. Well, no one but Miss Parsons. She unfortunately had a relationship with Henry in his youth and demanded to be paid for her silence . . . regularly."

My eyes rounded. "The tree! Is that why she comes to the magnetized tree?"

"To collect her money, yes. How did you know?"

I ignored Miss Seton's pointed glare. "What I don't understand is why Mr. Selkirk opened the hospital and later took all of us in."

She pressed her lips together. "Driven by some facet of his guilt, I suppose. He always wanted to help people. He was unique in that sense. I can only imagine his actions sprang from some futile attempt to atone for past mistakes."

Though I hated to admit it, she was probably right. "And the will?"

A breathy puff of a laugh. "It was Henry's one stipulation in all this, and I've always made certain Selkirk stuck to the arrangement."

"What was the stipulation?"

"Before we left France, Henry demanded that his two illegitimate sons be provided for. He would stand for nothing short of that. Whatever his faults, he cares deeply for certain people in his life. The first will was promptly drawn up on arrival following his implicit instructions. I'll just say, he wasn't too keen when you were added to the document recently."

"I see." And I did, quite clearly for the first time. Mr. Selkirk, my friend and doctor, had no choice in adding the marriage stipulation, not if he hoped to include me in the will and pacify Henry at the same time. Henry never would have allowed his sons to be cut out entirely. No wonder he spoke to me that day in the meadow.

Miss Seton stood. "Henry must be allowed to keep to his routine. He's fairly harmless now, but still a bit unpredictable at times. I know I can control him, and I promised to protect him."

"Control!" I coughed out the word. "Then why did he come into my room that night and fling a knife at my head?"

I thought the room had been shocked by the revelation about Mr. Cluett, but this was ten times worse. Mr. Montague gasped as Miss Seton jerked back.

I'd forgotten we'd kept the murder attempt—or whatever it was—a secret.

Mr. Lymington stepped forward. "What are you talking about?"

I tried to retract my outburst as far as I could. "A man came into my room some time ago. I've had no trouble since."

Miss Seton huffed. "Henry has been known to sneak into the house from time to time. He knows more about this rambling structure than anyone else, but I don't believe he would sling a knife at you for a second."

I inhaled a ragged breath. "I agree that Henry's life should remain constant for now . . . at least until the authorities can be sent for."

Mr. Lymington narrowed his eyes. "I shall ride at once for the magistrate."

"Agreed." Ewan gave him a slight nod and Lymington left at once.

Ewan turned back to me. "In the meantime, Henry shall be watched as always, but with two nurses at all times." He turned to Miss Seton. "I shall put you personally in charge of his care for the time being. And, Miss Seton, I would suggest you spend the next few hours remembering every detail of what happened in France and then here at Moorington Cross. The authorities will expect it all, as do I."

"Understood." Her voice was icy as she headed for the door.

Mr. Montague pivoted to follow her but paused to look back when Ewan spoke. "Don't do anything stupid."

Mr. Montague only smiled. "I have no intention of announcing my relationship to the man if that is what you mean to imply. I simply plan to keep an eye on our friendly nurse, who has been quite forthcoming with us, wouldn't you say?"

Ewan laughed to himself as he watched Mr. Montague disappear around the doorframe before he headed to the sideboard.

I followed him, a newfound hesitancy to my steps. "Why do you think Henry snapped after all this time? To murder his own doctor?"

Ewan poured himself a drink. "Perhaps he isn't as controllable as Miss Seton thinks."

I shrugged. "Maybe."

Ewan watched me over the rim of his glass. "I know that face. What is it?"

"It just doesn't entirely add up. The murderer killed the imposter in the bathtub. If Henry is the murderer, how did he get away from the cottage? He has a nurse with him at all times."

"He's escaped before, and Miss Seton said he knows the house. I assume that means *all* of the house."

"Yes . . ."

There was a knock at the door and Andrews entered carrying a silver salver that cradled a letter. "This just came for you, sir."

Ewan took the letter, then waited until the butler left the room to examine it fully.

I moved in close. "Who's it from?"

He scanned the outer script. "It appears to be the information we requested from Mr. Dodge in France." A pause and he tore through the wax seal, his gaze fixed to the paper. "He writes that the teaching hospital was initially manned by Mr. Selkirk like Miss Seton told us and"—his face blanched, his eyes rounding—"Amelia, come closer."

I edged in next to him so I could read the paper in his hand. His finger lit on the sentence he was reading. "See here. It says the gentleman who founded and funded the hospital, Mr. Cull, has a cousin, Cecil, who is still the owner of the current hospital."

Something caught my eye and I tore the paper from his hands and flipped it over. The wax seal—where had I seen that triangular shape before? My mind was blank at first, then the image crept forward into my thoughts. Major Balfour had been running his finger along the same wax seal on a letter he held in the blue salon the day I'd come upon him and Mrs. Fitzroy.

I held the seal closer. There in the wax were the letters BMH—Bordeaux Mesmeric Hospital. How did Major Balfour get ahold of the hospital's seal? "What did you say the cousin's name is?"

"Cecil."

My eyes widened. "That's Major Balfour's Christian name!"

From the periphery of my vision I caught sight of Ewan rubbing his chin, but his voice sounded far away. "You don't think . . ."

"That they are one and the same person. I most definitely do. Major Balfour had a letter with the same exact seal. How else could he get it?" It was as if I'd been in a dark room and someone finally lit a candle, but I couldn't dare look at what had been revealed. I was afraid of it.

Ewan was still talking. ". . . remember him telling me his cousin believed in mesmerism."

I felt myself nodding, but I didn't remember initiating the action. "Yes, his cousin was a strong proponent of mesmerism. And . . . oh, Ewan! Major Balfour told Mrs. Fitzroy he bought his commission after his cousin died under strange circumstances. It proved to be quite a difficult time for him."

His breath hitched. "Then that would mean—"

"If we are right about his real identity, Mr. Cluett—the imposter—and Major Balfour were loosely connected before he came to the hospital for treatment here in Britain."

"More than a connection, Amelia. If the real Mr. Cluett is Patient A as we suspect, as Miss Seton revealed, he is also the man who might have killed Mr. Cull—Major Balfour's cousin."

My stomach felt heavy, my muscles on edge. I attempted a close-lipped smile, but I could not stop the painful connections forming in my mind. "Which would give Major Balfour—or Mr. Cull, or what-ever his real name is—the perfect reason for murder."

Ewan's head flinched back slightly. "But that was not the real Mr. Cluett."

I shook my head. "And Major Balfour had no way of know-ing that."

Images dashed through my mind—conversations, clues. It was all coming together like a well-sprung carriage, driving me ever closer to the truth. "He was in the house; he had easy access to Mr. Cluett's bedchamber. Mr. Cluett was teaching him how to mesmerize. He must be responsible. Mrs. Fitzroy was certain it was a man she saw in the hall. And then she saw that flash. Remember? I don't know what that was—"

"His cane . . ." Ewan's voice was shaky. "The round metal handle. He keeps a vinaigrette in there, does he not?"

"Yes, the top pops open to reveal the vinaigrette, which he uses quite frequently to calm his nerves. It must have caught the moonlight while he was opening or closing it. If he'd just murdered a man, he would most certainly be off stride."

"But can we be right in all this? Why would he kill him now? He's been here for over a year."

My skin felt cold. "The will."

A furrow formed on Ewan's forehead. "The marriage clause."

"When Major Balfour learned of all the stipulations that day in the drawing room, he knew it was time to make his move. He's been against me choosing either gentleman from the start. He knew that if he could get me to walk away from both of them, the money would go back to the founders of the mesmeric hospital in France—in effect, him. It says right here in this letter that Mr. Cull's cousin is the current owner."

Ewan gave me a bit of a sheepish grin. "I will confess Balfour has encouraged my affections for you at every turn."

"And he cautioned me against the others. You know, Mr. Montague even mentioned something about Major Balfour encouraging him to press his case—to . . . well, kiss me, I mean. He knew very well that would do nothing but repulse me."

"I kissed you."

"That was different. I wanted to kiss you."

He settled his hands on my arms. "And I have half a mind to do so again right now."

"Wait!" My hand flew to my throat. "If Major Balfour was the murderer from the start, and Henry was not even involved, was Major Balfour also the shadowy person who entered my bedchamber?" A shiver ran down my back. "The person who threw that knife?" I shook my head. "I cannot believe it."

Ewan pulled me against him. "It is possible, particularly if Balfour thought you meant to follow the stipulation in the will and marry one of the gentlemen. We were both thinking along those lines at that point. If he killed once, he would have had no qualms about doing so again. It is a great deal of money in the end."

A wave of icy cold ripped through my body and I jerked back. "Mrs. Fitzroy! The one person who saw him the night of the murder, who could potentially attest to his guilt—he's driving her home. She's completely in his power. She told me only yesterday that she was beginning to remember more about that night and that Major Balfour was helping her through mesmerism. Why else would he be so keen to take her home, particularly with his feet the way they are?"

I nearly stumbled as I whirled to look out the window. "Oh, Ewan! She might be in terrible danger."

CHAPTER 29

W e gathered the household and hatched a plan at once to recover Mrs. Fitzroy.

Within seconds the halls became a flurry of movement with servants rushing about everywhere as Ewan, Mr. Lymington, and Mr. Montague took a harried leave of me and rode out that very hour. There was no time to waste.

All that remained for me was silence . . . and worry.

I was alone. Well, not entirely alone. Miss Seton pounded in and out of the house tending to Henry, and Andrews, who brought me tea and cake, popped into the library, where I'd settled in like a nervous little bird to wait out the afternoon hours.

Despite their presence I still felt abandoned . . . useless. I first attempted needlepoint, struggling in vain to squelch the horrid loss of control that ate away at me. Of course, there was no question of my joining the party, not with my condition, but to have to wait out the rescue at Moorington Cross when my dear friend's life was in danger seemed unimaginable. If only I could have ridden out with them, done something to help.

I tossed aside the needlework and propped my elbow on the arm of the sofa. My fingers found my forehead as I released a tight breath. That was the exact moment I saw it. The poetry book Ewan had been using so long ago. I retrieved the collection at once and flipped absently through the pages, unable to focus on the words. That is, until a slip of paper emerged. It had been tucked deep within the middle of the book. Carefully I unfolded the crisp white parchment to reveal vibrant ink. Whoever had written the flowing script had done so recently.

Leaning forward I shifted the paper into the light. An unfinished poem? I read the lines aloud:

> "Though winter's icy fingers claw desperately at
>   the soul
> The silent moments seek to alter:
> A tender look, a subtle touch,
> Is it the beat of her heart that beckons me near?
> Or . . ."

The last few lines were crossed out, and though I squinted to get a better look, I could only make out the final three words: *cultivated . . . urbane. . . . eloquent.* I stared down at the paper in my hands for some time, my throat growing thick, my fingers tingling.

Urbane?

Ewan!

My eyes widened as my gaze inched back down the page. He'd used those very words to describe me not so long ago. I shook my head as my finger retraced the script.

How many times had I seen Ewan scribbling something he never shared with me? That moment I found him working away at this very desk came to mind. How quickly he'd hidden what he was writing. How embarrassed he'd been.

A groove deepened on my brow as I tapped the book. He most certainly admired poetry, but could he actually be a poet himself? Moreover, was the entirety of this verse about me?

I inched the book closed, once more running my finger over the embossed cover.

E. H. Radcliff.

I froze. E. H. Radcliff. And narrowed my eyes. Was this the answer? Could the initials E. and H. actually stand for Ewan Hawkins? I rushed over to the bookcase and located Moorington's well-worn copy of *The Peerage of England, Scotland, and Ireland* that I'd seen several times before. It was a few years old, but it would do well enough for my search. Like lightning, my fingers flew through the pages until I found what I was looking for—the Baron of Torrington's entry.

Radcliff! I was in the right of it. Radcliff was Lord Torrington's family name.

I sat back down and flopped against the bookcase, a little stunned and a bit giddy. Dear, sweet, maddening Ewan had published his poetry under Lord Torrington's family name, and he hadn't even bothered to tell me. I bit my lip. Granted, he'd attempted to in a way.

My shoulders felt heavy. No wonder he'd pursued my thoughts regarding his "favorite" poet. My heart skipped a beat. How terribly dismissive I'd been.

I scrambled to my feet. With little else to do but worry and doubt, I had plenty of time to remedy such an unfortunate ignorance. I glanced over the massive bookshelves of Moorington's library. Even if it took me all afternoon, I'd find and read every last poem by E. H. Radcliff that resided within the house.

A small smile tugged at my lips. And I just might enjoy doing so.

My eyes fluttered open. I blinked again and again, all the while staring into a considerably darkened library. My vision was blurry at first, but it began to clear as I pushed myself into a sitting position on the sofa. The book of poetry I'd been reading slid quietly to the cushions beside me.

My head smarted as my thoughts cleared. I must have fallen asleep.

The gray afternoon had faded to night; the small fire still smoldering in the grate was the only light in the room. I sat still for a long moment, gazing at the fireplace, imagining what could possibly be happening with the rescue party. That is, until I heard what sounded like a swish of fabric and my heart pounded back to the here and now.

I thrust my head to the side, my muscles twitching beneath my skin. "Who's there?" A chill skirted across my shoulders as I squinted into the shadows.

"It's only me, Mrs. Pembroke." The voice that emanated from the corner of the room was cold and familiar—Miss Seton.

I could see her now, the nurse's thin silhouette captured by a sliver of moonlight as she approached.

Her voice was sharp. "Andrews asked me to seek you out when you didn't come to supper."

"Oh." I attempted to calm my scattered nerves as I ensured my coiffure was intact. "I had one of my sleeping spells. I certainly didn't mean to concern anyone."

"As I see." I thought I saw a flash of moonlight reflected in her eyes as the dark orbs shifted one way, then the next. "Since you seem more yourself now . . . I mean, if you haven't need of me, I would like to retire for the evening. I plan to stay at the cottage tonight. Henry's been restless and needs me near him."

Near him?

Her shadowed form edged toward the door.

"Wait." I held up my hand. "Would you step into the firelight for a moment? I have a few things I wish to speak with you about."

A quiet pause, then she sidled into the subtle waves of orange light hovering at the center of the room. And though she lowered her chin in mock deference, an underlying haughtiness still ruled her countenance, a bitter intensity she would never be able to shake, not with me at least.

I swallowed hard as I motioned to the opposite end of the sofa. "Please be seated."

She offered me a forced nod before perching like a viper at the far end.

I saw no reason for pleasantries. We'd never bothered with them before. "What exactly is your relationship with Henry?"

The fire's dregs led a pulsing dance of light across her face as she gathered her thoughts. "He is my patient."

Slowly I shook my head. "There's more. Isn't there?"

She rubbed her arms. "Not really."

"Are you in love with him?"

Her eyes shot up. "I do love him, yes. I always have."

"And Mr. Cluett—or rather, Mr. Selkirk—knew that."

"Bah." Her laugh was quick and deep. "Of course he did."

My lips parted, memories of my friend and doctor rising to the surface—how he'd always seemed somewhat troubled by Miss Seton, how easily she controlled everything at the hospital. It all made sense now. Mr. Selkirk, the imposter, had been afraid of his own nurse. Of what she knew, what she could reveal. And her heart belonged to a madman.

A smile emerged on her wrinkled face. "William Selkirk was nothing but a fool. No one in their right mind would have let Mr. Cull practice on Henry with such little experience."

My gut lurched. It wasn't what she'd said, but that name . . . It unhinged a memory. "What did you say?"

Again that insidious smile. "William Selkirk was a fool."

"*William* Selkirk?" Ice gathered in my chest as the room blurred around me. My gaze fell hard on my fingers. I drew in a quick breath and spoke again. "His name was *William* Selkirk." The name rolled thickly off my tongue. Then a bit breathier, "*Uncle* William."

My eyes slipped closed for a long moment. Why hadn't I made the connection before? Mr. Selkirk had always been so thin, so old, probably altered by the choices he'd made in his life, the guilt he bore. I never would have dreamed he and Uncle William could be one and the same person. I lifted my chin, the final piece of the puzzle clicking so neatly into place. "Mr. *William* Selkirk was one of my guardians."

Miss Seton gave a careless shrug. "You're only figuring that out now?"

Of course. The will. My connection to my beloved doctor. It all made perfect sense. He must have recognized me the moment I stepped foot in the hospital. He'd always acted so paternal, been so careful with me. And when he learned his days were numbered, he'd set out to provide for me one way or another. "I was only five years old when he handed me over to Mr. Stanley and returned to France."

"Naturally. He couldn't take you back there, not with everything going on with Henry. It was no place for a child."

"He was the only guardian who ever cared a fig for me."

She turned back to the window. "He revealed to me at one time that he felt rather sorry he couldn't care for you, but the hospital had to come first, you know."

My chest felt heavy.

A moment of silence crept between us, the weight of so many truths settling like layers upon my shoulders. So many of my friends I never really knew. "Do you think Major Balfour purposely came to this hospital to avenge his cousin's death?"

She nodded slowly, carefully, as if speaking the truth aloud might in turn put us in danger somehow. "Balfour was always a troubled soul. I thought it then. I think it now. Selkirk believed he could help him. He knew who he was from the start. He wanted to atone for the tragedy that befell his cousin Mr. Cull. They are both members of the Cull family. Major Balfour could not have used his real surname, not with what he apparently had in mind."

My fingers curled around the armrest. "If you knew who Major

Balfour was from the start, why didn't you say anything after the murder?"

She winced. "My only thoughts were of Henry. If I exposed Major Balfour, I would have had to expose Henry as well. And I had no way of knowing if Balfour was actually involved. I had my doubts, but I am sorry for them now."

"And Mr. Selkirk?"

"Like I said before, in the end Mr. Selkirk was nothing but a fool. He actually thought he could teach Balfour the finer points of mesmerism so he could, in effect, help himself. Selkirk believed most of Balfour's issues stemmed from the depths of his mind and that he was highly suggestible, ready for treatment.

"He was right, in a way, but wrong in so many others. Selkirk was extremely excited when he was able to get Balfour to drink that foul-tasting medicine with very little mesmeric effort. That's how Selkirk tested a patient's moldability—how effective his treatments would be. I think Balfour's easy acceptance was nothing but a ruse."

My thoughts felt heavy, my stomach sour. I couldn't help but remember my own first mesmeric session. I'd not been able to drink that horrid concoction at all, but others had. "Mrs. Fitzroy told me about how Mr. Clu—Mr. Selkirk—was quite effective in assisting her to tolerate the herbal medicine he prescribed to help her slee . . ."

I had just pressed my lips together to complete the word *sleep* when the truth flashed before me. "Oh my goodness. Could that be how Major Balfour did it? I'd never even considered such an angle."

"What do you mean?"

My heart was racing now, and I sat forward. "The night Selkirk died. What if Major Balfour managed to get him to take Mrs. Fitzroy's sleeping concoction, and he didn't realize he was ingesting it . . . perhaps through mesmerism?" I shot to my feet. "Mr. Hawkins said it looked as if Cluett, or rather, Selkirk, had been given something. And there was minimal bruising on his shoulders. If he'd been asleep or not in complete control of his faculties, Major Balfour could have simply held him under the water without much of a struggle, leaving the medicine to do the work. Selkirk's body would appear as if his death was an accident, or even better . . . a suicide."

Miss Seton didn't move, but I thought her a bit shaken.

"Mrs. Fitzroy said she was low on tansy oil for her sleep medication. At high doses, I know that herb is fatal. What do you think?"

Miss Seton's voice was flat. "I really couldn't say."

Images danced through my mind and all at once I knew I was right. Having someone take advantage of me while I was incapacitated had always been a great fear of mine.

I bit my lip. Major Balfour must have been keeping a keen watch on my friend since the murder, living in dread that she would not only remember she'd seen him in the hall, but perhaps also uncover the details of how he murdered the man he thought had killed his own cousin.

An insidious draft of cold air swept over me as I struggled to picture Mrs. Fitzroy's current plight. I pressed my hand to my mouth and shook my head. Surely Major Balfour would not harm her. He only meant to get her away from Moorington Cross as soon as possible. Yet everything I thought I knew about Major Balfour would have to be reexamined. He was most certainly a cold-blooded killer, and all my friends were in terrible danger.

The darkened house was eerily alive by the time I departed the safety of the drawing room and began making my way down the hall intent on my bed. Miss Seton had long since taken her leave and left me to my thoughts. I'd seen the murky clouds amassing over the course of the evening, yet for some reason I'd not expected a storm. It came nonetheless, almost as if summoned from the depths of my imagination.

In passing I peeked out an entryway window just as a sweeping howl rushed against Moorington's old stones, conjuring up a discord of popping and creaking. As I reached the turn in the hall near the east corridor, flashes of lightning snuck in through the slits in the drapes, illuminating slender patches along the walls and carpet, then vanishing into the gray abyss.

The hairs on my neck stood at rapt attention, and it was all I could do to keep myself calm and continue moving forward. One foot in front of the other, my heartbeat accelerating with each step. I simply needed to make it to my room where I could wait out the storm beneath the safety of my covers.

Another flicker of lightning, however, drew me to a standstill near the foot of the grand staircase. My breath stilled.

Had I seen something? Every muscle in my body tightened. All at once it felt as if the house had shifted and the room was not as it had once appeared.

Shrinking against the wall, I squinted into the gloom, my gaze darting one direction then the next. Then I heard it—the cruel moan of a floorboard—a long, measured complaint as if someone was taking a careful step.

Oh dear. My pulse throbbed and my vision blurred. I tried to will it away, but it was too late—the jolt of fear I'd been working so hard to keep at bay since the arrival of the thunder shook me to the core.

My hands. No, not my hands! I could feel the slow, treacherous paralysis taking over before I could process what to do. Somehow in my panic I managed to collapse backward against the wall, slowing my descent onto the floor, which left me propped on my side lengthwise, my back pressed to the cold wainscoting, one arm on the hard dusty floor beneath me—completely immobile. I could still see and hear everything, as was the way with my extreme spells. The front room lay quiet and still around me, the shadows in my vision fixed. Perhaps I'd imagined the sound in the first place.

But then I saw it—a darkened figure creeping across the entry-way carpet, a cane in his hand, propping each of his harried steps.

Major Balfour. At Moorington Cross? How was that even possible?

All sorts of possibilities raced through my mind. Mrs. Fitzroy was already dead . . . and Ewan? If I could have screamed, I would have. Anything to alert Andrews from his bed. Then the lightning struck again, illuminating not only the metal vinaigrette box atop the cane but also a pistol poised to shoot in Major Balfour's other hand. I knew then and there any sound from me and my life was over. He was here for one reason. My death would ensure him the money he so desperately sought, and his revenge on the man he thought was Mr. Cluett would be complete.

In his cautious wandering Major Balfour did not at first turn my direction. My earlier movements and collapse must not have been regarded, but for how long? I would be clearly exposed but for the shadows.

Terrified, I lay incapacitated, forced to listen to his hesitant foot-steps as he entered the drawing room and paced about like a lion on the prowl. I wondered if he could hear the pounding of my heart.

The footsteps grew louder, more determined, as I lay there unable to do anything but breathe. He was coming back my way.

"Mrs. Pembroke?" It was a whisper, a call.

Waves of terror spread over my numb limbs, chilling me to the core.

"I know you are here somewhere . . . I saw you through the draw-ing room window only a moment ago. I am certain you have not yet ascended the stairs, and I need to speak with you urgently."

Speak with me indeed. I'd already seen the pistol.

Thunder rumbled, shocking the old walls into a quiver. Major Balfour's darkened form emerged once more in the doorway, and I fought the mounting panic with everything that was in me. If lightning struck again, I would most certainly be exposed. Silently I prayed as tears filled my eyes.

Control. How many hours had I spent trying to harness such a vital concept? The one aspect of my life forever out of my grasp. A darker thought dawned. I'd fought my guardians, my husband, my doctor, always believing I'd find a way to shake free of dependence and finally dispense with the need to rely on anyone besides myself. Yet here I was, nothing but a helpless victim—forced yet again into complete vulnerability.

Major Balfour's raspy voice rent the night air. "Where are you, my dear? Why are you hiding?"

My chest burned, igniting my heart into a fresh round of wild beating. Then I felt it—a tingle at my toes. My body was waking up. The sheer exhilaration of hope coursed through my bones, and as I moved my foot an inch, inwardly I cried out with joy.

Then a streak of lightning flashed, and everything changed. I could see Major Balfour now in his entirety, standing in the center of the rug. A wraith illuminated by the ghostly white light of the storm—and he was staring straight at me.

"Ah, there you are . . . and yet, you didn't call out to me. Interesting."

His approach was slow, calculated, as if he didn't fully understand my current predicament. He'd never witnessed one of my more extreme spells. If only I could stall for time.

I tried my voice. "Please, Major Balfour. A question. Please. What are you doing here? . . . Moreover, why our doctor and friend—"

"That is two questions, my dear." A smile spread across his face. "So you do know all . . . I made the right decision to return. Mrs. Fitzroy was remembering too many details of that night."

My arms were partially my own again, and I was able to push myself into a sitting position. "Did you have it planned since the beginning?"

He seemed to think for a moment, bursts of lightning illuminating the twist of emotions on his face.

"Yes, I came to the hospital to kill Cluett." His voice sounded rushed and a little regretful, but no less determined; the pistol never wavered in his hands. "I daresay the fool recognized me when I arrived. I'm sure of it, even though we never spoke one word about my cousin. Cluett would have had no idea that, while I was recovering in a French military hospital from my injuries at Waterloo, my path happened to cross with that of a nurse who formerly worked with him. She saw the resemblance between me and my cousin at once and felt the need to unburden herself of the true story of his demise. I'd had no information until that point about the details of my cousin's death. I was told only of his drowning. Of course, then I had hours and hours to lie on that cot and think of what I must do."

He adjusted his stance. "My feet do pain me still, but I had no real intentions for improvement. I came here for the sole reason of learning something of my cousin's mesmerism before I disposed of the man who took his life. You're well aware I was never much of a believer in the medicinal powers of the *baquet*, but I've always been quite magnetized. Both my cousin and I possess the gift, and it proved a very effective weapon."

"You mean you managed to magnetize Mr.—"

"Mesmerize him, yes." He seemed terribly pleased with himself. "Cluett agreed to teach me and then fell quite nicely into my hands . . . just as Mrs. Fitzroy did."

A beat of fear coursed through my body. "Where is she? What have you done with her?"

"My dear, kind, gullible friend." He shook his head, his voice oddly affected. "I had planned to . . . well . . . you know. It was quite strange though. When the moment came, I found I couldn't bring myself to do it. We've a mesmeric bond I don't intend to break. She's currently safe at an inn, waiting for my return. I've decided to keep her with me. I don't know if I'd call it love, but there's something between us, and she can be a great resource when needed. After all, it was she who brought me the medicine when prompted and quite brilliantly possessed no memory of it."

"You used her. You're still using her."

A quiet smile. "To a point, yes, but unfortunately I was blindly unaware of her relationship with Cluett. It was only a short time ago that I discovered the connection during one of our sessions in the blue salon. I can forgive her to a point. Her mind troubled her greatly, and people do foolish things when they are not at ease."

"But why kill him?"

"Quite simply because the moment had come to avenge my cousin. I'd already begun gathering the personal information I needed to persuade you to reject both of your suitors, particularly if my attempts at matchmaking failed with you and Mr. Hawkins."

He caught my look of surprise. "Oh yes. I had the gentlemen investigated. Turns out neither is as destitute as they allowed you to believe. At any rate, Cluett worded the new will perfectly to benefit me, and I had no way of knowing if he might change it again. He was threatening to do just that, you know. He'd kept Mr. Hawkins in residence for just such a situation. No. I could not wait any longer. The time had come."

I could feel my back stiffening, growing stronger. "But Mr. . . . ." My mouth slackened. Should I reveal the mistaken identity? My stomach lurched. It wouldn't change my position or the need for Major Balfour to keep us all quiet. I plowed on. "Mr. Cluett was dying. Why not wait?"

Major Balfour huffed a laugh. "Cluett's complaint was a minor one. Male in nature. And though it felt like death to him, it would have taken years to reach that point, if it happened at all. He merely saw such an affliction as proof of his inadequacies as a mesmerist. As well he should have. He was losing his touch. No, when I heard the contents of the will, I knew the time had come."

Major Balfour extended his arm, the pistol glinting in the moonlight. "It is unfortunate that you are so resistant to mesmerism, Amelia. I would have been far happier not to have to kill you."

"What do you mean, 'resistant'?" Feeling was returning to my legs, the numbness retreating. I only needed a few more minutes.

Major Balfour crept closer. "Cluett spoke of your inadequacies often to me, which is why he was so frustrated with your care. No, I dare not chance my own future in your hands." He lightly shook his head, a sort of defiance about the movement. "I've given it quite a bit of thought, and I'm afraid this is the only way."

The moonlight flickered off the metal pistol as Major Balfour's finger inched inward on the trigger. The moment had come. The muscles in my body contracted to propel me into a roll away from the wall.

The blast was deafening, the resulting quiet surreal as the smell of gunpowder permeated the room. He'd actually done it. My dear friend had attempted to murder me, but he'd been too sure of himself.

I scrambled to control my legs, floundering on the cold hard floor, but I had no chance of regaining my footing, not yet at least. I could only hope Major Balfour did not possess a second pistol.

Desperate to get away, I used my elbows to crawl down the east hall. Every bony prominence screamed out in pain, but the rush of adrenaline had overtaken me, pushing me onward—faster, harder, more frantic—into the relative safety of darkness.

Time. All I needed was a little time, and I could flee the house for the cottage. But where to hide in my current state?

My gaze fell upon the large mahogany doors to the east wing, and I was thankful we'd left them unlocked after what happened to Ewan and me. I had the latch open in seconds. Then I heard the familiar shuffle of Major Balfour's injured feet and accompanying cane.

I managed to rise onto my knees once more and was able to move a bit more speedily than before, the carpet of dust not only aiding my flight but coating my gown and forearms. A sliver of moonlight lit my way back to the east wing bedchamber, where I'd spent so many hours before with Ewan. Without thinking I made my way behind the large poster bed and prayed it would take Major Balfour enough time to locate me that I could regain the use of my legs.

I set out at once to massage them, running my fingers up and down my numb muscles, rolling my feet at my ankles, my eyes ever conscious of the shadowed door. I had the merest vantage point just under the bed at an angle from which I hoped I could see Major Balfour's arrival, and from which I doubted he could see me.

Oh God, help my legs.

The large door to the wing slammed closed, then light splashed into the bedchamber, brightening every crevice of the forgotten room. I ducked to look at the door, and my heart seized. Major Balfour stood at the entrance holding a well-lit candelabra. The trail I'd left in the dust was perfectly exposed before him.

I clawed harder at my legs, willing them back to life, but Major Balfour did not immediately approach.

"I was at a bit of a loss just now since you evaded my pistol, but your retreat has given me a far better idea for disposing of you. I've heard these old walls won't withstand much. In many ways, a fitting end. Moreover, one that won't be questioned."

I heard a jangle of keys and shrank back against the wall. Did he mean to lock me in here and . . . then what?

A tint of amusement lit his voice. "The last time I left you here, I thought I had it all worked out. You fell quite nicely into Mr. Hawkins's arms, as I suspected you would. I congratulate myself on that at least. I knew you had it in you to give up Mr. Cluett's fortune for love. You only needed a bit of prodding, or rather, Hawkins did." He inhaled a loud breath as he strode to the far side of the room.

"It's too bad Mrs. Fitzroy started remembering things—the flash of my vinaigrette in the moonlight, the movement of the stone coat of arms. I could not chance the possibility you'd put two and two together. You've always been far too bright for your own good. Turns out I was right."

He continued stepping slowly about the room before he returned to the door.

"We both know there is only one way out of here. Goodbye, Mrs. Pembroke. I shall miss our conversation."

I sat petrified against the cold wall, my arm pressed to the side of the bed, my muscles quivering as I listened for his footsteps, but he didn't leave, not yet at least. What mischief did he intend? Miss Seton would return to the house at some point. I would eventually be found.

I sat quite still for several seconds, terrified to move, my head cradled in my hands. That is, until I smelled the unmistakable scent of smoke.

My head swam as I thrust myself onto my knees and squinted into the room, my fingers gripping the bed. Flames lapped up the heavy curtains like wild animals that hadn't eaten in weeks. Curls of smoke wound toward the ceiling and spread overhead like a turbulent sea. He'd been lighting every fabric in the room while he talked.

The old, dry boards that supported the ancient wing of the house would be no match for Major Balfour's fire. And he was right. It wouldn't take much before the whole thing came down.

I heard the final pounding of his footsteps as he disappeared beyond the bedchamber door. My legs were still not entirely responsive and I was forced to crawl, but I threw myself forward, chasing him. Smoke stung my eyes and I wrested a handkerchief from my pocket to hold over my nose and mouth. The fire was already spreading beyond the confines of the room, and as I rounded the doorway into the hall, I saw Major Balfour at the large doors leading into the house.

Smoke erupted from the room behind me in black puffs, claiming every last inch of breathable space. I had to stop him from locking those doors. My legs were weak, but I managed to rise onto my feet and stumbled forward. The key was in his hand, his attention focused on the latch.

It was my only chance. I lunged forward without a sound and crashed into his body.

His feet could not support the added weight and his knees buckled as the two of us slammed against the door, then the ground. His upper body was well tuned, and he grasped my hair, thrusting me against the nearby wall. "Really, Amelia. I didn't think you had it in you."

My vision tunneled. My head felt light, but I was able to grasp the sleeve of his jacket and hold on. Heat seeped into my lungs and burned my muscles. I cried out in frustration just as a rumble sounded overhead. All of a sudden flaming ashes showered down in the hall behind us. We looked up just in time to see the central ceiling board crash down where we'd been only moments ago.

Every muscle in my body throbbed with agony and my eyes stung. The smoke had grown thick, and the air was like soup drowning my lungs. Major Balfour paused, then released me to lean over, searching for something on the ground.

The keys? Had he lost them?

I felt along the wooden floor hoping to locate them first, but I was wrong. It wasn't the keys he was after but a second pistol. The flames illuminated the gun as he extended it toward me.

I froze, my mind darting in all directions, desperate for another chance at escape. But the situation had progressed too quickly, the balance of power now so terribly one sided. I was trapped—death the only outcome from the heat intensifying at my back.

Major Balfour's voice was darker than I'd ever heard it before. "You are becoming an irritation, Mrs. Pembroke." He steadied the pistol aimed at my heart as a menacing stare transformed the face I'd thought I knew so well. "I don't relish such a brutal end for you. The fire certainly would have been neater, but I have little choice now, and I must finish what I started."

"Everyone has a choice."

He gave a light shrug. "I suppose they do. You could have chosen to stay where I put you."

Pain filled me at his words, and I shrank to my knees, shock coloring not only my shaky movements but also my flawed thoughts. It was all over.

He adjusted the barrel of his pistol to match my new position. "Goodbye, Mrs. Pembroke."

A blazing streak of fire lit up the wall beside us, stilling his finger for the merest second.

It was all Henry needed. His massive body flew in front of me from the room on the opposite side of the T-sectioned hall, his shovel raised high to strike.

Henry? Had he been in the old wing all along?

The metal tool came down hard on Major Balfour's head at the same instant the pistol discharged.

A strangled cry and Henry's lifeless body engulfed Major Balfour as they both fell to the ground.

I sensed rather than heard the multitude of screams originating from behind the east wing doors. The resulting seconds felt like hours before Miss Seton, Andrews, and the other servants appeared. Hands were on my shoulders, a voice at my ear. "We've got to get out of here. Are you hurt?"

I shook my head, unable to find my voice. Henry Cluett had saved my life.

CHAPTER 30

I received word that Ewan, Mr. Lymington, and Mr. Montague were to arrive back at Moorington Cross late the following morning, having found Mrs. Fitzroy unharmed at the inn. They arranged to have her escorted to her son's house.

I wasn't sure if Major Balfour's leaving was a ruse to lure the others away from the house or not, but he'd certainly taken advantage of the opportunity to end my life.

I'd spent a great deal of the night pondering the terrible descent of my friend, but I knew quite well such thoughts did no one any good. If only Major Balfour could have understood that as well.

Thankfully the heavy rain from the storm made quick work of the fire, sparing much of the house. Andrews sent a groom for the authorities as soon as I was recovered, and the rescued Major Balfour was kept guarded until they arrived. I did not see my former friend again, although I was told by Andrews he'd been informed at last that he killed the wrong man, and it affected him greatly.

I stayed in my room all morning, perched upon my window seat until I saw three familiar horses trotting down the estate road.

Ewan. My heart swelled.

I met him on the lawn somewhere between the stables and the east wing. He caught me in a tangled embrace that turned all too quickly to a rather desperate kiss.

Gasping for breath, he held me at arm's length. "My groom told me everything." Then he crushed me once again against his chest. "I never dreamed Balfour would come back here. I don't know what I would have done if . . ."

We stayed tight in each other's arms for a timeless moment before gradually facing what was left of the east wing.

I pulled him close. "Don't ever leave me again."

A gentle smile spread across his face. "I don't intend to."

"Good."

He turned to face me. "I mean it." He paused to search my eyes, his hands slipping so neatly into mine. "You couldn't get rid of me now if you wanted to. It's biblical, you know. You and me. I believe the whole explanation is in Ecclesiastes—something about two being better than one, and that we were meant to help each other up. You cannot deny we were made for each other." He regarded his scarred hand, his tone turning serious. "I daresay the two of us have been fighting alone for independence, for respect from the world, long enough. Don't you think it time we do so together?"

"Are you sure?"

He tugged me closer. "You know very well I couldn't walk away from you, not any longer. My heart would not permit it."

"Nor mine."

He lifted my hand and kissed it, a wry expression settling in those light brown eyes. "You, my love, are the only person I know who elevates my thinking, keeps me honest, and pushes me when I need it. And in return, as your husband, I only hope I may find a way to open the world for you."

"What did you say?"

"Open the world—I plan to take you everywhere with me, you know, whether you want to go or not. No more staying in the house for you."

My smile widened. "No, the part about being my husband."

He cast me a daring look. "Have I not even asked for your hand as of yet?"

I shook my head.

"Heavens, allow me to rectify that at once." He dropped to his knee, his breeches splashing into the wet grass. "Amelia Pembroke, how can I even begin to assign words to what has dwelt within me since the moment I searched my room for that ridiculous little guinea pig of yours?" He stilled. "Plain and simple—I love you."

He ran his hand down his face and I moved to kiss him, but he held me off. "No, no, I have more. Surely I can do better than that." He cleared his throat. "My darling, I once thought myself a judge of true beauty—the sundry colors of a sunset cresting a hill, the eerie calm of the ocean after a storm. I've made it my life's work to put words to feelings, thoughts to experiences. But as I stand here and look at you, I am patently aware of the existence of something so brilliantly beyond description I . . . am speechless. Amelia Pembroke, will you marry me?"

My chest felt light and warm, as if I could fly away. "Without doubt or hesitation, yes." I tugged him to his feet and threw my arms around his neck. "I love you now and forevermore . . . even if winter's icy fingers claw desperately at your soul."

He jerked back, a questioning laugh on his breath. "What did you say?"

"Winter's icy fingers. By which I hope you meant the stipulations in the will, because otherwise I'd find myself quite concerned."

His eyes grew round. "You *knew*! You saw. How long?"

"Just yesterday. And I assure you I'm quite impressed. There's a great deal more to E. H. Radcliff than 'The Stubborn Swan.'"

He looked almost abashed, but his smile emerged readily enough. "I should hope so."

Ewan and I walked the remains of the east wing later that afternoon, my arm tucked possessively in his as I finally allowed myself to relive the full breadth of what I'd experienced. In many ways the idea of moving on from such a personal tragedy felt terribly distant, a dream we might never fully realize.

I peered over at my fiancé. I'd never felt more cherished, nor so sure of the connection we'd forged. Quite frankly, Ewan Hawkins was the best man I'd ever known, and he would stand by my side to face whatever was to come our way.

And there was certainly still much to be faced. I would have to approach Mr. Montague and Mr. Lymington to discuss the details regarding my pending departure from the house. After all, I had no claim to Moorington Cross, nor to any further hospitality on their part.

The sun was full and warm at our backs, the sky a sea of cloudless blue. One glance up at Ewan and I knew all that could wait. For now, I simply needed his calm strength, his solicitor's intuition, his warmth. It was time for healing, for the both of us.

I swung our arms a bit, sweet moments from the night we'd spent in the east wing drifting through my mind. How much had changed since that day, how much we'd endured.

Major Balfour had succeeded in one regard. He'd brought us together.

My gaze roved the manicured lawns before settling on the gated path to the cottage. I inhaled a long, measured breath before slowing our steps. "Why do you think Henry did it? Took the shot for me, I mean?"

Ewan was silent for a moment. "He must have known of Mr. Selkirk's intense regard for you."

I narrowed my eyes. "Then you think he knew that Mr. Selkirk changed the will to include me? That he knew I was Selkirk's ward at one time?"

"He must have. Servants, Miss Seton—anyone could have made him aware of what transpired. Mr. Selkirk may have spoken to him about you long ago. I daresay that's what drove him to address you in the meadow in the first place. Yet keep in mind, his thoughts were disordered." He nudged a loose board with the toe of his boot. "I do still ponder the existence of that document he mentioned. If only we'd been able to find the curst thing." He pointed into the rubble. "I checked what was left of the desk in the elder Cluett's room, as well as the exposed passageway—nothing."

I drew us to a firm halt, a distant thought rattling around in my mind. "You know, when Major Balfour was talking to me during my spell, he mentioned something I hadn't really thought about until just now. It was regarding that old stone coat of arms—the one in the hall beside Mr. Cluett's bedchamber. Major Balfour suggested that Mrs. Fitzroy had remembered it moving." My lips parted. "You don't think . . ."

Ewan met my inquisitive gaze with one of his own. "That there's another secret passageway?"

Slowly we shook our heads, the possibility too tantalizing to dismiss. "Shall we have a look-see?"

One second of shared silence and we bolted for the stairs, not stopping until we were face-to-face with the stone dragons in all their splendor. At once I saw the marking Mrs. Fitzroy had shown me on the nearby sconce and gave the iron emblem a twist. A *pop* and the stone shifted, releasing whatever held it tightly in place.

I shook my head. "No wonder Mrs. Fitzroy's ghost seemed to vanish. Major Balfour knew how to escape being caught. He then stumbled onto the murder scene at the exact right moment to throw off any suspicion."

Ewan nodded then motioned into the small opening. "Shall we?"

I secured a candle from the hall table and thrust it out in front of me, then crept carefully into what turned out to be not a corridor at all but a small room. We looked around, incredulous.

Dust blanketed every inch of the space, sealing the apartment in a timeless shroud. A desk stood at the center. Books were packed snuggly into a large bookcase. A delicate painting flanked the adjacent wall. Somewhat mystified, I edged closer to the artwork. It was a beautiful woman dressed in pale yellow, captured with a rather knowing smile. I stared at her face. She was almost familiar somehow.

Ewan drew in behind me. "What do you think this place was used for?"

"Some sort of an office, I suppose—a room for the Cluett family to keep things they did not want observed."

Curiosity swelled, and I tugged open one of the desk drawers. Empty.

My shoulders slumped, but Ewan was quick to nudge my arm. "Not there. Underneath."

A quick look and I crawled into the cavity, yet there was no hidden drawer. Thwarted again.

Upon resurfacing, I let my gaze tour the room. "Perhaps there's more to the secret, another hidden passage or chamber."

Ewan and I set out at once running our fingers over every inch of exposed wood and paneling. After several minutes I heard his voice from the other side of the bookcase. "What was it about that curse again?"

I checked. "What do you mean?"

"Wasn't it something specific about the family?"

The family. I'd already noticed the circular dragons that marked the entrances to the secret corridors—the same dragon that had been carved into the stone crest. I edged into view, pursing my lips. "Ewan."

Suddenly I was breathless with excitement. "What if the curse was not a real curse at all, but some sort of clue instead?"

I touched my forehead. "Even Henry indicated that what we were looking for was in the walls. And he mentioned the curse—I remember it all now. And . . . Ewan!" I focused in on a small crest at the base of the painting. "It's the Cluett family's coat of arms. Look here." I shook my head. "Henry was leading us here all along, and he didn't even know it. He told me that day in the meadow to follow the curse. He said he hadn't been able to find it."

Ewan smiled. "A Cluett family secret from long ago."

I felt around the small coat of arms until it popped suddenly to the side and the painting released from the wall. Ewan was next to me in a second and we peered into the opening.

A tiny cavity held a few papers tied together with a string. I lifted them out at once and moved to the desk.

It took me a moment to unravel the knot with my shaky fingers, but finally I held the first paper into the light. "Look. It's a letter written to . . . Miss Parsons of all people. And here—it's signed Robert Cluett."

My conversation with Miss Parsons at the tree jolted into my mind. "So Robert was Henry's elder brother. See here. He talks about his brother Henry . . . and not in a very good light, I might add." I pressed my forehead and looked at Ewan. "Miss Parsons told me she put something where the family would have wanted it to be. Could that be here? In this secret office? This has to be what she was referring to."

Ewan edged in closer. "Robert was murdered on the eve of his wedding, correct?"

"Yes, that's what I was told." I scoured the missive as fast as I could. "He writes that he was terrified. He says he sent this enclosed document to Miss Parsons." I lowered the missive to the desk. "Oh, Ewan. Robert's fear for his life only confirms Henry's guilt."

Ewan wrapped his arm around my back. "It is all done with now. One tragedy that only beget another."

I stared down at the paper on the desk. "But I don't think this letter is the document Henry was looking to find."

The feel of the room shifted as we both stared down at the other papers exposed on the desk.

Carefully I picked up the remaining documents, my heart thundering.

A marriage license? And underneath it a torn page from a church registry in Scotland?

Ewan shook his head, then lurched back, his face ghostly white.

I grasped his arm. "What is it?"

"The name on the registry page there . . . I know it." Achingly slowly he turned to face me, disbelief in his eyes. "Florencia Ayles was my mother."

I jerked my gaze back to the paper, reading it over again as Ewan collapsed into a nearby chair. "I don't understand."

"Neither do I." His hands were at his face. "It was my understanding that Lord Torrington was my mother's only spouse—that the child she birthed after her marriage was illegitimate. But if Mr. Robert Cluett married my mother on that date, this document proves otherwise. Look—it's nine months before my birth. Even if her pregnancy occurred before the marriage, the offspring would still be legitimate. But why wouldn't she acknowledge the connection? Why would she pretend as she did with Lord Torrington? She wouldn't have been ruined with proof of a marriage. And me . . . Well . . ."

"But did she have the proof?"

His eyes widened, the truth dawning.

I rested my hand on the desk. "How do you think these papers got here? Miss Parsons must have sealed them in this room as Robert asked her to. See here at the bottom of the letter. She did what she was asked to do."

"But when she found out he was murdered . . ."

"I cannot pretend to understand what drove her actions, but she told me that day at the tree that all she wanted to do was protect the Cluett family name. According to this letter, Robert was the one who wanted these documents hidden. He was afraid—not for himself but for Florencia. The marriage would have certainly been second to her very life. He might have known she was with child. I daresay he thought he was protecting them both—from Henry."

Ewan let out a sigh. "Henry must not have known that he caught my mother and Robert on their way *back* from Gretna Green instead of on their way there. And if the dates are correct, Henry set out for France rather quickly afterward, driven, no doubt, by his overwhelming guilt."

"And your mother would have been forced to pretend the marriage had not happened at all, that she'd not even run away. With no proof, she would have been ruined."

"It was my grandfather who forced her into the marriage with Lord Torrington." Ewan stared at the floor for a long moment. "Perhaps that's why she sent me away—I might have reminded her of Robert . . . or Henry, for that matter."

I rested my hand on his. "I don't think we'll ever know. It was still the wrong choice, a terrible choice—unconscionable."

"I know." Ewan's gaze slid back to the paper. "Of course, this does answer a question I've had all my life, something I thought would never be answered."

"What is that?"

He lifted his eyebrows and dashed a smile. "That I am a Cluett, through and through. Mr. Robert Cluett was my father, and Henry was right to send you looking for this. These papers change everything. My parents were married in the end. *I'm* the heir to Moorington Cross."

His smile deepened. "Dash it all, it may take some work to prove it, but who better to do so than me?"

CHAPTER 31

News of Ewan's inheritance spread through the house like wild-fire. Miss Seton was the first to depart, followed by a rather subdued Mr. Lymington, and last but not least by Mr. Montague, who seemed determined to establish some level of friendship with us before his departure.

Ewan was wary to befriend him, of course, but there had always been a certain likability to the cad that had wormed its way beneath my skin. I could already imagine inviting him back for a visit. After all, Ewan and he were actually cousins.

Over the following few days, the house settled rather gently into a time of healing and comfort for me as Ewan arranged a trip to London to meet with Mr. Huxley to prepare his case. That is, until one particularly interesting evening when Ewan took my hand most unexpectedly and ushered me onto the terrace.

The night was a blustery one, but warm, the rolling gusts sliding deliciously over my bare arms like a fragrant embrace.

I caught Ewan's roguish grin the minute I leaned against the stone railing. "Whatever have you got in mind, sir?"

"Lord Torrington and I have been to see the Archbishop of Canterbury."

A twinge tickled my heart. "Have you?"

He slipped his hand into his jacket pocket and pulled out a folded piece of paper. "He's agreed to the special license we requested."

I couldn't stop the smile that burst onto my face, nor the butterflies that filled my stomach. "I wasn't aware we had decided to wed in such a way."

He closed the space between us. "You told me long ago about your dream to visit London, to see Vauxhall Gardens, to tour the Royal Menagerie."

"You remember that?"

"I remember it all, Amelia." He slid his hand along my chin, plunging his fingers into the delicate strands of hair at the nape of my neck. "My dearest, I cannot wait one more second to share it all—our marriage, our life together. The future you dreamed of begins today. Goodness knows you've been in seclusion long enough. All loose ends are tied up here at Moorington Cross. And frankly, I'm not leaving here without you."

My throat felt thick. "No?"

"No." He laughed to himself as he tugged me closer and pressed his forehead against mine. "You've mesmerized me."

I looked up and met the kiss he was waiting for, my heart soaring, yet I pulled back to whisper all too eagerly in his ear. "Do you think that is because I am . . . Now what did my very own poet call me? Oh yes—cultivated, urbane, eloquent, and let us not forget . . . well read."

"Certainly well read."

"Yes, but most importantly, my darling, I'm yours forevermore."

ACKNOWLEDGMENTS

Travis, this book began and ended with you—your ideas, your strength, your love, and your Christlike example. My writing would never be possible without you.

Audrey and Luke, thank you for navigating the lockdowns of the pandemic with me. This book never would have been written, let alone edited or anything else, without your understanding and patience. I love you both.

Mom, with every passing year, I recognize more and more the mark you've left on my life. From the selfless years you raised me and my sisters alone, to the unending encouragement and love you show me every day. Thank you for being the person who understands me better than anyone else and believes so fervently in my talent. As I've said before, there is no one in the world like you.

Becky Monds and Jodi Hughes, my amazing editors—you take my words and make them sing. Thank you both and the entire team at Thomas Nelson for such incredible support.

And to my Lord and Savior Jesus Christ. To you alone be the glory.

DISCUSSION QUESTIONS

1. Over the course of the story, Amelia must come to grips with the fact that her narcolepsy with cataplexy will likely never improve. Have you or a family member had to accept a physical limitation and find a way to move forward with it?

2. At the start of the book, Ewan Hawkins has something to prove. Have you ever had to confront your own preconceived notions regarding something you feel to be a flaw?

3. Though mesmerism was an early precursor to hypnotism, it was ultimately very different and had no scientific basis at the time it was conceived. Faced with a desperate situation like Amelia's, would you consider alternative medical options, and how would God play a role in this decision?

4. Thanks to Mr. Cluett's will, Amelia is forced to choose between an unwanted marriage providing financial security and a marriage of love. Would you make the same decision she did if you lived in the Regency era? How would having friends who were dependent on you change your answer?

5. Who was your favorite character and why?

6. Do you think Mr. Montague learned anything over the course of his time at Moorington Cross?

7. It is clear from the beginning of the novel that Amelia simply wanted to belong somewhere. Have you ever felt like you were on the outside looking in?
8. Amelia felt trapped by her obligations. Have you ever wished you could step away from something weighing you down?
9. Narcolepsy caused Amelia to feel isolated. Having lived through the lockdowns associated with the global pandemic, can you identify with her in any way?
10. What characteristics do Amelia and Ewan possess that will help them move forward in their marriage after such a tragedy?

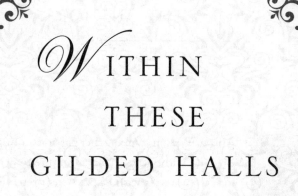

WITHIN THESE GILDED HALLS

When a treasure hunt turns deadly, Miss Phoebe Radcliff discovers all too quickly that she's trapped in a den of liars and can't escape the mysterious Avonthorpe Hall—not without confronting the demons from her past first.

ABOUT THE AUTHOR

Author photo by P. Gardner

Abigail Wilson combines her passion for Regency England with intrigue and adventure to pen historical mysteries with heart. A registered nurse, chai addict, and mother of two crazy kids, Abigail fills her spare time hiking the national parks, attending her daughter's diving meets, and curling up with a great book. Abigail was a 2020 HOLT Medallion Merit finalist, a 2017 Fab Five contest winner, and a Daphne du Maurier Award for Excellence finalist. She is a cum laude graduate of the University of Texas at Austin and currently lives in Dripping Springs, Texas, with her husband and children.

acwilsonbooks.com
Instagram: @acwilsonbooks
Facebook: @ACWilsonbooks
Twitter: @acwilsonbooks